THE VERMILION CROSS

THE VERMILION SAGA
BOOK 2

HAYLEY PRICE

A catalogue record for this book is available from the National Library of Australia.

National Library of Australia Cataloguing-in-Publication entry

Author: Hayley Price

Title: **The Vermilion Cross**

ISBN: 978-0-9756238-3-1 (Print)

ISBN: 978-0-9756238-2-4 (ePub)

ISBN: 978-0-9756238-1-7 (PDF eBook)

✾ Created with Vellum

This book is dedicated to my mum.

She wouldn't have understood half of it, but she would have been proud. Gone, but never forgotten.

At times this book will change point-of-view. Please note that each new scene does not necessarily follow the same timeline as the last.

A note for my American readers. This book is written in UK/Australian English. Many of the words will be spelled differently from what you're used to - colour, centre, grey, etc.

In addition, we do not share your fondness for the letter "Z". I realise you may find this difficult and offer my humble apologies. We make up for this by using a plethora of "L's where you would make do with one. Marvellous

---

All the writing and artwork in this book was created by a real person. No AI was used at any time.

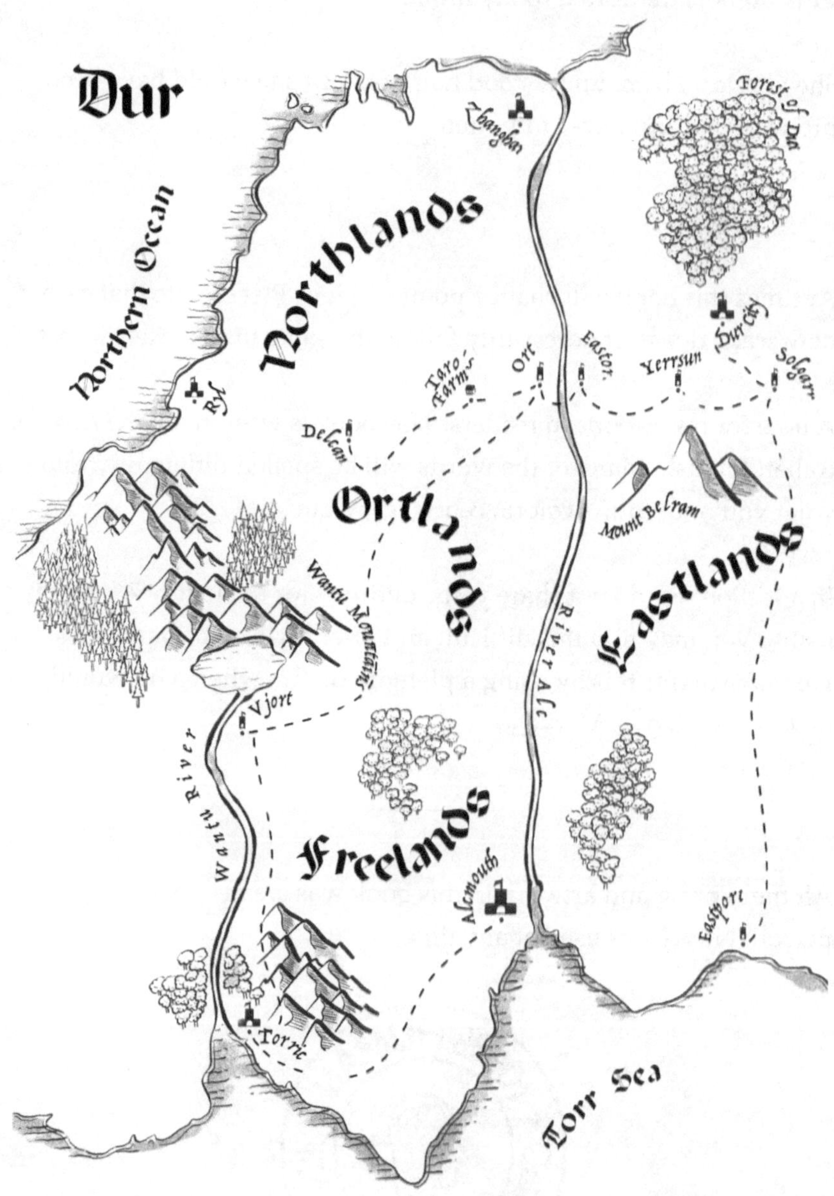

Dur
Northern Ocean
Northlands
Zhangban
Forest of Dul
Rf
Taro's Farms
Ort
Eastor
Yerrsun
Dur City
Solgarr
Delean
Ortlands
Mount Belram
Wantu Mountains
Eastlands
River Ale
Vjort
Wantu River
Freelands
Afemouth
Eastport
Torric
Torr Sea

ONE
A SORRY TURN

An eerie howl from the ropes and nets turned Jorinda's blood bitter cold in her veins as the wind hurled the little ship forward through the ominous swell. A large wave reared up before the vessel, a wall from the sea to the sky, and as the hull drove straight through it, water heaved over the bow and soaked Jorinda, who stood naked on the forward deck of the ship. The water tasted of blood, and she spat it from her mouth. It plastered her long brown hair to her head; her arms dangled loose at her sides as the wave crashed over her, and she stood as still as death.

A crowd of people faced her. She knew most of them, had encountered them at one time or another. Some had played a major part in all that made her the woman she had become, others no more than minor roles. At the rear of the crowd stood every man whose life she had taken on the orders of the Guild. They all stared at her with reproachful eyes, motionless and silent.

Between Jorinda and the crowd of silent onlookers stood a lone woman whom Jorinda did not recognise. Older than her by around ten years, the woman stood no more than two fingers taller than Jorinda but had a stocky build and an excess of weight, her feet bare below a simple blue dress of common making. A small scar ran down her chin and gave character to an otherwise unremarkable face. Contempt burned in her brown eyes, and Jorinda wondered if she had angered the woman. Had she refused to fashion a fine dress for the woman to wear? The stranger wore her long, straight, blonde hair scraped back into a horsetail, held in place by a blood-red ribbon tied with an expansive bow. The woman stood so close, Jorinda could have reached out and touched her.

Feet shuffled behind her, and Jorinda turned to face Arella and Deineike, one at each shoulder. Both looked on her with disdain, and they each held a fan in one hand.

Deineike sighed. "Jorinda. What have you wrought?"

Arella glanced at Deineike before she also spoke. "Corelle."

The confusion over the names prompted Jorinda to think back to happier times. *"Arella knew me as Corelle, but Deineike did not know me in those days. I became Jorinda before I met Deineike."* Jorinda turned again to face the scornful woman and the crowd behind her. Some in that crowd would call her Corelle, others Jorinda. Few would call her friend. Their hostility washed over her, as palpable as the wave that soaked her moments earlier.

Nothing could justify their scorn for her. She had killed some of them, but she had done nothing to most of them. What made them so angry at her? Even the ones she had killed had no right to anger, in truth. They had brought their ruin upon themselves through threats to her or those she loved, or had been killed on the orders of others. Their rage should be saved for those who paid for them to be dispatched wherever they travelled to afterward. Why had they all gathered here to fix their hateful gazes on Jorinda?

Exasperated, Jorinda could tolerate the silence no longer. "What do you wish of me?" Her voice screeched through the wind, the loudest sound she had ever heard.

They replied with one voice. "I love you." Their eyes spoke of hate even as their voices spoke of love.

A familiar soft metallic hiss whispered behind her, and Arella and Deineike both reached around her. A blade had sprung from each of their fans, and they drew them across Jorinda's throat in opposite directions. The blades opened two vermilion ribbons that criss-crossed her throat, and blood gushed out of her in a plume that arced down onto the feet of the unknown woman to paint them the bright red of the ribbon that held her hair in place.

Jorinda screamed as she awoke.

Wilash had not spoken for some time. Morose, he rode behind the members of the Torric Guild as they left the farmhouse of Amharkk Tyrk. Although Wilash had believed he pursued Corelle and the other woman to the farm, he had missed his guess, and they slipped through his fingers. His disappointment lay less in the fact he had not found the fugitive and more that he had misjudged her intentions—a misjudgment that might cost him his life once he returned to Zhanghar. He had failed to carry out Styrrach's orders, and that failure would not be well received. Death itself held no terror for him, but Guild justice did, and he shook with fear as he contemplated it.

The part of Wilash that had liked Corelle from the moment she arrived from Ryl with Arella rejoiced that she had escaped. He had watched the Guild turn the carefree, happy girl he first met into a moody, disaffected woman, and he held himself in some way to blame for the course her life had run.

Corelle had fled Zhanghar a year ago and earned Wilash's respect through her resilience and determination. He marvelled that she continued to avoid the grasp of the Guild, even burdened as she appeared to be by the other who travelled with her, whose injuries must be an impediment.

Another part of him could not forgive Corelle for the death of Arella, for whom he had cared a great deal, even though he bore some portion of the blame for her death himself. Arella had confided dark secrets to him, secrets she had kept from Corelle, but after all else, she might have confessed those secrets to her lover on that dreadful night, then paid a terrible price beneath Corelle's blade.

Wilash wondered how he would have acted had he found himself in those terrible circumstances in the room above The Ship's Yard. If, like Corelle, he had been betrayed to the Portreeve, with the Guild bent on his death to ensure the Portreeve's men could not take him alive, he could not say what heinous act he might have committed. After all else, he despised his part in the events that placed Arella under Corelle's knife—he had invited Arella to join the Guild, which set her feet on the road that led her to The Ship's Yard that night. He would be prepared give his life to unwrite that fate if he could.

Ahead, the Guild men turned south onto the Vjort to Torric road. None of them had spoken to him since they left the farm. He imagined his failure to read Corelle's intentions had cast him in a poor light with them, but in truth, he did not care about them or their opinion of him. As they rode on, the road became a street, flanked by houses instead of trees and pasture. The Senior Aide of the Torric Guild slowed his horse until he rode alongside Wilash.

The man lowered his voice, as though he did not wish for any but Wilash to hear him. "A sorry turn." Wilash grunted but did not reply. He had forgotten the man's name moments after they were first introduced. The Senior Aide lowered his voice further, little more than a whisper, almost inaudible above the steady clip-clop of the horses' hoofs. "I understand you played some part in the failed attempt to shroud the woman."

Wilash studied the short, slight man; his pallid skin, his dark hair cut close to his scalp, and his eyes that flitted about as if he expected danger to appear from every alleyway and shadow. He portrayed an air of menace, but he had been reluctant to enter the farmhouse and risk the chance of death under Corelle's blade. "Shroud?" Wilash did not recognise the term, and the man's implication it involved some failure on his part irritated him.

"The woman had been marked for shrouding in Zhanghar, had she not? You intervened in some way before the Portreeve could take her into custody. Unless I have it awry."

The man's words made no more sense to Wilash than the unusual names and speech of the family at the farm, and he frowned in concentration as he tried to harvest some scrap of comprehension from what he heard. "I do not know what you mean. What does 'shrouding' mean?" It rankled Wilash that the man suggested he had erred when he informed Styrrach of Pilos's betrayal of Corelle.

At that, a look of alarm crossed the man's face, the colour drained from it, and his whisper turned desperate. "Are you not the Senior Aide in Zhanghar?"

Wilash could not disguise the anger in his tone. "That I am not. I am nothing more than Styrrach's emissary on this gest, which has turned awry. Again, I ask you—what do you mean by this word 'shrouding?'"

A deathly pallor turned the man's face ashen. "I have spoken out of turn, and it will go better for us both if you forget you ever heard that word from my mouth."

The Senior Aide gathered up his reins as though to spur his horse forward and rejoin his colleagues, but Wilash could not allow the mysterious conversation to end on this unsatisfactory note. He grasped the man's reins.

The Senior Aide wheeled in his saddle and faced Wilash. A sudden, unexpected fury flushed his face. "Release my horse." Spittle flew from his lips, and he pulled at the reins to tear them from Wilash's grip. As he kicked the flanks of his horse, Wilash grabbed at the sleeve of his tunic to stop him but pulled him off balance, and the Senior Aide fell from his horse into the dust of the street. The other Guild members wheeled their mounts and stared in confusion as he hit the ground.

The situation turned perilous. Wilash had assaulted a senior member of the Torric Guild. Under different circumstances, such an insult would see Wilash die beneath the blades of the Torric members, but his stature as an honoured guest of the local Guild— a member of the Zhanghar Guild and trusted emissary of Styrrach —complicated matters. To cut down a person of such status would be unthinkable, but the Guild code also demanded vengeance for the assault on the Senior Aide. The others hesitated and seemed unsure how to react. Some reached for daggers while others looked on in consternation.

The Senior Aide climbed to his feet with some difficulty and glared at Wilash. Fury turned his face bright red and his voice into a low snarl. "You shall answer for this attack..." The man hesitated, drew in a sharp breath. "Not here, and not now, but you will answer." He held out a hand to placate his colleagues as they approached Wilash.

If they wished to kill him, Wilash could do nothing about it, one man alone against six. The Senior Aide's horse had wandered off as the man had fallen from its back, and one of his men gathered its reins, led it back to him. He mounted, and the six men rode off without another word.

Wilash hung his head in despair. Any doubt that Styrrach would have him killed on his return to Zhanghar for his failure here had vanished when he tipped the Senior Aide into the dust of a Torric street. He had come full circle and arrived in no better place than Corelle. His fate was written, and it would be his ruin. He could run, as Corelle had done, but he lacked both her ingenuity and her art. She had cunning and quick wits; his skills lay in the creation of weapons, not in the sly arts of an assassin. He had never killed; she would not hesitate to kill to escape and would prove difficult to take alive. In truth, Wilash could never be like her, and he must face his end with as much courage as he could summon. He nudged his horse into a gentle walk toward the Guild building.

As Wilash expected, Sisnop spat his fury at him the moment he entered the building. "Gillar urges me to dispense Guild justice upon you as payment for this insult." The Guildmeister stepped so close to Wilash, his spittle sprayed into Wilash's face as he hissed in anger. "I will not do so out of respect for Styrrach, but we will no longer tolerate you here. You will leave for the docks without delay and sail back to Zhanghar. Letters will follow, and the full account of your misdeeds will be told to Styrrach. I do not envy your fate. Leave us now." He turned and entered his office. The Senior Aide followed him and slammed the door, an over-dramatic display.

Wilash, who had already forgotten the Senior Aide's name again, stood motionless and stared miserably at the door to the Guildmeister's office. Some of the members slid daggers into their hands from wherever they had been hidden, and Wilash held up both hands to calm them. The Torric members glared at him, and Wilash wondered whether Corelle could take on so many if she were here. He doubted it; weight of numbers must tell in the end, and Wilash alone could not entertain any thought of victory. It might be less gruesome to die under their blades than suffer the justice that awaited him in Zhanghar, while those who slew him might incur Styrrach's wrath in payment for their part in his ruin. The thought that some vengeance might be wreaked on them for his unsanctioned death gave him no joy. He heaved a sigh, spun, and left the building without a word.

Wilash strode to the docks. His mind raced as he tried to unravel the cryptic remarks the Senior Aide had let slip in his small unguarded moment. How the man had mistaken Wilash for the Zhanghar Senior Aide must remain a mystery, but the larger puzzle concerned the use of the term "shrouding." What had it meant, this word Wilash had never heard any Guild member utter before? The man had implied Wilash had played some part in the failure of the Portreeve to "shroud" Corelle, and his words seemed to refer to her betrayal by Pilos, news of which Wilash had brought to Styrrach. He recalled that Styrrach had seemed angry in that moment, but the brief conversation with the Senior Aide made no sense. The word left him disquieted, and he resolved to understand it further. He would try to persuade Styrrach to elaborate on it before he ordered Wilash killed.

Several ships stood at the docks, so Wilash walked up the ramp onto the deck of the first one he came to and ordered a mariner to bring the master to him. The master said the ship headed south to a land whose name Wilash could not understand. For a heartbeat, Wilash entertained the idea he could sail away from Dur and the Guild aboard this ship, but he turned and walked back down the ramp to the dock, unable to commit to such a venture with little coin and no idea where the strange land the ship sailed to lay. The next ship along the dock would soon sail to Alcmouth, so Wilash used the Guild token to acquire passage. The token looked harmless enough—a small black metal circle with a stylised letter G etched on one side—but the Guild inspired such dread in all who came into any contact with it, no master would refuse to carry anyone who bore the small symbol. Such dread should have no place in anybody's life, but it seemed unlikely Wilash would be a part of the organisation that so frightened people for much longer.

The ship sailed through heavy swells in the Torr Sea, and when he did not fetch up over the rail, Wilash lay on his bunk in a foul mood. He ate precious little on the journey, and such fare as he managed to eat erupted back out of him almost as soon as he swallowed it. Three days later, one day out from Alcmouth, the master advised him he planned to sail on to Ort once he unloaded the ship's cargo in Alcmouth and took on new goods destined for the town. Wilash disembarked in Alcmouth and spent a few hours on solid ground before he boarded again and continued north on the same ship.

The journey north up the River Alc proved easier on Wilash's stomach, which boiled less within him in the gentler swell of the river. His demeanour improved, and by the time the ship docked in Ort, he resolved to leave the ship and spend a day or two in the town before he sailed further north. It seemed pointless to rush toward his ruin, and he decided to take a tankard or two of ale in Ort and try to find a woman to lie with for what might be the last time.

On each of the next three mornings, he woke with a headache, the stale taste of old ale in his mouth, and a woman whom he did not recognise next to him in his small bed. On the third morning, the folly of the stay in Ort overwhelmed him. He would not approach his end in this way. He wished to die with dignity, not fall into the Alc, inebriated.

He pushed the woman from him, and she did not awaken. In truth, he could not recall where he had met her or even that he had brought her to the room. He left two regals atop her discarded dress—an exorbitant sum, but he would have no need of coin where he would soon travel. He settled with the innkeep, and as he walked through an alleyway toward the docks, he fetched up the previous night's ale.

He found a ship that prepared to sail to Zhanghar and settled down against one of the masts to await his fate. The three-day voyage passed without incident, and as he entered the Guild building in Zhanghar, he guessed the letters Sisnop had promised to send had preceded him while he tarried in Ort. The three members in the parlour were circumspect and reluctant to make eye contact, and a broken chair lay in the corner of the room. Wilash had seen Styrrach's temper destroy furniture before, and the chair may have met its end on his account.

Porl entered the building soon after Wilash arrived and dashed into Styrrach's office. Moments later, he reappeared and beckoned for Wilash to follow him into the office. Styrrach stood with his back to the door, as he often did when he wished to assert his authority. The unnecessary display amused Wilash. None doubted Styrrach's authority or his prickly disposition.

"The deviant slipped through your fingers." Styrrach had not asked a question, and Wilash did not answer. "As it turns, word of her has preceded you. She sailed to Alcmouth. It seems she had retained her Guild token and used it to obtain passage for herself and her…companion."

Wilash nodded and felt foolish. He had reasoned Corelle would have insufficient coin to purchase passage from Torric aboard a ship, which may have been correct, but he had not considered she might have the audacity to use the token as a way around that inconvenience. He admired her initiative and courage, even though it seemed sure to bring his ruin.

It did not matter what he said now; lies or the truth would both condemn him. "I pursued her north and had not considered she might take ship, for I thought she would not have the coin. I had not the imagination to perceive she might be bold enough to use the token, nor that she might have retained it."

Styrrach gave a nod so slight, Wilash almost missed it. "Bold indeed, but it will not happen again. I have sent instructions that any woman who attempts to use the token is to be subdued and brought to me."

Wilash did not believe any mariner who worked on the rivers or seas could subdue Corelle, but he kept his opinion to himself. "A wise move."

Styrrach turned to face Wilash. A small stain marred the front of Styrrach's tunic, some food dropped, mayhap, but the Guildmeister's face betrayed no emotion, as ever. "Do you recall the day I came to your smithy?"

The change of subject took Wilash by surprise. His mind raced back to the day, so many years before, when Styrrach first appeared in his life. Wilash's parents had died from the fevers, and although he did his best to keep his father's smithy in business, he had proved in equal parts a brilliant weaponsmith and terrible businessman. Creditors threatened to close the smithy down, but Styrrach offered the young Wilash a way to stay out of the Debtor's Gaol when he invited him to work for the Guild and craft the weapons Wilash had a special talent for. How many times Wilash had regretted that day since then could not be numbered. "That I do."

"I saw a young lad with vast potential and great ability at a forge, and I saw skills I could harness in this venture." Styrrach waved a vague arm in the air as though to encompass all the Guild stood for. "I did all I could to protect you, for so many years. I sheltered you from the gests, treated you well. I arranged for you to work in the Portreeve's Offices so you could be kept untainted by the nature of our work. Some"—he flicked a glance at Porl—"believe I go too easy on you." He fell silent and stared at Wilash.

Wilash hesitated, uncertain how to reply—a situation he had grown familiar with over the years since he joined the Guild. He did not believe Styrrach's story about the job in the Portreeve's

Offices and felt it had little to do with any attempt to keep the taint of death from Wilash. Doubtless it came from Styrrach's disappointment that Wilash did not have the temperament to become a killer. "My thanks." Wilash could find no more to say. What other words could there be, after all else?

"You knew of the jade's deviancy, yet you chose not to speak of it to me. I sent you to Torric to return her to me alive, and you failed. Is this how you thank me for the care I have shown you for so long?" Wilash looked down at the floor but said nothing, and Styrrach continued. "To add further insult, letters come from Torric. The letters suggest you have thrown their Senior Aide from his horse in a fit of temper. This is intolerable. It casts the Zhanghar Guild and me in a poor light. A poor light indeed."

Wilash looked up and stared into Styrrach's cold eyes. Warmth never came to the Guildmeister's eyes even when he smiled. Wilash could offer excuses for the incident with the Senior Aide: provocation, a momentary lapse of judgement, some lie that implied the man had slighted Styrrach. Instead, Wilash drew himself up to his full height. Defiant and proud, he held Styrrach's gaze. "How do you propose to respond to my failures?"

Porl began an immediate response. "Guild jus—" Styrrach snapped his head around and shot his Senior Aide a ferocious glance that almost sloughed the skin from his body. Porl did not continue.

Styrrach turned his attention back to Wilash. "Do you offer no excuse I might consider to mitigate my response?"

Wilash shook his head, irritated by the facetious question. He stood at the door of his ruin but still had no answers to some of the questions the Torric man had raised. "*It is as well to be hanged for a mutton as for a lamb,*" he thought. He narrowed his eyes in defiance and clenched his teeth as he answered. "Tell me about the word 'shrouding' and what part I played in whatever turned on the night Corelle killed Arella. Then do with me as you will."

A slow, cold anger came into Styrrach's eyes. "Where have you heard this word?"

"In a tale, or part of a tale at the least, told to me by the Senior Aide in Torric. As you have heard, I then threw him to the ground. I wish to hear the full tale before my ruin falls upon me." The atmosphere in the room had become charged with such tension, Wilash felt he could grasp handfuls of it and force it into his trouser pockets. Porl seemed to hold his breath, and Styrrach's lips twitched. Whatever Wilash had stumbled upon by accident that day in Torric appeared to be of such magnitude, Styrrach might strike him dead on the spot rather than reveal it.

Styrrach clenched and unclenched his fists several times. Wilash could never recall such fury in the man. At last, the Guildmeister seemed to reach a decision. His lips were taut, his eyes flashed with fury, and he clipped each word as though he fought his rage. "That is not yours to know. You should forget you ever heard that word."

"The Senior Aide in Torric said much the same." Vitriol dripped from every word Wilash uttered. "I cast him down and brought my ruin upon me with him, but I will not forget what I heard. I insist you tell me."

Styrrach glanced at Porl, then returned his gaze to Wilash. "That is not yours to know." He repeated the words, slower this time. "Leave us. When you return in the morning, you will learn what fate is written for you. Do not hope for any favour based on the fondness I bear you." He turned his back on Wilash.

Porl drew in a sharp breath. Wilash could make no sense of what he had unleashed in the room. He stared in hatred at Styrrach's back for long moments while neither of the other men spoke. He wondered whether he could pull his dagger from his belt to stab Styrrach in the back before Porl struck him down. The Guildmeister seemed as angry as Wilash could ever remember, but Wilash's own fury matched Styrrach's. What could this secret be that so infuriated Styrrach? What inadvertent role had Wilash played in whatever deception this wall of silence protected?

Wilash would receive no further answer, so he turned, walked out of the office, and slammed the door even harder than the Torric Senior Aide had done. He glowered around the parlour, but the three members refused to meet his angry stare. He walked to his room, which lay undisturbed as expected, and lay on his bed, but his mind raced as he tried to grasp at some semblance of what he had stumbled into. Sleep eluded him for many hours.

Porl did not speak after Wilash slammed the door. Styrrach stood with his back to his Senior Aide as he replayed the conversation with Wilash in his mind. The Senior Aide in Torric had both misjudged and misspoken, a dangerous mistake. Styrrach must determine the best way to handle a delicate situation with the minimum of damage, which meant Wilash's fate was written.

He turned to Porl. "A sorry turn."

"Wilash has failed us. Worse, he has blundered into something about which he knows nothing and about which he must learn nothing, for all now depends on this. He must die, on the morrow if not tonight."

Styrrach favoured Porl with a cold glare. "Should Gillar not die? He let slip the beast that now roams our nightmares."

"Gillar has let us down, but to order his death in place of Wilash's might not be well received and might lead some to question your authority."

"None should doubt my authority." Styrrach kept his voice level, emotionless. "Do you doubt it, Porl?"

Porl's face flushed. "Never. It is absolute. Wilash's fate is written, nonetheless. He must die. Too much is at risk should he learn more of our business."

Styrrach contemplated the situation for some time. He had felt a rare empathy for the lad he found in the smithy. He had cared for him, more than Wilash even knew, but only Wilash's death could maintain the strict secrecy around Styrrach's operations, however painful it might be for him to issue the order. "Other matters must be considered also. Corelle may still be in Alcmouth, and she is an aggravation I wish to rid myself of. She has slipped from our grasp three times, and we cannot allow this to continue." Porl raised his eyebrows in mute assent. "Things might have been simpler if we had not selected her to be shrouded. No gain can come now if we attempt to guess anew fates that have already been written, but she is more resourceful than we believed. We should have made better use of such an asset, not discarded it."

Porl clucked his tongue against the roof of his mouth. "She is a deviant. Worse, her spirit failed her. She threw herself into the Guild; a poor decision. I admit I misjudged her character when she applied to join us, but her disillusion had become transparent to all. Have you not said at times that the single thing that spreads faster than enthusiasm is the lack of it? It would have infected the others in time. We made the correct decision, though it is ironic she has proved so difficult to kill."

Styrrach chuckled in spite of himself. "Wilash played his hand well that night. Though he did not know it, I could not gainsay his insistence before the others that we could not allow her to fall into the Portreeve's clutches. Had I refused to act, it might have brought things to light that lay concealed. The other, Arella; that might have been foreseen. Had she not warned Corelle, things might not now be so awry."

"That they would not." Porl hesitated. "Do we attempt to rewrite the fates?"

Styrrach turned away again. "That we do not. You are correct; we must focus on the solution and not dwell on fates we cannot unwrite." He paused as a sudden sadness settled on him. "Wilash must die, although it grieves me to say it. Not here though. For the affection I hold for him, I will not kill him, and I will not permit any who know him to do so."

Porl tutted. "That is unwise."

Styrrach wanted to be annoyed by Porl's defiance, but his Senior Aide had the right of it, after all else. "That it is, but my decision is final. We will send him to Alcmouth, and send letters to Balgow, who will shroud him there, and let that put an end to it. He will be banished; his punishment, to all eyes. He will be relieved he has not come to his ruin, my guess."

"And the woman?"

Styrrach could not repress a resentful admiration for Corelle's ability to remain one step ahead of them and for her ingenuity when they seemed to have her in their grip. Hiw had cornered her, but she had found a way to kill three men and escape. They were nothing more than couriers, of course—an error on the part of the Torric Guild. Regardless, she could not be allowed to learn any of the things Wilash had stumbled on. He could see only one solution. "It might be best if she has sailed south and never darkens these shores again." He sighed in resignation. "More letters will go to the other three Guilds, and we will again order her found, taken alive, kept silent, and sent to me. This must end. She vexes me."

"That she does. With luck, she fell overboard, and the fish have taken her. Curse her." Porl sighed. "What of the other?"

"I do not care about her. Let her be a plaything for the members who find them. Corelle is my concern, not this thing she toys with in her depravity." A lengthy silence settled on them both. At length, Styrrach sat on the chair next to his desk and looked up at Porl. "A sorry turn." He waved at his Senior Aide in a sign he should leave.

TWO
CAPITAL PUNISHMENT

THE NIGHTMARE OVER, JORINDA SAT BOLT UPRIGHT IN THE BED. Deineike sprang up beside her, threw her arms around her, and soothed her. Jorinda's heart pounded in her breast, and sweat soaked her body. Her tongue stuck to the bone-dry roof of her mouth, and her brown hair lay dishevelled about her shoulders.

Deineike pulled her closer, her voice soft, calm. "Another nightmare?"

Jorinda nodded, although she imagined Deineike could not see the gesture in the darkness. The room above an inn in Alcmouth had no window, but after the ship docked the previous day, they took the room because of its low cost. "Everybody I have ever met. Everybody I have ever killed, all gathered on the deck—you among them." She turned to Deineike's silhouetted form. "You killed me."

Deineike stroked the back of Jorinda's head. "I would never harm you. Ever." She kissed Jorinda's cheek.

"Arella too." Tears sprang to Jorinda's eyes as she whispered of the nightmare. "You both killed me with my own fan."

"The fan lies at the bottom of the Torr Sea. Unless a fish picks it up and learns to walk on the land, it can never hurt you again. It can never hurt anybody else, not ever. My love." Deineike buried her head in Jorinda's neck, and Jorinda relished her familiar smell. Her heart rate slowed, safe in the strong embrace of the woman she loved, but the nightmares had not stopped. Mayhap they never would, and her mind would unravel at some future time.

Jorinda lay back in the bed as she revealed more of the nightmare. "A strange woman appeared in the dream. I have never seen her, I am certain. She stood before me as you killed me. What does it mean?"

Deineike lay down beside Jorinda and wrapped her in her arms. "I do not know. I cannot interpret dreams, and I am certain I would not wish to interpret yours, for they are hideous."

"That they are." Jorinda lay silent in the darkness and replayed the nightmare. What did the woman whom she did not recognise signify? Guilt might explain her death by her own fan, gone as Deineike had said, cast into the Torr Sea as they sailed away from Torric. Why had she thrown it overboard? When Deineike urged her to throw the fan over the side, Jorinda acted on impulse. If she had hoped to cast the nightmares away with it, that hope had been dashed. The foul dreams that plagued her since she killed Arella had not ceased but had become more vivid, more powerful.

She had cast it from her for no reason but to satisfy Deineike, who appeared relieved when the fan sank beneath the water, and why not? It had brought nothing good into Deineike's life, had been responsible for injuries so terrible, they took her to the doorstep of death. Worse, the fan had killed so many people. It had killed Arella, and Jorinda had no longer wished to be near it. It had

Arella's blood on it, and her own guilt bound up in it. She had cast it from her and vowed never to kill again, so had no further need of it.

Jorinda had sworn other vows, of course, and broken them all. After she took Arella's life, she vowed to end her own, but she still lived. Would she break her vow never to kill again? To do so would further deepen her self-hatred. They were not safe while the Guild hunted them, nonetheless, and she might be required to kill again or be killed, and Deineike with her.

Would they be safe in Alcmouth? The vast capital city might hide them. To find two women in such an enormous city must be beyond even the Guild. Six or seven members served in Zhanghar. How many might there be here? Even if it were double the size, that amounted to no more than fourteen. Fourteen men to search for two women in a huge city—an impossible task, she guessed. Nonetheless, the Guild had dogged her every move since she had left Zhanghar. They must have a wider network of couriers and informants than she had appreciated. Even so…

She turned her head toward Deineike and whispered. "Are you asleep?"

"That I am not. I shall sleep when you do. Aboard the ship from Torric, you told me I must keep you safe, and I cannot do so while I sleep."

Jorinda gave a soft laugh. "No harm can befall me while my lover protects me. I am safe." Deineike's warm laugh at the jest comforted Jorinda like a soft blanket pulled around her. "We must make some decisions, and they will not be easy. I am unsure how safe we will be here in Alcmouth. There is a Guild here, and I am sure they will search for us. They will soon know we have arrived here. I could not avoid the use of the token, but it will prove dangerous. Styrrach will not rest until I am under his knife, and once he knows we are here, he will send word for them to search for us."

Deineike gave a short, soft sigh. "Alcmouth must be immense. Would they find us here? As long as we are careful, we are safe, are we not?"

"We may be, we may not. It is a conundrum. We could investigate what accommodations we might find, although our coin supply is not vast. I have no other useful skill but garment making, and it is dangerous, for the Guild knows of my abilities, and I suspect they will visit every garment shop in the city in they hope they can unearth me."

"Curse this leg. Until it heals, I cannot earn coin. The burden of my care restricts you also. Should we leave Dur altogether? You mentioned it in Torric."

Jorinda pursed her lips, still certain Deineike could not see the gesture. "I do not believe we have sufficient coin for such a voyage, and I fear to use the token again. Styrrach will take action to prevent that now we have used it to escape once. Mayhap he will introduce a different token, but I fear it will lead him to us if we continue to roll the dice."

Deineike paused before she replied. "He is sure to act to prevent your use of the token, but he cannot learn of it for many days yet. News of our arrival here cannot come to him before ships can sail north up the Alc, can it? He must then send letters back here, and they will take as long again, unless he possesses some charmed device he gazes into and sees all the instant it happens."

Jorinda laughed again. "My sweet Deineike. Your imagination is as vivid as the brightest ray of sunshine. I do not believe Styrrach possesses this wondrous item, but with all my heart I wish we could come by it. We could sell it for so much coin we could travel far beyond Dur and enjoy our life together in safety until your hair turns grey, and your bones creak whenever you move."

Deineike laughed and gave Jorinda's brown hair a gentle tug. "Your bones will creak long before mine. I am not much older than you and have cared for my body far more than you have."

Jorinda gave a derisive snort. "You have no knowledge of how many years you are, but you are now the expert on the difference in our ages?" They both laughed, the nightmare forgotten for the time.

Deineike seemed to reach a decision. "Let us investigate accommodations today. I weary of life in rooms and inns. We might find a small house we can occupy all by ourselves, with a small garden in which you can grow vegetables."

"*I* can grow vegetables? Why me, and not you?"

"I know nothing of how to grow vegetables."

Jorinda snorted. "And I know less than nothing."

Deineike did not reply for some moments. "A garden may not be necessary."

Jorinda smiled and turned to kiss Deineike. "I shall sleep if sleep will come. I am safe. You can protect me with your muscles and with carrots and cuces from your vast vegetable garden." She laughed again at the thought of the garden.

"Sleep then. While you sleep, I will throw the cuces into the street, for they are vile."

Long after Jorinda's breaths became the soft, rhythmical sound of sleep, Deineike lay awake. As they sailed away from Torric, she had been elated. Jorinda had avenged her mother's death and lifted that weight from her, or so she thought. Few enough days had passed since they had fled Torric, but she already felt a fresh despair. She kept it hidden from Jorinda, who needed no more cares heaped upon an already troubled heart. The burdens of Jorinda's violent past and her unassuaged guilt over Arella's death were enough for her to bear; more than she could bear, mayhap.

The murder of Deineike's mother had left a hole in her life, and to her horror, vengeance had not filled it. Her mother's killer had been slain, but the hole remained, and it dismayed her to realise it.

Against her own wishes, Jorinda killed the mariner because Deineike urged her to. Her love for Deineike overcame her better judgement, and she killed the man to salve the hurt in the woman she loved. To reveal to Jorinda that his death had not resolved Deineike's misery might destroy the younger woman.

Deineike hoped the vengeance on behalf of her mother would bring her peace over time. She did not wish to become like Jorinda; a tortured, nightmare-plagued figure full of self-loathing. For them both to be so broken would be insufferable, and it might be better if Styrrach's Guild found them rather than for them to endure such misery. Deineike fell into a troubled sleep, but it brought no relief from the emotions that crashed against one another within her.

Wilash rose early and pulled on a tunic Corelle made for him not long after she first arrived in Zhanghar. It seemed appropriate to go to his death in a tunic of such fine making. He would not slink or grovel; he would accept his fate dressed in his finest tunic and with his head high. He walked to the Guild building at a brisk pace. When he arrived, early, one other member sat in the parlour, but the others drifted in as time dragged by. It appeared the entire complement of the Guild had been summoned to witness his judgement, and Wilash did not doubt they would all participate in his Guild justice at some point. He did not resent them for it; it would be expected of them, and in any event, he did not count any of them as a friend.

Styrrach and Porl arrived last. Doubtless they had watched the building to ensure all the members arrived before they entered, to assure themselves of a grand entrance. Porl deferred to Styrrach, who gazed around at the assembled members. When he appeared content he had their undivided attention, he nodded to Wilash, who took a step toward him and stood straight and proud.

"Wilash, you have failed us." Styrrach dispensed with any preamble and did not deign to catalogue the failures he intended to punish. "You are banished to Alcmouth, where you will serve the Guildmeister, Balgow, in whatever capacity he determines appropriate. Do not return to Zhanghar. Your tenure in this city is at an end. You will leave for the docks without delay and take passage to Alcmouth."

The judgement shocked Wilash. He had expected death— nothing less could atone for the assault on the Torric Senior Aide, and he had failed to apprehend Corelle, which demanded more severe punishment. He had pushed Styrrach to the limit of his patience with questions about the word "shrouding." The decision made no sense. Banished to Alcmouth, nothing more? The punishment did not fit the crime, no more than a slap on the wrist. The other members remained silent and stared at the floor, mayhap unable to meet Styrrach's gaze, but they seemed as perplexed as Wilash at the leniency of the punishment.

Wilash looked Styrrach in the eyes. Neither of them spoke, and neither of them looked away. Wilash could stare into those cold, unsympathetic eyes all day if necessary. He would not lose this battle, his last moment of dignity, and he would not skulk away with his tail between his legs like a beaten dog.

At last, Porl broke the tension. "Your Guildmeister has spoken. You are to leave now. The penalty for defiance—"

"I am well aware of that penalty." Wilash flashed Porl an angry glance, then stared at Styrrach again.

Styrrach tore his gaze away from Wilash. "Then leave." The

Guildmeister walked into his office, Porl close behind him. The door closed, the final dismissal.

Wilash gathered his belongings together once more and headed to the docks to find passage south. The three-day voyage down the Alc passed without event. The river had been smooth on the journey south and had not troubled his stomach overmuch. Wilash did not plan to spend any time in Ort, but the vessel he travelled on planned to return to Zhanghar once its hold had been emptied and replenished, so he disembarked in the unfamiliar town.

When he reached Alcmouth four days later, Wilash had drawn an inevitable conclusion: nothing but his death could atone for the insult to the Torric Guild, and Styrrach would not be prepared to lose face. It followed that Styrrach must have told Torric he had arranged for Wilash's death and sent Wilash to Alcmouth for the execution of the sentence. Why Styrrach made that decision rather than kill him in Zhanghar, Wilash did not know, but he imagined his stay in Alcmouth would be brief and would end with his death in an alleyway somewhere away from curious eyes.

He walked down the ramp, stood on the Alcmouth dock, and looked up into a glorious blue summer sky. How many more such skies would he see before the Guild closed his eyes forever? Resigned to his fate, he sighed and trudged off toward the Guild building.

He reported to the new Guildmeister, who seemed surprised when Wilash explained he had been reassigned to Alcmouth. Wilash appeared to have arrived before the letters from Zhanghar that contained instructions for his fate, and he saw one last chance to get to the bottom of the mystery he had stumbled into on the outskirts of Torric. If he wished to learn any more, he must act fast. Once the letters arrived, his time would be limited.

The Guildmeister and Senior Aide in Alcmouth might know nothing about "shrouding," but that seemed unlikely. Wilash had once heard that the Senior Aide in Alcmouth had a fondness for ale, and he might pry some information from the man if he acted fast. He sought him out and invited him to a tavern to discuss his new assignment. They headed for the Senior Aide's favourite tavern; a small place tucked into the entrance of an alleyway in the poor quarter. As Wilash's eyes adjusted to the dim light in the tavernroom, the Senior Aide spoke to the innkeep in a hushed tone. The innkeep ushered two patrons out of a private booth at the rear of the room despite their protestations, and the Guild men took the table.

Wilash gave the innkeep four groats and a request for the ale to flow. Four groats would pay for vast quantities of ale, and regular fresh tankards appeared as the hours slipped by. Wilash had no wish to become inebriated himself, and he poured some of his own ale into the Senior Aide's tankard at every opportunity. The Senior Aide did not hide his captivation with the pretty face of the woman who served them. He pursued her around the tavernroom at whiles and badgered her to lie with him. The Senior Aide's attentions insulted her as much as they humiliated the man himself, who seemed oblivious to his shameful behaviour, but Wilash ignored it for his own benefit.

By early evening, the Senior Aide had become intoxicated, and he returned to the table after another failed attempt to exhort the server into a dalliance. "She is a rare beauty, that one." His words slurred, and his eyes struggled for focus. "I have tried many times to lie with her, but she plays reluctant. I will have her, nonetheless." His lewd smile sickened Wilash.

The man had become so inebriated, Wilash doubted he could perform even if she did agree to lie with him, and unless she became aroused by men who fetched up on her, she would leave the encounter disappointed. Wilash kept his counsel to himself and played his hand. "That you will. You could shroud her if she continues to rebuff you."

The Senior Aide looked askance at him, then loosed a loud, intoxicated laugh. Wilash ignored the ale the man spat over him in the process. "She would need to join the Guild first. And you of all people should know women will never again be permitted to join the Guild after the fiasco with your Corbelle." He took another swig of ale, spilled much of it down his tunic but appeared not to notice.

Wilash put him right on the name. "Corelle."

The man seemed not to hear Wilash's correction. "That went awry." With a concerted effort, the Senior Aide focused his eyes on Wilash's face. "Did the Portreeve not understand the instructions? Now I think on it, did she not kill you and flee? Oh no…" He chortled as he realised what he had said.

Wilash laughed with him, eager to sustain the conversation, although the man made no sense. "That she did." As though born to the role of a festival performer, he clutched at his chest and flopped face down onto the table while the Senior Aide roared with laughter.

"You appear to enjoy a good time." The Guildmeister had appeared unseen by either of them.

The Senior Aide blanched and fell silent as Wilash answered, "That we do."

Balgow fixed his gaze on Wilash. "Letters have come from Zhanghar. You preceded them by a few hours."

Wilash stared up at him, and the tension between them reminded him of the atmosphere in Styrrach's office a sevenday before. The Senior Aide half-rose from his settle but could not raise himself further, and he fell back in an untidy heap. Wilash ignored him and directed a quiet question at Balgow. "Do you intend to shroud me?"

The Guildmeister paused for several moments, then snorted.

"This word is unfamiliar to me, and I suspect it is to you also. I am here to warn you that my Senior Aide may well get you into a fist-fight if he drinks any more ale. I will take him home and allow you to enjoy the rest of your night. Tomorrow we can talk about the services you can render our Guild here in Alcmouth."

"That we can." Wilash thought Balgow might not have heard his soft reply.

The Guildmeister turned and summoned two men from behind him. Each of them took one of the Senior Aide's arms, and they pulled him to his feet. He swayed and almost fell despite their assistance. They helped him from the tavern and left Wilash alone at the table to ponder what he had learned.

Not much, he decided, and little of it made sense. "Shroud" did not mean a gest. The man had said the woman would need to be in the Guild, which suggested that whatever "shroud" meant, only Guild members could be "shrouded." Wilash could not unpick the reference to the Portreeve who had misunderstood instructions. It appeared more certain that in relation to Corelle, "shrouded" had some connection to her betrayal by Pilos. Wilash shook his head. It remained as unclear to him as it had been before he had entered the tavern, and he did not consider his new knowledge worthy of the four groats it had cost.

He drained his tankard, rose to his feet, and realised he had become inebriated despite his endeavours to avoid it. He had consumed far less ale than the Senior Aide, who must wake tomorrow as ill as could be endured. It had all been for naught. Wilash had learned little new, and the sand had fallen.

Wilash would live to see another day but imagined tomorrow would be his last, since the letters from Styrrach had arrived. Despite Balgow's sweetened words, it appeared Styrrach had sent Wilash to Alcmouth to die. For now, he needed a room where he could sleep. It need not be anything elaborate; he would not need it for long. He headed out into the street and took a series of random turns. An uneasy sensation grew within him as he walked, as though somebody watched him, so he doubled back and took time to stare into a shop window but could see nobody suspicious. He saw no evidence that anybody followed him, but his discomfort grew. Did Guild members crouch in the shadows, anxious for him to turn onto a quiet street that he would never leave alive? Wilash could not live his life this way. Either he would confront them or confirm that his imagination played tricks on him. He retraced his steps again and entered a dark alleyway he had passed mere heart-beats before, took five or six paces, then whirled around. He expected to see a figure silhouetted against the half light of the street beyond but saw nobody.

Hot breath behind him carried words from a familiar voice into his ear. "Do not move, or I will be your ruin."

THREE
AN UNEXPECTED MEETING

Deineike's urgent plea resonated in Jorinda's ears again. Jorinda had lost count of the number of times they had held the same argument in the days since they found the small cottage in the poor quarter in which they now lived, unable to afford anything more elegant. The cottage had a parlour and indoor privy downstairs and one small bedroom upstairs. They had never lived together in an entire building before, and Deineike seized on the sense of privacy to become even more noisy in her appreciation of their physical enjoyment of one another. At times, Jorinda feared Styrrach would appear in their bedroom, led to them from Zhanghar by Deineike's cries of passion.

As soon as they moved into the cottage, Deineike asked Jorinda if the splints could be removed from her leg. The cottage had a small yard at the rear, and she insisted she wished to plant vegetables in it as soon as she could bend with less difficulty. She argued that without the removal of the splints, she could not realise the ambition. At first, her continued fixation on a garden amused Jorinda, but the jest soon wore thin.

Deineike would not allow the subject to pass. "Please. It has been passes beyond number. Will the things stay on my leg for the remainder of my days?"

"How do you reckon the number of passes, who does not know how many years you are?" The incessant requests had worn Jorinda's resistance down, and it had been three passes at the least since the chirurgeon in Torric had applied the splints. She imagined they could now come off and free Deineike from their constraint.

"Please?" Deineike wore such a picture of desperation on her face, Jorinda could no longer resist.

She knelt beside Deineike, inspected the leg, but saw nothing to suggest the splints should remain. Where the bone had pierced the skin, the wound had healed, though a large scar had formed that seemed unlikely to ever disappear. The redness of inflammation had disappeared a long time ago. Jorinda sighed, defeated. "Very well. We will remove them." Deineike gave a loud screech of delight, and Jorinda covered her ears. "I will change my mind if you make that awful sound again."

"I apologise." Deineike gave Jorinda a demure look, but her wide smile returned straight away. "Take them off, I beg you. Free me."

Strips of cloth tied around Deineike's leg held the splints in place. The dreadful condition of the bandages on Deineike's arm had taught them to keep those on her leg clean, and they changed them often. Jorinda took great care as she unfastened them. "If you are pained—"

"I know, I know. I promise, I will tell you if I am in pain." Deineike's face flushed bright red with excitement. "It is a beautiful day. Take them off and let me walk in the sunshine."

"With your staff. You must promise to walk with your staff at all times and do not rush things. Short distances, no more, as you rebuild your strength."

Deineike pouted, but the excitement did not leave her eyes. "I promise."

With one last resigned sigh, Jorinda unfastened the last of the strips and removed the two pieces of wood that had held Deineike's leg straight for so long while the bone repaired itself. Jorinda helped Deineike to her feet and passed her the staff, then stood on Deineike's left side with one arm around her waist to hold her steady.

Deineike sighed. "I cannot bend it, not yet at the least, but that will come, we know this. It is like my arm." Her right arm had healed well and had almost full mobility now. Deineike exercised it every day, and Jorinda admired her resolute progress. No doubt the same process would now begin with her leg. Deineike's determination went far beyond Jorinda's.

Deineike insisted she needed to move around the room by herself for a few moments, and her brow furrowed in concentration as though she learned to walk for the first time in her life. She perspired and gasped for breath.

The apparent toll on Deineike's body concerned Jorinda. "Is all well?"

"That it is, although it seems more difficult to walk than I remember. Come, let us go and sit in the yard."

"What will we sit on?" No outside furniture had been provided with the cottage.

"The ground." Deineike laughed and hobbled toward the back door. Jorinda shook her head. Nothing could keep the older woman's spirit down, it seemed. She followed Deineike to the door and pulled it open, so the determined woman did not have to release her grip on either the staff or the wall she leaned on. With a grin, Deineike walked out into the sunshine, free of the splints for the first time in more than three passes. She struggled to lower herself to the ground while Jorinda hovered nearby, worried in case the older woman fell, until she sat, her right leg straight out in front of her, as inflexible as it had been in the splints.

Deineike patted at the ground beside her. "Sit with me." Jorinda sat, and Deineike kissed her lips. "My thanks." Her breathy voice suggested she had become aroused, and she kissed Jorinda, a deep, passionate kiss that inflamed the younger woman's own desire. Deineike's hand slid to Jorinda's breasts, and Jorinda gasped as Deineike aroused her nipples. Jorinda worried they might be overlooked in the little yard, although she could see no windows that looked into it. Deineike's hand slid between Jorinda's legs and chased her concerns away, and they made frantic love in the dust of their yard.

They lay in each other's arms in the warm sunshine afterward and chatted about Deineike's leg, the future of the vegetable garden, and whether they should remain in Alcmouth or move on. The warmth left the yard as the sun slid down the sky and behind the rooftops that surrounded the cottage.

Jorinda pulled her tunic around her as the chill nipped at her bare skin. "We should go inside."

"It has turned a little chilly, and to be honest—as I promised I would be—I confess I am in some pain now."

Jorinda became concerned, helped Deineike to her feet, and supported her as they went inside. "Can you climb the stairs?"

"I will try."

The stairs had been problematic when Deineike had worn the splints and proved no easier without them. They struggled to the bedroom, and both panted from exertion as Deineike flopped onto the bed. Jorinda slumped to the floor beside the bed, exhausted by the effort.

Anxiety chewed at Jorinda, and she feared they might have removed the splints too soon. "I will go out for some herbs. They will ease your pain and you may sleep. We will see what tomorrow brings."

Deineike gave a weak nod in response, and Jorinda headed down the stairs. She snatched up her coin pouch and headed out in search of a shop where she could buy the herbs to ease Deineike's pain. As ever, she resorted to her Guild training to throw off anybody who might follow her as she doubled back, stopped to stare into shop windows and took a circuitous route. After a few moments, her heart leapt, but not because she had been followed. Across the street, a face on the periphery of her vision demanded closer attention. Jorinda melted back into the early evening shadows of a doorway and stared in horror as she recognised Wilash. Thoughts raced through her mind as she glanced around to see whether any others loitered nearby. Had the Guild found her despite her diligence and sent him to kill her? *Deineike.* She slept alone in the cottage, and Wilash headed straight for it. Their ruin had found them at last.

He appeared unsteady as though he might be intoxicated. Would he come to kill her in such a condition? Movement could betray her, so she remained motionless as he passed opposite her. He must not see her until she had a plan. He wandered on, still unstable, and Jorinda followed him with all the care her Guild training had taught her. She hugged any available nook or cranny in the facades of the buildings she passed as they retraced her steps toward the cottage.

Wilash stopped to look around, and she sank back into the doorway of a house. Had he spotted her? Jorinda had always liked Wilash. His friendship with her and Arella had meant a great deal to them both, and it would be a pity to kill him. She raised a hand to her mouth in horror. She could not kill him; she had vowed never to kill again, and even if she had not, she had no weapon with which to take his life. The full weight of the desperate situation hit her, and she slowed her breaths, tried to remain calm. *"Never panic. No complication is irredeemable,"* she told herself.

Wilash turned and walked back the way he had come from. Had he noticed her and turned toward her to spring a trap? She reached behind her and tried the handle of the door. The door swung open, she stepped inside, then pushed the door closed until it left no more than a crack to peer through. Wilash stopped and gazed into a shop window across the street.

Jorinda glanced behind her, but if anybody occupied the house, they did not seem to hear her, and nobody came to investigate. When she turned back to the street, she saw no sign of Wilash, and she opened the door further, anxious. He had turned and set off toward the cottage again, so Jorinda slipped out and followed him. He passed an alleyway, and she dashed across the street behind him into the welcome shadow of the alleyway.

The sound of his footsteps should have grown fainter, but they grew louder, and she guessed he had turned once more. He must have seen her run across behind him and decided to confront her. Her mind strove for a plan, and she decided to lead him away from the cottage so he and any accomplices with him did not find Deineike. She ran a little further into the alleyway and crouched down in the darkness as he turned from the street and walked toward her.

When he had come within a pace of her, he whipped around, mayhap to summon his accomplices. Jorinda could not allow him to cry out to them, so she stood, moved up behind him without a sound, and whispered into his ear. "Do not move, or I will be your ruin."

His response took Jorinda by surprise. "Corelle. Why do you follow me? You have lost none of your skills, I confess. I did not spot you once."

Jorinda turned the few words over in her head. They implied she had followed him and not the other way around. He could not intend to kill her, if so. "Tell me why you are here before I send you wherever you travel to afterward."

"Corelle, Corelle." He slurred his words somewhat, but Jorinda could not miss the sadness in his voice. "If you do not send me there now, the Guild will send me there on the morrow. It matters not. I travel there either way." He hesitated. "Do not use the fan, I beg you. It is too fine a weapon. I do not deserve to die under its kiss. Find another way. Nothing you can do will be as brutal as Guild justice. You know this."

Jorinda tried to shake the confusion from her mind, failed. "Guild justice? What do you mean?"

"Styrrach sent me to Torric so I could return you to him alive, but I failed him. I also had not told him you lay with Arella, and it sits ill with him that you did. Even though they had learned of it, they said I concealed it from them, nonetheless." He spat on the ground. "Styrrach is little more than an animal, and I am no better. I spent years yoked to his Guild, and I have brought pain to you and death to she whom we both loved."

He sobbed as he spoke, and Jorinda's consternation grew. She sought clarification. "You mean Arella?"

"That I do. I regret all that turned that night. I would change the fates if I could and would be content to die under your knife to bring her back if it would re-write them. Now make it quick, but do not use your fan, I beseech you."

"How did you know they suspected I lay with Arella?"

He sighed. "They did not suspect. They knew for certain— Arella confirmed it to them." He wiped a tear from his eye.

Jorinda did not believe Arella would have told Styrrach of their relationship. "You lie. Why would she tell them this?"

Wilash looked at the floor. "There are things I do not trust myself to tell you. I would prefer to go wherever I travel to with these dark secrets locked inside me."

Jorinda tutted, irritated by murky words that made no sense.

She felt certain Arella would not have risked their lives with such a reckless admission. "Did you pursue us in Torric?"

"That I did. I failed to predict your use of the token, and you escaped."

Something he had said came back to her. "You loved Arella?"

"That I did, though not as you did. I loved her for her friendship and company, and for her spirit. I despise myself that I ever brought her into that wretched life, and you with it as it turned."

Tears stung Jorinda's eyes. The night in The Ship's Yard played itself out in her mind yet again. "You loved her." This time it had not been a question.

Wilash spoke again after a moment. "The other. Is she safe?"

Jorinda paused, uncertain who he meant. "The other? Do you mean Deineike?"

"I do not know her name. She suffered some injury when you killed Hiw."

"Deineike." A horrific thought came to Jorinda. "Does Styrrach know of her?"

"That he does, though I do not believe he knows her name. He does not care about her. He wishes you brought alive to him, but her fate will not be pleasant, nonetheless. You must protect her."

Jorinda considered this development. Wilash did not intend to kill them, but she could not unpick the story he had brought to her. "Why are you here?"

He laughed without mirth. "I am here be killed, 'shrouded,' my guess."

"'Shrouded?' What does this mean?"

His silhouette shrugged, and his head dropped forward. "I know not. Some scheme of Styrrach's, I believe. It involves Guild members and the Portreeve, but I know no more. It had been ordered for you that night, but Arella intervened. I have been sent here to be killed, after all else. Whether I am to be shrouded or fall victim to Guild justice, I do not yet know. It now seems you will be my ruin, after all else. That may be more apt."

Jorinda spoke her thoughts aloud as she strove to unravel all Wilash had said. "I must learn more of this. My betrayal runs deeper than I believed, that is clear now. Arella…" Her voice caught in her throat, and tears pooled in her eyes. Jorinda had killed Arella, but it now seemed clear others had her blood on their hands, beyond Pilos. It seemed she had not broken her vow, after all else. Other blood might need to be spilled in payment for Arella's life. Not by her though, she reminded herself. With the back of a hand, Jorinda wiped the tears from her eyes and spoke in a softer voice. "I cannot kill you with the fan. I no longer have it."

His silence stretched to many moments. "What became of it?"

"It lies at the bottom of the Torr Sea. I cast it there at Deineike's suggestion. I vowed to kill no more."

"You are unarmed then?"

She nodded, unnecessary in the dark alleyway. "That I am."

"Corelle—"

She interrupted him. "Jorinda."

"What?"

"I call myself Jorinda now. I abandoned 'Corelle' after I left Zhanghar that night."

"The Guild knows this, but they do not know what you now call yourself." He paused. "Jorinda." He lowered his voice as though he feared unfriendly ears lingered nearby. "You are in great danger. The Guild seeks you still. Styrrach wishes you brought alive to him, and Guild justice awaits if they catch you. You must arm yourself. You must protect yourself. You must protect…" He fell silent.

"Deineike." Had he forgotten her name already?

"I hear your care for her in your voice. You must protect her." He repeated his advice, firmer, more resolute. "You must arm yourself."

"I have vowed to her I will not kill again. I need no weapon."

He tutted. "A weapon has more than one use. It may serve as a threat, after all else." He fell silent again, then continued. "Take this. I crafted it. The blade is as keen as the fan's, and it may serve you in a time of need." He found her hand in the shadows, pressed the hilt of a dagger into it, and her fingers closed around it, an instinct. It had superb balance, and she could feel something carved on the handle, but as her vow burned in her memory, she dropped it.

Wilash tutted again and bent down. She could turn and run while he scrabbled around on the floor. He could not catch her if she ran, but he posed no threat despite the menace of the Guild he still served. He stood, reached for her hand again, and pressed the dagger upon her once more. This time she did not drop it, but deep within herself, she feared it betrayed Deineike and her vow never to kill again. "Its balance is unmatched by any blade I have ever held."

"My thanks. May it help you. I see now you do not intend to end my days with it. Your vow…" His voice trailed away to nothing.

"I wish to know more of this 'shroud' and of what turned that night. Tell me all you know."

"I have told you all I have learned. I am certain there is far more, but I know no more than I have already said. If I find out more…" He gave a short humourless laugh. "I am convinced I will die tomorrow and will learn no more."

Jorinda's tears came again. "Wilash…"

"Do not cry Corelle."

"Jorinda."

"Jorinda, that is what I meant. Do not cry, not for me. My fate is written, and in large part I have written it myself. Leave here, I urge you. Take Denkie—"

"Deineike."

He sighed. "Deineike. So many new names, and I have no time to learn them. Take her and flee. Styrrach will not stop. His obsession with you burns at his insides. More than ever since I questioned him about the events of that night, my guess."

Jorinda threw her arms about his neck to whisper her farewell. "Take care, Wilash." He wrapped his own arms around her and pulled her close to her. On a whim, she decided to trust him. "We live nearby. If you learn of any threat to us, will you warn us?"

"That I will, if I live to learn of it."

Jorinda told him the address of the cottage and stood on her toes to kiss his cheek. "Be safe, Wilash. I am sorry for my part in what has turned."

He sniffed. "It is I who should apologise."

She pulled away. "My thanks for the dagger. Deineike awaits. She will be worried by now." She did not wait for an answer as she brushed past him into the street and headed for the herb shop.

FOUR
HIDDEN AGENDAS

Klordia had worked at the Bailiff's Offices for three passes, work that both challenged and enthralled her. Her previous employer, the merchant Cheyn, had provided a recommendation that played a large part in her successful application for the job. She had worked for him for three years when the tragic death of a tally clerk in the Bailiff's tally office came to her ears. Cheyn had been sorry to see her leave his employment but supported her desire to utilise her superlative numerical abilities in the service of Dur.

The Duke's vast, complex business interests covered all Dur and beyond. Four other tally clerks worked in the small office alongside Klordia, two men and two women, all kept busy throughout the day as they tallied the chits and maintained the ledgers. Klordia thrived from the start and enjoyed the complicated tally work, the vast abundance of chits. She had already earned praise from her colleagues, the Senior Tally Master among them, for her diligence and strong commitment to her work.

The Senior Tally Master visited their office several times a day and spent some time in conversation with the clerks, almost always about their work. Klordia had not seen another Tally Master in the building and concluded the Senior Tally Master might have added the "Senior" to his job title to make his position sound grander. The Bailiff's tally office accounted all the Duke's tallies, but the Duke's Secretary had overall control of the Duke's personal finances. Klordia had not seen the Bailiff or the Duke, although two of her co-workers claimed to have once met the Bailiff at a function.

Klordia had always accounted the tallies with great precision and labelled the front of the tally ledgers with the pass, day, and year in which each began and ended in accordance with the system the scribe, Orthus, had created some five hundred and fourteen years earlier to mark the passage of time. The system had been named Thurology, rumoured to have been at Orthus's request. Few ordinary citizens used the system, but Klordia always imagined all tally clerks would both know and use it. It amazed her to find none of the other workers in the Bailiff's Offices labelled their ledgers, but Klordia adhered to the practice. Failure to do so would complicate any potential audit of inaccuracies.

The most favoured and longest tenured of the five tally clerks, Dathys, worked at the desk in front of Klordia's own. Along with the regular chit work, Dathys, and nobody else, tallied the levies the five cities remitted to retain their city charters, along with levies from large towns that aspired to city status. He towered over Klordia by more than two spans, a lean man who spoke little, and when he did, his soft voice could be difficult to hear. He never turned to engage any of the others in social intercourse throughout the day, as the others did from time to time.

Office rules were strict and forbade any ledger or chit to be left on a desk overnight, and each night they locked the tally ledgers and unaccounted chits in a cupboard. They all had a key to the cupboard, but another cupboard stood next to it that Dathys alone seemed to have a key for, and he would often take a ledger from it, work on it, then lock it away again without delay. Klordia imagined he accounted some tallies for the Duke's personal finances on behalf of the Duke's Secretary.

One morning, Dathys had not arrived an hour after the appointed start time. The tardiness surprised Klordia; he had not been late, nor missed a day in the office, once in the passes since she began her new job. When he arrived at last, his pallid face and sweat-beaded forehead betrayed his sickness. He sniffed and grumbled under his breath for an hour before he rose to his feet, shaky and in obvious pain.

Klordia watched in concern as he used one hand to steady himself. "Is all well, Dathys?" He did not reply, and without warning, he fetched up and fell to his knees. Klordia leapt from her chair and crouched beside him, a hand on his back. "You are unwell." The other workers also crowded around him, and he fetched up a second time. "Help me." Klordia looked up to the others in despair, and they helped Dathys to his feet.

They manoeuvred him to a settle against the rear wall of the office. One of the women ran for help, and two Portreeve's men soon appeared. Dathys had not spoken throughout, and Klordia guessed some meal had disagreed with him, or some malady laid him low. The Portreeve's men offered to escort him to a healer and carried him out between them.

A large pile of vomit lay on the floor and on Dathys's desk. Its smell turned Klordia's stomach, and she imagined they would all fetch up from the stench, so she went in search of some cloths and a pail, then drew some water into the pail to clean the unpleasant mess from the office.

Klordia tackled the floor first and retched many times as she wiped up the contents of Dathys's stomach with the cloths. As she wiped the last of the vomit from his desk, she spotted a ledger he must have worked on as the illness took him. The ledger had been spared the ignominy of Dathys's vomit. She returned the pail and threw the cloths into the receptacle in the rear alleyway that held any rubbish that needed to be taken away and burned.

When Klordia returned to the office, she thought the ledger should be returned to the cupboard, since Dathys would be unlikely to return to work that day. Out of diligence, she decided to account any untallied chits in the ledger before she replaced it in the cupboard. There were no chits in the slot cut into the inside of the ledger's binder, where untallied chits were stored until they were entered. Conscientious as ever, she checked whether the ledger recorded levies, since if it did it must be stored in the separate cupboard. She had no key for that cupboard, but imagined the Senior Tally Master would have one. As Klordia turned to the first page, she raised a hand to her mouth in shock. She had never seen a ledger so full of credit entries, all for enormous sums. Many of the individual entries involved sums greater than all the chits she might have accounted in an entire pass for Cheyn.

The credits must represent levies, but the sheer size of them baffled her. Cheyn had contributed a levy, but he had never contributed anything close to the amounts she saw in this ledger. The businesses involved must have revenues beyond the wildest imaginings of anybody in Dur if they paid such enormous levies on those revenues. Klordia scanned the business names in the ledger. Several of the names were tally houses in Alcmouth, but most of the names were unfamiliar. Against each business name, a letter had been scribed—A, T, Z, and R. She guessed they represented four of Dur's five cities, Alcmouth, Torric, Zhanghar, and Ryl. The letter D did not appear; Dur City's levies must be accounted in a separate ledger.

At the end of each pass, a line ruled off and summed the credit items, and one debit entry appeared on the debits page. The debit appeared every pass, always accounted as "Styrrach"—whatever or whomever that might be—and Klordia calculated Styrrach always received seventy percent of the credit amount in each pass. Why had a large part of such enormous levies been paid to an entity other than the Duke? Klordia could not answer her own question. Did Dathys take part in some fraudulent manipulation of the Duke's coin? She could not believe he would do so, nor that he would maintain a ledger of such nefarious activities in plain view in the Bailiff's Offices.

The door opened, and the Senior Tally Master entered. "I hear Dathys is..." His voice trailed off as his eyes settled on Klordia, who glanced up from the ledger, and he hurried across the office to Dathys's desk. "What is this?" He pointed to the open ledger.

"I..." Klordia became flustered, unsure how to respond, guilty she had been caught as she studied the ledger. "Dathys left this. I thought to lock it away. It is...I am concerned by..." She had failed in her feeble attempt to explain the ledger. Cowed by his stern gaze, she felt her cheeks burn as she flushed with embarrassment.

"You are concerned? By what?"

"These entries. There is—"

He raised a hand to stop her. "Come. Bring the ledger to my office and explain your concerns. Doubtless it is naught but a dummy ledger like the one I showed to you as a test of your abilities at your interview." He turned and left the office without another word.

Klordia gathered up the ledger. The other three clerks stared at her in curiosity, but she shrugged her shoulders and followed the Senior Master to his office. His assistant waved her straight through into the Master's office. The Master gestured at the horrible, uncomfortable chair before his desk that she recalled from her interview, and he stood to one side of the chair.

His emotionless voice disturbed Klordia. "Tell me what concerns you."

"The Duke's finances are raided, it seems, and paid elsewhere. Large parts of it, at the least."

He laughed. "That is preposterous." Klordia detected little humour in his words despite the laughter. "You are mistaken."

"I am sorry Master, but when numbers speak to me, I am never mistaken. These ledgers tell the tale as I have recounted it to you. You must investigate, for somebody cheats the Duke. It is clear."

A dark frown swept across his face. "You are mistaken. Leave the ledger here and return to your work."

Klordia bit her lip, deep in thought. Though she worked in the Senior Tally Master's area, the Duke's Bailiff employed her, and she had a responsibility to ensure all tallies and chits were accounted without fail. The strange ledger must be investigated. The Master's spurious suggestion that she had seen a dummy ledger had been false, and he did not attempt to continue the pretence. The ledger suggested the existence of potential theft, and she would be negligent in her duty if she let it pass.

She drew in a deep breath. "I do not understand the full implications of the ledger, but they tell me enormous sums of coin are remitted as levies, and most of those levies are not paid to the Duke. With respect, I ask you again to investigate the ledger." His contemptuous stare beat down on her, and her heart raced at many times its normal rate, but she had an obligation to protect the Duke's finances. She must not wither.

He stared at her in silence, and his temples throbbed. What reason did he have to be angry at her? She might have uncovered nothing more than some game Dathys played in a ledger of his own construction. If so, he might have done nothing more serious than to allow games to waste time he ought to have devoted to his employer's business. At worst, he had some involvement in a fraud of immense proportions. The Duke could be nothing but pleased to learn the Senior Tally Master's office had uncovered this fraud, so the Senior Master's fury seemed inappropriate.

"You are mistaken." His voice sounded like an angry growl, and the menace in it increased Klordia's anxiety. This day had taken a sorry turn, but she could not turn away and pretend she had not seen the ledger entries.

Klordia must see the matter through. "I would like permission to bring this ledger to the Bailiff so he can judge whether I speak the truth." She had made a bold move; a threat to go above his head. He must now investigate the ledger himself rather than be cast in a poor light if he ignored her, and the Bailiff saw she had the right of it.

He stood in silence for some moments, then smiled. "Klordia, you have done diligent work in this office during your employment with us. I should not have doubted you, and I apologise. I must be certain you have seen a major discrepancy, and I am sorry I pushed you so hard. Explain what you have found, then leave the ledger with me, and I will investigate it. We will get to the bottom of this mystery, and if you are right, you will be rewarded."

"I am right, though I wish no reward."

"Quite. Then I shall reward you now. I grant you the remainder of the day as a boon, for your diligence. Now, explain the story you see in these numbers, then go home. By the time you come to work tomorrow, I hope to have unravelled your mystery."

Doubt about his sincerity nagged at her, but Klordia could see no way to pursue the matter further now he had agreed to investigate. "You will bring the ledger to the Bailiff's attention?"

"As soon as I can arrange an appointment." She showed him the entries, and he appeared to be shocked. "What is this 'Styrrach?'" He turned a pointed stare on her, and she again became nervous.

"I do not know." She had mumbled, but she focused on a clearer tone. "A person, or a business? Such vast sums of coin must be easy to trace."

Satisfied he understood her concerns over the unusual ledger, Klordia felt exhausted and decided to take up his offer. The Master rang the bell on his desk as she turned to leave, and his assistant passed her as she went through the door.

Balgow summoned Wilash into his office the day after the encounter with Jorinda. Guild justice must await him, but he remained surprised Styrrach had sent him to Alcmouth to meet his fate. He would not, however, waste the brief time left to him on any attempt to understand that puzzle.

The Senior Aide joined them. He looked discomfited, and Wilash did not doubt Balgow had compelled the man to reveal the full details of the evening in the tavern. He must also feel dreadful after so much ale, a thought that brought Wilash a perverse pleasure.

Balgow did not waste time on preamble. "We have a gest for you."

Wilash had not expected those words. "A gest? I do not understand."

"You do not understand what a gest is?" The Guildmeister laughed and looked at his Senior Aide, who laughed on cue.

"I know full well what a gest is." Wilash could not keep his voice civil. "I do not understand why you assign one to me when we all know the fate written for me."

Balgow's face took on a confused expression, as though he could not unravel Wilash's implications. "Your fate is to carry out a gest for me. It is a simple one, as it needs to be, for I understand you have never killed." He smirked.

Without a sound, Corelle rose from behind Balgow, and a slash of her fan across his throat wiped the conceited grin from his face. As lithe and supple as a dancer, she took two steps and stabbed the Senior Aide in the heart with her new dagger. Wilash shook his head, and the vision disappeared from his mind. Wishes; nothing more. He sighed. "Very well. I shall gather my intelligence today. Who is to be my mark?"

Balgow laughed again. "Wilash, do not fret. We have already gathered the intelligence for you. It is simple, as I have said. A woman. Even a novice such as you cannot fail to overpower and kill a woman."

"A woman?" Wilash's unease increased. Something must be awry.

Balgow's contempt flew from his mouth in droplets of spittle. "You do know what a woman is? We hear your friends lie with each other like animals. Do you also? This might explain why you are unfamiliar with women." The Senior Aide appeared to find this hilarious and laughed loud and long. "We seek two of your friends, by the way." The Guildmeister made the comment sound like an afterthought. "It will go ill for both of them when we find them."

Wilash's body shook as he fought to control his temper, with little success. "I imagine you believe those words. Beware, Balgow; she whom Styrrach seeks will not fall to your inebriated Aide, nor to such limited skill as you might possess, as most of your hapless victims have."

Balgow snarled and took a step toward Wilash, then appeared to think better of whatever his intentions had been. He drew in a deep breath before he continued. "The woman you are to kill works for the Bailiff. She will be detained at work tonight and will emerge well after dark. She will be directed out of a rear door that gives onto an alleyway. No eyes will see you there, and you will take her. Her name is Klordia, and she is unmistakable, I hear. She is an older woman, short and fat." He snorted as he said "fat."

"Fat?" The ugly insult seemed unnecessary to Wilash.

Balgow replied through clenched teeth. "Fat." Spittle splattered onto Wilash's face as the Guildmeister said the word, and Wilash balled his hands into fists at his sides as he wondered what impediment made the man spit so much when he spoke. "Do your ears fail you? She is fat and undesirable. And tonight, she will be dead. You are a novice, so Sky will observe and assist if the fat old woman proves too much for you to handle alone." Balgow laughed again, a bitter sound, full of mockery and disdain.

Wilash focused on the mention of the sky as he battled the urge to punch Balgow in retribution for the man's humiliation of him. "Sky?"

The Senior Aide joined the conversation at last. "That is my name, although you did not care to learn it last night."

Wilash gave a derisive laugh. "Sky? Your parents called you this?"

Sky bristled with indignation. "That they did. What of it?"

Wilash's sarcastic sneer seemed to increase Sky's irritation. "They possessed a wealth of imagination, I see this. The name does suit you, however, as bland and unimag—"

"Enough." Balgow interrupted the petulant exchange. "Have you grasped this simple information? Are you prepared to accept the gest? You know the penalty if you do not."

Wilash did not reply for some time. The gest jarred with him. Other than the honour gest on Corelle, he could not recall a gest on a woman in all his years in the Guild. The mark seemed to be a simple employee of some kind. She struck him as unremarkable, not the successful business owner whose life some disgruntled competitor might buy, or a philanderer, his death paid for by a husband jealous of his wife's dalliances. It would be dangerous to kill an employee of the Bailiff, and it would be absolute madness to kill that employee in the shadow of the Bailiff's Offices. The gest must be a diversion with no purpose other to bring about Wilash's ruin. If Sky could stay sober, Wilash guessed he would deliver the fatal blow. Wilash realised the Sky would fall on him, and he laughed aloud at his own jest.

Balgow snarled. "What amuses you? Do you accept the gest?"

"That I do." Wilash turned and left. He would not permit anybody to dismiss him with a derogatory wave or an insult, not ever again. He wearied of the schemes of these vile wretches. He cursed the day he had ever met Styrrach. That day had been his first with the Guild, and he expected this day to be his last.

With nothing to lose, Wilash headed for a tavern to drink an ale or two and pass his last hours with some degree of enjoyment, but as he walked away from the Guild building, a thought occurred to him. What if they did intend to kill a woman? It seemed inconceivable, yet so inconceivable, it might be genuine. His father's words came to him again. *"The tale must be true that could not be invented."* He did not fear death, but he feared to kill a woman at the command of these unprincipled murderers. How could he save her if they did mean to kill her? He already knew the answer to that question.

By the time Jorinda had returned with the herbs the previous night, Deineike had fallen asleep, but this morning she drank a cup of the herb-infused brew and set off to walk in circles around the small room while Jorinda watched on in concern, anxious lest she fall. The taller woman's right knee would not bend more than the tiniest amount, but at the least she could walk with the aid of her staff, and her progress amazed Jorinda, who marvelled again at Deineike's irrepressible spirit.

As she walked, Jorinda told her of the meeting with Wilash, and Deineike frowned in concentration. "You are certain he meant us no harm?"

"That I am. He expects to die today." Sadness washed over Jorinda at the thought. She pointed to the dagger on the table. "He gave me the dagger, though I did not wish to take it. It felt as though I betrayed you when I accepted it."

"You did not betray me. We should hide it away somewhere, nonetheless." Deineike walked close to the table and glanced down at the dagger. "It looks well made."

Jorinda laughed. "It is little better than the item you once offered to protect me with." She laughed at her jest. In truth, the dagger's workmanship could not be faulted. The magnificent carved bone handle sat in her hand as though it had been created for her, and no weapon she had ever held equalled its exceptional balance. Its edge glinted in the light from the window, as sharp as the blade in her fan had been, a slight serration near the tip the sole mark on it. A small "W" had been set into the top of the pommel. Wilash had given her a fine weapon, as fine as any she had ever seen.

Deineike smiled at her, then froze as a gentle knock came at the door. Jorinda held a finger to her lips, ran to the door without a sound, and strained her hearing for any telltale signs of who might be without. The knock came again, so soft that had the women been in the yard, they might not have heard it.

A familiar voice spoke. "It is Wilash."

Jorinda looked over to Deineike, who remained rooted to the spot, a mixture of puzzlement and fear on her face. Although Jorinda did not believe Wilash meant to harm them, some threat might have coerced him to lead the Guild to them, and he might be prepared to watch them through sad eyes as they died moments before the Guild took his own life. She shook the conflict from her head. How could she believe he would betray them after all he had said last night? He would give his own life to spare theirs. Had he not said as much?

"Corelle? Are you within? I need your help. Please." He sounded desperate, and Jorinda had to act. Either they could wait in silence and hope he left, or she could open the door and see what turned. It would require great trust to open the door, and she had Deineike to consider.

Deineike solved Jorinda's dilemma. "What do you want?" Jorinda gritted her teeth and bowed her head as Deineike yelled the question. The cat was now out of the sack, and Jorinda sighed at Deineike's incomprehensible lack of patience in this life-or-death situation. Why could she not have shown the same patience she displayed as she recovered from her dreadful injuries?

Jorinda pulled the door open and hissed at Wilash. "Come inside. Hurry." He stepped into the cottage, and Jorinda risked a brief glance in both directions outside before she closed the door. She spotted nobody else in the street.

Wilash gazed at Deineike and held out his right hand. "I am Wilash. I meet you at last."

Deineike did not take his hand. To release her staff to do so might have resulted in a fall, but that had nothing to do with her reticence. "I hear you have tried your best to meet me before today. Had you done so, it might have gone ill for me."

He lowered both his hand and his head. "It is true." He sounded as sad as the previous night. "I apologise. I have brought naught good to your life, and now I must beg for your help. You must despise me, but I should expect nothing less."

Deineike's blue eyes studied him while Jorinda stayed silent—she could say nothing of value. After some time, Deineike responded. "I am Deineike." The introduction broke the lengthy silence, and though Deineike did not smile, Jorinda sensed she had decided not to order Wilash to leave. "You were a friend of Arella's and are a friend of Jorinda's. Welcome to our home."

Tears dripped from his eyes, and he did not raise his head. "You knew Arella?" His voice became even sadder as he spoke Arella's name.

Deineike replied, a sadness in her voice also. "I knew her, and loved her, before you knew her, I believe."

Wilash's head snapped up and around to shoot a quizzical look at Jorinda, who shrugged her shoulders. "It is a complicated tale."

He turned his gaze to Deineike. "I stand humbled before a remarkable woman. I am grateful I did not meet you before."

Deineike laughed. "A compliment dressed in an insult's clothing, I think." Her eyes sparkled. Jorinda thought her at her most beautiful when she laughed.

Wilash joined in the laughter, the tension in the room dispelled by their merriment. "Indeed. My tongue betrayed me before a smile that brings light to my last day. My thanks for your welcome."

Jorinda wiped at her eyes, lest the tears gathered there betrayed her. Wilash had the right of it. Jorinda had never met a more remarkable person than Deineike, and the more she came to know her, the more the older woman surprised her. Less than a pass ago, Wilash had hunted them both, bent on their ruin, yet Deineike welcomed him to their home like a neighbour, new to the area, who brought the traditional bread gift into their house.

Jorinda had not, however, missed his reference to his last day, and she strove to keep any edge from her voice. "What brings you here, Wilash?"

He turned to face her once more, while behind him, Deineike lowered herself into a chair. "I have been assigned a gest. I suspect the gest is a fabrication; nothing more than a ploy to have me at a certain place at a certain time. The gest will be my ruin. There is doubt in my mind though, for the mark is a woman. If for some reason this woman has become embroiled in the schemes of the Guild, then I fear for her life. I do not fear for my own, but I would not see her killed. I beg you for your help."

Jorinda chewed at the inside of her cheek, reluctant to become involved. More lay at stake for her than a stranger's life. To save Wilash, she might have been prepared to do some small thing. For a stranger who might not even exist, she did not wish to take any risk that might put Deineike in danger's path. Jorinda's own life mattered nothing to her, but Deineike must be kept safe at all costs.

Wilash seemed to sense her reticence. "You have much to lose, I know this. I ask a great deal of you, when a pass ago I would have subdued you and cast Dankie to an ill fate with Guild members." Deineike corrected his mangled attempt at her name. "My apologies." He blushed as he mumbled his miserable response. "Corelle, I cannot see this innocent killed before me, nor by me. I beg you to help me."

Again, Deineike corrected him. "Jorinda."

Wilash sighed and corrected himself. "Jorinda."

Jorinda had no desire to be involved but felt obliged to show some interest. "How would you have me help with this?"

"I had hoped you might have some thoughts of your own on this aspect, I admit it. Could you intercept her and warn her before she comes to the alleyway?"

Jorinda frowned. "What alleyway?"

"She will leave the Bailiff's Offices by a rear exit into an alleyway. If she comes at all, I am to kill her there. I reason she does not exist other than as an excuse that puts me in the alleyway where a Guild blade will send me wherever I travel to afterward. But she might exist, and I would not have her drawn into my downfall and lose her life in the process."

Jorinda stared at him, incredulous. "The Bailiff's Offices? You realise every Portreeve in the land seeks my neck for a hangman's noose? You would have me risk my own life, walk into the Bailiff's Offices to save this woman, who by your own admission might not even exist?"

Wilash nodded, miserable. "I know it is much to ask, but I can trust nobody else in Alcmouth. You are right to question my state of mind. It is madness, but I can think of no other way to save the woman." He fell silent and his head dropped again.

A heavy silence fell over the room. Each appeared to battle with their own thoughts. Jorinda could see no way to help Wilash. She felt sorry for the woman and for Wilash, but she must prioritise Deineike's safety. "I am sorry, Wilash. I am obliged to keep Deineike safe. You may have compromised that already if anybody followed you here—"

He interrupted her. "Nobody followed me."

Jorinda glared at him. "You thought so last night, but I followed you."

Wilash let out a dejected sigh. "That you did, and I did not mark you."

A further silence descended on them until Deineike broke it. "Jorinda, you cannot let this woman die. I cannot stand by and watch you condemn her to die from our fear and inaction."

Jorinda looked askance at her, a broken thing who could walk no more than a few steps unaided, victim of unspeakable horrors visited on her by the two monsters who stood before her, but whose concern appeared focused on a total stranger. "Deineike—"

Deineike interrupted Jorinda yet again. "We will help Wilash as best we can."

Wilash exhaled loud and long and whispered in reply. "My thanks." He turned to Jorinda. "I know all there is to know about this so-called gest. What information do you need?"

Jorinda struggled not to laugh at the farcical situation that had developed in so few moments. "I know not, in truth. My lover has the plan, it seems."

Wilash turned again to Deineike. "You are a remarkable woman. I rue the day I joined the Guild more than ever now I have met you. In some small way, I feel my involvement in the pursuit of Corelle led you to the injuries you have sustained. She is fortunate to be your lover."

Deineike corrected yet him again, but with laughter in her eyes. "Jorinda."

Wide-eyed, Wilash looked at Jorinda, who held both arms out from her sides, palms upward. "She will vex you."

FIVE

TWO BODIES, TWO BOOKS

WILASH EXPLAINED ALL HE KNEW, AND JORINDA CONSIDERED THE information for some time. "You are certain her name is Korldia?"

Wilash wore a bashful look. "That I am not. I am clumsy with names, but that is how I recall it."

Deineike's brow furrowed as if she could not get her mind around the name. "It is an awkward name."

He shrugged and still looked embarrassed. "She should be easy to recognise, after all else. She is short, older, and overweight. There will be few women in that alleyway tonight who will fit this description."

Deineike seemed to voice her thoughts as they formed in her mind. "The moment she appears, we will greet her as old friends. We will urge her to come with us for a goblet of wine or a meal, some celebration of our reunion. We must impress upon her the urgency of her fate but not alert others to the ploy."

Jorinda remained determined Deineike would play no part in her attempt to save the woman, and she strove to sound as forceful as possible. "There is no 'we' in this. You will not be there. It is too dangerous." Wilash agreed with Jorinda.

Deineike gave them each a look of defiance. "Well done, both of you. You agree with one another. I will be there lest things go awry. The Guild may be less enthusiastic to spill the blood of innocents."

Sadness clouded Wilash's eyes. "You are not innocents in their eyes."

Jorinda remained resolute. She must keep Deineike out of the night's events. "You will not go, or I shall not."

Deineike laughed. "You would let me go alone? This will not happen. I know you, Jorinda. I will go, and you will go also. I might fall if you are not there to lean upon." She laughed again, and her eyes sparkled.

Deineike's laughter dissolved Jorinda's resolve as fast as it arrived, and she shook her head in resignation. "You are impossible."

Wilash drew in a sharp breath before he added his own thoughts. "Then we have a plan. You take her to safety, and I will tell the Guildmeister old friends appeared, and you all went off together. Guild rules did not allow me to spill the blood of innocents. After that, I will take my chances. I imagine my life will be forfeit in atonement for all I have brought to the three of you." He nodded as though to himself, mayhap an affirmation that his fate was written within their plan. "There is no more to discuss. I will take an ale, I think, then go to the alleyway and whatever fate is written for me."

It surprised Jorinda when he left in such a hurry, but in truth, it suited her. She yearned to spend some time alone with Deineike and dissuade her from any part in the night if possible. They both embraced Wilash, Jorinda held the door open, and he vanished up the street. He left with no farewell, and she wondered whether he felt too many words would have been required to say that farewell.

Jorinda tried for an hour but could not persuade Deineike of the foolishness of her involvement in the scheme. In truth, part of her wished Deineike would argue for neither of them to go. Jorinda considered the entire situation dangerous and the plan, if it could be called such, inadequate at best, disastrous at worst.

Outside, daylight changed to twilight, and they must act now or never. Jorinda decided not to take the dagger, but even as she told Deineike, doubt ate at her. The words she spoke might have been intended to reassure herself as much as Deineike. "There will be no need for bloodshed. The dagger will not be necessary to persuade this Korldia to come with us. It will remain here."

"So be it, if that is your decision."

Deineike's ready agreement sounded treacherous in Jorinda's opinion, and she chewed at the inside of her mouth as she brooded. "If we must go, we must go now. One of us walks at a pace unfit to be called movement." Deineike poked her tongue out at her. Jorinda narrowed her eyes and pouted, one last attempt to dissuade her lover. "I have a better use for that tongue."

"We will investigate those thoughts when we return." Deineike laughed, but at once, she raised her hand to her temple and pain flashed in her eyes.

Jorinda knelt before Deineike and wrapped her arms around her. "What is wrong?"

Deineike's bright reply seemed forced. "A small headache, nothing more. It will pass. Let us make ready."

Jorinda studied her lover's face but saw no grimace of agony or any further hint of pain. "Let us go then, fools that we are."

"Pick up my staff please."

Jorinda sighed. How Deineike imagined she could be of help in this madness if she could not stand without assistance, Jorinda could not calculate. She bent to pick up the staff from the floor, and when she stood again, Deineike had already risen, one arm on the table and the other outstretched for the staff.

The walk taxed Deineike's stamina, and they stopped many times for her to recover her strength. She leaned on Jorinda, and they both panted as they approached the square. They had not seen the Bailiff's Offices before, and Jorinda had never seen a building so magnificent in her life. Its size alone stilled her breath, and the ornate carvings in the stonework and woodwork, which represented various scenes of Dur life, astonished them both. Jorinda recognised a depiction of Zhanghar's square on one corner of the building and thought one of the carvings might represent the River Wantu as it flowed through Vjort. The front door had been fashioned from two enormous pieces of stained Ortwood. The women stood for long moments and gazed on the building in awe.

Darkness cloaked the city before they found the alleyway behind the colossal building that housed the Offices. Jorinda did not wish to enter the alleyway from the square, and more time slipped by as they searched along the next street until they found a smaller entranceway that led them into the middle of the alleyway from a different direction. Anxious they might have already missed the woman, Jorinda lay on the ground and peered around the corner of a building.

Lantern light spilled from some windows opposite the Bailiff's Offices and combined with the moon to provide a faint glow within the alleyway. A low wall ran down the alleyway close to the Bailiff's Offices, and two men dressed in the unmistakable red tunics of the Portreeve crouched behind the wall. Some paces behind them, another crouched figure hid, but that figure did not wear the Portreeve's tunic. A Guild member, she guessed, sent to slay Wilash if the Portreeve's men failed. Jorinda had no wish to be taken into custody by the Portreeve's men and, anxious for both of them, stood and eased Deineike back into the shadows where she raised a hand to the older woman's mouth.

Jorinda lowered her hand, and Deineike whispered, fear in her voice. "What is it?"

"The Portreeve's men wait there." Jorinda pointed toward the two figures in the red tunics.

Deineike peered forward and squinted as she attempted to see through the darkness. "I see them. Two of them. What does it portend? Do they wait for us?"

Jorinda considered this. She thought it unlikely, for they could not have known she and Deineike would come unless Wilash had betrayed them, which she did not want to believe. The men had been sent to kill or capture him, she guessed. They must be linked to the mysterious 'shrouding' Wilash had referred to the previous night. "I think not. They complicate the situation, nonetheless. Another hides some way behind them, a Guild member, I think. We should leave. The place reeks of danger."

Deineike seemed to have lost her initial fear. "That we will not. We are here now. We will see how the fates are written."

Jorinda sighed at Deineike's willfulness and cast around for a better place where they might conceal themselves. A small construction some steps from one of the buildings opposite the rear of the Offices caught her eye. It might be a privy or a storehouse, but to her dismay, two further figures lurked there. "There." She pointed to the shadowy figures. "Two more."

Deineike peered in the direction Jorinda pointed. "I do not see them. Your eyesight is better than mine."

Jorinda tutted. The situation had taken a sorry turn, and she feared they could not emerge from it alive. They had been drawn into events more complex than anticipated, and to proceed might bring their ruin. She shook her head and muttered, "This has turned awry. Deineike, we must leave now. Death lurks here, and it may be ours."

At that moment, a small door in the rear of the Offices opened and two figures appeared, silhouetted against the lantern light from within—a tall, slender man, and a woman, far shorter and stout. They exchanged words Jorinda could not hear, and the woman stepped out into the alleyway before she turned to speak to the man. Jorinda gasped as the lantern light washed over the woman's face.

Jorinda stared at the woman from her nightmare on the night they had arrived in Alcmouth. There could be no doubt. Short and overweight, with a plain face so like the face of the woman in the nightmare, she could be no other. She wore her long hair scraped into a horsetail, held there by a bright red ribbon, and she wore red shoes. Jorinda's blood had coloured the woman's feet the same red in the nightmare, and as she stared at the woman, all thoughts of the plan vanished from her head.

The door closed, and the woman walked toward Jorinda and Deineike. She would pass close to them if she headed for the opposite end of the alleyway or the small entryway Jorinda and Deineike had used.

Deineike hissed at her. "Jorinda. She is headed this way. We must act now." Jorinda could not move, aghast at the woman from the nightmare made flesh before her. "Jorinda." Despite Deineike's frantic whisper, Jorinda did not reply.

As the woman drew near, Deineike hobbled out of the shadows. "Korldia." She yelled the name, her left arm toward the woman, who stopped in her tracks to gaze in surprise at the woman who appeared out of the shadows and limped toward her. It took long painful moments for Deineike to reach her and pull her into an embrace. Deineike whispered something to the woman, but Jorinda could not hear the words.

At the sight of Deineike and Korldia in furtive conversation, Jorinda's inertia fell from her at last. She cast another glance around. The four Portreeve's men had not moved, but the two behind the wall whispered to one another. Wilash had not appeared, and the Guild man crouched so low behind the wall, Jorinda could no longer see him. Deineike had now become bound up in the night's events, however, and Jorinda could not stand by and watch.

Jorinda pushed herself forward and cried the woman's name. "Korldia. It has been too long." She folded the surprised woman into her arms and whispered in her ear, urgent and breathy with concern. "Your life is in grave danger. We can help you, but you must treat us as old friends whom you have not seen for some time." The woman blinked at her in obvious surprise as Jorinda kissed her cheek and raised her voice for the benefit of the Portreeve's men. "How do you fare?"

The woman blinked again, still pressed against Jorinda, and whispered in alarm. "My name is Klordia, not Korldia. Is this linked to the ledger?"

Jorinda cursed to herself that Wilash had misremembered the name. She had no idea what Klordia meant by "the ledger," but reasoned it might calm the woman if she agreed. "That it is." Jorinda feared their whispers might be overhead in the quiet alley-way, which would bring them all undone. Sweat trickled down her forehead.

Beyond Klordia, the two Portreeve's men emerged from behind the wall and moved toward them. Deineike stood nearby and shuffled her feet, nervous. The women had one last chance to save the plan, and Jorinda whispered again, agitated. "We are all in peril here. We may escape if you play your part."

The men had reached them, and Jorinda heard the other two on the move also, though she did not look in their direction. One of the men spoke, all business. "Is all well, ladies?"

To Jorinda's relief, Klordia answered him. "That it is. I have not seen my dear friends for some time. I recognise you. I work in the Bailiff's tally room."

"I have patrolled that area and believe I have seen you there. But unless I miss my guess, your name is not Korldia."

Klordia laughed. "That it is not, but my friends have ever been fond of a goblet, and they have taken several tonight." The man laughed also, less enthusiastic. He turned to look at Jorinda, who heard footsteps close behind her even as movement caught her eye further down the alleyway.

Deineike took an unsteady step toward the man. "We drank such fine wine. Had I known we would meet Korldia…Klorida… our friend, we would have saved a goblet for her. We did not." She giggled and leaned on the man as though her she had lost her balance for a heartbeat. Indeed, she may have, and Jorinda's heart raced in her breast despite her attempts to control it. "Why her parents chose such a compilcat…complicated name, I will never know." Deineike giggled again, and Jorinda thought the deception might be over-played.

The men looked at each other. Their faces suggested they could make no sense of what they witnessed and could find no reason to press the matter since the three women stood with their arms about one another, to all appearances old friends reunited as they claimed.

The man lowered his chin in a gesture of farewell. "We bid you a good night, then. I suggest you head for your homes, since these dark alleyways are not the place for ladies." None of the other men had spoken, and Jorinda imagined he may have been the senior man.

Klordia answered him. "Good night to you, and sound advice. We shall away and find a goblet for me, though none for you." She wagged a finger in Deineike's face, and they watched, anxious, as the four men wandered off down the alleyway.

Klordia turned to Jorinda. "Let us leave this alleyway and find somewhere safer where you can explain what has turned."

Jorinda cast about. Still no sign of Wilash, and she wondered where he had got to. She took Deineike's left arm and draped it over her own shoulder. "She is injured, as you see. In truth, she should not even be here." She glowered at Deineike.

Deineike gritted her teeth and muttered, "A goblet might ease my pain."

As they moved to leave the alleyway, a shadow to one side of them formed itself into the figure of a man. Jorinda hoped Wilash had arrived at last, but she did not recognise the newcomer. Deineike's left hand slid down Jorinda's back and fell to her side.

The stranger spoke, mockery in his voice. "My thanks. That performance entertained me no end. How you two came here, I do not know. The traitor Wilash played some part in it, my guess, but unless I am wrong, I have before me three desirable birds, and I believe I will pluck the feathers from you all. We will deal with Wilash afterward."

Jorinda glared at him. "Who are you? Stand aside, whoever you are, or I will be your ruin."

He laughed. "You do not know me, but I know you, Corelle—or whatever you now call yourself. Your description is known to every Guild member throughout Dur. Styrrach ensured we all knew of your treachery."

Klordia drew in a sharp breath. "Styrrach?"

The man ignored Klordia's question. "You should have been shrouded in Zhanghar. That would have been a kinder fate than the one Styrrach now has planned for you."

At the mention of the Guildmeister's name, Jorinda's stomach knotted, and she could not keep a vitriolic snarl from her face. "Stand aside. Your life hangs by a thread."

He laughed again. "You could strike me down unseen in this alleyway, and you would not hesitate to do so. You would not allow yourself to be taken if you could prevent it. You are unarmed, for you would have acted by now were it otherwise. Instead, I will kill you, but first, you will watch me take the lives of these others."

Klordia screamed as he drew a dagger out of his belt, and his free hand shot out to grasp Jorinda by the throat. He straightened his arm and held her at arm's length as he squeezed. He stood no more than a span taller than her, but he possessed formidable strength, and his grip constricted her throat. She could not suck any air into her lungs.

As Jorinda reached up to pull his arm away from the vicious hold he had on her, Deineike pressed something into her hand, and she recognised Wilash's dagger; its balance in her hand convinced her it could be no other. She had left it on the table in their cottage, and while Jorinda had been distracted by the staff, Deineike must have picked it up.

The man turned to Klordia, and she screamed again as he raised his dagger. Jorinda's head swam, and her vision blurred as his hand squeezed ever tighter. No air reached her brain, and if she did not act without delay, she would faint. To her surprise, Deineike's left hand shot up and grasped at the man's shoulder-length hair. She pulled it down, hard, tore some of it from his scalp, and he yelped in agony. Instinct took over, and Jorinda brought the dagger up while the pain distracted him. His height and the arm that squeezed her made his throat an awkward target, but she reached over his arm and slashed inward. The dagger caught him close to his left earlobe, and she dragged its blade downward. Although it bit deep into his cheek, his jawbone saved him from fatal injury. The blade skipped downward and ploughed a deep furrow in his neck toward his breastbone.

He screamed in anguish and released his grip on Jorinda's throat to press his hand to the wound in his neck as he swung his own dagger in a wild arc in a last gasp attempt to save himself. She stepped inside the arc of his swing, his arm bounced off her shoulder, and his dagger missed her flesh. Jorinda reached up with her left hand, pulled his arm away from his neck, and slashed the dagger across his throat under his jaw, calm, calculated. The keen blade caught his artery, and his blood spurted out across her and Deineike. The two cuts formed a deadly vermilion cross, and he slumped to the floor as his life pumped out of him. Klordia fetched up, and Deineike stood in shock, the man's hair still clutched in her fist.

Jorinda pulled Deineike's arm over her shoulder again. "We must go."

A man's voice echoed in the alleyway, and Jorinda froze. "I heard a scream." One of the Portreeve's men had returned, but before Jorinda could offer any explanation for the scream that had prompted his return, he flicked his eyes down to the figure of the man at their feet. He scrabbled at his belt and opened his mouth as though to call out something, but he made no sound. Blood trickled from his mouth instead, and his eyes widened in surprise. He fell forward onto his face with a gruesome thud. Wilash, who must have approached him from behind, held a bloodied dagger in his hand and gazed at the man's body in disbelief.

Jorinda bent down and checked the Portreeve's man's neck. She found a faint pulsing, and she slashed at his artery with her own dagger. Klordia fetched up again.

Jorinda urged them to action as she took Deineike's arm yet again. "We have to leave. This man's companions will seek him soon enough." They turned toward to the entryway, and Deineike also fetched up as she limped alongside Jorinda. They paused where the entryway spilled out into the street. Jorinda and Deineike were soaked in blood, so Jorinda knelt to cut a strip from the hem of Klordia's dress and used it to wipe the worst of the blood from their faces.

She turned to Klordia. "Where do you live?" Shock appeared to have rendered Klordia immobile. She stared forward, did not blink, and would not meet Jorinda's gaze. Jorinda grasped her shoulders. "Where do you live?"

Klordia seemed to speak out of some instinct. "Two streets away. I have a room. It is close to my work."

"Lead us there, and hurry." Klordia appeared rooted to the spot, and Jorinda hissed at her again. "Klordia. We are in great danger. Lead us to your home now. Every heartbeat hastens all our ruins."

Wilash's voice startled Jorinda. "I killed him."

Deineike fetched up again, and Jorinda tutted. They had all sunk into a deep state of shock at the precise moment she needed them to be lucid and on the move to somewhere safer. "By the fates." She grasped Klordia's chin and hissed, furious, into her face. "Lead us to your house, or I may as well kill us all where we stand and spare us all from Guild justice."

Klordia blinked, but at last she turned and walked away from the alleyway. Jorinda hurried Deineike along behind her, but thanks to Deineike's injured leg they soon fell behind Klordia, who seemed oblivious to the fact. Jorinda muttered under her breath. She had saved the woman's life, and now the wretched creature seemed determined to leave them behind and make good her own escape while ruin caught up with the rest of them. She cursed their ill fortune.

Klordia stopped at a street corner ahead of them, and at last she looked back and appeared to notice how far ahead she had moved. To Jorinda's relief, she waited for them to reach her. "This is my street. Come. My home is not far."

They followed Klordia, who reduced her pace so Deineike and Jorinda did not fall so far behind. Wilash made no attempt to help Jorinda, and she struggled to assist Deineike alone, but time spent on any attempt to persuade him to help would be time wasted. Klordia stopped at the door of a house, pushed the door open, and they hurried inside while Klordia closed the door behind them. She led them down the hallway toward the rear of the house where she fumbled in the small bag she wore strung across her shoulder, took out a key, and used it to open an inner door that led into a room.

Klordia located a flint and lit a lantern. She lived in a sizeable room, with a bed, a table, a vanity stand, and a large cupboard near the fireplace. Jorinda helped Deineike over to the bed and sat her on it. Klordia slumped into one of the two chairs at the table, her head in her hands. The colour had drained from Wilash's face, and he stood inside the door with the bloodied dagger still clutched in his hand. Jorinda had not checked whether he had concealed the dagger as they hurried from the scene, but she reasoned they would have attracted a great deal of attention with or without the dagger had they encountered anybody on the street.

Their luck had held, but she dared not push it further. Jorinda stood before Klordia. "Where are your clothes? We cannot stay here, but Deineike and I must change our clothes."

Klordia looked up at her. "What? My clothes? Why?"

Jorinda longed to slap her. It might bring her out of the stupor she appeared to be in, but she resisted the urge at great cost to her temper. "Deineike and I must change. Our clothes are covered in blood, and we must draw as little attention to ourselves as we can."

In a voice little more than a whisper, Klordia replied with another question. "Can we not stay here?"

Through clenched teeth, Jorinda replied as she struggled against her fury at the inane questions. "That we cannot. The Portreeve's men recognised you. They will know where you live, or they will soon find out from your employer. We must be gone as soon as we can. Where in the Five Cities are your clothes?"

Klordia pointed at a curtain hung against one wall. "There."

Jorinda suspected Klordia had not understood the question. "In the window?"

"It is an alcove, not a window. I keep my clothes behind it. The curtain hides them. In case a visitor…" She appeared to lose the thread of her thought, and Jorinda stepped over to the curtain and whipped it aside. Three chests sat behind it in a small alcove, along with two tired pairs of shoes and a pair of ankle-height boots. She opened the first chest and peered into it. It held a few plain dresses of common making, and she snatched out the first one her hand fell on, then pulled it over her head. The dress fit well enough for her purpose, and she tore off her trousers, wriggled out of her tunic beneath the dress, and threw both on the floor.

Anxious, she pushed the dresses around as she tried to find the largest, but they all appeared much the same, so she pulled a random dress from the trunk and held it toward Deineike. "Put this on. Use the curtain if you wish privacy." Wilash turned away, to allow them some modesty, she guessed.

Deineike sounded pitiful. "It will not fit. I am too tall."

Jorinda answered in a terse voice as her irritation grew more fervent with each beat of her heart. "A dress that is clean, but a poor fit, is preferable to a fine, fitted one that drips with blood." The others appeared determined to bring about their ruin as well as her own. She turned to Wilash. "Wilash, you must help me with Deineike, for we must hasten from here. The Portreeve will be here at any moment, and we must not be here when they arrive. And put away your dagger, please."

He turned to face her and nodded as Jorinda turned again to Klordia. "Rouse yourself, Klordia. We are away." When she turned back to the bed, Deineike's struggles to pull the dress over her head might have been comical in less dire circumstances. She had managed to shed her tunic, and Jorinda stepped over to her and helped her pull the dress down. Folds of excess cloth across the bust betrayed Klordia's ample bosom and fuller figure, and Deineike's extra height left the dress not far beyond her knees. It must do for now, Jorinda decided. She reached under the dress, fumbled loose the button of Deineike's trousers, and pulled them from her.

Klordia spoke from behind her. "How can you be so calm?" At the least, Klordia had risen to her feet, Jorinda noted with relief.

Jorinda threw Deineike's trousers onto the bed. "One of us must remain so, since the three of you have become…" No number of insults would improve the situation, she reasoned. "I am sorry. I am more used to death than you." She managed a weak smile. "I am as frightened as you, if I speak the truth." She laid a hand on Klordia's shoulder. "Let us hurry to our cottage. It is a good distance from here, but we will have some time to form a plan there. We cannot stay here."

She rounded them up and badgered them out into the hallway. If any other residents of the house heard them, they must have judged it prudent not to pry. Wilash took Deineike's right side, Jorinda took the left, and they moved at a better pace than when they had fled to Klordia's house.

As they struggled down the street, Jorinda cautioned them. "Please, by all the fates. Control your stomachs. If you can manage it, leave no trail of your insides for them to follow us by."

Deineike raised a hand to her mouth, but if she had been about to fetch up, she controlled the reflex. "I hate you." Despite her half-hearted jest, Deineike moaned as they spirited her along, as strange a sight as any who might observe them would ever have seen.

They bypassed the square to reach their cottage; Jorinda had no wish to meet the other Portreeve's men again. The trip took longer than it had taken Jorinda and Deineike to reach the Bailiff's Offices earlier. Jorinda found it somewhat easier with Wilash's help, but Deineike suffered, and it tore at Jorinda's heart to continue without pause rather than stop to allow her any short spell of relief. Jorinda insisted they find detours that avoided inns and taverns. It added time to the journey, but she deemed it best to avoid any patrons who might come out of such establishments.

The journey took over an hour, and at times, Jorinda thought Deineike had been rendered unconscious by her pain as her head slumped forward and her feet dragged along the street behind her. After a few heartbeats, she would snap her head up, shake it, grit her teeth, and attempt to move her feet to help Jorinda and Wilash.

Jorinda battled her guilt as she dragged Deineike along through such pain, and she fought back tears as the full horror of the night threatened to overwhelm her. She struggled to stay as calm as she could, although the others sighed and moaned and appeared ready to give up, to sit in the street until the Portreeve's men arrived and took them off to the gallows.

Despite the late hour, two people turned a corner and walked toward them, and Jorinda saw no alleyway she could turn them all into to avoid the pair. When she judged they were within earshot, Jorinda turned to Wilash. "Father, I swear it. This is the last time I rescue her from that tavern." She hoped the flimsy tale would deflect curiosity and might persuade the strangers against any offer to help. Deineike still clutched her staff in her right hand, which may have weakened Jorinda's deception. One of the two whispered to the other, and they both laughed. The pair passed by, and Jorinda led her little group onward toward the cottage and whatever fates were written for them.

SIX

CONVERSATIONS IN THE NIGHT

They came to the street where Jorinda and Deineike had their cottage, and Jorinda stopped them at the corner with an urgent whisper. "Wait here while I walk forward and make sure none watch for us. If I scream out, turn and walk away. Do not follow me." She stared at Wilash since he must now step up as leader while she moved forward alone. He nodded again but did not speak.

Jorinda moved forward with great care and used the shadows to hide herself from any eyes that might look for her. She spotted no figures crouched hidden nearby, and no curtains or window shutters twitched in the vicinity of the cottage. To her relief, when she tried the door, she found it intact and still locked, unlocked it with the key hung on a leather string around her neck, and slipped inside. She closed the door behind her and stood motionless for several heartbeats while she listened for any sound as her eyes adjusted to the darkness within. Satisfied, she slid outside again and ran back to the three dejected figures at the corner.

She whispered again. "Hurry. We are safe for now. Once we are inside, we can determine what we do next." She slipped back under Deineike's left arm, and they reached the cottage. Once inside, Jorinda closed and locked the door, then slid down it until she sat on the floor, her back against the door and her head in her hands.

The others watched in silence as the tension knotted Jorinda's stomach, and she wept at last. Her tears poured down her cheeks for some time. She had broken her vow and killed twice. The tension that coursed through her as she marshalled the others throughout the fraught hour and more of their escape had drained her, and her body shook and spasmed. They had survived for now, though for how long, Jorinda could not guess.

The tears poured from her for yet another vow broken and all the trials her ill-conceived decision to join the Guild had brought. When she joined the Guild, she hoped it would help to protect the woman she loved. Instead, it had led her to kill Arella and countless others. It had led Deineike to the brink of death and placed Wilash and Klordia in mortal peril also. How could she live with herself another heartbeat? The time had come to fulfil the vow she had sworn that night above The Ship's Yard and put an end to a life full of death before she wreaked any more havoc in the lives of those who did not deserve it. She reached toward the dagger she had pushed into her boot after she had slit the throat of the Portreeve's man.

Deineike's soft voice stopped her. "Jorinda, my love. What must we do?" Jorinda looked up at the three shadows, who had not moved. They still gazed down on her as all her self-hatred and guilt poured from her eyes with the salt sting of remorse. They needed her, and she could not abandon them yet.

Jorinda gave an involuntary laugh. "Light a lantern to begin with, by all the fates." Deineike hopped to the table, found the flint, and light burst from the lantern. Jorinda looked at her companions, and they were a sorry sight. Klordia's dress looked ridiculous on Deineike, a terrible fit. Klordia had lost her ribbon on the journey, and her blonde hair lay strewn about her face. Wilash blinked as if in disbelief, and he still held the dagger pressed against his leg. She shook her head. "How we have come here alive, the fates alone know, but we must prepare to leave before the sunrise. We cannot stay in Alcmouth."

Klordia drew in a sharp breath. "I want to know what in the Five Cities turned tonight. It seems I am a fugitive, although I have done no wrong."

Jorinda gave a sarcastic laugh. "You are welcome. You have done no wrong, yet the Guild assigned a gest on you that would have seen you dead had I not intervened. But by all means—"

Deineike interrupted, and her blue eyes flashed in anger. "Jorinda. What is wrong with you? How can you speak to her so?"

Klordia began to cry, a hand across her eyes. Jorinda felt a twinge of sympathy, but in truth, she and Deineike once more found themselves in extreme danger and must flee. She blamed Klordia, for none of the night's events would have unfolded but for her.

Through her sobs, Klordia searched for more answers. "What is a 'gest', and what is the Guild? What is this 'Styrrach' that…vile man mentioned? I saw it in the ledger, but I do not understand any of this."

Wilash reached out a hand, awkward, and smoothed some of Klordia's hair back from her face as he attempted a simple explanation to a complicated question. "The Guild is a clandestine group of hired killers. They sent me to that alleyway tonight to kill you. That is a gest—a mission to take the life of another for coin." Her hand fell from her eyes, and she stared at him open-mouthed. His words seemed to shock her, and she turned as white as the petals of a daisy. "Styrrach runs the Guild in Zhanghar, but I cannot tell you anything about this ledger you referred to."

A question in Jorinda's mind would not be ignored. "Why does the Guild wish you dead?"

Deineike spoke in a soft, compassionate tone. "Tell us what the ledger is."

Klordia turned to her, and although Jorinda could not tell what Klordia saw in Deineike's eyes, she drew in a short breath and appeared more composed. "I am a tally clerk at the Bailiff's Offices. I found a ledger there that contained entries I could make no sense of. Vast amounts of coin—levies, I thought—and the greatest part of it seems to be paid to this Styrrach."

The other three stared at her as her words continued to pour out. "I asked the Senior Tally Master to bring the ledger to the attention of the Bailiff, and he assured me he would. He required me to stay at work longer tonight and give him a detailed explanation of all the ledger suggested. He seemed grateful I had brought the matter to their attention. He said the main doors would be locked at that time of night and asked me to leave through the rear door. The events that then turned, I have no explanation for and cannot understand."

After many moments, Wilash broke the silence that ensued. "This man is involved in the gest then, since the Guild told me you would be detained tonight at your work. He delayed you on orders from the Guild."

Jorinda could not believe her ears. "How can this be? How can the Bailiff's Offices be involved with the Guild in these things?"

Deineike snapped her fingers. "The Portreeve is involved also. His men went there to capture Wilash as he tried to kill Klordia." She seemed to realise they all stared at her. "There can be no other explanation. They were not there to take some break from their work. They must have been there to take Wilash into custody. They knew he had been sent to kill Klordia."

A scornful look came to Klordia's face. "You rave. The Bailiff and the Portreeve, their hands in the gloves of some group of animals that kill for coin? It is not possible. I can scarce believe such an organisation even exists. Do you torment me for some perverse sense of pleasure?" Tears came again, and Wilash squeezed her arm, affectionate and concerned.

With a sigh, Jorinda swept away Klordia's doubt. "The Guild exists. I know this, for I belonged to it."

Wilash paused, then confessed his own guilt. "As did I."

Klordia looked at Wilash with red-rimmed, tear-stained eyes. "I cannot believe it of you." She sniffed. "I can believe it of this." She waved an arm toward Jorinda.

"*This?*" Jorinda snarled at Klordia as she reached toward her boot.

Deineike held out a placatory hand. "Jorinda, calm yourself." She turned to Klordia. "Klordia, I understand why you are upset. I beg you not to judge any of us by the things you have seen tonight. There are things here none of us can comprehend, and we must work out what they signify and what we must do. Let us remain civil to one another while we do so."

Wilash, who had nodded several times as Deineike spoke, agreed with her. "Deineike speaks the truth. You judge Jorinda for the death of Sky, but I also killed tonight."

Klordia shook her head in violent denial. "That you did not. You did nothing worse than injure that man to help us. She cut his throat in cold blood as he lay helpless."

Jorinda's voice grew louder as her frustration reached fever pitch. "He would have drowned in his own blood had I not done so. Wilash had stabbed him in his lung. Would you have left him there to die in agony? I gave him a quick death. And you, of course, forget that I saved you from…Sky?"

Wilash shrugged. "He told me his name, and I derided him for it. Now he is dead. His name is ash now, as is he, in truth."

Deineike returned to her earlier point. "It is clear why the Portreeve's men were there, whether you will believe it or you will not. They are somehow bound up with the Guild, and it with them."

Wilash's confusion and misery turned to anger. "It is hard to see it another way. They waited for me to kill Klordia, and I would be taken to the gallows in punishment."

Klordia gave Wilash a brief smile. "I do not believe you would have killed me."

Klordia tried to cast the night's events in a light favourable to Wilash and unfavourable to Jorinda. Annoyed, Jorinda spat out, "That he would not. In fact, he begged us to help him save your life, and as a result, Deineike and I must once more flee, the Guild and the Portreeve at our backs. Your gratitude for our involvement warms my heart." She could not resist the sarcastic rejoinder. Every beat of her heart increased her dislike for the ungrateful Klordia.

Klordia's face flushed with anger, and she balled her hands into fists. "You must flee because you killed those men, not because of me."

Jorinda clenched her teeth again, irritated by Klordia's prickly demeanour. "I killed those men because of you."

Deineike let out a heavy sigh. "Can we put aside these differences and recriminations while we decide on our best course of action?"

Klordia held her head high, proud or stubborn. "My course is clear. I have killed nobody, and I will not run. To do so would make me an accomplice in the murder of two men. I will go to the Portreeve and explain what turned. I will be exonerated and return to my life."

Jorinda snorted and shook her head, and even Wilash and

Deineike looked askance at Klordia. Wilash replied before Jorinda could make another barbed comment. "Klordia, you will be killed. You should have been killed tonight. Whatever you uncovered in that ledger marked you for death. Like it or like it not, you are a fugitive now."

Deineike seemed to have recovered her composure. "Can we at the least agree the Portreeve and the Guild are somehow entwined in this scheme, whatever its end?" She stared around the room, hands on hips.

Jorinda accepted Deineike's conclusion. "That we can, or I can, at the least." It seemed impossible to arrive at any other explanation. Wilash nodded, a look of misery on his face. Klordia looked reflective, almost as if she had not heard the question.

Deineike continued. "Then we face two choices. We flee, or we fight." She looked at each of them in turn. "Since only one of us can fight, we must flee."

Klordia snapped her fingers in the air, realisation in her eyes. "I did not see levies. They run two books." Klordia's words seemed unrelated to the conversation, and Jorinda looked at her in confusion as she pressed on. "The amounts in the ledger were vast. If they did represent nothing more than simple levies, the revenue that generated them would be enormous. So enormous, in truth, the person who earned them would be richer than the Duke. How could I have missed it? Numbers never hide their secrets from me." She fell silent and shook her head from side to side for some moments.

A puzzled expression on her face, Deineike pushed her to explain further. "What are two books?"

Klordia's face radiated joy as if the topic excited her. "I have heard of it, but I never believed it existed. They keep two sets of ledgers. One is false but will stand any scrutiny, for the numbers in it make sense. The other is factual, and all the dirty secrets of what is hidden are accounted within it." They all wore puzzled expressions, and she huffed in exasperation. "Wilash, you send me five hundred regals as your so-called levy."

Jorinda sneered. "It seems Wilash has come into a great fortune."

Klordia shot her a hateful glance but ignored the jibe. "I account the levy in my factual ledger, which I keep secret. I then account a far smaller levy in my false journal, the one that is made public and will stand any audit."

Deineike stared at Klordia, and her brows knitted together. "What of the difference? I cannot understand what happens to the excess coin."

Klordia glared at her. "Then do not interrupt me. The difference is sent to this Styrrach. He receives seventy percent, or three hundred and fifty regals. The other one hundred and fifty regals are accounted in the false ledger as Wilash's levy."

Deineike seemed intrigued, but Jorinda had lost the thread some time before. "Why does the three hundred and fifty go to Styrrach?"

Klordia opened her arms before her, palms to the ceiling. "I cannot answer that question."

Deineike pressed on even as Jorinda gave up any hope she would ever understand. "How much coin did they send to Styrrach?"

"Enormous amounts. Thousands of regals each pass. All from different businesses, tally houses for the most part, as far as I could tell."

The concept of so many coins baffled Jorinda. "How do they transport such numbers of coins?"

Klordia shrugged again. "I cannot explain this."

"They do not." Deineike grew more animated. "The amounts are too great, and I imagine the weight of thousands of regals would sink any ship. The ledger records how much Styrrach receives, but some other arrangement exists for him to take possession of the coin."

Jorinda did not know how much thousands of regals weighed and doubted it would sink a ship, but other questions nagged at her. "If you are right, and this is no more than a record, why does Styrrach not keep the record himself? Why does he allow it to be handled in the Bailiff's Offices?"

Wilash had said nothing for some time, but now he intervened. "The real levies are accounted there. It may be simpler to keep all the ledgers together."

Klordia seemed thoughtful, but she favoured Wilash with a coy smile. "The simplest answer is often the truth."

Jorinda could see no connection between the coin paid to Styrrach from the levies and the deadly work of the Guild. "It is not clear to me why the Guild kills people over this. How is the work we performed for Styrrach linked to this?"

Wilash shook his head as if to imply he reached for candles in the dark. "The deaths of Guild victims are linked to the vast amounts of coin in some way. People who might betray them must be eliminated, people such as Klordia." He shrugged as though he had no real idea of the answer.

When Klordia spoke again, her voice became quiet, as though she feared to be overheard. "I have a further concern. Individual businesses do not send their levies straight to the Bailiff. The Portreeve of each city sends the Bailiff any surplus levies he does not need for the management of his city. The amounts I saw are far greater than I would have expected those excesses to be."

Deineike seemed uncertain when she replied, her brow furrowed and her words hesitant. "Might the Portreeves pay these huge sums to retain city status? To reward the Bailiff for the prestige of the charter?"

Jorinda saw a flaw in Deineike's argument. "That would make sense but for the fact that most of it is sent to Styrrach."

Nobody spoke. Jorinda struggled to believe such an organisation could exist. The Portreeves and the Bailiff, the law of the land, bound up with clandestine killers. She could see no rational explanation for it. More than that, it went against everything all Durfolk believed. No citizen would believe such corruption existed in the highest offices in the land. Even Jorinda found it difficult to believe, and she had seen some elements of it play out that night.

After all else, it sounded no less outrageous than all she had believed about the Guild before this strange night. Would disgruntled Durfolk pay coin to bring about the deaths of those who had fallen out of favour with them? Most people would laugh at her if she suggested such a thing happened right under their noses. She returned to the more urgent issue. "We appear to have uncovered something we can do little about, but we have more important things to decide. We are not safe in Alcmouth. If we are correct in what we have deduced, then our peril is greater than we have guessed up to this point. We must leave without delay. The question is where we go, not whether we go."

Deineike seemed to have more questions, but she nodded. "Let us try to sleep for an hour or two, then return to this issue. We are all exhausted and will make better decisions if we get some sleep."

None disagreed, so Deineike crawled up the stairs with some difficulty. Now she had turned her thoughts from Klordia's tale, her exhaustion became palpable. Wilash lay down on the floor, and Klordia sat in a chair. Jorinda remained seated against the door for a time, and when she heard Wilash's breaths become deep and regular, she guessed he had fallen asleep. Careful to avoid unnecessary noise, she went up the stairs and lay down next to Deineike, who turned and wrapped her arms about her.

Deineike's breaths soon suggested she had also drifted off to sleep. Jorinda told herself she would stay awake in case danger came to the cottage, but the night had drained her, and she fell asleep in moments. When Deineike's soft shake dragged her awake, daylight seeped through the shutter. The previous night had not been a nightmare, and they must now flee again or risk Guild justice at Styrrach's hands.

SEVEN
DECISIONS ARE REACHED

Jorinda and Deineike went downstairs, and they all gathered in the parlour—Klordia and Deineike in the room's two chairs, Jorinda and Wilash on the floor. They ate some bread and meats, then returned to the events of the previous night.

Klordia gazed at Jorinda, earnest and uncomfortable. "I spoke out of turn last night. I apologise."

Deineike had not expected the apology, but it seemed appropriate. She waited some moments, but Jorinda did not reply, and Deineike felt some answer must be made. "You were tired and shocked. Jorinda understands." By rights, Jorinda should have acknowledged the apology herself, but Klordia could not begin to comprehend the things that ate at Deineike's lover.

Jorinda crossed her ankles before her and looked at Wilash. "Where in the Five Cities did you get to last night? Why did you arrive so late?" Jorinda's vitriolic tone spat sharp needles of accusation at Wilash.

He looked crestfallen. "I lingered in the tavern overlong and lost track of the hour. I am sorry. Some Portreeve's men walked away as I neared the alleyway, so I hid. I heard a scream, then one of them ran into the alleyway, and I reasoned things had turned awry. I am sorry."

Jorinda tutted, and Deineike understood her lover's frustration. Things had turned awry, and Wilash's tardiness had complicated the situation. Blame does not put bread on the table, as the Dur expression went, so she hoped Jorinda would drop the subject. The younger woman gave a heavy sigh and seemed to weigh his explanation, her brow furrowed, her mouth crooked, then shook her head and continued. "Regardless, we must decide where we go now. Deineike and I are not safe here and will leave this morning. We do not ask you to come with us. Danger follows us all, but it dogs my footsteps more than most. If you wish to travel with us, you may, but we will not think any worse of you if you go your own ways."

Wilash drew in a deep breath. "We could leave Dur, head for a different land."

Jorinda's hair swished from side to side as she shook her head in rejection of the idea. "Deineike and I do not have enough coin for such a voyage. I no longer have my token. I hid it in my fan, but I would be loath to use it even if I had retained it."

Wilash looked despondent. "You could not, for Styrrach has ordered you to be taken into custody if you attempt to."

Jorinda gave a derisive snort at his explanation. A dreadful fate would await any mariner who tried to apprehend her. Such thoughts were unhelpful, and Deineike shook them from her, scattered them into the motes of dust that hung in the ray of sun through the window.

Klordia looked horrified. "How then will we leave, if not by ship? I cannot walk from the city. It is beyond me."

Wilash appeared to weigh their options before he spoke again. "We could sail to Ort, then travel inland to Vjort or Delcan."

Jorinda sighed again and seemed exasperated. "We cannot take ship. The cost would be prohibitive." She drummed the fingers of one hand on her leg.

Wilash looked thoughtful. "I have my token, though I do not know whether it would be challenged if I tried to use it with you present. I confess, I do not know whether women in the company of a man might be covered by Styrrach's order. We could claim you are my family." His words carried little conviction.

"It seems risky." Jorinda's lack of faith in the suggestion showed in her face, and Wilash nodded as she spoke. He might be grateful she had swept his idea away.

Any decision they made would be rife with risk, but Deineike wanted decisions without the fruitless back-and-forth of the night before. "Everything is risky. We must choose the lesser of all the evils that lie before us. We must leave here, and a ship seems no riskier than any other means. We cannot go to Vjort, but we might settle in Ort."

Wilash jerked forward, his eyes bright with excitement, as though some fresh thought had come to him. "Or Dur City."

The suggestion puzzled Deineike. "Why Dur City?" She had never been to the city in the Eastlands. Mayhap nobody had. It might not even exist. The foolish thought almost brought a laugh to her throat. She swallowed it, anxious not to make light of their situation.

Wilash replied so fast, his words almost stumbled over each other as they competed for release. "Ort is a waypoint on the river, and Guild members may come there at times. Dur City is further to the east and difficult to reach, so it is unlikely they would ever visit. There is no Guild there, and I hear it is vast. A large city is easier to hide in than a small town, and with no Guild presence, we have only the Portreeve to worry about. One fewer snake in the pit, so to speak."

Jorinda appeared unconvinced. "The Guild and the Portreeve are one as far as our safety is concerned."

Deineike pondered this. She had not realised no Guild existed in Dur City, could see no reason why it did not. "Why is there no Guild in Dur City?"

Wilash looked thoughtful again. "In truth, I do not know."

Jorinda seemed to have no answer to the question either. "Styrrach sees no reason to run a Guild there, or the Portreeve there is not bound up with Styrrach and the levies, my guess."

Klordia snapped her fingers together and startled Deineike, who had become lost in her thoughts about the inconsistency. "It is landlocked." The others stared at her in confusion as she expanded on her thought. "Dur City is landlocked, and goods do not arrive there by ship. That must be why they have not established their Guild there."

Jorinda disagreed at once. "Ort is on the river, yet there is no Guild there either. It is not even a city."

Wilash nodded, though his words did not confirm which of them he agreed with. "You have the right of it. It is a mystery."

Deineike grew ever more frustrated. "Good. This tale needs further mystery. It had become too simple for my tastes." Her jest lightened the mood for a moment, and the others managed laughter.

Jorinda held up a hand for silence, keen, it seemed, to pursue a thread of thought that wriggled in her mind. "Why is Ort not a city? I have wondered this before."

Klordia frowned in concentration. "Insufficient levies?"

Jorinda shook her head, and Deineike wondered whether Jorinda intended to disagree with every word Klordia spoke. "It is large. Larger than Ryl, my guess, almost as big as Zhanghar. It is on the Alc, and a great many ships must pass through it every day. A town so large must be able to raise sufficient levies to justify city status."

Tears appeared in Wilash's eyes. He hung his head and stared at the floor in misery. Deineike leaned down to him and stroked his neck in concern. "Is something wrong, Wilash?"

"I apologise." He sniffed and wiped at his eyes. "I had a memory of last night, of the man on the floor and my dagger covered in his blood."

Jorinda shook her head, laid a compassionate hand on his arm. "You did not kill him, Wilash. I killed him. Do not burden yourself with that guilt. It is mine to carry."

Despite Jorinda's attempt to brighten his mood, Wilash continued to berate himself. "The man did no wrong. He went about his business, and I took his life away from him." His voice had become deathly quiet, but it resonated with his pain.

Klordia gave Wilash an affectionate smile. "That you did not. Jorinda has the right of it. You injured him in defence of us all, nothing more. You should not dwell on it." Jorinda did not react to Klordia's words.

Deineike could not stand to see Wilash look so crushed. "The fellow had some part to play in the fates written for us. Like as not he would have killed or arrested us if you had not intervened. The Portreeve's men might have had some involvement in the gest."

Jorinda threw out yet another objection. "I do not believe they had any role in it." Deineike shot Jorinda a stern glance, afraid her words might compound Wilash's misery, but it seemed she would not be deterred. "The Portreeve and the Bailiff may be caught up in it, but I am sure the Portreeve's men are not. I also do not believe all members of the Guild are aware of the things we have discussed."

Wilash looked up, his eyes wide. "You have the right of it. When the Torric man talked to me of you and the shroud, he mistook me for the Senior Aide, not an insignificant member. When he realised his mistake, his reaction showed he knew he had spoken out of turn. The members are pawns in this, as are the Portreeve's men. Styrrach grows rich from this, and the other Guildmeisters, I imagine. The rest are toys they play with as they see fit."

Jorinda looked up at him with horror on her face. "They play with them as they see fit, then they discard them when it suits. Styrrach orchestrated my betrayal himself. That must be the "shrouding" you mentioned."

Wilash's face grew pale. "Can it be? I suspected the Guild had some link to the betrayals, but to suggest Styrrach betrays his own members to suit his own ends…" He fell silent.

Jorinda shook her head and seemed shocked at the explanation she had latched onto. "Pilos said as much with his last words before I cut him down. 'Am I to be killed for what I did, then? Has Styrrach betrayed me?' He has repeated those words many times since, in my nightmares. I guess Styrrach ordered him to betray me to the Portreeve. I could make no sense of his words—until now." Deineike winced at the horrified look Klordia shot at Jorinda as she spoke of Pilos' death, but Jorinda seemed not to notice.

Wilash spoke slow and quiet, afraid to ask, it seemed. "Why would Styrrach betray his own?"

Jorinda took a long breath, as though she sought answers from the air itself. "Who knows? They may have felt I had served any useful purpose they had for me. The same happened to you, last night. The Portreeve's men were there for you, not us, for they could not know you had asked us to intervene. You had been sold to them by the Guild and would have been hanged."

Wilash furrowed his brow, clenched his teeth together. "Corelle, there is something else—"

The conversation had deviated far enough from the original point and must be returned to that issue, so Deineike interrupted whatever Wilash had been about to say. "None of this helps us with the decisions before us. Where do we go, and do we travel together or apart?" Wilash gave her an angry stare but abandoned whatever he had been about to say.

Heartbeats passed, then Jorinda announced, "I will go to Ort."

"Why Ort?" Deineike would rather leave Dur altogether if some means could be found. She feared for her life after the previous night.

Jorinda shrugged, almost an apology. "I have no explanation that would make sense. I feel some answer lies there. It has never been granted city status, and there is no Guild there, despite its size." She flashed a smile of regret toward Deineike. "I fear to travel by ship, since the use of the token is dangerous. It will be a trial for you to ride so far, my love. I realise this."

Klordia did not look at Jorinda as she spoke to her. "You have the right of it. None of the coin came from Ort. It all came from Alcmouth, Torric, Ryl, and Zhanghar."

The conversation had once more strayed from the point, like a cat that cannot be forced to do its owner's bidding, but Deineike could not resist the temptation to press Klordia to expand on her statement. "How do you know this?"

"The entries had the letters of each city next to them. None had an 'O'."

Jorinda's voice spat her disappointment at Klordia. "Why did you not mention this last night? Ort has some significance in all we have discussed. I must go there and learn why it does not pay coin to Styrrach, unlike those four cities."

The question annoyed Klordia; her cheeks red, her jaw thrust forward, eyes narrowed. "My thoughts were jumbled last night." Deineike imagined Klordia and Jorinda were heat and cold, fated never to exist together.

Wilash intervened even as Jorinda drew in a breath to respond to Klordia. "I will travel to Ort with you if you desire it. I have brought even more troubles down on you here. We must chance the journey by ship, though it may prove risky. To ride would take too long and would be beyond Deineike."

The final decision on whether Wilash travelled with them must be left to Jorinda, since he had been a friend to her before Deineike had known her. Jorinda glanced up at him and nodded. "Your company would be welcome." Wilash gave her a grateful smile.

Klordia's prickly demeanour vanished, replaced by a sorrowful air. "I am unlikely to live until nightfall if I remain here alone. I will travel with you." Self-pity dripped from the tally clerk's words, her face.

Deineike could never have anticipated Jorinda's next question to Klordia. "Do you fear me?" Deineike sighed. Why did Jorinda re-stoke this fire?

Klordia stared at the floor. "Who would not fear you? You frighten me more than death itself."

Jorinda crumpled in on herself, as though Klordia had pulled a part of Jorinda's pain out of her body and displayed it for all to see. "I am death. I travel with death. I am its boon companion, and even when I vow never to kill again, death bids me do its work."

Deineike could not sit by and let Klordia's disapproval of Jorinda inflict another wound on her lover's battered sense of her own value. "You killed to save us." Klordia flicked her head up at Deineike's words. "You broke your vow out of necessity, not choice. Your actions saved Klordia and me from death. You could not have stood by and watched that man kill us, even if it brought your own ruin. Last night does not condemn you. We are grateful for your intervention."

Deineike shot Klordia a glance that implored her to voice some support. "Deineike speaks the truth." Klordia's voice contained little conviction, but Deineike hoped it would suffice.

Jorinda muttered and shook her head in disagreement. "You drip honey on rancid bread. Arella would have another opinion."

"That she would not." Deineike's temper flared as Jorinda

attempted to close yet another door to potential redemption. "Arella's decision came from her love for you. You have been forgiven for that moment."

"By you. Not by her." Tears pooled in Jorinda's eyes, a small brook that at any moment might turn into a torrent of grief, guilt, and shame.

Klordia's voice sound thin and reedy among such dark tension. "Who is Arella?"

Klordia tried to stoke the fire, but it could not stand, and Deineike's terse reply did not hide her irritation. "I am sorry. That is not yours to know at this time." She hoped her fierce stare would convince Klordia the conversation had ended.

Jorinda, however, did not get the message. "My lover. I killed her."

Klordia raised a hand to her mouth, shocked, and Deineike tutted. Unless she could snatch Jorinda from the brink of despair, she would remain mired in her misery, and they would be lost. "Others have Arella's blood on their hands. You alone are not to blame. You both became caught up in all we now discuss. She gave her life in the knowledge that the alternative would bring death to both of you."

Jorinda snorted. "My blade ended her life. Your excuses do not exonerate me."

Wilash spoke up, and not before time, in Deineike's opinion. "I am responsible also. I brought news of your betrayal to the Guild building, where Arella heard my words and made her decision. For night after night since that moment, I have blamed you, but I now see you were a piece of some larger puzzle. Do not hold only yourself to account for this, Corelle."

Klordia frowned. "Corelle?" She sounded confused. "You mentioned that name last night also."

Deineike sighed, frustrated beyond words. "Jorinda." Like a leaf that drifted on the breeze and would not fall to the ground, the conversation insisted it must wander further from the decisions they must make. "Corelle is the name her parents gave her."

Klordia shook her head. "A pretty name. Nicer than Jorinda. That is a killer's name. I understand why you changed it."

Deineike ran out of patience, slammed her hand down on the table, and they all started. "By the fates, I believe I will kill you both if this argument continues. We have agreed to travel to Ort. You must leave this thread unworried lest it unravel in our hands, and we all swing from the gallows before the day is ended. We must decide how we travel. You squabble over scraps that do nothing for our cause."

The arguments frustrated her, and she could not fathom why Jorinda and Klordia bickered with one another when they all stood in such a parlous place. Wilash seemed surprised, Klordia cast her eyes down to the floor once more, and Jorinda might have nodded, but Deineike could not be certain.

Nobody spoke, and the decision appeared to fall to Deineike. "We will take a ship. The risk is immense, but we are beset by risk whichever way we turn. We must use Wilash's story that we are family." The ploy seemed unlikely to succeed, but if nobody acted, they would all sit in the cottage until the Guild or the Portreeve arrived. Nobody objected, and the atmosphere remained solemn.

Klordia raised a concern the others had overlooked. "Will they not watch the docks?"

Jorinda nodded. "That they may, but I can spot any who hide in search of us, and they will not see me. What we will do if they are there is a stream we must ford when and if we reach it. The Guild will hear of our voyage soon enough if we use the token, but there is no difference between a hideous death in Ort or in Alcmouth. Once news of our voyage is known, the Guild will search Ort, as will the Portreeve, since the two appear to act as one. We must discover all we can as soon as possible, then make our next decision."

Deineike doubted Klordia's resilience for the fugitive's life. "Klordia, would you rather sail south and leave Dur and the danger that exists here?"

She turned pathetic eyes to Deineike. "I am the only one who understands the financial manipulation involved." Deineike believed she had grasped the principles well enough but did not gainsay Klordia. "I have no wish to sail away alone to a land where I would not understand the ways of life or indeed the language." Klordia gave Wilash a coy glance as she spoke, but Deineike decided to stay silent, since everybody else seemed far too eager to accept excuses to deflect the conversation away from the course of action ahead of them. Better not to spark another flame that ran in a different direction but brought no benefit.

Deineike stood. "So be it."

Jorinda, it appeared, had not shaken off her dark mood, but she seemed motivated to act now a decision had been reached at last. Without warning, a sharp pain jabbed through Deineike's forehead, and she sat with her head in her hands for a time, unable to focus. Jorinda became concerned about another headache so soon after the one the previous evening, but Deineike passed it off with a jest. She blamed the arguments between Jorinda and Klordia, and as the pain became more bearable, she announced herself ready to leave.

Klordia and Wilash had no packs, and Wilash had nothing but the clothes he wore. Klordia, at the least, had the two dresses Deineike and Jorinda had worn the night before, since they now had their own clothes. Jorinda thought it too dangerous for Wilash and Klordia to return to their rooms to gather belongings for the journey and suggested they should purchase any items they needed as they set out.

Jorinda walked ahead of the others and left Wilash to help Deineike. He stood two spans taller than Jorinda, and Deineike found his support more beneficial. Jorinda checked every direction at every corner. At times, even Deineike could not see Jorinda, and she marvelled at the furtive way the shorter woman moved through the streets.

It took them almost an hour to reach the docks area, and Jorinda told them to wait a street away while she investigated. Deineike sat on the ground behind one of the many statues of the Duke that festooned Alcmouth. Either the capital city's citizens felt more affinity for the Duke than those in other towns and cities or he lauded himself more here than elsewhere. Wilash stood in quiet conversation with Klordia while Deineike flexed her leg as part of her daily routine as she progressed toward full mobility.

Jorinda had been gone longer than Deineike had anticipated and worry nagged at her. She caught Wilash's eye and beckoned him over. "Is there any sign of Jorinda yet?"

"None yet. Do not fret. She is without peer in the arts of the Guild."

"That may be so, but those skills tear her apart." Wilash looked miserable at Deineike's correction, and she regretted the way her instinctive reply had hurt him. "You have the right of it. She hides from sight well, more so when I need help of any kind."

She laughed at the weak jest, and he smiled at her. "You are special."

His reply embarrassed her. "Help me to my feet so I can walk around for a time. It will be good for my leg." With his assistance, she struggled to her feet and walked in small circles for a few moments. The flexibility of her knee had already improved somewhat; she looked forward to full recovery. She chewed at the nails of her spare hand as she hobbled about, anxious for Jorinda to return and afraid of whatever had turned at the docks.

EIGHT
A VOYAGE BEGINS

Deineike had chewed her fingernails in worry for some time when, at last, Jorinda scurried round a nearby corner. Deineike smiled in relief as they huddled together to hear her news.

"Two Portreeve's men patrol the docks. I saw no Guild members, and the Portreeve's men chatter non-stop as they wander up and down at a continuous pace. If we time our dash right, we can be aboard a ship while they are at the opposite end of the docks."

Deineike chewed at her lower lip, anxious about the injured leg. "I fear I cannot dash."

Klordia agreed. "The same. I am not built for speed."

Jorinda seemed ready to hurl some insult, but a stern glance from Deineike appeared to change her mind. "I misspoke. I meant that if we time our movements, we ought to encounter little difficulty. We should move closer. I have seen a ship I think will be suitable."

Wilash helped Deineike, which left Jorinda free to check for danger as they moved ahead, wary. Ahead on the docks, mariners and dockhands bustled up and down ramps as they carried goods on and off ships, into and out of tally houses. The air filled with jovial banter and curses alike, and the thick scent of exotic goods and spices filled Deineike's nostrils. She breathed in the fragrance, a welcome reprieve from thoughts and conversations that teetered on the edge of capture and death more often than she would like.

The Alcmouth docks were the busiest Deineike had seen, and the frenetic levels of activity captivated her. She had not anticipated they would return to the docks so soon, bent on departure, yet here they were. With a sigh, she wished she could somehow write different fates for herself. They took refuge among a jumbled mass of boxes strewn around outside a tally house, and Jorinda pointed to a ship she thought would be suitable, although two others were closer.

Wilash pointed to the ship moored closest to them. "Why not that one?"

Jorinda did not look at the vessel. "It is a southern ship, with three masts. It will return south to whichever land it calls home."

"And that one?" Klordia pointed at the second ship along the dock. It had only two masts, but Deineike noticed the name on the rear of the ship—The Jorinda.

"The other suits us better." Jorinda offered no further explanation, and Deineike remained silent, uncertain how she could explain why the ship did not suit.

Wilash insisted. "It seems ready to leave sooner than the third." He had the right of it. A mariner stood at the top of the ramp, ready to push it down to the dock so the ship could sail from the dock.

Jorinda wheeled on him and gave him a fierce glare as she made no effort to restrain her anger. "You may board that ship if you wish, for I do not tell you what you can and cannot do, but I will not sail on it. I have travelled on it before. It is The Jorinda, and if you cannot comprehend why I do not wish to sail on it, then board it, and farewell to you."

Wilash's mouth opened wide, and he seemed lost for words for a time. He gathered himself and looked again at The Jorinda. "You took the name of a ship?" He seemed aghast.

Jorinda's face twisted into a picture of fury. "Forgive me. I am unable to create the pleasant names my parents could." The bitter glance Jorinda shot at Klordia sent chills down Deineike's spine.

A tense silence settled on them. Jorinda's mood had become blacker as the morning had progressed, and her acerbic tongue surprised Deineike. It fell once more to her to deflate the over-wrought atmosphere. "The other will serve. A slip of the tongue on The Jorinda could lead to complications we should avoid if possible. Agreed?" She glared at Wilash as she spoke, and he nodded, a grim look on his face.

Klordia laid a hand on Wilash's arm. "The Portreeve's men are at the far end of the docks. We should board."

Jorinda's curt reply, for once, seemed justified. "That we should not. We must board at the last possible moment. The Portreeve's men might check the vessel as it prepares to depart, or someone from the crew might find a way to indicate to the Portreeve's men or a dockhand that something is awry. The less time there is for such a complication, the better."

Klordia's endless capacity to find holes in any plan resurfaced. "What if the Portreeve's men are at this end of the dock as the ship prepares to move away?"

Jorinda's snarl did not lessen. "Then we may need to find another. Escape is an imprecise art."

Wilash held his dagger, and Deineike whispered to him. "Put your dagger away, Wilash. It will not be needed."

As he hesitated, Jorinda asked him to hand it to her, studied it, then handed it back to him with a slight nod. Pride flashed in his eyes for a heartbeat as he tucked it into his belt, then he smiled at Jorinda and said, "It is a twin to the one I gave you."

Jorinda returned the smile. "I see this. It is the equal of its twin. Your skills as a weaponsmith are unequalled."

"My thanks. I thought I might name them."

Jorinda stared at him, then she laughed and shook her head. "You would give names to weapons?"

Wilash joined in the laughter, although his cheeks burned so red, Deineike imagined she could have warmed her hands on them on a cold winter's morning. "It crossed my mind. Though it does seem foolish now I give the idea voice." Deineike could not grasp what they found so comical about the concept of names for weapons, but the levity improved the atmosphere, to her relief.

The Portreeve's men wandered back in their direction, so they crouched out of sight among the boxes. Jorinda peered around a box for a time, then beckoned for them to stand again. "They have their backs to us, and the crew is ready to cast off. The Portreeve's men are closer than I would have liked, but we must either take our chances or await another vessel." Nearer to them, The Jorinda had already moved out into the current and swung south toward the Torr Sea.

Klordia seemed to have a ready stock of awkward questions at her disposal. "Do we know this ship even travels to Ort?"

Jorinda looked at the ground and shuffled her feet. "That we do not. It is a gamble. I could not run up and ask them." She gave a hopeless gesture with her arms, and Deineike's heart sank. She had not considered the ship's destination.

"That you could not—but I can." With that, Wilash walked out onto the docks while the others hissed at him to return. He ignored them and, hands in his pockets, wandered over to the nearest dockhand, who stood by a rope at the stern of the ship. After a brief conversation between the two men, Wilash scanned the length of the docks toward the Portreeve's men. The dockhand glanced upward at a call from the deck above, and Wilash seized the opportunity to give a stealthy wave in the direction of the three women, then sauntered toward the ramp as Jorinda hoisted Deineike's arm about her shoulders, and they moved toward Wilash and the ship. Their every movement suggested they were up to no good. If the Portreeve's men glanced backward, they would be undone.

Their fortune held, and they reached the ramp where Wilash studied the ship, a picture of innocence. By the time they reached the bottom of the ramp, the dockhands at the front and rear of the ship looked ready to uncoil the taut ropes between the ship and the metal hooks on the dockside. Wilash hurried up the ramp and onto the deck, and the three women followed him.

The dockhand at the bottom of the ramp gave a shout, and Deineike looked along the dock again in concern. If the Portreeve's men heard the shout, they did not turn to investigate it, and the four fugitives reached the deck as the ramp fell to the dock below. The bow rope had already been thrown aboard, and the bow of the ship drifted out into the river, but the stern rope remained attached to the dock. The dockhand at that rope, who seemed uncertain of what took place above, looked up at the ship's crew with a look that suggested he awaited instructions from them.

Wilash tugged at the sleeve of a nearby mariner and opened his clenched fist. The mariner blanched and waved at the dockhand, who unfastened the rope and threw it aboard, and the ship moved out into the current. Deineike guessed Wilash had shown the mariner the Guild token. It must have struck a dread into his heart as cold as the bleakest winter day.

Wilash turned his attention to the women. "Come. We must find the master. The vessel must not be allowed to return to the dock." They followed Wilash toward the stern where the master commanded the ship from a raised deck atop the cabins below. Six passes ago, these things were unknown to Deineike, but the voyage from Torric to Alcmouth had taught her much. Wilash bounded up the steps at one side of the deck, and they followed. By the time they had reached the top of the steps, Wilash had already engaged the master in hushed conversation.

As they drew closer, the master glanced at them, and his face turned ashen. "You have women with you. Do they travel under this token?"

Wilash stuck to their story. "That they do. They are my family. What of it?"

The master glowered at Wilash, his face hardened and uncompromising. "I am under orders to detain any women who travel under the token, at Styrrach's express command. I must summon my crew and take them under guard."

Jorinda stepped forward and stood in front of him. They almost touched one another, though he towered over her by two spans. Her face distorted in obvious fury, her lips taut, her eyes narrowed. "Your crew would regret such a move, and so would you, for a heartbeat. You know the organisation we work for, which stands behind this token?"

The master's face turned bright red. "I know the organisation, and well. But this man has claimed you are his family. Did he lie?"

Jorinda did not hesitate. "As far as your crew is concerned, we are his family, but we are all Guild members, and friends of Styrrach's. Do you know him?"

The master shook his head. "That I do not. The order came from another, but Styrrach's command is attached to it. I know he is to be feared."

Jorinda sneered. "That he is, as am I. The woman he seeks is called Corelle, and I also seek her. If you hinder us in our search, it will take me a single heartbeat to ensure your heart beats no more, master. Do you wish it?"

He hesitated, then cast his eyes downward. Jorinda's threat seemed to have cowed him. "That I do not."

"Then sail on to Ort and leave us to enjoy the wind in our hair while we journey with you."

The master seemed to claw for some dignity he could rescue from the situation. "Very well. You may sail with us, but rest assured, the Guild will be informed of this as soon as we arrive."

"You will have their gratitude." Jorinda smiled, danger in her demeanour, in every word. "They may even let you live, despite your threats when first we spoke. Whilst I imagine you will omit the details of those threats when you present your report, I will not."

Deineike imagined the Guild would kill the man when they learned he had failed to take them all into custody, but they were in an impossible position, and she chose not to dwell on his fate. The master summoned an officer who had stood to one side as he spoke with Wilash and Jorinda. He instructed the officer to find a cabin for the four travellers, who would sail with them to Ort as guests of the ship. What the officer had made of Jorinda's part in the conversation, where she pitted her menace against the master's resistance, Deineike could not guess.

It had not surprised her when Jorinda succeeded in the bluff, since Klordia had the right of it earlier that morning. Jorinda became as fearsome and dangerous as a cornered animal at moments such as these, and few could stand before the shadow of death she became. It puzzled Deineike how much Jorinda had changed, by all accounts a simple girl, raised to be a garment maker, yet somehow transformed into a cold-hearted killer, an instrument of ruin who showed no mercy to any who stood in her way. The burden of death had been unkind to Jorinda as her guilt grew with each body in her wake, an added weight she struggled to carry even as her deadly blade added to it like bloodied stones piled on her back.

A mariner showed them to a cabin, and Klordia collapsed into a chair, her face pale, drawn. Deineike feared the woman might now initiate another round of insults and incrimination, but she appeared drained by all that had turned since the previous night and sat in silence with her eyes downcast. Jorinda stood in one corner of the cabin, her breaths long and deep. Deineike had noticed her breathe in this deliberate way before when Jorinda became agitated or threatened and imagined the Guild taught it as a means of self-control. Wilash, as ever, remained silent, a man of few words as far as Deineike could figure him.

The small cabin held six bunks, little more than hammocks strung along the walls. It would be unpleasant to spend several days in the small space in the company of the others, but they had no alternative. There were three mismatched chairs, and Deineike wondered why there were fewer chairs than bunks. No furniture other than the chairs and the bunks occupied the sparse accommodation, but it would serve.

As the ship gathered speed before the wind and rode out into the centre of the river, it pitched and rolled, and Deineike's stomach soon reminded her of its distaste for water-borne travel. Wilash appeared afflicted in the same way, but Deineike's stomach roiled, and she limped back to the deck to fetch up over the rail.

The first day of the voyage passed without event. They stayed in the cabin for most of the time unless Deineike or Wilash went out to the rail. Klordia seemed unaffected by the motion of the ship, and she comforted Wilash as he heaved his stomach into the wind that carried it backward and downward, down into the blue water that agitated his stomach in the first place. Jorinda brought a pail into the cabin, but the smell of it soon became so unpleasant they abandoned the idea.

The wind dropped on the second day, and the swell reduced. The ship moved through the water at a slower pace but also pitched and rolled far less, which brought some relief to Deineike's stomach. Wilash invited Klordia to take some air with him, and they went out to the deck. Deineike and Jorinda had not enjoyed any time without the pair's company for almost two days, and Deineike yearned to forget her stomach's woes for a time. A wooden bolt slid into a holder on the frame of the cabin door in place of a lock, and she manoeuvred it into place, then pushed Jorinda down onto one of the bunks and clambered on top of her as passion built within her.

Jorinda's eyes filled with lust. "Will this thing hold the weight of both of us?"

Deineike kissed her, and their tongues danced in each other's mouths. She gave a series of desperate moans as she pulled Jorinda's tunic up and lowered her head to lick at a nipple until it stood hard and proud on Jorinda's full breast. Jorinda's hands moved through Deineike's hair, and she pushed Deineike's head lower in search of satisfaction from other regions. Deineike surrendered to the pressure and found Jorinda wet and swollen. She tasted like fine wine and gasped with pleasure as Deineike's tongue flicked at her. Jorinda's body shook as Deineike coaxed her to a peak of ecstasy.

That first fulfilment would not be the last, and each of them took satisfaction from the other for close to an hour. The bunk did not collapse, and afterward, they lay together, spent and sated. The cabin must reek of their passion, but Deineike did not care. "By the fates, you arouse me so. I cannot keep my hands from you most of the time. I love you."

"I love you also." Jorinda gave a short laugh. "Your leg did not seem to trouble you for an hour or so."

Deineike purred with contentment. "I forgot I had legs. You took me where there is no pain, as you always do." She let out a satisfied sigh, and Jorinda blushed.

Jorinda nuzzled into Deineike's neck. "Let us leave the door locked. Those two can find another place to sleep. Let us spend the rest of the voyage in this cot and forget all our troubles for a few days."

"That does tempt me." Deineike kissed Jorinda's forehead. "My stomach, however, will be certain to interfere with that plan, I am afraid."

Jorinda laughed and kissed her as footsteps approached the cabin, and the handle of the door twisted. Deineike guessed either Wilash or Klordia stood outside the door, but whoever lingered there hesitated. She imagined they weighed the implications of the locked door, and after some moments, the footsteps moved away again. For half of another hour, Deineike and Jorinda chatted about frivolous subjects or enjoyed the silence that never became uncomfortable between them.

At once, Jorinda seemed to return to all the problems that had beset them over the last days. "Do you imagine the Duke is involved in this venture?"

Deineike groaned. The short time they had spent making love had been a calm shelter from those matters, like a drink of cool water on a hot day. "Let us not think on that now. I tire of it We are hunted, and the whys and whats of it do not concern me. I wish to know some peace. Let Styrrach make his fortune. Why should we care how he comes by it?"

After a time, Jorinda continued, darkness in her words, her voice, her eyes. "I loathe him, Deineike, more so now I believe him implicit in my betrayal and the death of Arella. I long to kill him and take the coin he has hoarded. I will buy you a fine house with it, I think." Jorinda half-smiled, mayhap in a bid to brighten the mood.

Deineike held a finger to Jorinda's lips. "Do not speak of death, even his. You vowed never to kill again, but two nights ago, you did so, in difficult circumstances. Have you re-acquired your taste for it? Would you have killed the master of this ship?" Even as she asked the question, Deineike feared the answer. How could either of them bear a life in which Jorinda must threaten or kill anybody she perceived as a threat?

Jorinda ran her fingers through Deineike's hair. "That I would not. I sought to convince him to allow us aboard. If he is frightened enough, he may not even tell the Guild he transported us. Styrrach will be displeased with him if he learns of it, which may turn in our favour." Her answer lacked sincerity, like a half-truth a child might offer to a parent to avoid punishment for some wrongdoing.

Deineike lay on her stomach and raised herself onto her elbows, although the bunk swung from side to side and threatened to tip her out. "I hate Styrrach. I have never met him, but I hate him for all he has done to you and Arella. You have survived, and you are here with me now, but there is terrible pain in you. He is to blame, and I despise him for it. Nonetheless, I believe the more you kill, the deeper you will sink into the darkness, and I fear it will consume you in time. Let us talk no more of it, I beg you."

Jorinda kissed her forehead. "I shall talk no more of it, then." She fell silent.

Deineike pulled her closer. "My thanks. You have earned your reward." Her fingers drew a gasp from Jorinda, who reaped her reward in full for a further hour.

NINE

A FAMILIAR FACE

DESPITE THEIR WISH TO REMAIN LOCKED IN THE CABIN, THE DAY SLIPPED away, so they strolled to the deck to take some fresh air.

The wind whipped their hair about their faces as they emerged onto the deck in the warm sunshine of a summer day. Wilash and Klordia leaned against a rail at the side of the ship; they had been on deck for some hours now. They must have guessed what took place in the cabin when they found the door locked and decided to remain on deck for such time as the lovers required.

Jorinda had no desire to while away her time in the company of Klordia and would not allow Deineike to persuade her otherwise. "She is ungrateful and spiteful. Do you deny it?"

Deineike gave a sad shake of her head. "She rankles you; I see this. I do not think her any more spiteful than you. She does not appear grateful you saved her life, but she may not yet have come to a full realisation in her imagination of everything that turned in the alleyway. She can never have seen its like in her life."

Jorinda walked to the opposite side of the ship, peered over the side, and wondered if she had been churlish when she refused to join Klordia and Wilash. The older woman irritated her and seemed determined to argue with or insult her whenever she could. Deineike found good in Klordia, but Deineike would find good in a wild animal as it tore out her throat. Jorinda looked sideways at Deineike, who joined her at the rail. She had done nothing to earn the love of this magnificent woman, but she had it. She kissed Deineike's cheek, and the dark-haired woman smiled.

A small commotion came from behind them, and they turned to look. Five mariners gambled at dice in the warm sun, and raucous laughter and jeers filled the air as one or another lost some small part of his wages. Deineike did not watch the game or the mariners who played it for long, and she returned her attention to the water as it flowed past below them.

Jorinda continued to watch the game for a time. She thought she detected an unusual movement in the way one of the mariners cast the dice, but she could not be certain. The man won two games in a row, and Jorinda became convinced he rolled the dice in a strange way. He won for a third time, and his opponent grabbed at the winner's arm. The boisterous crowd fell silent in a heartbeat. The two men strained against one another, and in the tussle, a die fell from the sleeve of the victor's tunic. The loser stared at it, incredulous, as Jorinda sneered. The winner must have swapped the die for one loaded in his favour. While she had never seen such a thing before, she imagined it might not be uncommon. The men played for groats; mere trifles. No doubt they would curse at each other for a time before harmony returned, and they would all go ashore together and become inebriated once the ship docked in Ort, the incident forgotten.

As she had anticipated, the loser shouted at the other, "You think you can cheat me?" and pushed at him. Beside Jorinda, Deineike stiffened, and Jorinda turned to gaze at her. Deineike stood as still as death, the colour drained from her face. Her eyes stared out across the river as though she watched some event a great distance away. Her white knuckles stood out against the natural colour of the backs of her hands, and she gripped the rail so tight it seemed as though she feared she might be cast overboard.

Deineike's change of demeanour worried Jorinda. "What is it?" Behind them, the small fracas seemed to have concluded, and a few peals of laughter could even be heard among the angry shouts.

Silent and slow, Deineike turned to stare at the dice players. As Jorinda watched in horror, Deineike's mouth opened, then closed again, she blinked, and collapsed to the deck. Her head struck the boards, and she lay motionless at Jorinda's feet. Jorinda yelled, "Deineike," and the mariners looked over. Jorinda bent to clutch at Deineike's neck, where she found a slow but steady pulsing. A careful inspection of Deineike's head revealed no evidence of any cut from the fall, and no blood.

A voice asked, "What has turned?"

The mariners gathered around them, but she did not look up. Jorinda positioned herself so she could cradle Deineike's head in her lap. "She has fainted."

Wilash's voice cut through the general hubbub. "Deineike. Are you hurt?"

Jorinda looked up at him, tears in her eyes. "She has fainted. Help me get her to the cabin, please."

The mariner who had lost the game bent down and took one of Deineike's arms. He hesitated for a moment as he hovered above her, stared at Deineike's face, and squinted as though he tried to place her in his memories. Others took her legs, lifted her, and carried her down the stairs to the cabin. They laid her with care on one of the bunks and lingered, unsure what to do. Jorinda whispered Deineike's name over and over and searched for some sign of consciousness, but no flicker of an eyelid or movement of her lips came to encourage her.

The master appeared. "How is she?" Somebody must have brought news of Deineike's fall to him, but Jorinda did not reply.

Klordia joined them with a pail and a cloth. She dipped the cloth into the pail, brought it out wet, squeezed excess water from it, and wiped Deineike's brow with tender strokes.

Wilash seemed flustered, and he waved at the mariners who crowded around. "Please, so many in the cabin, there are too many. Allow us to tend to her. Our thanks for your help and your concern." He ushered them out, and once they had all gone, he closed the door. "What has turned?"

How could Jorinda trust her voice to form words? A cold dread took hold of her breast and tightened her throat as though it squeezed the breath from her. "She fainted. She has had headaches since the fall from the horse. She may have had another, and it led her to faint." She stroked Deineike's hair and smoothed it back from the wan face. Klordia continued to dab her forehead with the wet cloth, which also wet Deineike's hair. Jorinda leaned forward to whisper as her tears dripped onto the unconscious woman's face. "Deineike, do you hear me? Come back to us, my love."

Moments went by, and Jorinda's anxiety increased as Deineike did not regain consciousness. Wilash and Klordia spoke words of encouragement, but Jorinda found no solace in them. Deineike had gone to this place before, in Torric, and had journeyed to the threshold of wherever she would travel to afterward until she returned after several days. With luck, she would come back sooner this time. Jorinda could not stand to lose the love of this woman now after all they had been through together—could not face another day if she might never again see those expressive blue eyes and the smile that so often sprang to those lips.

Deineike's eyelids fluttered, and Jorinda stroked her hand. "Deineike? Can you hear me?"

Deineike's eyes snapped open, full of terror. She lay motionless for a heartbeat, then grabbed at Jorinda's tunic with both hands. With an urgent dread in her voice, she whispered, "He is here." She looked about, fear on her face.

Jorinda's relief gave way to confusion. "Who is here?"

"He is aboard this ship." Deineike's voice grew louder, filled with horror and panic, and her frenzied eyes stared up at Jorinda. She tugged at the tunic so hard, Jorinda had to brace herself against the bunk with both arms so Deineike did not pull her down on top of herself.

"Who?" Jorinda's confusion threatened to overwhelm her.

"Him. He is here. The man who killed my mother."

Jorinda closed her eyes, perplexed. Deineike's words made no sense. The fall must have dislodged something in her head. How could she have seen a dead man on the ship? Had the fall from the horse damaged her more than the chirurgeon believed and brought on visions? When Jorinda opened her eyes, Deineike still stared up at her, her breaths heavy and her tearful eyes full of panic and desperation.

Jorinda could stand the confusion no longer. "He is dead. Has he returned from wherever he travelled to?"

From behind her, Klordia's voice asked, "Who is dead?" Jorinda ignored Klordia's question, resented her unwanted intrusion into the moment.

"Jorinda, Jorinda." Deineike's tears intensified, and her hoarse whisper grew more difficult to hear. "What have I done? What have I done?" Jorinda's thoughts raced hither and thither as she tried to find some small piece of reason to latch onto. "My love, I am sorry. What have I done?" Deineike released Jorinda's tunic and covered her eyes with her arm as sobs tore through her body.

Klordia spoke again. "Who is dead? Who does she mean?"

Jorinda looked up at the wretched woman and fought down a desire to strike her chubby little face over and over. "Be gone, jade. Do you wish to taste the kiss of my blade?" Klordia blanched.

Wilash kept his voice soft, but he leapt to Klordia's defence. "Corelle—"

Jorinda interrupted Wilash, turned her ferocious stare on him. "Jorinda." At the tone in her voice, he took a pace backward, his hands raised in appeasement. In tears, Klordia also stepped back, and Wilash took her in his arms.

Jorinda looked down at Deineike as sobs continued to wrack the tall woman's body. What had she meant? "Deineike, how can he be here?"

Deineike stuttered, each word interspersed with colossal sobs that tore through her. "I must have been wrong. My mother's killer is not dead. He is here."

Jorinda stared down on the woman she loved and tried to comprehend what she heard, words that suggested Deineike had been wrong in Torric and the man Jorinda killed that night had not been the one who murdered her mother—yet it could not be, for Deineike had been adamant. *"I am right, and he must be killed for what he did."* She had said it, even as Jorinda insisted she might be mistaken. *"I am not mistaken. Do you doubt me? Do you think I lie?"* The words returned to Jorinda, as clear as if she stood once more on the docks, as if she stared at the intoxicated mariner who danced before them, whose throat her blade would slit later that evening. The wrong throat; an innocent throat.

Fury welled up inside her, burst from her like water from a pot boiled too long. "You were wrong? You were wrong?" She glanced up at the ceiling. "I killed him, Deineike. I killed him for you." She wiped at tears that streamed from her eyes, but Deineike did not reply. "I killed him." Deineike flinched as Jorinda's voice rose to a yell.

"That you did. I am sorry. What have I done?" Deineike's plaintive voice could not assuage Jorinda's fury, and she rose from the bunk, flicked a glance at Wilash and Klordia. They each stood with a hand to their mouths and appeared no more able to comprehend Deineike's tale than Jorinda, who stepped a pace away from the bunk where Deineike's desperate sobs continued unabated.

Jorinda grasped for explanations in an inexplicable moment. "You are wrong now; you must be. You insisted you could not be mistaken in Torric, so you must be wrong now."

Deineike's sobs grew even louder. "His voice..." She seemed to choke, and she coughed for several heartbeats. "It is him. I am sorry. My love, I am sorry."

"You have already apologised. Your sorrow is noted." Jorinda growled with fury, and Deineike turned onto her stomach to bury her face in the small pillow. Her entire body convulsed as sobs ripped through it. "Your sorrow will not rewrite the fates. I killed him, and I did it for you. I killed an innocent man because of you." The vitriol she poured into the last word could not be measured as all her anger, all her doubts, and all the things she despised about herself became focused in that word. "How could you do this to me?" Jorinda strained for control, desperate to scream at Deineike, to curse her and abuse her, to strike her. "How could you?" She struggled for breath to speak as despondency and anger welled up inside her.

Deineike raised her head, her eyes red-rimmed and puffy, her nose red around the nostrils. Her tongue licked at her swollen lips like a reptile as it tests the air for danger. She looked distraught, devastated. "I am sorry." Jorinda tutted, irritated by the constant apologies. "I curse that we did not take the other ship. This turn would not have—"

Jorinda's shout interrupted her. "You blame me for this? This has become my fault, since I refused to sail on the ship I took my name from? You now seek to lay this at my door?" It beggared belief that Deineike had implied Jorinda's refusal to sail on the other ship played some part in the tragedy that unfolded in the small cabin.

"Forgive me, I did not mean that." Deineike buried her face in the pillow again.

Jorinda narrowed her eyes, tautened her lips. "I should have left you to die beneath that horse and gone on my way." Behind her, Klordia gasped.

Deineike's head snapped around, and her blue eyes stared at Jorinda, pained. "Jorinda, you do not mean that. I love you."

Jorinda pounded her fists on her thighs as frustration and rage consumed her. "How do you know I do not mean it? You cannot tell one murderer from another, it seems, yet you know all my intentions."

Deineike continued to sob. "I am sorry."

"Do not say that again." Jorinda raised her fists before her as she screeched at Deineike. "Stop it. Do you hear me Deineike? I will not hear it again." In that moment, she believed she could pummel Deineike with her fists. She must leave before she succumbed to the instinct. Furious, she spun and pushed past Wilash and Klordia, but she paused at the door. "I cannot bear to look on you." Jorinda shook with fury as she stalked out of the cabin.

"Jorinda." Deineike's plaintive cry came from behind Jorinda as she walked up the short flight of steps onto the deck. The mariners, who must have heard the argument, busied themselves about the deck and ignored her. She stomped to the bow, where she slumped to the deck. Tears poured out of her, and she screamed her agony into the wind.

Deineike buried her face in the pillow and wept. Violent sobs ripped through her, and her entire body ached. Her heart had been torn asunder as Jorinda had said, *"I cannot bear to look on you."* How had Deineike done this to the woman she loved more than life itself? She had destroyed everything that mattered to her with one small mistake, and the void inside her where her heart had been torn out might never be filled.

It had been no small mistake for the man in Torric, she reasoned. He had died, his family and friends robbed of him—and the blame sat at Deineike's door. How could she have been so adamant she had been right yet have been so wrong? Had her grief and desire for vengeance so clouded her judgement, she saw her mother's killer in any face that resembled the one she saw as a child? The moment she saw the mariner today, she realised her instincts in Torric had been wrong. His eyes and his voice were unmistakeable. He had even said some clumsy thing like the last words her mother ever heard. Deineike had been wrong in Torric, and it tore her apart now.

Even worse, Jorinda might not come back to her. Deineike might as well have driven a dagger into the heart of the woman she loved when she added this horrific burden on top of all else Jorinda endured. How could Jorinda survive now she knew she had murdered an innocent man because of Deineike's mistake? After all else, his death had brought Deineike no more than temporary relief from the pain that had dogged her since the monster who now worked somewhere on the ship murdered her mother. Had it all been worth the heartache that now sat at her door like an unwelcome visitor in the still of the night?

A terrible thought occurred to her, and she raised her head from the pillow. Wilash and Klordia still gazed at her in equal parts concern and confusion, and Klordia sobbed. Deineike whispered to Wilash. "Wilash, go to her. Check she is well. I fear she may…do something rash. Let no harm come to her beyond the pain I have already caused, I beg you."

For a moment, he seemed unable to grasp her intent, then he nodded and left the cabin. Klordia watched him leave, and her sobs grew louder as he disappeared from their view.

Anxious to calm the distressed woman, Deineike pushed aside her concern for herself for a moment. "Klordia, Jorinda did not mean those words. She would not hurt you. She is a good person. Her anger at me got the better of her for a time. Do not fear her." What else could be said? What Deineike had revealed had hurt them all and may have broken Jorinda beyond repair. It must be made right.

Deineike did not know how long she cried into the pillow, but the tears would not stop. Klordia moved around the cabin for a while, then left. Deineike desired no company, filled with revulsion at herself for what she had done to Jorinda and hatred for the mariner who had killed her mother. Jorinda had not fulfilled Deineike's vow after all else, and grief returned to torture Deineike, stoked the fire that smouldered in the hole left in her life by her mother's murder.

It had grown dark outside when footsteps approached the cabin. Deineike hoped it would be Jorinda, but Wilash entered. "Jorinda sits at the front of the ship and will not suffer me to come close to her. No harm has come to her though. She weeps, but she is safe."

"My thanks." Deineike could coax no more words from her lips before she buried her head in the pillow once more. Klordia returned to the cabin, but Deineike did not look up. Klordia and Wilash each climbed into a bunk on the opposite wall, and soon enough, their soft, rhythmical breaths indicated they slept. Jorinda did not return to the cabin, and at length, Deineike's grief and incessant sobs took their toll on her body. She fell into a fitful, nightmare-filled sleep.

Deineike woke before the dawn. Wilash and Klordia still slept, and when Deineike sat up to check the other three bunks, no shadowy figure lay in any of them. Dismayed, she pulled herself to her feet and hobbled to the door, then out onto the deck to look for Jorinda. The sun would soon come over the horizon as the first light of day chased away the dark of the night. Daylight should drive off all the night's horrors along with the darkness, but Deineike feared today's sunshine could not penetrate the shadows of all that had turned yesterday.

Loath to walk the deck in the half-light lest she trip and fall, Deineike stood at the entrance to the cabin area until the sun peeped over the horizon. As the light improved, a shadowy figure huddled at the far end of the ship faded into view. Deineike limped toward it and found Jorinda seated on the deck, her knees drawn up, her arms around them. Her head lay on her knees as though she slept, but as Deineike drew closer, she heard Jorinda sob.

"Jorinda." Her lover did not look around or raise her head. "Jorinda, may I sit with you?" Jorinda still did not move or speak. "Please?" Deineike waited, but Jorinda did not move and gave no sign she had even heard the words, so she moved closer. "Jorinda?"

Jorinda did not look up, but she spat out a reply at last. Her words sounded angry and bitter. "I do not own this ship. I imagine you may sit where you will."

Deineike paused, mulled Jorinda's words as the chill dawn wind tugged at her hair, her clothes. Jorinda had not said she did not want Deineike's company, and in the absence of further encouragement, Deineike decided to sit next to her angry lover. As she struggled to sit on the deck unaided, her knee still stiff, she placed a hand on Jorinda's arm. Jorinda did not shrug the hand away, and once Deineike had lowered herself to the boards, she laid her head on the younger woman's shoulder. "Please forgive me. I could not stand to be without you. I have made a terrible mistake—"

"That you have." Jorinda made no attempt to disguise her fury or lack of patience with Deineike's clumsy attempts to explain and beg for forgiveness.

Deineike fought back tears. She felt no anger at Jorinda's reaction, only remorse for the dreadful thing she had done. "I have brought pain that should not have been laid on you, and because of me, you killed an innocent man. I cannot imagine how that must feel, and I am so sorry. I will do anything to rewrite the fates and make amends, if it is within my power. Please forgive me, I beg you. I love you. I do not have the words to explain how much I love you." She fell silent and cursed her inability to express her emotions better. Tears she could no longer hold back flooded from her eyes onto Jorinda's tunic.

The ship crested a large swell and dipped forward. The movement alarmed Deineike, but Jorinda did not react. Deineike's stomach, however, responded as expected, so she struggled to her feet and headed for the rail. She did not reach it in time and fetched up on the deck. Miserable, she stood with her outstretched arms on the rail, her head between her arms, parallel to the deck. The sight of her vomit on the deck at her feet compounded her wretchedness, and her stomach heaved again, a retch that produced no vomit.

To Deineike's surprise, Jorinda placed a gentle hand on each hip and guided her forward until she leaned against the rail. Jorinda held Deineike steady against the movement of the ship as she continued to retch over the rail, but nothing more came from her stomach.

She wiped her mouth with the back of a hand and turned to face Jorinda. "I imagine there is nothing but my innards to be expelled."

"When did you last eat?"

Deineike thought back over the last day. "Breakfast yesterday, I believe."

"You should eat."

"I could not face it, and I fear its stay in my stomach would be short-lived after all else." Though she tried, she could find no joy or mirth to bring a smile to her lips.

Mariners moved around on the deck behind them. Deineike worried she might again see the man who had murdered her mother, might faint again, or attack him and be hurt. Would Jorinda aid her if the man struck her? "I must go back to the cabin. I cannot stand to see him again."

Jorinda sighed, as if moved by Deineike's undisguised anxiety. "I will help you." She draped Deineike's arm over her shoulder. "I am angry beyond words, and my help does not signal anything other than a recognition of the fact your leg has not yet healed. You suffered terrible injuries on my account, and I cannot neglect my responsibility to help you, but do not imagine you are forgiven for this torment you have put me through."

Deineike turned and kissed her cheek. "I know. I love you."

Jorinda turned her head away. "You must sweeten your breath, and soon. The smell of vomit is unpleasant." They hobbled toward the stern.

"I am sorry. I will do so once we are in the cabin.

"Deineike, please do not continue to apologise. You are sorry for all you have wrought. I understand, but I am weary of that word."

Deineike's sobs grew louder. "I am sorry." She tutted. "I cannot help it. I am beside myself with remorse, and I am desperate to make things right."

"Time may heal these wounds. Who can say? Let me say this now, once. I will not kill this man whom you now claim to be the real murderer of your mother. I will not have any more blood on my hands over this matter."

"I understand. I will not ask it." Deineike drew in a sharp breath. "I will say this, however. You must apologise to Klordia for the threat yesterday. Your anger should be directed at me, not her. No doubt you spoke out of turn, overcome with frustration. You are a kind person, Jorinda, even though Klordia cannot or will not see it. Think on it, please." Jorinda made a sound that might have been a huff of agreement or dismissal. Deineike could not tell and lacked the courage to press the matter further.

When they reached the cabin, Jorinda helped Deineike to a bunk and laid her down on it. Klordia watched them from her bunk, a puzzled expression on her face as they passed her, but Wilash appeared to sleep on.

Jorinda lifted Deineike's legs up onto the bunk and did not turn around as she spoke. "Klordia, I do not wish you to believe things are peaceful between Deineike and me. The injury to her leg is my responsibility, and I cannot ignore her need for help as she moves around. I will say no more on that matter." Klordia did not respond. "One thing further I must say. You and I are destined never to be friends. We rankle one another, and to me, you are like a cut that will not cease to bleed. I cannot say why, and I cannot say it will ever be otherwise. My words to you yesterday cannot be justified, nonetheless, and were not meant, in truth. I apologise."

Deineike gave Jorinda a weak smile, but Klordia did not reply. The anger fell from Jorinda's face for a time, but Klordia seemed not to notice, her own face stony and unmoved.

Jorinda turned and walked to the door, where she paused. "Deineike's stomach is unsettled. I will see whether I can find some food she might keep down. We cannot allow her to eat nothing." She disappeared into the corridor.

Wilash's voice startled Deineike. "You are unwell?"

Despite her weariness, Deineike found the strength to reply. "You heard what she said?"

"That I did. A sorry turn, the events of yesterday. I do not understand, and it is not my place to do so. I am sorry to see your relationship sundered, and I hope things will come well for you both. Do not push this. Jorinda must come to you in her own time if she comes at all. You could alienate her forever if you push her too hard."

Deineike managed another weak smile. "I do not think I have ever heard so many words from you since I met you, but those words are wise. My thanks."

Klordia spoke at last, and her face took on a more sympathetic aspect. "What help can I be?"

Deineike took a deep breath. "None, unless you can arrange for this accursed vessel to have wheels affixed so it travels on the land." She owed them some explanation for all they had witnessed, but the story would be difficult to tell. "A man killed my mother when I was a young girl. I saw a man in Torric whom I believed to be the one who murdered her. My mother slept with men for coin. Wilash knows this, my guess, but you…" Deineike had rambled, and she focused harder on her words. "A man killed her, and I saw it happen." Klordia swung her legs from the bunk with compassion on her face as tears came anew to Deineike's eyes. "I swore I would avenge her, but I never saw the man again until that day in Torric. I had suffered terrible injuries when I fell from a horse, and I could not act on my own behalf. Jorinda tried to persuade me I must be mistaken, but I felt sure I had the right of it. Although it cost her to take his life, Jorinda killed him to ease my pain. Yesterday, I saw again the man who killed my mother. He is aboard this ship. I had begged Jorinda to kill the wrong man." Deineike fell silent. Enough had been said, and fresh tears streamed down her face.

Klordia's soft voice held compassion, not recrimination. "I am sorry for all that tale recounts." Wilash also looked at Deineike with tears in his eyes.

Deineike closed her eyes against the distress that engulfed her. "As am I. The vengeance I believed had been served brought me only temporary satisfaction. It did not return my mother to me, and it did not lessen my loss. The wrong man died, the murderer lives, I am unfulfilled, and I have estranged the woman I love. All for naught." She turned away from them and sobbed again, and she struggled to breathe through the spasms that wracked her body.

When she turned back to face them, they both stared at the doorway open-mouthed, where Jorinda glared in anger at Deineike.

Deineike gasped. "Jorinda." How much of the conversation had she overheard?

Jorinda crossed the room and placed a few pieces of bread on Deineike's bunk. "Eat this if you can. It looks stodgy and may bind your stomach somewhat." She glowered down as Deineike picked up one of the pieces of bread.

"My thanks. I shall try to eat some of it now." Deineike words laboured to take wing between her sobs.

Jorinda's cold, flat voice chilled Deineike. "Your misplaced vengeance did not satisfy you the first time and may never do so. You were foolish to hope it would." Deineike could find no words to fashion a response. Everything had now been laid waste, it seemed. The long pause that ensued seemed as though it might never end until Jorinda spoke again at last. "It brought me no peace to do what I did either, and now it has brought me untold misery. I will seek another cabin for the remainder of the voyage."

Deineike reached up and grasped Jorinda's arm. "What then?" This latest development terrified her, and she feared Jorinda might be lost to her.

"We will reach Ort. I will stay there for some time while I decide what to do next."

The emptiness in her voice sent shivers of dread through Deineike. "What of me?"

"You are free to go where you will. Your decisions are not mine to make."

Deineike's throat constricted and threatened to choke off her voice. "Can I not remain with you, in Ort?"

"You are free to go where you will or stay where you will." Jorinda moved away, but Deineike would not release her grip on her arm.

Deineike looked up into the reddened, angry face that loomed above her as Jorinda attempted to pull her arm free. "Jorinda, I have broken your heart; shattered it into myriad pieces. I hate myself for that. But I remind you, you also broke mine, in the inn in Torric. Please, search within yourself. Please forgive me. Please."

Jorinda's face turned dark with fury as she hissed out her words between clenched teeth. "Do you seek to equate the two circumstances? They are not the same. You had the freedom to choose whether you remained or stayed when I told you that tale."

"You had the freedom to let that man escape with his life. Indeed, you told me you would not kill him."

Jorinda's eyes glared down at her in anger. "I had the freedom to choose? That I did not. You used me. You took advantage of my skills to bring you vengeance, and that vengeance has not sated your grief."

Despite her grief, her fear she might lose Jorinda, Deineike's own anger built within her at Jorinda's accusation. "I did not take advantage of you. I asked you to let me kill him myself. You would not permit it. You knew best." She spat the last three words out.

"That I did, for you would have died otherwise. You trapped me between doubt and uncertainty. I could let you suffer, or I could kill. I decided to kill, curse me. And kill I did; but I killed"—Jorinda's voice rose to a crescendo—"the wrong man." Deineike started and squeezed Jorinda's arm. She opened her mouth to argue further, but the memory of the mariner's dance swam before her eyes, and remorse flooded through her.

Deineike looked down, ashamed she had become angry and attempted to cast Jorinda in an unfavourable light. Dejected, she whispered. "I am sorry."

Jorinda prised Deineike's fingers from her arm. "Eat your bread." She turned and left.

Deineike sobbed so loud, she might have been heard in both Alcmouth and Ort, and she buried her face in the pillow as she had done the previous night. Had she driven Jorinda away forever? She could not bear the thought. Once again, she grew angry because Jorinda had reacted with such fury to the revelation she had killed the wrong man. Deineike had erred, but how could anybody punish a simple mistake with so much rage?

Deineike could not sustain the anger. It had not been a simple mistake, in truth. It had cost a man his life and cost Jorinda still more of the low regard she held for herself. Deineike pushed away the fury that threatened to take her in its grasp, and the face of the dead mariner again appeared in her mind. Guilt replaced her rage. Anger had no place in these considerations. Jorinda had anger enough for both of them, and who could blame her?

Deineike's heart softened, and she hoped Jorinda's might also, that the younger woman would find forgiveness in her heart as Deineike herself had when Jorinda had revealed her past; not the least that she had killed Arella. Life without Jorinda would be unbearable, and Deineike could not conceive of it. She would do all in her power to set things right between them. For now, Jorinda felt darkness and pain, and Deineike could do no more than hope some light would shine into Jorinda's heart and illuminate a path to forgiveness.

Klordia and Wilash walked from the cabin without a word and left Deineike with her own abject misery for company. Tears poured from her, and she pounded a fist on the bunk. She did not eat any of the bread.

TEN
A MEETING WITH FRUSTRATION

BALGOW STARED AT THE CRYPTIC LETTERS IN HIS HANDS, DISCONSOLATE. The letters came from Glailam, the Duke's Bailiff, and despite the vague language, the letters carried a clear, simple message. The Bailiff would meet him in The Riverside Tavern at the sunset that night. Glailam had never sent letters direct to Balgow before. All previous contact between them had been done by messages between the Guild's couriers and the Bailiff's emissaries. In truth, meetings between Balgow and the emissaries took place on precious few occasions, since contact between them would be risky to the Bailiff's position if it became public knowledge. The Duke's own Bailiff consorted with the leader of a band of clandestine killers? It would be considered outrageous. That had been made clear long ago, and Balgow had never challenged it.

The brief letters gave no reason for the meeting, but Balgow needed no explanation. Sky, Balgow's Senior Aide, had been found dead in an alleyway behind the Bailiff's Offices, and a Portreeve's man with him. Balgow knew the circumstances that led to the deaths, for he had orchestrated them himself. The mark's body had not been found, and he imagined she had escaped.

He believed the traitor, Wilash, had killed both men, although it beggared belief that Wilash, a novice who had never killed before, had bested a well-trained, skilful killer like Sky. The death of the Portreeve's man also posed a conundrum, since there should have been more than one in the alleyway to arrest Wilash after he killed the woman.

The plan had been simple enough. The Portreeve's men were to wait in the alleyway until Wilash moved to attack the woman, then arrest Wilash, who would be hanged before the sunrise. Sky could kill the woman afterward if Wilash had not done so before the Portreeve's men arrested him. What had turned so awry?

Like a horse that faces the wrong way in the traces, speculation went nowhere and achieved nothing useful. New revelations soon found their way to him, however, and they disturbed him. There had been four Portreeve's men there that night after all else, but Wilash did not appear. Two women had met with the mark; the Portreeve's men described them as old friends. With neither criminal nor crime in evidence, the Portreeve's men had few options, and they withdrew. They decided to return to their homes but heard a scream. Two of the women were in their cups, and the men believed it nothing more than the hysterical laughter of inebriated women, but the senior man went back to investigate, nonetheless. The others, unconcerned, returned to their duties.

Both bodies were discovered the next morning, their throats cut, and the Portreeve's man also stabbed in the back. The manner of the deaths and the presence of two mysterious women led Balgow to conclude the fugitive, Corelle, had been one of the women. How she had injected herself into the plot he could not see, unless Wilash had betrayed the Guild and involved her. The more he brooded on it, the more Balgow convinced himself he had the right of it. He soon discovered the address of the intended victim, Klordia, and he and four of his members went to her room. They found the bloodied clothes of two women, but the bird had flown, and Wilash with it.

Searches revealed nothing. The Portreeve's investigations turned up somebody who claimed to have seen four people late at night some distance from Klordia's room, a family who carried an intoxicated daughter home. The "family" must have been Wilash and the three women, but no matter how hard the Guild searched the area where the four had been seen, they turned up no further information.

Three days had passed, and they had found nothing. Wilash, Klordia, Corelle, and the other had fled. Where they went, nobody knew. Some discreet enquiries at the docks revealed nothing. The Portreeve should have swarmed the city's docks and stables, but because the bodies had not been discovered until the next morning, precious hours had been lost, and the escape had been made.

As if that were not bad enough, Balgow felt compelled to send letters to Styrrach to explain how both the attempt to shroud Wilash and the gest had gone awry, and there would be no good news from Zhanghar when a reply came back.

Balgow stared again at the letters from the Bailiff. He could not ignore the summons—he must go to the Riverside Tavern tonight, but he feared the outcome. When he first made the plan, Balgow thought himself clever enough to kill two birds with one rock. Wilash or Sky would kill the woman and satisfy the Bailiff's gest, and Wilash would be hanged by the Portreeve, as directed by Styrrach. Indeed, Balgow had imagined Styrrach would send letters of commendation and a reward, whereas it now seemed Styrrach would shroud Balgow instead. Worse, Balgow's "reward" might be Guild justice. Styrrach would appoint a new Guildmeister in Alcmouth, and Balgow would be forgotten, his body never found.

He fumed at the fate written for him. He had served Styrrach and the Bailiff well, and others had failed, not him. How had Sky allowed a woman to best him after Balgow had mocked Wilash and laughed that Sky would be on hand if it proved too difficult for him to slay a woman? Why had the senior Portreeve's man not insisted all four of them investigate the scream? Incompetence—and incompetence Balgow's life would pay for. He tore the letters into pieces, threw them to the floor, and stamped on them in temper.

In truth, Sky had been a problem for some time, and Balgow's attempts to ignore the issue would cost him. Sky drank too much, had become prone to fits of misery, and often complained to Balgow about how hard he found it to manage the pressure of Styrrach's dictates. Had Sky stirred something in Wilash that night in the tavern, something that led the traitor to seek the help of Corelle? How had he contacted her? Wilash might have betrayed the Guild long before the incident in the alleyway. More speculation, no more answers.

Sky. What a ridiculous name. Balgow doubted the man's parents had given him such a dull name. He imagined Sky had invented it and took some perverse satisfaction from it.

As the sun sank below the city skyline and cast long shadows into Balgow's heart that threatened to darken it forever, he set off for The Riverside Tavern and the meeting with the Bailiff. Inside the tavern, he lurked in the shadows of a back room. The Bailiff himself did not bother to appear, and when one of Glailam's lackeys entered the room, insult had been added to injury.

The lackey gave Balgow a scornful smile. "The Bailiff is unhappy at this turn. A Portreeve's man has been killed. The Duke himself has asked for an update on the situation, and this embarrasses the Bailiff. The Bailiff wishes to know how you permitted this simple task to turn so awry."

The lackey did not use Glailam's name. Doubtless some scheme designed to intimidate him, but he would not allow it. "I do not answer to the Bailiff. I answer to Styrrach, and the Bailiff would do well to remember his own position, which is tenuous if he does not remain loyal and treat Styrrach's trusted aides with respect." The man seemed taken aback, and Balgow struck a more conciliatory tone. It made little sense for him to attract enemies where friends would serve his purpose better. "This need not turn awry for us, must it? There have been some errors, but the situation can be redeemed."

"That it can." The lackey's voice dripped with smugness, and he wore the smile of a savage beast as it salivates before it bites the head from its victim. "The Bailiff will cast this in his favour. He will say the Portreeve's man saw two assassins attempt to kill a woman and lost his life as he attempted to defend her. The man's family will be well compensated and will say they are proud of the actions of this hero. Though they are distraught at his loss, they will take comfort that he acted with such honour. After all else, he even managed to slay one of the assassins before the other struck him down. The other will be apprehended in, say, two days?"

Balgow clenched his fists in fury. The Bailiff would turn the Guildmeister's woe to his own favour and leave Balgow to deal with Styrrach's anger. Glailam ordered Balgow to shroud one of his members into the bargain. Balgow stared Guild justice in the face, while the Bailiff would fall into the privy and emerge covered in the scent of fragrant flowers. He pushed a reluctant smile to his face. "Of course. I will select a member to be shrouded, and the Portreeve will know where to apprehend him, along with evidence of his heinous crimes, two days from now." Balgow had no choice but to go along with the plan. His life might depend on it.

"The Bailiff, nonetheless, seeks assurances no such mishaps will occur in future, and you will do all in your power to bring to book with the utmost discretion those who wrought this ruin. The Bailiff wishes no further public displays of this kind."

"I remind you again; I answer to Styrrach. If that is what Styrrach wishes, that is what will be done."

A lengthy silence passed as Balgow waited for a response. "I shall report your words to the Bailiff." The lackey turned to leave.

"Wait." Balgow worried his anger might land him in further trouble. "Let the Bailiff know we seek those who carried out this attack with every resource at our disposal. We believe a fugitive from Guild justice, a woman named Corelle, had some involvement. Styrrach already seeks her, and the search intensifies after this misstep." It hurt him to yield so, but he could ill afford the enmity of the Bailiff. He had no wish to have his neck stretched by the hangman's noose.

"Corelle, you say? A woman? Did the Bailiff have knowledge of this woman before this incident?"

Balgow's misery grew. "That he did not, my guess. She should have been shrouded in Zhanghar but made her escape through the intervention of others."

"She seems to mock you. Has she emasculated you all?"

In Balgow's mind, the lackey's neck made a pleasant sound as it snapped in his hands, but he fought to control his anger. Bailiff's men waited outside the door, and Balgow's life mattered to him. If he could, he intended to find some way to emerge from this mess alive. "That she has not. She will be beneath Styrrach's blade within days. We close on her already."

The scornful, contemptuous smile returned; the vile little man had perfected it. "This news will comfort the Bailiff. If there is no further information..."

"There is none. I shall attend to the matters we have discussed without delay." Balgow watched in anguish as the lackey left. The Guildmeister stayed alone in the room for a time, livid at the arrogance of this lapdog of the Bailiff. Balgow took the risks, while the

Bailiff grew fat on the profits of the operation. Glailam sat comfortable in his luxurious Ortwood chairs and never once faced the dangers and day-to-day intricacies of the management of the Alcmouth Guild.

Balgow stomped out and walked back to the Guild building to address his members. He had summoned them, convinced there would be news to impart after the meeting. He ranted at length about the inadequacies of the Bailiff and his unreasonable demands on them all. At the end of his tirade, he placed an honour gest on all four fugitives.

One of his members broke the stunned silence in the parlour. "Is Corelle a part of the honour gest, then? Is she not to be taken alive to Styrrach?"

Balgow could not stand to lose face again this night. "I will deal with that issue. The honour gests are assigned." He retreated to his office where he cursed his luck and the intervention of a woman who should never have been allowed to leave Zhanghar alive but had now brought him to the door of his ruin.

ELEVEN

HARSH WORDS, HARSH RATIONS

Jorinda sat at the bow of the ship for the rest of the day. None of the mariners spoke to her, but the man who had become the centre of her pain appeared on the deck once. She now loathed him as much as Deineike must, though for less pragmatic reasons. His actions, and Deineike's subsequent error when she mistook another in his stead, had created a rift between the two women that Jorinda could see no way to repair.

It devastated Jorinda to overhear Deineike reveal to Klordia and Wilash that the death of the mariner in Torric had brought the older woman no redemption. Bad enough an innocent man had lost his life under her blade, and against her better judgement, without Deineike's confession that it had not healed her grief. The flames of anger had been further stoked when Deineike insisted Jorinda's terrible admissions in Torric inflicted comparable hurt on the older woman.

Jorinda had slept little the previous night. Her eyes ached from tears spilled and from exhaustion intensified by nightmares in which she slaughtered men, women, and children without end as they all cried their innocence while she slit their throats with a fan, an image of Deineike's face on its folds.

She looked backward at the sound of footsteps. Wilash and Klordia emerged from the cabin, but she did not join them. She desired no company. Jorinda had intended to apologise to Klordia even before Deineike urged her to, though it cost Jorinda much pride to do so. The ignorant woman had not even acknowledged the apology, and Jorinda fumed until she remembered the boot had been on the other foot in the cottage when Klordia had apologised to her. Her chin fell to her breast in shame. She had sunk lower than ever before. Her life amounted to nothing, a series of mistakes and missteps that led her here. Estranged from Deineike, locked in a ceaseless duel with Klordia, and her self-esteem in pieces around her like a broken reflecting glass.

Wilash and Klordia did not meet Jorinda's eyes as they sat close together on two upturned pails on the deck some way from her. They talked in hushed voices, laughed often, and touched one another in small ways; a hand on an arm or a leg, or Wilash might brush a piece of Klordia's hair from her eyes. Their mutual attraction could not be missed. Jorinda disliked Klordia, but it pleased her Wilash might have made a connection with the woman he had been ordered to kill.

Why did Klordia see Jorinda as a monster and Wilash as blameless? They had both joined the Guild, although she conceded they were two quite different people. Wilash, kind natured, almost never lost his temper, while she often succumbed to angry outbursts and violence.

Deineike did not appear through the day as the boat sailed on toward Ort, and as darkness closed in, Wilash approached Jorinda. "We plan to take some food. Will you join us?"

She flashed him a grateful smile. "My thanks, but I am not hungry."

He nodded. "Jorinda, do not spend another night outside on the deck, I urge you. Find a bunk. It would be pleasant to enjoy your company in our cabin."

"My company would be far from pleasant."

"Nonetheless, we would enjoy it, and Deineike has need of some hope. Do not dash her on the rocks of her agony."

Jorinda shook her head. "That may come at some future time. At present, any words between us might be destructive."

Wilash glanced away for a heartbeat, as though to compose himself. "You know I loved Arella, and I care for you. I have known Deineike for such a brief time, but there is such goodness in her, Jorinda. Do not cast her from you over her mistake. She has stood by you when few would. What she did to you, you have done to her, tenfold."

Jorinda choked on fresh tears. "How can the two be compared? I knew nothing of her when I did the things I did. Deineike had the choice to order me gone from her life—I gave her that option. She made her decision, she remained, and I loved her without question. She asked me to kill that man in Torric because she knew full well the thing that lurks within me and used it to her own end—and now this turn comes about, and I have an innocent's blood on my hands."

"They were all innocent."

She sighed, frustrated by the grain of truth in the wheat field of his claim. "Some were, but most deserved the justice I dispensed. Hiw, he whom you sent after us, is such a one."

"Styrrach sent him, not me." Jorinda drew in a breath to protest, but Wilash held up a placatory hand. "I do not argue the point. For some, then, you had no call to end their lives."

Jorinda wiped the tears from her eyes, tears that glistened on the back of her hand like daggers of grief that sought her heart. "I need time. For now, I cannot find forgiveness in me. She did not mislead me on purpose, I accept this. But she begged me to kill, and I killed an innocent. It sickens me."

Wilash took a moment to reply. "I understand. Take some time, but for all that is good in her, please do not destroy her. Sleep elsewhere if you must, but visit her tonight, to make sure she still breathes, at the least. I ask it for the friendship between you and me."

She sniffed. He had backed her into a corner, but she had no quarrel with him. "Very well. You ask it for friendship, and I will do it. You have the right of it, I see this. I cannot let her shatter to the point she opens her wrists or throws herself from the ship. I may as well follow her if I add that burden to the load I already carry."

He nodded, turned, and disappeared through the door at the rear of the ship that led to the cabins and the common area where the mariners gathered to eat. Jorinda pondered his words for a time. Wilash spoke little enough, but his words were often wise. Did he speak so little because he weighed his words with care to ensure he used those that were appropriate?

Darkness had fallen, and the lanterns hung on each of the two masts had been lit. Jorinda rose, went through the outer door, then into the cabin. Deineike still lay in the bunk Jorinda had placed her in earlier. The bread lay untouched on the bunk next to her.

Deineike lay on her back with an arm across her eyes, and no sound of tears could be heard. Jorinda judged her to be asleep and tiptoed across the cabin to look down on her. She reached out to stroke the black hair strewn about the pillow.

Deineike's voice startled Jorinda. "I love you so much, more than I have words to say." She had not been asleep, after all else.

"How do you fare?"

Deineike lowered the arm from eyes red-rimmed and shot through with bloody spiderwebs. She wore her agony like an open wound, and Jorinda choked as her throat tightened. Her own eyes stung with tears.

"I am well."

Jorinda could not fathom where Deineike found her strength. Her appearance cried out that she suffered, but she attempted to make light of her situation and deny her pain. "That you are not. I see that." Jorinda sighed and sat on the bunk beside her. "You have not eaten. Did I not say you should eat some bread?"

"That you did, but I could not face it. I am sor..." Deineike turned away as tears threatened again.

Jorinda also looked away and wiped tears from her own cheeks. When she looked back, she gave Deineike a soft smile. "I imagine you are sorry."

"That I am." Deineike laughed, though the laughter soon faded.

Jorinda picked up a piece of the bread. "Will you share some bread with me? I have not eaten for some time, and I am hungry."

Deineike tried to smile. "I will join you." Jorinda helped her to sit up, and they nibbled on the bread, though they each managed only a small piece.

The taste of the bread revolted Jorinda, and she wrinkled her nose in disgust. "That may be the vilest bread in Dur."

"Worse food exists, doubtless, but if it does, I hope I never encounter it." They laughed a little. "If this bread is intended to relieve my stomach, I fear it will fail, for my stomach cannot tolerate it."

Jorinda exhaled a long breath. "Deineike, tonight I will sleep elsewhere. I must have some time to weigh all that has turned." Deineike nodded, a mournful expression on her face. "Tomorrow, you can sit with me at the front of the ship, and we will see what changes a night of sleep has brought to my thoughts, if any."

Deineike's unhappy eyes stared up at Jorinda as tears spilled down her cheeks. "I believe I will have time for you, although my stomach oftentimes makes unscheduled demands on me." She gave a pained smile.

Jorinda laughed at Deineike's jest. She had done as Wilash bade her and given Deineike a thread of hope. The blue-eyed woman needed nothing more, it seemed, but remained ever optimistic in the darkest hours. In truth, Jorinda felt pleased to see Deineike smile and even laugh a little. Her beauty shone brightest when she laughed. Her eyes sparkled, and her perfect lips turned upward at the corners into a huge smile that could light a fire in Jorinda's heart, and elsewhere, in truth.

Anger still fumed inside her, but she could not hate such a gentle, considerate woman, one who wore her pain and remorse in such plain sight. She reached out and stroked Deineike's cheek. Deineike moved her head into the touch, and Jorinda leaned down and kissed her forehead. "Sleep now. You must be tired. You look terrible."

Deineike smiled again. "My thanks. You have ever been quick with a compliment." Jorinda moved to the door. "Jorinda." Jorinda turned to look back at Deineike, who still sat up in the bunk. "Sleep well, my love. I love you." Deineike blew her a small kiss, and Jorinda smiled.

"You also." Jorinda walked into another cabin, occupied by four mariners. Three of them sat on chairs and wagered on a card game, while the fourth watched from a bunk. The buzz of their conversation ceased the instant Jorinda walked into the cabin.

She counted eight bunks in the room. "Is there a bunk in this cabin nobody occupies?" One of the mariners pointed at one of the bunks, the bottom one of a pair. Jorinda crossed the cabin and lay down on it. "Please, continue your game." She drifted off to sleep within a few moments.

The next morning, Jorinda woke late. The exhaustion of the previous two days had kept her asleep through the noise of the mariners as they rose for their duties, it seemed. Two men still slept in their bunks, and one of them snored. Some mariners must watch over the ship all night, and these two may have been part of that duty last night and would now sleep for some part of the day. She climbed from her bunk and visited the vanity area, where she washed her face with cold water and used a finger to rub the white paste, used throughout Dur, over her teeth to sweeten her breath. Even these simple acts made her feel much improved, since she had not performed them for almost two days now.

When she entered the common area, some of the bread had been set on the counter along with some cold meats. She ate some of the meat but did not take any of the horrendous bread.

A man's voice came from behind her. "You do not care for our bread?"

Jorinda did not turn, but she recognised the voice. "That I do not. It disgusts me." She did not add that he also disgusted her, but she thought it.

"We agree, but it binds the stomach, and in heavy seas, that can be a boon. How is your friend?"

She turned to face the man whose debt had been paid by another's blood. "You killed her mother."

He blanched. "I know nothing of this accusation. You will withdraw it."

She shot him a cold, mirthless laugh. "Have you heard of the organisation behind the token?"

Fear crossed his face, and he looked down as he mumbled, "That I have."

Jorinda repeated the accusation. "You killed her mother."

He shuffled his feet. "In truth, I recognised her when she fainted, although she was so young that day. I had quaffed ale all day and became inebriated beyond all reason. I have never forgiven myself. I did not mean to kill her. I sought only to frighten her. She attempted to cheat me, and I wished to show her I am not to be cheated, but it turned awry. Inebriation, nothing more can explain it. I have never so much as struck a woman since that night, but I cannot atone for it."

Jorinda fixed him with a cold stare, spoke in a voice to match. "Your blood could atone for it."

He took a step backward. "Please." His eyes widened in fear, his hands held toward her in a further silent plea.

"If I wished you dead, you would already float in the Alc, food for the fish. I will say this, nonetheless. Do not ask after her. Do not visit her. If you see her on the deck, do not loiter where she can see you. And do not give me cause to regret that I allow you to take another breath, not ever. It would be no chore to take you. Now, eat this vile bread and keep out of my way. I will go to the deck." It gave her some small measure of satisfaction to intimidate the man, but it also concerned her she might have killed him with little thought or remorse.

He moved into the room, cowered back against the wall, and she stomped out onto the deck. Wilash and Klordia were already seated on the same upturned pails as yesterday, and Jorinda stopped to enquire after Deineike.

Klordia answered. "She slept long last night. She still slept when we left the cabin."

Jorinda nodded. "I will leave you to your conversation." An unexpected lightness came to her step, and she attributed it to Klordia's news that Deineike had slept. Last night's visit had been good for them both, it appeared. Jorinda left the pair to their romance and went to the bow. She sat down and gazed over the water as the boat ploughed north toward Ort.

Deineike limped along the deck behind her little more than an hour later. "When will we reach Ort?"

"Tomorrow, I believe." Jorinda patted the deck beside herself. "Come, sit with me. I would welcome some company."

Deineike sat, slow and careful, and Jorinda did not help her, prepared to do so if asked, but aware of Deineike's stubborn, independent streak. "You could have had company. Wilash and Klordia are not far from you."

Jorinda gave a small laugh, keen not to draw the lovebirds' attention. "They have eyes only for each other."

"More than eyes."

Jorinda looked at Deineike, open-mouthed, curious. "What? Tell me."

"They lay together last night. They thought me asleep. In truth, they awakened me. He is noisy, and she is a screamer."

Jorinda flicked a glance at Wilash and Klordia, then grabbed Deineike's arm. "Do you tell the truth? I heard no screams." She laughed.

"She buried her face in a pillow, but she screamed." They both laughed for a time. "I am pleased. I like Wilash and Klordia, although I know you do not care for her."

Jorinda could not deny it. "That I do not. I cannot say why. We stroke each other's fur against the grain. There is naught to be done about it. What is scribed, must be."

Neither of them spoke for a time, but Deineike broke the silence at last. "What will you do once we reach Ort?"

Jorinda huffed out an uncertain breath. "I do not know. The things we discussed at such length in Alcmouth, how we would bring down Styrrach and expose the Bailiff's corruption, these things have not been mentioned since we boarded this ship."

"That is my fault." Deineike sounded mournful.

Jorinda placed a hand on her arm to reassure her. "That it is not. I have not relished the topic, in truth. I care nothing for this 'two books' issue. I do not care if they make coin by legal, illegal, or any other means that exist. I care that for some reason, Styrrach arranged for me to be taken and hanged by the Portreeve. I wish to get to the bottom of why. Arella paid a terrible price for this treachery, and there must be an accounting."

Deineike laughed. "Do not say that before Klordia. She will lecture you for half a day on the whys and whats of how to tally that accounting."

Jorinda smiled, amused by the jest. "That she will. I must know whether the Portreeve in Ort is involved. If he is, then I do not understand why there is no Guild there. That will occupy me for a day or so while I make some enquiries, then I shall see what I do next. Doubtless I will move on. Ort will not be safe. The Guild will hear we have travelled there soon enough."

Deineike sat in silence for a time and fiddled with the bottom of her tunic. She did not look up when next she spoke. "Jorinda?"

"Deineike?"

Deineike continued to fiddle. She had something important to say, and Jorinda waited for it. "May I stay with you? In Ort, I mean. For a time."

Jorinda stifled a sigh she longed to set free. She owed Deineike the care promised to her in Torric. Whatever else had passed between them, Deineike's injuries remained Jorinda's responsibility, and she had sworn to help until the damage healed. Although the tall woman could now move around unaided, she still struggled, and Jorinda had not yet discharged her obligation. Beyond that, the love between them must be considered. She could not swear she wished to live without that love, but her anger at the needless death of the wrong man created a rift between them, and she could see no easy way to heal it, though she wished she could.

Arella once said something about Deineike; Deineike had needed her more than she had needed Deineike. Jorinda understood now. At times, Deineike proved a strong and capable woman. She made a life for herself after Arella abandoned her, but she appeared more comfortable when subordinate to another, content to defer to another as long as it allowed her to love and be loved. Deineike seemed to need an inequality in her relationships, one where she valued herself less than the woman she loved, and it did not seem to concern her.

Jorinda looked into the desperate blue eyes. "Deineike, you are a strong woman, compassionate and warm. You could achieve so much. Why do you rely on others so? Why must you need another to the exclusion of your own ambition? It is strange to me."

Deineike's eyes filled with tears, and Jorinda cursed herself. She had brought more sadness to this selfless woman whose life had been so turbulent. "I only asked if I could stay with you. I wish to set things right between us. I love you; you know this. I could not live if I did not have you."

"Do not say such things." Jorinda battled to keep any edge from her voice. "It is not true. Did you say the same to Arella, or think it, at the least?"

Deineike lowered her head and her voice. "That I did. I thought it many times."

"Yet you still live and are a woman of great character. You lack confidence in yourself for some reason. You should not. You are…" Jorinda found it difficult to articulate her thoughts and Deineike's tears distracted her.

"I do not wish to live without you. Is that a crime?"

Jorinda could not constrain her resigned sigh. "That it is not, and you know this. You must be stronger, more independent. There will not always be an Arella or a Jorinda to beat your problems away for you. You do not need us, in truth. You are the better woman. The best woman I have known in my life."

A cry came from behind them. "Craft astern." When the two women turned to look, a larger, three masted vessel cut through the water some way behind their own ship. It sat low in the water, but it looked sleek and fast. Awkward, Deineike turned where she sat but did not watch the ship for long. Jorinda stood to watch. The ship gained on them, and she chewed at her lower lip.

Deineike gazed up at Jorinda, her head to one side, confusion in her eyes. "You are worried?"

Despite Jorinda's concern, Deineike seemed unbothered by the other ship. Had she not understood the risks it might portend? "What if the Guild pursues us?"

Deineike reached a hand up to Jorinda's thigh, spoke soft words. "That seems unlikely to me. How could they already know we flee aboard this ship?"

Jorinda continued to worry at her lip, distracted. "You have the right of it, I am sure." She could not shake the sense of concern despite Deineike's words.

Deineike remained calm, mayhap to reassure Jorinda. "There is nothing we can do, in truth. We cannot ride away from any pursuit. We are trapped aboard this wooden box that floats atop the water. Come, sit. I believe you worry over nothing."

Jorinda's exasperation grew. "This is what I meant earlier. You take charge in a stressful moment; you calm me and allay my fears. Once the moment passes, you will again become the helpless, needy little girl who begs for any boon I might cast your way."

Deineike blinked away her tears, her hand still on Jorinda's thigh. "I cannot become somebody I am not. I apologise for my limitations."

"You need not become anybody else. The strength you seek from others is already within you if you could grasp it. Your life would be richer if you did."

"As yours is?" Deineike lowered her eyes as soon as she spoke.

The words scarred Jorinda. They were hurtful but true. Jorinda's strength had carried her through times few could have endured, but she despised herself and believed herself a monster. Deineike had a sweet, affectionate nature despite her neediness.

"Jorinda, I am sorry. I should not have said such a horrible thing. Forgive me."

Jorinda wished she had never loved Deineike with all she was, that she could react to those words with anger and push her off the ship into the river. Instead, she ruffled the dark hair. "You spoke the truth." She sighed and glanced back at the ship. It sailed faster than them without question, but Deineike had the right of it. It would catch their ship and either pass them by or disgorge a horde of Guild members who would swarm aboard. Nothing could be done about the outcome except await it. She sat on the deck again.

Deineike returned to the issue of their fate in Ort. "You have not answered my question. Not in a way I desire to hear, at the least."

As Deineike had done, Jorinda now fiddled with an imaginary thread, though she chose the hem of her trouser leg. "Deineike—"

"I do not believe any pleasant tale begins with somebody who sighs my name."

Jorinda glared at her. "You cannot listen to somebody speak without you interrupt them. Are you aware of it?"

Deineike sniffed and wiped at the tears that still rolled down her cheeks as she mumbled a reply. "I am an imperfect woman. This has been laid bare before me this morning. I will strive to improve myself."

Guilt tore at Jorinda's heart. How could she continue to be so cruel to Deineike, who wanted nothing more than to love Jorinda despite her evil nature, and to be loved in return? "I spoke out of turn. The constant interruptions are sweet, though I fear I must live two lifetimes to complete all I wish to say." She managed a smile, and to her relief, Deineike returned it. "You may go or stay wherever you will. I have told you this already. You may stay with me in Ort while I seek my answers if you wish. Do not read into this that all is now right between us. I am obligated to tend to you until you can walk unaided again. And I do care for you. In time, things may be right between us. I cannot see what fates are written."

"I wish to help you. With the mystery of the Guild, I mean. I will help you seek your answers if it lies within my power."

"My thanks."

Deineike kissed Jorinda's cheek, lay back on the deck, and closed her eyes. The wind added a chill to an otherwise warm, sunny day, but not enough to make it uncomfortable to sit at the bow of the ship. Jorinda thought Deineike had fallen asleep after a time and allowed her to go undisturbed. The trials she had endured since Wilash first came to the cottage must have left her exhausted. Tiredness wore Jorinda down, but she would not allow herself to sleep until she determined what the ship behind them portended.

Jorinda thought long on the disagreement between her and Deineike. She tried to convince herself she had over-reacted to a trivial matter, and she should wake Deineike, drag her to the cabin, and make passionate love to her. That would make light of the fact she had killed the wrong man, however, and that affected her, more than she would have expected. Until her resentment at Deineike's involvement in the murder of the mariner faded, Jorinda could not suppress her anger or her misery. Deineike had not intended the mistake, and Jorinda guessed the older woman also punished herself for the loss of an innocent life. She sighed, frustrated by the complexity of the situation. Deineike must salve her conscience herself while Jorinda, likewise, attended to her own considerations on the matter. Until she calmed her fury and purged herself of the guilt she felt, they would be estranged with no way to tell whether that estrangement would pass.

Jorinda looked behind her as the sun slid across the sky and the midday passed. It surprised her how much closer the other ship appeared to be. It might draw level with them within two or three hours. She shook her head, uncertain of what might happen then.

Deineike's voice interrupted her thoughts. "I have slept long, it seems."

The sleepy surprise in Deineike's voice coaxed a laugh despite Jorinda's worries about the ship and the tense situation between the two women. "That you have."

"Why did you not wake me?"

"Your body does not lie to you. If you sleep, it is because you need that sleep. I did not wake you, though I missed the pleasure of an interruption to one of my stories."

Deineike pushed at Jorinda's leg in jest. "Away with you, tease." Her eyes sparkled as she laughed, and she poked her tongue out at Jorinda. She sat up and looked backward. "I saw you look at that ship. It is close now."

"That it is. That it is."

Deineike struggled to her feet. "I must walk a little. I shall do so without your aid, since I must become more independent if I am to win back your heart." She smiled, one of her beautiful smiles that further tore at Jorinda's already shattered heart.

Jorinda returned the smile and pointed at Wilash and Klordia. "Be off with you, then. Check on the lovebirds."

Deineike laughed and set off down the deck. She still used the staff, and Jorinda wondered whether she might progress better without it, although it doubtless reduced the risk of a fall. The unpredictable movement of the ship made it difficult to walk even without the hindrance of a damaged leg, but Deineike's stomach seemed to cope better with the movement of the ship today as if she had become more accustomed to it.

Deineike stopped to exchange some words with Wilash and Klordia and laughed aloud at something they said. After a few moments, she continued onward and passed through the door to the cabins. When Jorinda glanced at the other ship, the gap between the two vessels had grown smaller. The mariners and master of her own ship appeared unconcerned by its presence, and she tried to convince herself the bigger ship posed no threat to her or her companions.

She looked forward again. All she could gain from her observations of the other vessel would be a stiff neck, she decided. After some time, she heard Deineike's unmistakeable shuffle behind her and the tall woman's shadow fell across her. Deineike reached a hand down and offered Jorinda some cold meats. "I brought you some lunch."

Jorinda took the meat. "My thanks." Deineike huffed as she lowered herself to the deck. She seated herself to Jorinda's left, where she blocked the sun, so Jorinda shuffled forward to find the warmth again. She pretended to be offended. "You did not bring me any bread?"

"That I did." Deineike seemed to struggle to keep a smile from her face. "I found it so desirable, I ate it all myself on the return journey." They looked at one another for a heartbeat, then both burst into loud laughter.

Jorinda wrinkled her brow as she sought for a word in the recesses of her memory. "That bread is...oh, what strange word did Taro use? When he asked you to clean out the barn?"

"Muck?"

"That it is. Muck. That bread is muck." They both laughed again, recent woes forgotten for the moment.

Another hour passed as they chatted about titbits. Deineike's mood appeared to lighten, and Jorinda hoped some sadness might have lifted from the other woman. No doubt her unhappiness would return that night when Jorinda again slept in a different cabin, but she might bring some joy to her for now, and the beautiful smile appeared more often as the day wore on.

A cry came from behind them, and they turned. "Craft abeam." To Jorinda's surprise, the larger ship had already pulled alongside them, some distance from their own vessel. Mariners scurried around on the deck of the other vessel, busy with their work. They had dark brown skin and reminded Jorinda of the crews of some of the ships they had seen that fateful day at the Torric docks. Jorinda studied the crew but did not recognise any faces. It seemed the Guild were not aboard, after all else, and her concerns had been for naught.

The faster ship soon passed them, and cries in an unfamiliar tongue carried to them on the wind. The ship had almost passed them when a mariner at the stern appeared to notice the two women watch his vessel overtake their own, and he favoured them with an exaggerated kiss that he blew toward them from the palm of his hand. They laughed, and Deineike waved back at him.

Another cry came from behind the women. "Wash inbound." Jorinda had not understood all the cries from the mariners as the ship drew closer, then passed them. She imagined they were language unique to mariners.

She turned to Deineike. "Do you understand these things they say about that ship?"

"That I do not. I guess it is some shippy thing."

Jorinda stared at her with a gasp. "'Shippy?'"

"Shippy. Things related to ships."

"I do not believe 'shippy' is a word."

"What then?" Deineike seemed put out by the contradiction.

Jorinda considered the problem, but other factors intervened before she could arrive at a decision. As the other ship pulled ahead of them, it churned the water behind it, and the waves struck their own vessel, which pitched up, then down again as it wallowed from side to side in the violent, broken water behind the large ship. A wave splashed over the bow of their ship and soaked them. The cold water shocked them after the warmth of the sun, and the salt taste surprised Jorinda. In truth, the river flowed between the Northern Ocean and the Torr Sea, little more than a passage the two seas took to meet up with each other, so it made sense it would be salt water rather than fresh.

Jorinda's mind flashed back to the nightmare when the wave had crashed over her on the deck of a ship, but Deineike crawled toward the rail and distracted her. Their ship bobbed about in the water as the other vessel pulled away ahead of them, and the movement had brought Deineike's stomach undone. As before, she did not reach the rail before she fetched up, and Jorinda leapt to her feet to help her up so she did not have to drag herself through her own vomit. As Deineike donated the cold meats to the fish in the river, Jorinda glanced toward the stern. Wilash also hung in misery over the rail while Klordia fussed around him. Jorinda could not stifle laughter.

Deineike moaned, miserable. "My thanks. I am pleased you find such joy in my distress."

"I am sorry. Wilash also suffers with you. It must be unbearable."

"It is." Deineike fetched up again.

TWELVE

A CLOSE SHAVE

ONCE DEINEIKE'S AND WILASH'S STOMACHS CALMED, JORINDA, Deineike, Wilash, and Klordia passed an hour in the communal area and ate a meal of meats and cheeses. Deineike smiled when Jorinda pressed some of the bread on Klordia, and the three of them broke into wild laughter at the look of disgust on her face as she attempted to chew it. Wilash took a small piece of it, from some noble sense of empathy with Klordia's misery or from idle curiosity.

He chewed it, thoughtful. "It is unusual. It is too salty for my tastes, and almost too stodgy to swallow. There is something in its taste I cannot place." He frowned as though he sought to identify the taste.

Jorinda pressed him to agree it tasted horrible. "It is vile though, is it not?"

"That it is not. I would not say I like it, but it is tolerable." They stared at him in wonder.

He must have a sturdy stomach to tolerate the taste of the bread, and Jorinda pictured his misery as he fetched up over the rail earlier. She laughed. "I understand it binds the stomach against the motion of the ship." They all roared with laughter as Wilash tore off a huge piece with comic flair and crammed it into his mouth.

Jorinda bade them goodnight, and as expected, Deineike's mood deflated the moment she realised Jorinda would spend the night in a different cabin. Klordia scowled, and Wilash shook his head, a sad expression on his face. Jorinda could not find the strength to explain all that boiled within her, and she trudged, dejected, back to the cabin where she had slept the previous night.

Seven mariners played at cards in the middle of the room as she entered. As it had the previous night, the room fell silent as she walked in. The man who killed Deineike's mother sat at the card table, and the colour drained from his face when he looked up at Jorinda. He scooped up his coin, ran from the room, and his friends stared after him. One large mariner with an enormous beard rose, hands on hips. He glared at Jorinda as she lay down on the same bunk as the previous night, but Jorinda ignored him and closed her eyes.

A man's voice, filled with resentment, invaded her attempt to sleep. "You sleep here again tonight?"

She guessed the voice belonged to the big man, but she could not be certain since she did not open her eyes. "That I do."

"Why must you spend your nights here and drive our friends out? You have your own cabin, and your companions would doubtless appreciate your company more than we do."

Jorinda believed Klordia might have some thoughts on the matter, but she kept her own counsel on the issue. "I am here to mind my own affairs rather than intrude on another's." She hoped her words sounded as sarcastic as she intended.

"You deemed it your affair to threaten my friend earlier."

"He is a murderer." There were some intakes of breath at this.

"You lie. He denies it."

"Strange. He denies it to you while he admits it to me."

The man fell silent for a time, but he had not finished. "I doubt this so-called Guild exists. I believe it is nothing more than a fancy tale designed to frighten others so they will not resist freeloaders and ne'er-do-wells."

Jorinda still did not open her eyes. "Are you frightened of me, then?"

"That I am not. I think we could all take some pleasure from you and awake on the morrow unharmed."

One or two of the others muttered at this. Jorinda thought one of them said, "That we would not." She sat up and stared at the big man. All the men stood behind him, but two backed away a pace.

Jorinda cocked her head to one side. "What is your name?"

He stood taller as he spat out his reply. "Wilke."

"I have some advice for you, Wilke. Death is permanent, and yours would be the first. There are six of you, and you might overpower me, but you would die." She turned her gaze to one of the others. "You would be next. Others among you also. Come, who wishes to die next, after these two?" She gave them a cheerful smile.

Some of the men looked down, and none of them said any word of encouragement to Wilke. Doubtless, his bravado relied on assistance from his companions, and she imagined he now felt disappointed none of them shared his enthusiasm for a fight. He misjudged a simple human frailty that Jorinda exploited. Many might overpower one, but some might die in the process, and nobody wished to be among the dead. Someone in the Guild once called it, "Risk and reward." The reward must be greater than the risk for any endeavour to be worthwhile. People's feet often turned coldest when the risk included death.

Wilke would not admit defeat. "How would these deaths come about? You, a tiny woman, would slay us all?" His companions did not join in with his laughter.

He had pushed her far enough, so she reached down into her boot and took out her dagger. She tapped its blade up and down on her left palm as she stood and strode toward him. The others backed away. As quick as the crack of a whip, she reached up to grab a handful of his beard, and her dagger slashed upward to cut it from him before he could react. She extended her left arm, opened her hand, and his beard cascaded to the floor as she snarled at him. "Had I wished it, you would lie dead now where your beard lies." Frenzy and fury could bring a person undone. When Jorinda killed, she stayed calm, clear of mind, and let her Guild training guide her. Her temper might flare later, but she remained cold and dispassionate while she wielded her blade.

Wilke raised a hand to his now uneven beard. He said nothing, but his eyes blazed with hatred. The other men all moved back to their bunks. They abandoned Wilke, and his life hung in the balance. Jorinda's eyes never left his, but she remained conscious of the others in the periphery of her vision, wary of any change of heart among their number.

Jorinda whispered, "Do you wish death, Wilke?" He lowered his head at last and backed off. She had won but had created an enemy in the process. She might not survive the night in the room once asleep, so she decided to leave. She stopped at the door. Without a backward glance, she said, "The man who fashioned this blade once said he thought he might give it a name, though I believed him foolish. From now on, however, I will call it Wilke. Then I shall never forget you." She left the room, closed the door, and as the nerves she had held at bay throughout the encounter took hold, something akin to fear coursed through her, and her body shook. Despite her previous words of revulsion for the craft of death, Jorinda had been prepared to kill Wilke, had it come to that. She shook her head in resignation. What had she become?

In the cabin where Deineike, Wilash, and Klordia already lay in their bunks, a lantern still burned on the table, and Jorinda imagined they had been in conversation about her decision not to sleep in the cabin. Deineike's eyes lit up as Jorinda entered. Jorinda picked up one of the chairs, placed it against the door, and slid the bolt into place. Wilash sat up in his bunk, and curiosity replaced excitement on Deineike's face. "What has turned?"

Jorinda sighed, disappointed at the way the night had turned. "A disagreement. Doubtless nothing will come of it, but the chair will warn us if something does turn awry and the bolt can be disabled from without."

Klordia narrowed her eyes. "A disagreement? With whom?"

Jorinda sneered. "One of the mariners. It seems I overestimated my charm, and I am not as popular as I believed."

Klordia stayed silent, although Jorinda did not doubt she had suitable responses ready and available, and Wilash lay down again. Deineike moved in her bunk as though she made room for Jorinda, but Jorinda put out the lantern and climbed alone into the nearest bunk.

After a few moments, Deineike's voice whispered through the darkness. "Jorinda?"

Jorinda sighed. "Deineike?"

"Tell me the nature of this disagreement."

"It matters not. I no longer wish to sleep among them."

"You prefer our company then?"

Jorinda smiled in the dark. "You do not smell as bad, although Wilash snores even louder than them." She grunted as a pillow struck her in her legs. She taunted his poor aim. "You almost missed me."

His voice growled back at her. "I aimed at Deineike." They all laughed, and the atmosphere became less fraught.

Sleep eluded Jorinda, although she heard the others drift away as she lay awake in the bunk. Doubtless the killer had poured out the whole story to the others earlier, which had driven Wilke to challenge her. As luck would have it, the ship would reach Ort the next day, and they could leave it behind. Life would become unpleasant aboard if the crew turned hostile.

Nightmares plagued her when sleep came at last. Taro stood before her, and he whimpered and protested his innocence as she slit his throat while Styrrach watched on. Styrrach goaded her to kill Taro again and would not be silenced, and Taro rose from the floor. Jorinda slit his throat over and over as Styrrach urged her to kill him again and again. She woke in a cold sweat before the sunrise and pressed her pillow to her face to muffle the sound of her tears.

When Wilash stirred, Jorinda slid from the bunk and went up to the deck as the first light broke over the eastern horizon. She walked to the bow and stared ahead, eager for any glimpse of Ort. Some mariners moved about behind her, but she did not turn. Word of the confrontation of the previous night would have spread through the crew like a fog that crawled over the morning land, and she remained alert for any sound of threat. Deineike's unmistakeable limp came from behind her, and she sighed. The burden of the physical and emotional care of the older woman had taken a toll on Jorinda. She might be better alone, where she need care only for her own fractured mind.

Deineike slid her arms around Jorinda's waist, and she whispered, "Are you all right?"

"That I am."

"What happened last night? Did it have something to do with that animal?"

Jorinda imagined she meant her mother's murderer. "That it did not. One of the mariners fancied himself braver than it turned, that is all."

Deineike kissed her shoulder. "I am sorry. This is all my fault."

Jorinda unpicked Deineike's clasped hands from her stomach and turned. "That it is not. He rolled the dice. He will be more cautious in the future, I hope." Deineike's face lay half in shadow as the light improved and the sun peeked over the far horizon, but that did not make her any less beautiful. She had a statuesque, powerful body and a face that could turn rancid water into fine wine.

Mischief sparkled in Deineike's eyes. "What goes through your mind?"

Reconciliation still felt some distance from Jorinda's heart, but for the first time since Deineike had laid bare the terrible mistake, Jorinda thought there might come a time when they could repair the rift between them. "I think you are a temptress sent to torment me."

Deineike looked coy. "Temptress? Do I tempt you then?"

Jorinda laughed and felt the sting of heat in her cheeks. "You can tempt me, but you can rile me with similar ease. You are desirable…curse it, that is wrong…" Deineike said nothing. "Deineike, I cannot explain myself. By all the fates, interrupt me, and save me from myself."

Deineike kissed her nose. "Let us eat. I will even let you help me walk this morning if it will rescue you from your own bluster."

"That it will. My thanks." Deineike leaned on Jorinda, and they walked at Deineike's slow pace to the common area. Several mariners sat on the benches with food before them. The room fell silent as they entered. Jorinda had grown accustomed to the reaction. As all eyes turned to them, Jorinda stood at the door, and Deineike leaned on her, confusion on her face.

Jorinda looked from one to the other but could not see the killer, although she spotted Wilke, his face clean shaven this morning. No doubt he had been unable to sport the shame of the uneven beard. For some moments, they exchanged cold, hard stares. Without warning, Jorinda said, "Boo," and Wilke started while some of the others stifled laughter behind their hands.

Jorinda helped Deineike onto a bench and took some meats from the counter before she sat next to Deineike with her back to the wall. She whispered, her head close to Deineike's, keen to keep their conversation private. "Try to keep this down today, if you can."

The master appeared. Jorinda had seen him on no more than a few occasions throughout the voyage, and she guessed he had avoided them as much as he could. "Will you leave us in Ort?" It seemed he tired of his passengers.

Jorinda gave him the news she imagined he hoped for. "That we will."

The master seemed relieved. "We will dock there later this morning. We will not be sorry to see the backs of you."

Jorinda fought to control her anger at his rudeness. "We feel a similar disdain for you. Although I shall miss Wilke." She turned her gaze on him. "How fortunate I carry something to remind me of him in the future." Deineike stared at her open-mouthed, a slice of meat in her hand above the platter that held their breakfast.

Wilke sneered at her. "I would not lie with you if you were the last woman in the land."

"Woe." Jorinda once more hoped her voice dripped with sarcasm. "I shall have to find another to lie with in that case." She turned to Deineike and kissed her. Some mariners gasped, and she pulled her head back. Deineike had not returned the kiss despite Jorinda's belief she would welcome a passionate kiss after all that had turned in the previous days. Deineike's face turned bright red instead.

The master shook his head and left the room. Some of the men rose and followed the master, and the others looked away from Jorinda and Deineike. Once the women had finished their breakfast, Deineike limped from the room, but Jorinda continued to eat for a few moments before she followed her to the cabin.

As soon as Jorinda closed the door, Deineike wheeled on her. "What did you mean by that display?" She snarled, and her fists clenched and unclenched.

"What is wrong? Have you not begged me for days to come back to you? I kiss you, and all your professed love for me vanishes."

"I love you; the fates know I do. But I will not be used as part of whatever vendetta you pursue against the fellow who insulted you. That matter lies between the two of you. Do not compel me to be a part of it."

Wilash and Klordia sat on two of the chairs, horror on their faces. Wilash gave a discreet cough, and they both rose and left the cabin.

Jorinda looked at Deineike's red face and angry eyes. The reaction mystified her. "Would you rather I had slit his throat?"

"Some evil has passed between you and him, my guess, doubtless the dispute you spoke of last night. Do not toss me onto the fires of your own hatred. I will not be a toy you play with as you see fit."

"That you will not. The man who killed your mother lies at the heart of the argument. In his place, an innocent man died at your request, but you need not worry. You need no longer be part of this disagreement, though you lie at the core of it." Jorinda turned, pulled the door open, and stomped to the bow of the boat.

She sat cross-legged on the deck and stared forward, disconsolate. Her life continued to be a quagmire of bitterness, betrayal, and disappointment. She had killed the mariner for Deineike, then learned she had killed the wrong man. Although she had refused to kill the mariner aboard this ship, she had warned him away from Deineike. That warning brought threats of violence and rape against her, all thanks to Deineike's stupid mistake. Jorinda had been compelled to take action to keep them safe and had again been insulted this morning. Her response to that insult had angered Deineike, even though she had begged Jorinda for days to forgive and reconcile with her.

Everybody arrayed themselves against her, even Deineike. Jorinda had been dealt a terrible hand in life. She had tried to play it as best she could, but the unfairness of that unplayable hand could not be defeated. Jorinda bent her head and cried her frustration to the river.

THIRTEEN
THE FRIENDSHIP AND BEYOND

WHEN JORINDA LOOKED UP, SHE SAW BUILDINGS AHEAD, AND SHE imagined they must be close to Ort. She longed with all her heart to leave the ship and her companions. Let Wilash and Klordia care for Deineike; Jorinda had done all she could. Deineike could now walk unaided, and Jorinda had kept her word. Jorinda would move on alone and learn all she could of the things they had uncovered.

Why did she seek to solve the mystery of the shrouding and the Bailiff's role in Styrrach's organisation? Even as she asked herself the question, she could find no answer. Styrrach must lie behind her betrayal and the death of Arella. She could journey onward to Zhanghar, kill Styrrach, then end her own life and make good on her vow from The Ship's Yard. Vengeance followed by her own swift death would satisfy her.

She heard footsteps and turned, ready to pull her dagger from her boot, but the footsteps were Klordia's. Her nemesis, doubtless come to gloat as Jorinda fell at last to the lowest point of her entire life. Klordia stopped when Jorinda's eyes met hers, and the older woman fidgeted from one foot to the other.

Jorinda had no patience for uncertainty and hesitation this morning. "What is it?"

"Deineike has taken to her bunk, once more distraught and in tears. Are you the monster you appear to be?"

Jorinda's lips peeled from her teeth in a vicious snarl, but Klordia stood her ground. "Would you have me say you are correct? Very well, I am a monster. A creature without morals or compassion. A killer with no heart. The thing your mother said would come for you in the night if you misbehaved, made flesh. There, you have heard what you came to hear. Leave me be." She turned to face the bow again.

"She is a sweet girl."

"She is no girl."

"To me she is. A kind, thoughtful girl, torn to pieces by your cruelty to her. Did you ever love her?"

Jorinda turned to look at her again. "You speak of things you know nothing about, and you place yourself in peril. Do you forget I am a monster?" Her voice had become a growl, and the furious snarl had not left her face.

Klordia flushed, but she did not leave. Wilash came out onto the deck behind her, but he lingered near the door. "That is your way, is it not? Threats, violence, and murder are all you know. You can do no other, my guess."

"You guess wrong. I am as fine a garment maker as you could hope to meet. Any item I make would be far beyond the coin you earn in your sorry little job in the tally office. The sweet girl in your cabin wears clothes of my making. I am a garment maker by profession. The art of death is a hobby to me."

Klordia shook her head, disgust in her eyes. "I see no redemption for you, although Deineike does. You do not deserve her. Nonetheless, I beseech you to go to her and apologise for the myriad ways in which you have abused her love and her good nature. Spare her any more of your cruelty."

"Or?" Jorinda shook with rage, astounded that this woman whose life she had saved, with no evidence of gratitude, would speak to her with such rudeness.

"Or? Or she may die of a broken heart, if that concerns you. I doubt it does. Apologise to her. Then leave her, for you will bring nothing but darkness to her door, and she will never again know joy if she remains with you. I know this."

"You know much, who did not know us at all a sevenday past." Jorinda's rage built within her, and her hand strayed toward her boot. What right did Klordia have to speak to her this way? The woman knew nothing of what Deineike had put her through, or of what she had put Deineike through.

"Anybody could see it."

Deineike's face swam into Jorinda's mind. Her wide smile sparkled in her blue eyes, but she cried, and her eyes and nose turned red as tears spilled down her cheeks. Too often on this voyage, Jorinda had seen that version of Deineike, and she could not deny Klordia's words. Deineike did deserve better than the fates written for her since the night she had arrived at Taro's farm. Whether she could ever find such fates while she stayed with Jorinda could not be guessed, but she deserved them if they could be written.

Jorinda stood and pushed past Klordia, then past Wilash. She did not speak to either as she strode to the cabin. As Klordia had said, Deineike lay face down on her bunk with her face pressed into her pillow, and her sobs rent the air. She did not look up as Jorinda entered.

"Deineike."

"Go away."

Deineike's muffled voice stung Jorinda. She had never told Jorinda to leave her, as far as Jorinda could recall. "I have hurt you. I have come to apologise."

"My thanks." Deineike did not lift her face from the pillow.

Jorinda stood forlorn. She had gone too far, if Deineike had grown so distant from her. "Ort approaches. Or rather, we approach Ort." No response. "In Torric, I swore I would leave you if you asked me to. I swear it again. Tell me to go, and I will leave the ship, and you will never see me again. You might then find joy." Jorinda hung her head, and myriad thoughts crowded in on her, none of which brought her any pride. Her behaviour had been terrible, unforgivable, and there could be no explanation other than Klordia's, that the garment maker's daughter had become an irredeemable monster.

Deineike turned her head to look at Jorinda, though she did not rise from the bunk. "I say the same now as I did then. You want me to order you to leave, but I love you. Why would I wish this?"

Jorinda swallowed hard, tears not far away, and she doubted she could hold them back. Guilt had woven itself into her life, but she could attempt to atone for this latest act, at the least. "I should not have behaved as I did this morning. Filled with anger, I used you. I desired revenge for his insult. I know no way to take revenge unless I kill, so I sought an alternative. I used you, and I am sorry."

"That you did. You are flawed, I know this. Klordia—"

"Klordia." Jorinda spat the name from her mouth like a fly that flew in, uninvited and unwelcome.

"Jorinda, why do you despise her so?" Jorinda could not reply, did not know where to begin any explanation, so Deineike continued after a moment. "Klordia told me I should leave you, that I cannot be happy while I stay with you. She means well, but she is wrong. We have been happy. We were happy in Vjort, and in Torric, until I…" She paused.

"That we were."

"I believe we can be happy again, but we must find a way to ease the pain that consumes you from within. We can do that together. I fear you cannot do so alone, and you will destroy yourself. Your mind is torn by all that has turned in your life, and I fear I have damaged it further by the mistake revealed on this voyage. Even so, your reaction has been too extreme. Do not walk away from me, I beg you. You will bring your ruin upon yourself, I am certain."

"I do not fear death. I would welcome it, in truth."

Deineike wiped at her eyes. "I would not. I would be shattered beyond repair. I do not wish death for you. I wish you to find happiness." She hesitated, and Jorinda did not interrupt her. "I love you, and you love me. I know you are angry with me, but you still love me. I will not send you from me. I wish to rebuild our love, and I wish to rebuild you, for I accept I have torn you down with my stupidity. Give me that chance, please. I urge you."

Jorinda saw no reason for Deineike's words and had never understood why Deineike had forgiven her in Torric when such horrors had been revealed to her. Here, after all that had turned, Deineike sang the same song. She pursued Jorinda's redemption even though Jorinda had long since abandoned any hope it could be found. It could not be fathomed.

Deineike broke the silence. "Jorinda?"

"I know not. I cannot think. My mind twists and turns and comes back whence it departed. Your friend thinks me a monster, and I do not disagree with her."

Deineike smiled. "She is wrong. She does not know the Jorinda I know. You have made hard choices, and they have oft gone awry. You are no monster. You are a good person who sometimes makes bad decisions."

"We shall see." Jorinda had believed herself ready to leave Deineike not an hour ago, but decisions taken in anger often did not stand the scrutiny of a cooler temper. "I thought I might travel on to Zhanghar and seek out Styrrach."

"Jorinda, do not speak of death again. You kill a part of yourself with every life you take. Death has led you where you now find yourself. Other ways must exist to bring him down, and we will seek them together in Ort. If we do not find them, we will make new plans. We decided yesterday to follow this course. Let us keep to it."

Deineike had the right of it; she had touched on the absolute truth of it. A part of Jorinda had been cut away with every breath she had cut forever from her victims. They had arrived at a decision yesterday. The incident with Wilke that morning had clouded her mind, but she would not turn from the earlier decision, after all else.

Deineike moved in the bunk and held her arms out toward her. "Come, lie beside me for a time before we prepare to leave this ship." Jorinda shuffled forward and Deineike reached out for her, then pulled her down beside herself on the bunk, where she held Jorinda tight and kissed the top of her head. "Promise me something."

"What?"

"Learn the name of this wretched ship, and no matter if we must sail on this river a hundred times, let us never, ever, board this vile thing again."

Jorinda smiled. "Agreed."

They lay on the bunk and chatted for around an hour. Deineike stroked Jorinda's hair throughout and kissed her often. How could it be so pleasurable for her to do nothing more than lie in a cot with Jorinda? Deineike seemed to find more pleasure in the simpler things in life than Jorinda could.

Shouts and sounds of movement came from the deck, and Wilash appeared. "We will dock in Ort soon." The women roused themselves from the bunk and gathered their belongings together as Wilash continued. "I must find a garment maker as soon as I can. I tire of these clothes and must have others." He had worn the same clothes since they had left Alcmouth; they had not bought any on their way to the docks as discussed.

When they went out to the deck, the ship had almost arrived at the docks. The large vessel from the previous day had docked in Ort, but little activity could be seen around it. The master of their own ship stood nearby, and Jorinda sidled over to him, determined to throw further confusion into the tale of their journey.

"We journey on to Zhanghar to meet with Styrrach."

"Then I am grateful we can no longer be of service to you. We return to Alcmouth tomorrow."

"I will pass on your regards to Styrrach." Jorinda moved toward the ramp as two dockhands prepared to raise it up to the deck.

Wilke stood nearby, and he mouthed words she thought might be, "Good riddance." Jorinda changed course to walk toward him, but Wilash grabbed her arm and pulled her toward the ramp again. She contented herself with a snarl and an exaggerated slash across her throat with a finger.

Klordia joined them as they waited to leave the ship, and once the mariners had secured the ramp, they stood to one side while their passengers descended to the dock. Jorinda walked to the stern, then rejoined the others. "The Friendship. The name could scarce have been more inappropriate."

Deineike gave a soft, amused smile. "It is a clever name, none-theless."

Wilash seemed baffled. "Clever? How so?"

"Friend. Ship. It is a pun." They debated Deineike's opinion but could not reach any agreement, and their thoughts turned to accommodation.

Klordia seemed to have some knowledge of Ort. "I believe a smaller settlement lies on the other bank of the river. Eastort, if I have the right of it. We could stay there. It should be less expensive, and we are less likely to be sought there since we would be expected to stay in Ort."

Jorinda wondered how Klordia knew of Eastort. "How would we travel there and return to Ort?"

"I know not, but I am happy to enquire." Klordia wandered off while the others sat on crates on the docks until she returned. "There is a small boat that is rowed across from time to time. That is the most common way to cross the river to and from Eastort."

Defiance flashed in Deineike's eyes. "I will not ride in a small boat across that infernal river each day. If you are set on this course, then throw me to the fish now. My stomach could not stand it."

Wilash also opposed the idea, so they agreed to seek rooms at an inexpensive inn. Klordia could not be persuaded to stay in an inn near the noise and smell of the docks, and they trudged some distance away until they found one suitable to them all. Jorinda felt uncomfortable with the cost, but tiredness overwhelmed her, and she did not wish to search any further afield.

To reduce cost, they took two rooms, and Klordia and Wilash's enthusiasm to share a room left Jorinda in the other with Deineike. It had one bed, two chairs, and a table. A nightstand that held a vanity bowl sat against one wall, along with a few small cloths and some soap. A small trunk lay in one corner in which guests might store clothes or other personal items, and it could be locked as a safe place to leave coin or small valuables. They told the innkeep they were a family. Jorinda thought the age difference between Deineike and Klordia looked insufficient for the explanation that Deineike might be her daughter, but he had not challenged them on the claim.

They arranged to meet up and discuss the next move after they had rested a little from the journey, and Wilash and Klordia knocked at the door of the women's room after an hour or so. Wilash addressed the issue that had lain unmentioned as they had sailed north. "I am afraid to pursue the matter now we are here. I doubt we can trust the Portreeve."

Klordia supported Wilash, which suggested they had already discussed the matter. "I agree."

Deineike stared at Klordia, irritation in her eyes. "You were reluctant to believe the Guild and the Portreeves work together when we discussed it in Alcmouth. What has changed your opinion?"

Klordia glanced at Wilash. "Some words Wilash said to me on the journey north."

At first, when Jorinda asked Wilash to explain his thoughts, he seemed reluctant to speak, but he relented. "When you killed that man in Torric, information on his death and your movements around the tavern through the day came to the Guild within an hour. Of course, the Portreeve's men would investigate such a brutal death, but the Guild knew too soon. I wondered on it at the time, and I now realise Deineike guessed the truth. The two are bound up together."

Jorinda muttered as fury washed over her again at the reminder of the mariner. "The man I killed. The wrong man, you mean. A pity that piece of information did not come to me before I took his life." An awkward silence fell on the room. Jorinda's ire had been rekindled by the thought of the man's blood as it had gushed from his throat, and all for naught.

Wilash coughed. "A plan has come to me nonetheless, and one I must take part in despite my reservations."

Deineike cast a sad glance at Jorinda as she asked him to explain. "What is this plan?"

"I will request an audience with the Portreeve for Jorinda and me." Jorinda's head snapped up at Wilash's words. He held his hands up before him. "I know. It is dangerous, and his staff may deny us, but I am certain we can discover his involvement if we meet with him. If he is involved, of course"

Jorinda shook her head. "Why do we wish to meet him? He may well be involved, and if he is, he will hang us as soon as rope can be found. It is too dangerous."

"That thought had occurred to me, but another has nagged at me, one that suggests he might not be bound up with Styrrach. As you said, this large, wealthy town sits on the river, and a great many ships pass through it. Despite that, it is not a city, and there is no Guild here."

Jorinda shook her head again. "We do not yet know in what way the Guild is caught up in this thing. The absence of a Guild here does not prove the Portreeve plays no part in the scheme. Your plan is too dangerous."

Deineike seemed thoughtful. "There is one way to find out."

Jorinda threw up her hands in exasperation. "You may have the right of it, but to meet with him is also a way to learn he *is* a threat to us. We might be clapped in manacles before we are shipped back to Styrrach to meet ends none of us would relish."

Wilash nodded. "It is risky, more so as we have the blood of a Portreeve's man on our hands, but it could provide valuable information."

Klordia drummed her fingers on the table. She sat in one of the chairs, leaned forward as she spoke. "The alternative is to leave here and forget we ever discovered any hint of these things. I favour that option, and in his heart Wilash does also, but questions gnaw at him as they do you, Jorinda. I fear this move, but if you both wish to know answers, then it seems the best idea we have for now."

Deineike nodded her agreement. "Jorinda, the alternative is to kill Styrrach, and I believe we both agree that will not help you. We should meet the Portreeve, or we should move on as Klordia says. Time is against us. Styrrach will know soon enough we have arrived here."

"He may, or he may not." Jorinda considered all she knew, all she guessed. "The Friendship will return to Alcmouth. The Master may not talk to the Guild, but if he does, it will be many days before he can do so, since there is nobody here he can contact. Letters will take more time to reach Styrrach in Zhanghar. We can be far from here before anybody arrives to search for us." Wilash nodded his agreement, and Jorinda pressed on. "I also told him we would journey on to Zhanghar. Styrrach may not believe that, but if he does, it might buy us more time while they seek us there." Jorinda saw another, less attractive option, of course. If the master sent letters by courier from Ort, Styrrach might arrive within a sevenday. She did not give that thought voice.

Jorinda burned with desire for vengeance on Styrrach. It ate at her that he had betrayed her and other Guild members to the Portreeve, and she would be happy to break down any barrier in her way to see him dead under her blade. The issue of the coin and the two books did not matter to her, but if it created an opportunity to kill Styrrach, she would grasp it. If the Portreeve in Ort did play some part in the scheme, it would be dangerous to meet him, but if she killed him, it might bring Styrrach to Ort, which might give her a chance to kill the Guildmeister. She could not pass up that opportunity.

Deineike had already said she wished to stay in Ort with Jorinda, but Wilash and Klordia need play no further part in this. Danger lay in every move, and neither of them would be any help in the work that must be done. Jorinda turned to Wilash. "You could leave. It is unnecessary for you to place yourselves at risk."

"The plan is unlikely to succeed without me."

"You think not?" His words angered Jorinda. There would be little she could not achieve without his aid.

Before Wilash could reply, Deineike threw out a question. "How would we obtain audience with the Portreeve of such a large town, and why must you be involved?"

Wilash's face brightened. "This is the best part of my plan, in truth, and the only part I have any confidence in. I will say I am Jorinda's father, I own a successful garment shop in Ryl, and my daughter makes the finest clothes in all Dur. I wish to relocate to a larger town or city and open my shop there. I will pay levies, and I wish to meet the Portreeve before I arrive at my final decision. The Portreeve of Zhanghar has already expressed his desire for me to relocate to his city."

Jorinda nodded at the merit she saw in the plan. "I am certain that would gain an audience. My father's shop does indeed pay levies in Ryl, and the Portreeve's wife there wears my making to balls with all her rich friends. They favoured us with much custom, none of which makes this clever scheme a sensible course to follow." Despite her lack of enthusiasm, Wilash looked pleased, and Klordia looked at him in adoration, mayhap more pleased than him.

Deineike seemed convinced Wilash's idea made sense. "We must do it. I do not care how Styrrach or any of them earn their coin, but somehow their scheme brings death, and that is shameful enough in itself. We cannot allow them to avoid punishment for the death of Arella."

Jorinda felt the familiar stab of guilt at the mention of the woman she had murdered. "I killed Arella."

Deineike fixed Jorinda with a pointed stare as she spoke. "Her death came because of their scheme. There must be some justice, or all we believe about Dur falls apart around us like a spider's web that can no longer support the weight of our expectations. We will seek an audience with the Portreeve and trust our luck one final time."

The plan carried great risk and little chance of success. Deineike had played her best card last, however, and the death of Arella could not be allowed to pass without some attempt to find out what lay behind it. Jorinda's guilt demanded it. Deineike had known that, of course, and had said it for that reason, though doubtless her own grief over Arella's death drove her to seek answers also. Jorinda relented, outnumbered. "Very well. We may all die in the execution of this plan, but we will make this last attempt to find out more. If we fail to gain an audience, I make no promise to stay in Ort." If the plan failed to produce a meeting, she might follow her earlier thoughts, travel onward to Zhanghar and face whatever fates were written for her.

Wilash nodded. "I would rather not undertake this at all, but the things done to you and Arella cannot be forgiven, and I played some part in it. I must atone, so I will do this."

With the decision taken, Wilash and Klordia wished to venture out into the town and find a garment shop. They would try to arrange the meeting the next morning. Jorinda sat on the bed, miserable. Wilash had stoked her memory of the death of the mariner on the Torric docks and re-opened old wounds in her, and she could not shake the guilt or the anger. Deineike sat in a chair at the table, her chin in her hands as Jorinda sat on the bed and swung her legs back and forth in distraction while her mind leapt from one cheerless thought to another in time with them.

At length, Deineike spoke. "Something troubles you."

"Rare are the moments when nothing troubles me." Jorinda's melancholy crushed her beneath its weight, and she did not know how long she could continue to carry it around. Death seemed preferable much of the time, and without the joy that had existed at whiles in her relationship with Deineike, the burden became unbearable.

"We could walk the streets, take some air."

Jorinda watched her feet kick back and forth below her. The argument on the ship had surprised her. She and Deineike both lost their tempers so fast. They could be calm one moment, then in a heartbeat, they screamed angry words at one another. Deineike's attempts at reconciliation had calmed Jorinda for a time but had never salved her black mood for long. So it had turned for Jorinda of late, it seemed. Serenity would not linger within her for long before the anguish inside her again pushed her to the limit of her patience, and she found it difficult to control her fury.

Guild training had instilled in her a calm that stood her in good stead as she performed her deadly labours. She never killed in a rage, not even Hiw or Pilos. A calmness came on her as her blade took its victim. In the last few passes, there had been signs of irrational temper—Rewherran had sparked it, for one. Deineike could also send her into a frenzy of violent temper she could not contain, despite the love she bore for the tall woman. It could not be fathomed, this contradiction. Did Deineike have the right of it? Had Jorinda's mind unravelled?

She turned forlorn eyes toward the tall woman at the table. "Am I beyond redemption?"

Deineike drew in a sharp breath at the apparent unexpectedness of the question. "My love, you are complex. You are terrible and you are wonderful. There is a little girl in you still, though she does not often emerge. I suspect you suppress your better natures so you can fuel the fire of your hatred for yourself. When you are with me, I feel safe. None can harm me because you would lay down your life for me, if need be, and I feel no threat from you. Klordia would tell a different tale. That is the dichotomy of you."

Jorinda smiled. "I do not think I know this word."

"Dichotomy? It means contradiction." Deineike blushed even as she smiled. "I have used many words but provided no answer."

"That you have."

Deineike looked into Jorinda's eyes, a small smile on her lips. "That you are not."

"What?" Jorinda could not decide what question the negative response answered, or whether she had been corrected for some wrong thing she had said.

"You are not irredeemable. I will help you while you permit me to. I fear you cannot find peace alone. If you push me away now, then I believe you will be lost. That is why you must find it in your heart to forgive me. Unless you forgive me, you can never forgive yourself."

Jorinda again watched her legs as they swung from the edge of the bed as she weighed Deineike's words. Deineike had the right of it but had missed the mark in one respect. Jorinda would not be lost without Deineike; she had already lost herself, long ago. Deineike might salvage enough of her to patch together a passable likeness of Jorinda, but her restoration could never be complete. Too much of her had faded beyond recovery.

They would not salve any wound while they sat around and maundered; it might even serve to drive the two of them further apart. Deineike had suggested a walk, and Jorinda now desired fresh air and whatever sunlight remained in the day.

"Dichotomy. I like this word. Let us walk a while and you can find other new words to teach me."

Deineike smiled, held out a hand, and they went down to the street.

FOURTEEN
AN APPOINTMENT IS MADE

THEY SET OUT THE NEXT MORNING TO ARRANGE A MEETING WITH THE Portreeve of Ort. A restless night had not improved Jorinda's opinion of the plan, but her last desperate plea for the others to abandon it fell on deaf ears.

Jorinda would have preferred to visit the Portreeve alone. She wanted to keep Deineike safe from harm if things went awry, and Klordia had no interest in the death of Arella. Since Wilash's infatuation with Klordia had become obvious, Jorinda did not want him captured if things turned awry. Klordia already loathed her, and if the tally clerk blamed her for the death of her new love, her hatred could only increase.

Wilash, however, reminded her she could not go alone. Few women in Dur ran successful businesses without a husband. If he did not pass himself off as her father and the owner of the shop, the story would have little credibility, and she would not gain the audience they desired. Jorinda recalled a similar conversation with her father, and it felt so long ago that for a moment she wondered if it had all been a dream. Saboti and Orgel ran their own shops in Ryl, after all else, so Wilash might not have the right of it.

Next, Klordia insisted she must go with them, since she believed herself the one best suited to explain the intricacies of the tallies and the ledger. Deineike argued; she had also grasped the concept, and Jorinda watched with faint amusement as the two exchanged the harshest words she had seen pass between them since she and Deineike met Klordia.

Jorinda stepped in to end the argument before it became too heated, but when she said she did not care about the two books situation, the others shouted her down and said nothing but the entire story would persuade the Portreeve to intervene. Jorinda tried to remind them they only wanted to learn whether the man worked with Styrrach, but that led to a lengthy, tense debate about how much help the Portreeve could give them to bring about the downfall of Styrrach and the Bailiff. Tired of the argument, Jorinda relented and agreed they needed someone in a position of authority who believed their story and would help them, or they may as well abandon the matter. They chipped away at her resistance until she agreed the entire "family" should present themselves at the Portreeve's Offices.

Jorinda did wring one concession from them. Wilash agreed to flee with Klordia and Deineike if things did take a sorry turn, while Jorinda would attempt to provide some distraction. The midday had almost arrived by the time they resolved all the arguments, left the inn, and climbed the hill to the square.

The Portreeve's Offices were housed in an impressive building, though it lacked the pomp and grandiosity of the Bailiff's Offices in Alcmouth. Large Ortwood doors stood open at the main entrance, and coloured glass gave a bright look to the exterior, with beautiful, carved blocks of pale stone that made up the façade. If their own arguments had frustrated Jorinda, a worse system worked against them at the Portreeve's Offices. So many pompous oafs stood guard between the Portreeve and any interaction with the citizens of the town, Jorinda tutted as she fought her desire to kill them all.

The first clerk denied them an audience outright. He told them every three passes, the Portreeve devoted a day to all the grievances and requests the citizenry cared to lay before him, and they could not meet with him at any other time. The last meeting had taken place not long ago, and the next one would not occur for more than two passes. That did not suit Jorinda, who snarled at the clerk until he relented and agreed to consult somebody senior.

The man summoned another clerk who summoned another who, while still a clerk, claimed to be a senior clerk. It seemed the levies did little but provide jobs for intolerable upstarts with little to do but deny the payers of those levies access to the Portreeve to whom they paid their coin.

The senior clerk listened to the other clerk's explanation of their visit, then turned to them. "What is the nature of your enquiry?"

Wilash took control, as would be expected. "I own the most successful garment store in Ryl." He sounded so proud of the shop, even Jorinda half-believed he might have some share in its ownership, but she winced as she realised they had overlooked one of the more important elements of their tale. The clothes Wilash had bought for himself and his "wife" were not of a quality to back up his claim, and while his "daughters" wore Jorinda's making, their rudimentary clothes had been designed for day-to-day use, not to impress officious clerks.

The senior clerk's face made it clear he did not believe Wilash, and Jorinda wracked her brains for a solution. "Do not judge us by these clothes. We took a ride this morning and came here straight from the stable."

He did not seem convinced. "I see. Did you enjoy your ride?"

Jorinda beamed at the man. "That we did."

He looked her up and down, and Wilash seemed to feel the tale needed some further embellishment. "My daughter Cor...inda. She is the finest garment maker in Dur."

"Corinda. Do I have the correct pronunciation?" Jorinda nodded, irritated by the close call. They had not planned names beforehand. They must be the worst fake business owners in all Dur, and the worst prepared. The senior clerk gave her a stiff, formal bow as he greeted her. "My pleasure, but what interest does a garment shop in Ryl hold for our busy Portreeve?"

Wilash took over again. "I intend to relocate the business to a larger city where my daughter's making can attract more appropriate clients." Wilash seemed more comfortable in this aspect of the lie. "I pay substantial levies to the Portreeve in Ryl, and a meeting with your Portreeve might seal the deal of my relocation, if I feel his management of the city is competent."

The man steepled his fingers before him. "Town, I fear. We have no city charter."

Wilash's face fell in either a priceless piece of theatrics or genuine distress because he had been caught in another slip. Jorinda could not guess which as he continued. "Not a city? That is a disappointment. I would not wish my levies to pay for any cause less prestigious than the retention of a city charter. A meeting may not be required, after all else." Wilash fell silent, while Jorinda coughed and covered her mouth with a hand, fearful her enormous smile might betray her admiration of the brilliant delivery of the line.

The clerk's stiffness crumpled as though he felt he had cast Ort in a bad light and must redeem the situation. "I assure you, we are close to a charter. Indeed, another generous contributor might raise our levies to a level that proves acceptable to the Duke. I should be able to fit you into the Portreeve's schedule, after all else." Jorinda cheered in silence.

"It will not be for several days though." Jorinda groaned in silence.

Wilash pressed for an earlier appointment. "That will be difficult, for we do not want to tarry in Ort overlong. We have been impressed by Tarjkay in Zhanghar, and if your Portreeve cannot see us, then I fear…" He left the threat in the air like last wisps of cloud before the sun burned them away.

Deineike spoke for the first time since they had arrived. "Father, I desire to ride more in the delightful lands around the city." She gave the clerk a coy look. "I apologise, town. Let us extend our trip until the Portreeve can see us. It can be no more than one or two days, I am sure." She placed a hand on the arm of the senior clerk and fluttered her eyelashes in a way Jorinda had never seen before.

The man reddened and gave a cough before he spluttered, "The riding is indeed…nice here." He might not know one end of a horse from the other, but Deineike's charm had him smitten in a heartbeat until he seemed to pull himself together. "Remind me, what is the name of the Portreeve of Ryl?"

"Ferdan." Jorinda hoped the Portreeve of Ryl had not been replaced since Ferdan had visited her father's shop some years before. She pushed on. "His beautiful wife, Glorya, refuses to wear any making but mine to the Portreeve's Ball every three passes." She did not add that his beautiful wife had refused to pay for any of the dresses Jorinda had made for her.

The man smiled. "Indeed, they are both known to us. Such fine people. We wish they visited us more often." Jorinda wondered whether they had ever bothered to visit Ort, which seemed unlikely if they were caught up in Styrrach's scheme.

Wilash's simple reply conveyed a close friendship with the Ryl Portreeve. "He is kept busy with the management of a city."

The senior clerk, however, seemed unimpressed. "I see. My assistant here will take your details and we shall see you again in, say, three days?"

Wilash loosed an intolerant sigh. "That is an inconvenience, but it will suffice, I imagine. My daughter will get her wish and will ride to her heart's content for some days, it seems."

The senior clerk gave a small bow. "I will take my leave of you."

He gestured at one of the other clerks, who picked up an impressive hide-bound journal from his desk, opened it, and reached for a scribing tool. "I will make your appointment. Three days from now, at two hours after the sunrise, will that suit?" Wilash tutted but agreed, and the clerk continued. "I will need some details. Formalities, you understand, but necessary." He smiled, but Jorinda imagined that a wild animal about to devour her might give her a warmer, friendlier smile.

The man dipped the nib of the scribing tool into an ink pot, ready to scribe in the journal. "Name?" He looked up at Wilash.

"Balgow." Wilash could not be caught out a second time and had been prepared. Jorinda recognised the name from somewhere but could not place it.

"Your birthplace?"

Wilash hesitated. "My birthplace? Why do you need to know this?"

The clerk flashed the insincere smile again. "Formalities. I apologise, but we do record this information if you still wish the appointment."

Wilash grunted. "Zhanghar." The man gave him a confused look. "I moved to Ryl in my teenyears." The man scribed in his journal, and Jorinda let out a small breath, relieved Wilash had navigated the awkward moment.

The man turned to Klordia. "Name, madam?"

"Klordia." Jorinda tensed. A dangerous move, to use her real name.

"And where were you born?"

"Gzark."

The man looked up, a curious look on his face. "I am not familiar with this town."

"It is not a town of Dur. It lies in a land to the south. My parents brought me to Dur as a small child." Jorinda worried the elaborate tale might bring them undone, even if it had been the truth, but Klordia showed no sign of hesitation or concern as she spelled out the name of the town. "G. Z. A. R. K."

"I see." He scribed again. "I am sure it is most pleasant." He sounded even more officious than the senior clerk.

He turned to Deineike, who had formed a plan of her own, it seemed. "Dankie." Jorinda smiled. Deineike had used one of the names Wilash had mangled her own into when they first met. "My birthplace is Ryl." She smiled at him, sweet and suggestive, and he reddened. What a perfect actor, Jorinda thought. She had not known Deineike possessed such skills.

He turned to Jorinda. "Name?"

She remembered the bizarre name Wilash had used when he introduced her. "Corinda."

The tool scratched on the parch. "Corinda. Born?"

"Ryl." If their "father" had moved to Ryl in his teenyears, where else might his daughters have been born, after all else?

"There. We shall see you in three days, and the Portreeve looks forward to his meeting with you. Farewell." He closed the journal and turned his attentions to matters more important than them.

Outside, Jorinda exhaled long and loud, and once they were well clear of the square, she stopped. "I do not believe I have ever been involved in such a bizarre conversation. How we succeeded, I shall not know even as I go to my Pyre."

Deineike's laugh disguised a grim truth. "The clothes were a disaster. We ought to have known better. Especially you since it is your area of expertise."

Jorinda blushed. "A mistake, I admit it. In three days, we must array ourselves in finery that will impress the Portreeve. I need to buy some materials, and I fear the next three days will involve little but making."

Klordia seemed confused by the need for new clothes. "Will our clothes matter? Once we are in the meeting, we will drop the charade, will we not?"

Jorinda shrugged. "We will do so if we feel it safe. If we suspect we are in danger, we may deem it wise to pursue the falsehood until the meeting ends."

Klordia looked pensive for several heartbeats. "You are right. Very well. I await your making. It will be agreeable to dress in finery fit for a Portreeve's wife, whatever else turns."

Jorinda gave her a smile even as she felt her cheeks redden further. She accepted the small compliment as an attempt to ease the tensions between them, regardless of whether that had been Klordia's intent.

Deineike laid a hand on Jorinda's arm. "I will come with you to buy the materials. Wilash and Klordia may do whatever they wish with the rest of the day." She gave Klordia a sly smile, and Klordia also blushed.

Jorinda tutted. Wilash and Klordia had time for frivolity while she must craft four outfits in three days. "I will need you to come to our room later, please. I must fit you for the clothes or the making will be awry." She hoped she sounded as sullen as she felt.

Wilash and Klordia gave them some coin to put toward what would be an expensive task, and Deineike and Jorinda set off to find a garment shop where they could purchase the materials for the making that lay ahead of Jorinda.

Jorinda referred to the comment that had made Klordia blush. "You seem certain of their intentions."

"That I am, for she is quite smitten by him. She has confided as much over the past days."

"I have seen them together. It does not surprise me."

"I did not know she came from outside Dur, did you?"

Jorinda wrinkled her nose in distaste. "She is not from any land I would care to visit."

"You are too harsh on her. She has been through much since we surprised her in that alleyway."

"As have we all."

Deineike glanced sideways at Jorinda. "Gzark. It does not fit my tongue well. Unlike you."

With a wicked smile, Jorinda could not resist a suggestive retort. "You prove my point. It is not somewhere desirable to visit, if your tongue does not fit it." They both laughed, and as their amusement faded, Jorinda touched Deineike's arm. "You acted with such conviction. Those poor men. They may never recover from your charm."

Deineike laughed. "Did I go too far? I found it fun to tease them, I admit it."

"I enjoyed your performance."

Deineike lowered her head and looked bashful. "Are you jealous?"

"That I am not." Deineike looked a little disappointed. "You would as soon lie with a pitchfork as a man. I had no need of jealousy."

Deineike smiled, but her disappointed look remained. "Wilash made me laugh. His complaint about the city charter clinched the deal, I think."

"That it did. A moment of inspiration."

They walked around the better quarter for almost half of an hour until they found a shop that sold everything Jorinda needed. The materials cost more than Jorinda would have liked, but she haggled the price down somewhat, and they returned to the inn. Jorinda's days and nights would be busy until the meeting, but she would have time to ponder the conundrum of her relationship with Deineike while she worked on the making. Deineike would doubtless be enthused to help tomorrow, but she would soon become bored and might wander off to walk the streets or take a ride, the better to back up their story when they returned to the Portreeve. Once it occurred to her, Jorinda believed it a good idea, and she suggested Deineike might indeed rent a horse and take a ride outside the town. Deineike appeared reluctant but promised to consider the idea.

They reached their room and Jorinda set to work at once. She measured Deineike with meticulous care, then laid out the design to begin the arduous making.

FIFTEEN
A MEETING THAT DISAPPOINTS

Styrrach read the letters again. Balgow had lost his mind and had not scribed the letters in the usual cryptic manner. Rather, the entire woeful tale had been laid out for any to read; a mistake that could bring them all undone, had the letters fallen into the wrong hands.

He handed the letters to Porl and waited, impatient, as his Senior Aide read them. Porl looked up. "Unbelievable."

Styrrach agreed. "That it is. A gest gone awry, Wilash not shrouded, Corelle slipped through his fingers, and his Senior Aide dead, along with a Portreeve's man. What can have turned?"

"I have always had my doubts about Balgow. He has the biggest city, but he is the least competent. I prefer Krage. Should we move Krage south in Balgow's place?"

"That would be preferable, but it would be as difficult to pry him from his beloved Ryl as it would to dig a stone from a horse's hoof with a tuber." The last paragraph of the letters infuriated Styrrach the most. "He assigns an honour gest on Corelle and believes he can justify it with cries of his pride and his station. He knows full well, I have forbidden any but me to kill her. If one of his members fulfils the gest, how can I strip the flesh from the killer's bones for disobedience when his own Guildmeister ordered it?" He opened and closed his fingers into fists of frustration.

"Agreed. Balgow should be shrouded for that insolence alone. Do you think Corelle will remain in Alcmouth?"

Styrrach imagined the jade would flee the capital as soon as she could. "That I do not. I am unsure whether she will drag these other three along with her, since such a ragtag group would attract attention. She may deem it appropriate to travel alone now, and we may lose her if she does. Alone, she could travel anywhere—even beyond Dur."

"It seems unlikely this tally woman would throw her lot in with a killer such as Corelle. She must have seen the deaths of the men, since Corelle killed them to save her, unless I miss my guess."

"At Wilash's behest. He and Corelle throw in together to betray us, after all we have done for them."

Porl's gentle cough sounded apologetic. "Forgive me, but you should have killed Wilash yourself."

Styrrach glared at him but could not disagree. "I am too kind."

Porl emitted a laugh as dark as night. "That you are."

Styrrach reflected on the mess that had turned in Alcmouth. Incompetents had failed him, Corelle had slipped through their fingers once more, and she now posed a great danger to his enterprise. The tally woman from Alcmouth might have revealed all she had deduced from the ledger somebody had been careless enough to leave in plain sight for her to poke her nose into. If so, the two of them would soon enough reach a conclusion that might lead them to talk to the authorities. How fortunate Styrrach owned the Bailiff and the Alcmouth Portreeve, although other Portreeves might listen to such a tale. That pompous idiot in Ort for one, whose honourable character had seen him reject Styrrach's offer once already. Dur City had never been approached, and the traitors might find a sympathetic ear there. How to resolve this conundrum?

The Guildmeister came to a decision. "You and I will take over in Alcmouth. We will shroud the buffoon who has failed us there. Krage will take over here for a time, though he will not deign to stay overlong, I am sure. His Senior Aide can manage Ryl while we find somebody suitable to run Zhanghar. We must seek someone to take control in Vjort once that is finalised, and it is as easy to search for two Guildmeisters as one."

"Vjort is sealed?"

"All but. The emissary Hiw escorted there before he made his own mistake in this ceaseless tragedy has sent further letters. The Portreeve has been contacted and is ready to join us. It has cost us dear, but I want that Wantu silver, and I cannot let Vjort pass."

"You had not mentioned this before."

Styrrach fixed Porl with a cold stare. "Do you run this enterprise, or do I?"

"You do."

Styrrach said no more on the subject. He did not need to. He ruled with an iron glove, and none dared gainsay him. "We will break our journey in Ort to see if we can bring the upstart there aboard. If he rejects us again, the Bailiff can continue with his plan to replace him with one who is more...pliable."

"We leave for Alcmouth, then?"

"That we do. Send letters to Krage on my behalf and begin enquiries into someone suitable for Zhanghar in the longer term."

"It will be as you say."

"We will take your three best men with us. I wish to clean up the operation in Alcmouth, and we will have it run right. It is time to show these people Styrrach is not to be trifled with. I will favour nobody in future. Those who disappoint me..." He did not finish the sentence. He picked up Balgow's letters, tore them into tiny pieces, and scattered them on the floor.

Jorinda, Deineike, Wilash, and Klordia sat in the reception room in the Portreeve's Offices. They had arrived early, had already waited well beyond the appointed time, and Jorinda grew angry. The delay increased her anxiety, and she imagined all manner of things might have gone awry. Above all, she feared the Portreeve had betrayed them, that he played some part in Styrrach's organisation and now plotted their capture.

If things turned awry, they could fight, at the least. Wilash carried their two daggers in the waistband of his elegant trousers, hidden by a fine quality wescoat. Jorinda had crafted fine, high-quality dresses for the three women, but she could not conceal a dagger in hers. Cloaks would not suit the summer warmth, even if she had time to create them, and boots did not suit such dresses. After all else, she had finished the making with no time to spare, with small adjustments required almost until they left the inn for the meeting.

Klordia wore a purple dress, demure but shot through with highlight stitches of blue and with an elaborate bodice of lace and chiffon. Deineike's dress had a lower neckline than the others to match the flirty persona she had created on their first visit, which Jorinda captured in a cream dress with large, showy red buttons down the centre. A lace hem stopped short of her shapely ankles and strapped shoes completed her somewhat suggestive appearance. Jorinda wore a dress like the one the Portreeve's wife had first become smitten with, lime green, and made of satin that shimmered and reflected in the light as she moved. The hooped skirt perfectly offset her full bosom, constrained within a bodice that buttoned down each side and tapered toward her slender waist. Their clothes cast them as the owner and workers of a shop that would produce high quality garments the good people of Ort would clamour for from the first day the shop opened.

The senior clerk appeared. "I apologise for the delay." He turned to Deineike. "Did you enjoy your rides?"

Deineike glowed with joy. "That I did. I do not believe I have ever seen so pretty a waterfall as the one I found to the north of the city."

He smiled. "I confess I have never been there. I must remedy that."

Deineike clapped her hands together in excitement. "I shall take you when we move here."

Jorinda tired of the flirtation and wished Deineike would stop, but she could not tell whether jealousy or fear of some slip motivated her. A few days before, she had denied she had been jealous of the act, so she imagined fear of a mistake drove her irritation this morning. Although Deineike had agreed with Jorinda's suggestion she should take at least one ride, she took none. The waterfall story did not sound unreasonable since waterfalls must exist somewhere to the north, but Deineike pushed their luck with the continued flirtatiousness.

The clerk's face lit up. "That would be delightful." Something caught the man's eye, and he looked down the corridor. "Ah, the Portreeve is ready for you now. Follow me please. Again, I apologise for the delay."

He led them into a large office. Two enormous Ortwood desks stood at right angles to each other, a clerk seated behind each, the desks piled high with journals, ledgers and parch. A door led off to the left, which the senior clerk held open while he gestured for them to enter the office beyond.

They entered the Portreeve's enormous office—the biggest single room Jorinda had ever been in; larger than some tavern-rooms designed to hold large numbers of patrons, with a carpet so plush, she felt she left the ground and walked on air. The walls, covered by a patterned wallpaper that exuded wealth, were bedecked with artwork. A large couch surrounded by armed chairs stood under the window.

The Portreeve sat on the couch, a tall, slender, elegant man with slick, coiffed short black hair and green eyes that smiled with the same extravagance as his lips. He stood as they approached, then gestured at the chairs. He wore a fine quality tunic, similar in design to the ones they had seen on some of his men in the corridors of the Offices. His black trousers had a sharp crease down the centre of each leg. Several large golden rings adorned his fingers, and his black shoes were buffed to such a high gloss he could have used them as a reflecting glass. He sported a perfect clean-shaven look, and Jorinda guessed he might be forty years; two or three more, even.

He addressed them as they moved toward the chairs. "Please, sit. I apologise for the delay. I became detained by a delicate matter. My name is Raolos. You are Balgow?" He extended a hand to Wilash.

Before they left the inn, Wilash had explained why he chose the name of the Alcmouth Guildmeister. He reasoned that if the Portreeve did form part of the organisation, he might know the Alcmouth Guildmeister's name and would not take a meeting with one who pretended to be him. Jorinda thought it unlikely, but the deed could not be undone. She would have been far more anxious at the time Wilash proffered the name had she remembered where she had heard it before.

Wilash spoke as he sat. "Well met." Klordia and Deineike also sat, but Jorinda remained on her feet. If things turned awry, she must react without hesitation and might be delayed by attempts to rise from the snug embrace of an expensive chair.

Raolos studied their clothes. "What divine dresses." He appeared sincere. "My wife will beg me to procure you a shop next door to our own home the moment I describe them to her, I am sure."

Jorinda blushed, felt the familiar warmth as blood flowed to her face. "My thanks. They are only suitable for travel, of course, crude making compared to my best work." She blushed even more at both the unwelcome praise and her own conceit, but the part must be played well.

Raolos seemed taken aback. "In that case, you will never have a day off in Ort, I am sure. Our citizens do love to dress in their finery at any opportunity and would welcome another fine garment shop in the town."

Her face burned at his flattery. "My thanks. It would please me to ply my trade here." Flustered by the high praise, Jorinda hesitated as a thought came to her, one that could prove Raolos's innocence or guilt at a stroke. It would surprise her companions, and carried a burden of risk, but she committed to it, anxious to uncover the truth without further accolades from the Portreeve. "I must ask a question, if you will pardon my forthrightness. Why does this fine town have no city charter? Does Styrrach not recommend you to the Bailiff?" She played a dangerous hand as she mentioned Styrrach. Their fates hung by a thread.

Raolos's face froze, and darkness entered his eyes. Jorinda cursed her clothes. He had recognised the name, and they were undone, but she must wait for Wilash to pass her a dagger. She moved in front of Deineike, the better to protect her.

Raolos spoke at last. "You know this name?" The others sat motionless. They could not know what to do now, Jorinda guessed. The cat was out of the sack, and it had taken mere moments for it to obtain its freedom. By any measure, the meeting had not gone as they had planned.

Jorinda regretted her uncharacteristic impetuosity, but despite the clear doubt and fear on the faces of her companions, she must remain decisive. "That I do, and I curse it throughout the length of the land."

He stared at her for a time as she met his ferocious look with one of her own. She would not back down, no matter what turned, and Deineike attempted to intervene. "Jorinda—" Jorinda held up a hand to silence Deineike. She had played her hand, and now she must see how the cards fell.

Raolos's next words sounded confused. "Jorinda? Or Corinda, which? All is not clear to me." Jorinda admired his statesmanship, to have memorised names he could not have come across before this morning. "You are not garment makers at all, I reason."

Jorinda held her head high. "That I am, and I made all these clothes you see arrayed before you. My father owns the finest garment shop in Ryl, as we have said."

He glanced at Wilash. "Then I am confused. What business have you with the snake your daughter has named?"

Jorinda did not relax. This could be mere deception. "My father owns the shop, but this man is not my father, he is my friend. We have all suffered at Styrrach's whim. We have cheated death by the narrowest of margins on his account, and now we seek answers."

Raolos gave a curt nod. "As do I, about more than Styrrach. Let us discuss the outrageous deception you have perpetrated on me. Should I summon my men?"

Deineike intervened for a second time. "We apologise for the deception, but it is necessary. We must know whether we can trust you."

He turned to face her. "I guess Dankie is not your real name either. The answer you seek lies within your question, of course. In what context do you wish to trust me?"

Jorinda explained. "Styrrach has infiltrated the highest offices of this land in some illicit enterprise we do not yet understand in full, and he orders people killed in the service of this enterprise."

Raolos's face flushed red with anger, and he spoke through clenched teeth. "I know some of this, for I have been approached by him. Or by his emissaries, I should say, if I speak the truth."

Jorinda drew in a sharp breath. She had not anticipated this development. "How did you respond?"

His face and neck burned with apparent indignation. "This town should be a city. It is far bigger than Ryl, and might be as wealthy as Zhanghar, though it is smaller. But the charter will not be granted because I told Styrrach I would have no part in corruption and deception. I suspected violence lay behind his offer and his enterprise, which I wish no part of. As a result, he seeks to bring me undone."

The answer puzzled Jorinda. "How does he seek to achieve this?"

Raolos's face turned redder, and the veins at his temple throbbed. "I hear rumours the Bailiff seeks to remove me from office and replace me with another, a lackey for this Styrrach, my guess."

Every word the Portreeve spoke brought fresh intrigue Jorinda could not unravel. "We seek to bring them all undone, but we cannot. We are fugitives, hunted throughout the land by Styrrach's killers. We do not understand everything, but here is what we can tell you, some of which you may already know."

Jorinda looked at each of her companions in turn, a silent question. "*Can we trust him?*" That had been the meeting's purpose meeting, after all else. They each nodded, and between the four of them, they revealed all they had learned; the two books system, the link between the Portreeve and the Guild, the murders. They also told him their real names.

Raolos leaned forward as he listened, then pondered it for some time. "Some of this I already knew. I had not heard of this Guild, other than a vague hint about an organisation that would come to Ort to whom I could talk if Styrrach's scheme encountered resistance or difficulties. His emissaries told the tale in mysterious terms, and I did not grasp its full intent."

Jorinda mumbled an answer as she pondered his words. "That organisation is the Guild, the clandestine killers who kill business owners on Styrrach's command. We did not know why we were assigned these gests, and you have added confusion to the matter."

Raolos seemed confused. "We?"

Jorinda had thought aloud, and it had undone her. She had let slip that she once belonged to the Guild. "Those of us who belonged to the Guild. I used to be a member."

He considered this for a time. "I beg you to tell me no more of your involvement in it. You have not yet confessed to a murder, and in any event have not killed here, where I have jurisdiction. Do not force me to act on any crime you may have committed. I cannot turn a blind eye to a fact, so let us keep these things hypothetical."

Deineike let out a long, slow breath. "The Guild pursues Jorinda and has almost caught her on many occasions. Will you help us? We must flee if you will not, for we are not safe here."

He turned again to Deineike, who had tears in her eyes, and he handed her a kerchief he produced from a pocket in his wescoat. "I would help if I could, but I am powerless. I have already said the Bailiff seeks my removal, and your tale suggests he cannot be trusted. His involvement sickens me. The people of Dur have been betrayed. Everything they believe is a fabrication because of the actions of these people, in truth."

Wilash stood. "You said the Guild would intervene if you encountered problems?"

Raolos turned to him. "So they suggested."

Wilash stared at Jorinda, his voice the softest of whispers. "The gests do not come from Styrrach. They come from the Portreeve when some difficulty crops up in their operation." Jorinda raised a hand to her mouth. Wilash had seen through the worst part of the tale yet. The Portreeves in Ryl, Zhanghar, Alcmouth, and Torric had ordered the deaths of the very people they ought to have served.

When they explained what Wilash had deduced, Raolos became furious. He clenched his fists and turned his head away from them. Jorinda understood his anger. That the highest office in the land might be embroiled in so heinous a crime defied belief. All for greed, it seemed; nothing more. It shocked Jorinda to her core, and Deineike shook her head as if to deny what her ears heard.

Klordia stared at Wilash open-mouthed. "The Portreeve ordered me killed?"

Jorinda answered before Wilash could speak. "So it would appear. The Portreeve or the Bailiff. What you saw in that ledger threatened them, and they wished to remove you. They called on the Guild to do it." Jorinda reached out to the older woman and touched her shoulder. "I am sorry, Klordia." Tears pooled in Klordia's eyes, and she gave a small nod. She looked so distraught at the revelation, Jorinda felt genuine pity for her.

Raolos appeared not to notice Klordia's distress as he turned to face them again and leaned forward, eager and excited now. "How can we bring them down? Name it, and I will provide it for you, if it is within my power."

Jorinda hung her head. One hole remained in the puzzle, and she could not close it. "The shroud. That is the element I still do not understand. Why do they shroud us?"

Raolos looked at her, puzzled. "What is this word?"

This time, Wilash provided the fastest response. "We do not know. We believe the Guild betrays its own members at whiles to the Portreeve, but we do not know why."

Raolos shook his head. "I cannot help you with this. It is a mystery to me."

Jorinda looked up, filled with despair. "We can do nothing. The

Bailiff himself is involved." She drew in a sharp breath. "Raolos, you seem a decent man, outraged by the greed and the evil of these people, but you cannot prevent it. If the highest authority in the land seeks to remove you rather than provide a sympathetic ear, we are undone, after all else. I imagine they cannot kill you because you hold high office and are well thought of, so they seek to replace you, which is their best play. Once you are removed and forgotten, you will be found in the River Alc one morning. We must all flee. We are undone." She hung her head. Klordia's soft sobs disturbed the unhappy silence that fell on the others.

Wilash spoke in little more than a whisper, as though afraid to be heard. "There is one thing we could do, although only one of us can do it."

Deineike's strident reply contrasted with Wilash's hushed tones. "That she will not. I will not permit it. Do you hear me, Wilash? I refuse it. Do not say it, now or ever."

Raolos wore a confused look. "What is it that so outrages you?"

Jorinda sighed with frustration. Her loyalties clashed; her desire for vengeance against her love for Deineike, who often insisted Jorinda should not kill again. "Wilash wants me to kill Styrrach, and I should do it for the damage he has wrought on us and others whom we loved."

Raolos shook his head in an assertive denial of her words. "I cannot hear this proposition. It lies beyond what I can do for you. If you say you will do it, I will have you arrested and tried for any deaths I can prove you to have been involved in. You will be hanged. Do not test me on this, Jorinda. There will be no talk of murder." He stared at Jorinda, anger in his eyes.

Deineike agreed with him, for different reasons. "Jorinda, my love, Raolos has the right of it. You must not do this. We have discussed it. There is little of you left to save. Do not lose that which remains." Tears fell from her eyes into the crumpled kerchief on her lap.

Raolos looked down on her, a compassion in his eyes that caught Jorinda unawares. "You call her your love. I have heard rumours of love between two men or two women. It is not viewed with any favour in Dur. We are an imperfect people, but I believe we will grow to be kinder to those who are different from us. I fear it will not be in my lifetime or my son's, but it must come. The day must come."

"My thanks." Deineike forced the words out between her sobs.

Jorinda saw no solution to the issues they had discussed. "Then we are done. After all else, our outrage cannot bring this down. Our lives are in jeopardy, and we must flee." Her weakness frustrated her. Styrrach had won, and they could do nothing. The corruption ran too high for them to combat.

Raolos mumbled, and Jorinda could not tell whether he spoke to them or himself. "Haste will not serve. If the Bailiff decides to replace me, I have the right of appeal to one higher than the Bailiff."

Klordia gave a startled gasp. "The Duke?"

Raolos looked into Jorinda's eyes. "The Duke. He is the highest authority in the land, not the Bailiff."

Jorinda pondered his words but found no solution in them. "He will never accept your word over his own Bailiff. I see no hope in this."

Raolos sighed. "It may be the last roll of the dice. We must have proof for him to remove the Bailiff from office, and we should not rush to admit we cannot find it. Where are your accommodations?"

Jorinda had forgotten the name of their inn. "We have rooms at an inn toward the docks."

"I will arrange more satisfactory accommodations. Please, stay in Ort a day or two while I think more on this. We may devise a plan that gives us some chance of success. If we cannot, you will leave the town and find a life elsewhere where you may be safe, I hope."

Jorinda nodded, defeated "And you?"

A stubborn pride came to his face. "I shall stay and fight the schemes of the Bailiff as long as I can. Ort has always been my home, and I will not desert these people. I will not leave them in the clutches of this evil. I will not surrender without a fight." He rose, walked over to a large desk against one wall, and rang a bell that sat on it. The senior clerk came into the office and the two men conversed in hushed tones for a time before the clerk left again, and Raolos turned to them. "I have a house for you. One of my men will take you there soon. Will you sup a goblet of wine with me while we wait?"

Klordia looked horrified. "The hour is early for wine."

He nodded and gave her a warm smile. "That it is, but I feel we have need of it for our disappointment and frustration, at the least."

Jorinda could not recall a time in her life when she had felt more despondent. Because of Styrrach, Arella had died by her hand, and he seemed determined not to rest until the four of them also lay dead, and Raolos with them. Unless she killed Styrrach, she could do nothing to prevent that outcome. It might give her some small sense of vengeance to kill him, but vengeance for her mother's death had not served Deineike well, and if Jorinda killed Styrrach, she would either swing from the gallows or fall under the blades of the Guild members she once worked alongside. Even if she survived, his death at her hands might alienate Deineike, and Jorinda weighed her choices against that risk. Deineike had made it clear she did not want Jorinda to kill Styrrach.

A clerk entered with a cask and five goblets, and Raolos poured some wine into each goblet. He raised one to each of them and sipped at it as Jorinda picked up another. She enjoyed wine but knew little about it. Raolos had served an expensive variety, she guessed; smooth and rich with the strong taste of a fruit that might have been cherry. Jorinda smiled at Raolos as she sipped. "It is a delicious wine."

He made another appeal to her vanity. "That it is. And those are fine dresses. I wish you would open a shop in Ort. You would do exceptional business here." Raolos looked down into his goblet and did not see Jorinda's face turn bright red.

The others took a goblet each, curious no doubt as to how good the wine would prove.

Wilash gasped. "Never in the Five Cities have I tasted wine such as this."

Deineike replied, "I have." She gave Jorinda a suggestive glance that brought heat to her cheeks again.

SIXTEEN

THE BEDROOM CONUNDRUM

ONE OF RAOLOS'S MEN ARRIVED AND LED THE FOUR COMPANIONS TO the Portreeve's house. It stood on the side of the hill, one street from the square, with views over the river and the eastern lands beyond. Inside, two enormous parlours and a separate scullery made up the ground floor. A flight of stairs led upward from the long entrance hall to two higher floors. Deineike hobbled around one of the parlours and marvelled at the splendour and size of the house as Jorinda smiled at her from the doorway.

Wilash and Klordia offered to walk over to the inn, settle with the innkeep, and bring back their belongings. Once they left, Deineike urged Jorinda to sit in the parlour with her for a time, worried the meeting with the Portreeve had devastated Jorinda, that she might take off in pursuit of some rash action and come to some harm.

"Are you all right, my love?" Deineike placed a hand on Jorinda's knee to reassure her Deineike stood beside her no matter what.

"That I am not." Jorinda sounded as miserable as Deineike had anticipated. "We have lost, Deineike. Our fates are written. We are fugitives for the rest of our lives. I curse the hand we have been dealt." She fell silent.

"We have each other if you will have me. All is not lost while we have our love."

Jorinda's eyes filled with tears. "Klordia does not think I deserve you, and she has the right of it."

Deineike snorted. "I have never heard such nonsense. Why do you give credibility to every word that demeans you or casts you in an unfavourable light? Klordia knows nothing. None of us is given that which we deserve, only the fates that are written for us. My fate is written that I should have your love, and I count myself grateful for that fate every time I touch, kiss, or see you. I have damaged the love between us for now, but I will work to restore it."

Jorinda managed a weak smile. "You are kind."

"You asked me why I subjugate myself to you. In truth, I do not. I love you, but I also need you. Without you, I am incomplete. There is no Deineike unless there is Jorinda. You believe you will not always be there. The day I lose you, I will lose myself. That is the truth of it."

Jorinda did not reply. Silence had always existed between them, and they felt no need to fill it with nonsense. They might chatter about something that caught their interest, something that had turned for one or other of them, but they were content also to say nothing, to do nothing but rest in each other's company.

A thought occurred to Deineike; a thought that worried her. "Jorinda, I hope you do not plan to go to Zhanghar to kill Styrrach."

Jorinda sat in silence for a time, then exhaled a long breath. "How can I? There is little left of me, and if I kill him, it might destroy what remains. It would be no easy task to take him, in truth. He is surrounded by trained killers and will be no slouch with a dagger himself. I see no good outcome in such an endeavour."

Deineike sighed with relief. "Good. That is the right decision. We must decide what we do next, and it is my hope we decide it together. I love you."

Jorinda smiled. "You are as good a person as I have ever known. Arella cast you aside to join the Guild. I loved her, but I now see she had poor judgement. It would be better to live in a hole in the ground with you than to live without you in the grandest home in the land."

Deineike took Jorinda's hands in her own. "Her loss brought your gain. I am glad she cast me aside. After all else, if she had not, I would never have met you." She laughed as Jorinda blushed. "We must work on your inability to accept a compliment of any kind. You are deficient in that area."

"That I am." Jorinda hid her face behind her hands, and Deineike dropped her own hands to Jorinda's thighs.

Deineike laughed, stood, and pulled Jorinda to her feet. "Let us go upstairs and choose our bedroom while they are out. We may take the pick of them."

They took their time as they climbed the stairs. Deineike still struggled to ascend stairs and found it even more difficult to descend, although her knee flexed more each day. They investigated the three bedrooms on the first level. Any of the three would have been the biggest bedroom either of them had ever slept in, and a separate privy served the three rooms.

When they reached the uppermost floor of the house, however, they needed to look no further. The size of one of the two bedrooms on that floor took their breath away. Cupboards had been built into one wall from floor to ceiling. Deineike could walk upright into them, pass through them, and emerge from the far end. Rails within the cupboards would hold dresses such as the ones they wore, and smaller items of clothing and possessions could be stored on or in the vast collection of shelves and drawers. A couch sat in a bay window that looked toward the square, and the summer sun twinkled on the surface of the river as it wound past the town in the distance.

The room captivated Deineike. "I claim it."

"It is a fine room. Though I feel some guilt that you should claim it when Wilash and Klordia have no opportunity to argue their right to it."

Deineike threw herself onto the bed, which felt small in such a large space. "I feel no such guilt. It is ours. What is the phrase? *'Earliest to bed wears the best nightclothes.'*"

Jorinda laughed. "That it is not. It is, *'Earliest to rise wears the best clothes.'*"

"Bah. I had the right of it, near enough." Deineike patted the bed. "Join me. This room arouses me."

It had not escaped Deineike's attention that Jorinda had said "you" rather than "we" when Deineike claimed the room, but she felt sure she could persuade Jorinda to join her in the huge bed. Jorinda, however, hesitated, and Deineike wondered if she had pressed the younger woman too soon. They had not been intimate for many torturous days, and Deineike burned with desire. She unbuttoned the bodice of the dress Jorinda had made for her, slid it from her shoulders, and fondled her small breasts as her breaths became faster and heavier. Although Deineike ached for Jorinda, her lover did not move, and she looked uncomfortable.

Deineike could not abandon her primal need now. "Do it for Wilash and Klordia, if you will not do it for me." The husky tone in her voice came from her desire to be fulfilled, and she resolved to pleasure herself if Jorinda could not be persuaded.

"How do you reckon that?" Jorinda's breaths grew heavier, and her face flushed. Deineike did not believe Jorinda could resist her own desire for much longer.

"If we make love in this bed, they can no longer claim the room. Do not let them make an argument. Snatch it from them before they see it. Take me, I beg you. I cannot wait a heartbeat longer."

Jorinda made her wait a heartbeat longer, but no more.

Wilash and Klordia strolled to the inn. They enjoyed each other's company, and their despondent mood lent no speed to their feet. They found a small park on the way, a lush green lawn surrounded by flowers and shrubs. Benches were scattered around the park, and they sat for some time to discuss the meeting with the Portreeve and what they might do. They came to no decision and continued toward the inn.

Wilash's concern for his friends worried at him. "I imagine Deineike and Corelle have much to say to one another after the morning's events."

"That they do. Do you think they will resolve their differences?"

"I hope so. I like Deineike." Wilash smiled as he thought of the tall, dark-haired woman whose sweet vulnerability belied great inner strength. Deineike could stand to love a woman whose violent past would have sickened almost anybody.

"As do I."

"You do not like Corelle." Anybody could see the two women did not get along.

"Do you not realise her name is Jorinda?" Klordia laughed and laid her head on Wilash's shoulder for a heartbeat.

Wilash joined in the laughter. "To me, she will always be Corelle. I think you would have looked with more kindness on the Corelle I first met. She enjoyed life more then. The Guild did not serve her well, and she changed. She is worse than I first thought when I encountered her in Alcmouth. There are things she does not know about Arella, and I cannot tell her. They would…" He hesitated, unsure how he had stumbled and let slip even the smallest hint of the dark secret Arella had made him swear to never reveal to anybody, not even Corelle. Despite his vow, he had tried to reveal it in Alcmouth, but the moment passed, and he had kept his secret.

"Things? What things?"

"I am sworn to the utmost secrecy. I cannot tell anybody. Not even you."

"I understand." Klordia took Wilash's hand. "I do not like Jorinda. I try to, but I cannot find it in me. She is cold, and violent. I fear her, and I fear for Deineike."

Corelle, or Jorinda as Wilash should call her, had many faults, but he did not share Klordia's concern for Deineike's safety. "There are a great many people in this land, and Corelle would kill almost any of them if need drove her. You, me, anybody. There is one she would not, I think. Deineike need not fear her, my guess. Though they are estranged over the unfortunate incident and death of this mariner, I believe Jorinda loves her. I do not think that has changed, for I believe she loves Deineike more than life. I cannot conceive of such a love. Deineike is safe, I am certain."

Klordia walked beside him, silent, for several paces. "I love you."

Wilash turned to look at her. He had not expected the admission of love and had not considered the question of how they felt about one another. They had lain together, and it had been unlike any of the women he had lain with before. He and Klordia made love together, gave and took in equal part. They enjoyed each other's company, and he cared for her—but did he love her? He could not say he did. "You are sure of this?"

She laughed. "That is not the response I had anticipated. You are a man of few words, and when those words come, they are not always what people expect. I am sure, although I do not ask you to bleat the same in response if that is not how you feel. If things go well, you may come to it in time, if that is the fate written for us."

"I care for you." Wilash spoke with caution, uncertain of the situation or how he felt. "If time permits, that may become love, who can say? We are pursued by men who, if they find us, would cut our lives shorter than we would wish."

"We do not need to remain with the two girls. We could leave here and go somewhere safer. I think this Styrrach yearns to place Jorinda under his knife but cares far less whether our lives come with hers."

Wilash agreed with her, but he could not turn his back on his sense of loyalty to Corelle. "You have the right of it, my guess. I played some part in the death of Arella, and I hunted Deineike and Corelle. Deineike suffered terrible harm because we pursued them. She almost died, and I cannot abandon them until they decide they have no need of me."

Klordia's laughter rose into the air. "They have no need of you, Wilash. They only need each other. I wish Deineike could find someone more suitable, but for whatever reason, her fate is entwined with Jorinda's. Without Deineike, Jorinda will break and pass from the land soon enough. If they have each other, they have all they need."

"You may be right."

"You are not responsible for Deineike's injuries, in any event. Another is, if I have remembered the tale right."

Wilash shook his head in rejection of her words. "The Guild hunted her, and I belonged to the Guild. I cannot absolve myself of my part in her injuries. When Deineike told us of the death of the mariner, I knew some of the tale, though I said naught. I knew Cor… Jorinda killed that man, although I did not know the reason for it. When she killed him, it convinced me she had not yet left Torric. I sought her there."

Klordia stopped, and her brow wrinkled as she gazed into his eyes. "I am not sure I know the full extent of this tale, and I fear to hear it."

"Nonetheless, I must tell it. You must know me if you are to say you love me. I pursued them from Torric, or I thought I did. I thought they would flee on horseback, but Jorinda bested me when she had the courage to use the Guild token to secure passage on a ship. She risked all to save Deineike. I pursued them to kill Deineike and bring Corelle to Styrrach. Jorinda." He found Corelle's new name difficult to remember despite the many days that had passed since he had first heard it. Klordia lowered her eyes to the ground but said nothing, so Wilash continued. "You judge Jorinda to be a monster. She risked her own life to save Deineike from the same justice she spared Arella from when she killed her. There is good in her you do not allow credit for. There is evil in me you will not see either."

Klordia reached up and cradled his face in her hands. "This tale changes nothing. I love you. I will try to like her, but I doubt I shall succeed."

They walked on for a time in silence until a thought came to Wilash. "I had not realised you come from a land other than Dur until the other day." He had intended to speak of it earlier, but each time he thought to raise it, he felt it may be an invasion of some part of her she might prefer to keep private.

"I came here as a young child. I remember nothing of Gzark. In truth, I am not even certain where it is, but it is my birthplace, and he asked for my birthplace." A mischievous smile flitted across her lips.

Wilash laughed. "That seems fair." They spotted the inn ahead. "I like Raolos. He is honourable."

"That he is. He is handsome also." Wilash did not reply as he held the door open for Klordia to enter the inn. "You are not jealous?"

"That I am not. The fates are written. If you find another more attractive than me and leave me, I can do nothing about it."

Klordia made a sound that sounded like a snort. "Please tell me you would at the least ask me to stay before you cast me away for the fates."

"I might." Klordia must have guessed he had teased her, and she gave a gentle laugh, like the sound of water as it tinkles from a pitcher into a cup.

They gathered all the belongings from both rooms, pushed their own limited belongings into Jorinda's and Deineike's packs, and carried them down to the tavernroom. They settled the amount owed and left to find their way back to the house. The grey of twilight had replaced the daylight before they returned, and no lanterns shone within. They called to the two women as they entered, but silence called back to them. They climbed the stairs to the first floor and walked into a large, airy bedroom that would suit. They took their belongings out of the packs and placed the packs on the landing near the stairs, then went back into the room, lit a lantern, and were soon in each other's arms.

Klordia did not suppress her screams with a pillow. In such a large house, she doubted she could be heard, and she abandoned herself to her pleasure without restraint.

SEVENTEEN

THE INCIDENT ON THE STAIRS

Deineike fell asleep after they made love. Jorinda had not wanted to succumb to her desires. Deineike looked beautiful in the dress Jorinda made for her, and when she slipped it from her shoulders and fondled herself, Jorinda burned with desire. Although she resisted for as long as she could, her passion overtook her, and they made fervent love. Deineike gave her vast pleasure, far more than she took for herself. Jorinda guessed Deineike pleasured her in the hope it might help heal the rift between them.

Now they had been intimate and Deineike had fallen asleep, Jorinda sifted through the emotions the lovemaking awoke in her. As darkness drew in, she lit no lantern. Deineike lay with an arm draped across Jorinda's stomach, who did not move lest she woke her. She had lain with Deineike again, and while it would heal some part of their estrangement, she remained unsure she wished for a full reconciliation. At times, she did, but at others, the memory of that night on the Torric docks came back to taunt her, and Deineike had been responsible for those memories. Forgiveness must wait for now.

Jorinda heard Wilash and Klordia return to the house and call to her and Deineike, but she did not respond. They did not wake Deineike, and Jorinda had no desire to spend time with Klordia. The screams of ecstasy soon convinced her; Klordia had not wished to spend any time with her either.

At one point, Deineike awoke and murmured, her voice heavy with sleep. "I told you. She is a screamer."

Jorinda laughed. "That she is."

"Do I scream?"

"That you do."

"Then you have fulfilled your bargain." Deineike's hungry tongue danced in Jorinda's mouth. "Make me scream again." Her fingers drove other thoughts from Jorinda's mind, and they made love again.

They both fell asleep afterward. The nightmares had become more intense since Alcmouth. Jorinda would often awake in a cold sweat, and on occasions would spring from the bed to stand naked and confused while Deineike comforted her and attempted to soothe her, and with Deineike's help, Jorinda found it easier to regain calm after the nightmares.

Jorinda sat upright in the bed, snapped awake from a vivid dream in which she pleasured herself among the bodies of every victim she had ever taken while Deineike looked on and shouted words of praise that did not make her blush. Deineike woke with her, folded her into her strong arms, and whispered into her ear to calm her.

Jorinda sobbed, a dull ache in her stomach. "I cannot tolerate these nightmares. Will they never end?"

"I know not. We must find some salve for the things that eat at you. That may drive the dreams from you."

"I doubt such a salve exists." Jorinda's despondency had not lifted since Deineike had fainted on the ship. Brief moments of relief came and went but brought no permanent peace.

"We will find it. Do not despair."

Do not despair. Three words, so easy to say. They meant all, and they meant nothing. Noise, nothing more. They brought Jorinda no comfort. "I do despair. It does not help that you urge me not to."

Deineike said nothing for a time. Jorinda took her silence to mean she had little to offer save exhortations to repair her fractured mind. She pushed Deineike away from her and climbed from the bed.

"Jorinda? Where do you go? It is dark still."

"My mind fails me, not my eyes." Jorinda cast about for some clothes but could only find the dress she wore to the meeting with Raolos. Her other clothes must be in another room with Wilash and Klordia. She tugged the bedroom door open and went out onto the landing.

"Jorinda. Come back. You have nothing on but your skin. You cannot wander the house naked."

"That I can." Behind her, Deineike whispered a soft curse, but Jorinda walked down the stairs. A light sprang up behind her, and she glanced back in surprise before she continued down the stairs. Doubtless, Deineike had lit a lantern, she reasoned. She turned again, and Deineike stood at the top of the stairs with a lantern in her hand, as she had guessed.

"Jorinda, come back to bed." Deineike's urgent whisper rattled through the silent house like the hiss of a horde of insect wings.

"Where did you find a flint?"

"What? It lay beside the lantern."

The answer baffled Jorinda. "How did you know this? Have you been here before?"

Deineike shook her head. "That I have not, ever. I can think of no more logical place for it. Where would you have placed it? In the privy?"

Without warning, Deineike clutched at her head and bent forward from the waist with a short cry of pain. Anxious, Jorinda took one step up the stairs. "What is wrong?"

Deineike forced herself upright again. "It is nothing. A headache; nothing more. Come back to bed, please."

Wilash's voice startled Jorinda. "Corelle? Are you all right?" She turned to him, below her on the next landing, and he gasped and looked away.

Klordia appeared behind him, a lantern in her hand. "Jorinda? What are you about?"

"I search for my clothes."

Wilash spoke again. "You should not be up and about at this hour. It is the hour to be in your bed."

Jorinda looked down at him, but he still looked away from her, even though he spoke. "Why will you not face me?"

"Because you are naked."

His answer aggravated Jorinda. "Do I offend you? Am I not attractive?"

From above, Deineike's plaintive voice grabbed Jorinda's attention. "Jorinda, by all the fates."

Klordia picked up two packs and threw them part way up the stairs. She stood on the tips of her toes and spoke into Wilash's ear as he bent to bring his ear to her mouth. Jorinda could not hear what Klordia said, but she looked around at Deineike, tearful at the top of the stairs, a hand at her temple. At that moment, the ridiculousness of the situation and her behaviour pulled her mind back into sharp focus.

Jorinda turned to Wilash and Klordia again. "I apologise. I do not know what came over me. Please, we should all go to bed." She picked up the packs in one hand, turned, and went up the stairs.

She placed an arm around Deineike's waist and guided her back to the bedroom as she whispered, "Come back to bed. I am sorry for this behaviour."

Jorinda helped Deineike back into the bed, blew out the lantern, and lay in Deineike's arms. Deineike drifted off to sleep, but Jorinda lay motionless with Deineike's arms around her. What had turned, she could not quite determine. She had lost control of herself for those moments and had seen herself almost from outside her own body. It had been the most extreme reaction to the nightmares yet, and try as she might, she could find no explanation for it.

To her relief, sleep came at last, and the sun shone through the bay window when she woke. In their passion, they had not closed the shutters the previous night. The memory of the incident on the stairs came to her mind. Deineike still slept, and Jorinda did not move, reluctant to wake her since that would bring questions she could find no answer for. Had her mind come unravelled? The way she had behaved embarrassed her. It seemed to make sense at the time, but now it seemed only someone who had lost their mind would behave in such a way.

Deineike's eyes opened and gazed into Jorinda's, and Deineike smiled. Jorinda's heart fluttered as Deineike's lips turned upward into that radiant smile. Jorinda touched the tip of Deineike's nose before she voiced her thoughts. "You are beautiful when you smile."

"Only when I smile?"

Jorinda sighed. "I am sorry. About last night. I cannot explain it."

Deineike touched Jorinda's cheek. The tender touch promised warmth and comfort as if she might never need to fear anything while that hand could reach out and touch her. "Do not dwell on it. It matters not." Deineike's eyes lit up. "Let us rise and dress. I wish to go out and find somewhere that will sell us a breakfast."

"I do not believe I have ever done such a thing." Jorinda wondered where such food might be procured.

"I have not either. It will be fun."

"It may well be fruitless."

"Nonsense. You lack the imagination to conceive it." Deineike gave a jovial laugh. "A suitable place must exist at the docks somewhere. How else do all the dockhands and mariners eat in the morning?"

"In their homes? On their ships? I do not know. You worked at the docks. Did you see such an establishment?"

"That I did not." Deineike extricated her arm from beneath Jorinda and slid from the bed. "That does not mean it does not exist." She smiled.

"The docks are some distance from here."

Deineike picked up a pillow and threw it at her. It missed by some margin and landed on the floor beyond the bed. "You are a killjoy. Rise, sluggard. I wish to explore this notion."

"Very well." Jorinda could see no way to dissuade Deineike from the idea, and she rose from the bed.

Deineike pushed some clothes around in the packs and pulled out a tunic and some trousers. She pulled the tunic on with no difficulty, but the trousers proved a struggle and she almost fell, but Jorinda caught her. Deineike muttered, angry. "Curse this leg."

"It will mend. It mends well already, in truth. You got one leg into your trousers and are not quite out of breath."

"It comes easy to you to mock the afflicted. I see this."

Deineike's eyes twinkled as Jorinda teased her. A bead of sweat trickled down the taller woman's forehead, her hair lay in disarray around her face, and Jorinda felt a tingle in her sex as she drew Deineike into her arms and spoke, breathy with desire. "Let us break our fast here. I desire to eat but am certain no shop sells what my tongue craves." She pushed at the trousers, which slid down Deineike's left leg and pooled at her feet.

The sun had climbed high in the sky before they rose again from the bed. They washed at the vanity bowl, found clothes, then dressed before Deineike took on the descent of the stairs. Halfway down the second flight, she paused. "We should have taken a room on the lower floor." She leaned on the rail and panted as though exhausted.

"There is no hurry. The room justifies the wait." Jorinda descended the stairs ahead of Deineike, ready to catch her if she fell. That might see them both crash down the stairs, but at the least Deineike might land on her and avoid further injury.

Once they reached the parlour, Deineike collapsed into an armed chair. In the scullery, Jorinda found some bread, meat, and cheeses on the small table. Wilash and Klordia must have been out to buy provisions. Jorinda scooped some food onto a small plate and carried it back to the parlour, then sat on the floor at Deineike's feet as they ate. She brought cups of water for them afterward.

Deineike's breaths had returned to normal by the time they finished the food, her flush had faded, and her normal complexion had returned. The exertion of the stairs had drained her, and Jorinda guessed an exchange of rooms with Wilash and Klordia might be warranted, despite her words as they descended the stairs. She checked Deineike had regained her strength. "How are you now?"

"I have recovered." Deineike smiled down at her. "I desire fresh air, I think. May we walk outside?"

"If you feel you are up to the task, we can go."

Jorinda stared into Deineike's blue eyes. Those eyes were so expressive, no lie could pass Deineike's lips that could not be seen in her eyes. "I think I am."

Jorinda saw no deception. "Last night, a headache came upon you—not the first in recent days. I worry you have sustained further injury from the fall on the ship."

Deineike sighed. "They are frequent, and painful. There is

naught to be done. Healers can restore broken bones, but none exist that can restore broken minds, I fear. If one does exist, we are both in dire need of them." She smiled.

"That we are. Come. Let us see whether the sun on our faces will ease the aches in our heads."

"You are all I need to restore any ache. Some more than others." Deineike flashed her a suggestive smile.

Jorinda felt the familiar blush. "All is not yet as it used to be, Deineike."

Deineike nodded. "It is better than the last few days, none-theless. I am certain things will again be right between us, and I can forgive myself."

Jorinda smiled. "Forgive yourself, for any doubts that linger about the love between us are mine to resolve."

Deineike gazed into Jorinda's eyes for a time. "I love you."

"That you do, and it seems you never tire of the words." Jorinda stood and extended a hand to Deineike.

Deineike allowed herself to be pulled to her feet. "I must say it. That will never stop."

Jorinda teased her as she pulled the door closed behind her. "Never?"

Deineike stopped and stared at Jorinda, earnest, her reply breathy and urgent. "Never."

Deineike's husky voice aroused Jorinda. "What in the Five Cities are you? You need say but a word to me, and I wish to throw you to the ground and ravish you."

Deineike laughed. "That might lower the standard of the neigh-bourhood."

Jorinda scoffed. "It would improve the standard, and all the local women would queue for days for a moment in your arms."

Deineike's laughter grew louder. "We must make haste to find this healer who can set your mind right, for it has passed beyond reason."

Deineike walked at a faster pace as each day passed, and with the aid of her staff and occasional help from Jorinda, they covered a substantial distance as the day slid away, and the warm sun chased some of their recent troubles from them. Each new discovery enthralled them as they explored Ort; here a park, or a beautiful garden in some large house, there a narrow alleyway that led them to a different street with more sights to see, bright coloured houses and delightful little shops that sold trinkets, clothes, and foodstuff.

They found a small shop that sold various cakes and each bought a pastry to eat as they walked on a little further. They sat together on a low wall as the sun sank down the sky.

Jorinda studied Deineike for any sign of distress from the exertion. "We should return. We have covered some distance from the house, and the return journey is uphill."

Deineike gave her an earnest look. "I am not tired, I swear."

"You may be before we return. I have no fantastic means of transport if you cannot continue."

Deineike laughed. "That disappoints me. I only stay with you against the chance of a journey through the skies upon your wondrous device."

Jorinda gazed up into the blue sky above them. "I wonder if one day we might learn to fly up there with the birds." The thought distracted her from Deineike's care for a moment.

Deineike replied, serious, her brow furrowed by thought. "I do not think so. I do not think we are meant to be in their domain."

"What of my device? You would not need wings to ride upon it."

"That I would not, but what if I should fall from it?"

Jorinda laughed. "You have the right of it. We are both of us in sore need of this healer. Our minds are lost to us." Deineike took her hand, and panic squeezed Jorinda's heart, which pounded faster in response.

She pulled her hand from Deineike's, and the older woman frowned. "What is wrong?"

"I fear to show such affection in the street. It could be dangerous."

"None see us. The street is deserted."

"Nobody knows who watches from behind a window, unseen by us."

Deineike sighed. "Little enough in this land is fair, and I curse this more than any other thing, that I cannot take the hand of the woman I love in public." She wore a mask of sadness on her face.

Jorinda longed to hold her but could not shake her concern. One day, as Raolos had said, people might be free to love whomever the fates wrote for them without fear. That day had not yet arrived in Dur.

Deineike tilted her head to one side. "Do you have your dagger with you?"

"That I do. It is in my boot."

Deineike took her hand again and gripped it tight. "Do you see us?" She shouted too loud for Jorinda's comfort.

"Shhh."

Deineike looked at her with misery in her eyes. "You, who could slay any who dared to insult us for this simple gesture, you are afraid to hold my hand. This saddens me." She released Jorinda's hand.

Jorinda shook her head. "You are a mystery. You tell me if I kill again, I will be lost forever. Now you would have me kill somebody who objects when you hold my hand."

"I did not ask you to kill. I pointed out..." Deineike fell silent and tapped her hand on the wall for several moments. "Let us head back. The journey may be hard, as you say. This wall has blocked the sun from my heart." Jorinda sank into despair at Deineike's terse tone, but so much had become bound up in her reluctance to hold Deineike's hand, she judged it prudent to let the moment pass. She wondered again at how the mood between them could change in a heartbeat. Had it always been thus? It had, she guessed, and her troubled mind had more to do with it than she allowed before.

Jorinda, it turned, had been correct; Deineike tired some way from the house and requested a short break. Jorinda looked around at the unfamiliar streets as Deineike leaned against a wall, her face redder than Jorinda would have wished, and her breaths rapid. It must be difficult to walk with so awkward a gait, and Jorinda guessed from the haggard expression on Deineike's face that her leg pained her. They had walked too far. Deineike had grown unused to such exercise as she recovered from her injuries, and they should have been less ambitious in their first endeavours. Jorinda cursed herself for the oversight that now saw Deineike so exhausted.

Despite Jorinda's wish for her to rest further, Deineike wanted to be on the move, and they set off again. Jorinda wished she knew the town better. They might have taken a circuitous route, and there could be some shorter, more direct route back to the house had she been more familiar with their surroundings. A tavern's sign waved in the light breeze, and Jorinda suggested they enjoy a goblet of wine to allow Deineike time to recover some strength. Deineike agreed, so Jorinda looked inside the tavernroom before they entered. She did not wish to find Wilke or Styrrach within, as unlikely as that seemed. Better over-cautious than dead.

Two patrons sat in the tavernroom, a pair of men seated at a table in a corner who spoke to one another in voices Jorinda could not overhear, so she returned to Deineike and, against all her Guild training, helped her to a table near the door. They sat side by side on the settle and ordered a goblet of red wine each. When the innkeep brought it over, Jorinda sipped at it. "It is a good wine, but it does not match that which Raolos poured for us yesterday."

Deineike took a drink from her own goblet. "That it does not. I imagine we will be glad of that when we pay for it, however. I suspect we would have been horrified by the price of Raolos's wine." Deineike gazed around the tavernroom and the patrons, then sipped at her wine again. "Why does the innkeep manage the tavernroom?"

"Who else?"

"You miss my point. Why does the tavernkeep not manage the tavernroom, or the innkeep the innroom?"

Jorinda had never given the matter any thought. "That is how things are."

"Too much in this land is 'how things are.' We fear to challenge what we cannot understand."

"You would reform Dur so an innkeep can serve ale in his innroom? I wish you luck in this venture. We must first be able to hold hands in public or fly with the birds, I think. I prefer to resolve those issues before I address the tavernrooms of Dur."

Deineike smiled, and the innkeep, who had glanced over at them, appeared to misread the smile. "Do you wish something more? Another goblet of wine?"

Jorinda gave him a contented smile. "Our thanks. All is well for now."

To Jorinda's surprise, Deineike spoke to him. "I have a question, if you have a moment."

"Of course." He came to their table.

"Why is this area"—she gestured around the room—"called a tavernroom whether we are in a tavern or an inn?" Jorinda sighed. Why could Deineike not leave the matter alone?

The innkeep had not quite grasped the depth of Deineike's question if his answer meant anything. "That is simple enough. It is the area where the patrons drink."

Deineike appeared to consider this response. "That does not explain it in full."

He blinked. "Forgive me. An inn is little more than a tavern with rooms that may be rented for the night. The tavernroom is the room in the inn or tavern where the patrons drink, and since people enter a tavern to drink and nothing else, the tavernroom is the area of an establishment where they drink."

Both women furrowed their brows. Jorinda thought she understood, despite his clumsy explanation. In spite of her earlier doubt, he had understood the question, while Jorinda had not understood his answer.

Deineike would not let the matter end unresolved, it seemed. "Why, then, are you the innkeep in this tavern?"

"That I am not. I am Syme."

They looked at him for heartbeat, then all three of them laughed.

A smile lit up Deineike's face. "Shame on me. Forgive my rudeness, Syme."

Syme gazed at Deineike in admiration. "Your smile could dress the vilest insult in fine clothes, and anybody would be grateful you cast it at them." Jorinda saw no false flattery in his face and could not disagree with his assessment of Deineike's smile.

Deineike seemed uplifted by Syme's compliment and friendly demeanour. "I think I will have another goblet of wine after all. This tavern is as pleasant a place to while away an early evening as any I have encountered."

"My thanks. Do you live nearby?"

Jorinda became guarded and answered before Deineike's relaxed, friendly nature could bring unnecessary complications upon them with an ill-conceived response. "We visit Ort for a short time."

He looked thoughtful. "A shame. Such company is as rare as it is welcome. The locals are not as attractive. Now, I shall bring you more wine."

He returned with two more goblets even though Jorinda had

not asked for another, and three men and an older woman entered the tavern. The newcomers were loud and boisterous and called for a cask of wine as soon as they seated themselves, so Syme placed the two goblets on their own table and scurried off to attend to the new arrivals.

Deineike finished off the first goblet and nodded her head toward the newcomers. "These are the less attractive folks to whom he referred, my guess."

"I hope you do not intend to become so intoxicated, I must carry you home."

"That I might. I seem to recall that on previous occasions, wine has made you amorous."

Jorinda chuckled. "So that is why you ply us with alcohol. You have no need of wine. You need do no more than look at me or touch yourself, and I am wet."

"I should like to test that theory." Deineike's voice took on a sultry tone, and her eyes narrowed.

Jorinda lowered her voice to a whisper lest other patrons overheard her. "Syme might object, but you would find I am correct."

Casual and discreet, Deineike dropped her hand to the settle and touched Jorinda's thigh. Jorinda pulled the table closer to them, and Deineike raised her hand to Jorinda's waist, then unfastened the top button of her trousers. Jorinda stared into her wine and parted her legs. They had passed into the realm of madness, but it excited her so much, she could not bring herself to stop it. Deineike undid a further button, reached inside the trousers, and Jorinda could not stifle a small gasp as Deineike slid a finger inside her. She felt the heat in her face as her cheeks reddened, and her breaths became more rapid.

Deineike leaned so close, her lips brushed Jorinda's ears as she spoke, as quiet as a teardrop as it runs down a cheek. "You did not lie."

Jorinda looked around. Nobody appeared to have noticed them, but despite the fiery need within her, the foreplay should end before they lost control and became a spectacle. She reached a hand under the table and pulled at Deineike's arm to encourage her to remove the finger from within her and the hand from her trousers.

Deineike took her hand out of Jorinda's trousers, but she had one last torture to inflict. She raised the finger to her lips and slid it inside her mouth. Jorinda gripped the settle as her excitement crested, then shook as it burst within her.

Deineike took the finger from her mouth and picked up the second goblet. She took a sip and whispered over the lip of the goblet, her eyes full of sexual tension. "This wine is inferior to that which I drank a moment ago."

Jorinda shook her head. "You are impossible."

"Would you have me any other way?"

Jorinda smiled. "I would have you any way you present your-self, you know this. But no, I would change nothing about you, unless you interrupted me less."

"I do not believe I have interrupted you for days. I have attempted to avoid it, even when you have rambled on and on."

Jorinda laughed. She had enjoyed the relaxed time in the tavern, but a lengthy walk awaited them before they reached the house. "Let us finish this wine and head back. I would like to reach my bed before morning, and you walk at a laggard's pace."

They finished the wine and Jorinda settled with Syme, who would take no more than a groat. Deineike seemed refreshed by the break, and they managed a better pace than they had before the tavern.

As they walked, Deineike turned to Jorinda and asked, "How much did you pay for the wine?"

"A groat. He would take no more."

"That is precious little for four goblets of wine."

"That it is. It may be the best groat I have ever spent."

Deineike laughed. "Soon we shall be home, where more value awaits you for your groat."

Jorinda quickened her step somewhat and hoped Deineike could keep pace with her.

EIGHTEEN

BAD NEWS TRAVELS FAST

Two more days passed, and the four sat in the parlour at times, talked back and forth about the situation, but came up with no new suggestions of merit. On the morning of the third day, they agreed their frustrations could not be satisfied, and they must decide where they would head next.

Deineike wondered whether the Portreeve might have some thoughts that could help them, but Klordia believed he would have summoned them if he wished to share any opinion.

Deineike gave a sad sigh. "I like Ort. I wish we could stay here, in truth."

Wilash did not share her enthusiasm. "I feel it is much like any other town."

Deineike disagreed. "We have found a tavern we are fond of."

Jorinda blushed with a twinge of embarrassment as she thought of their first visit to the tavern. The incident had excited her, and they had returned to the tavern the next night, but they lacked the courage to attempt it again. The moment had been unique, it seemed. "And a cake shop. I fear I would need bigger clothes if I stayed here. Those pastries are delicious but are designed to bring coin to the garment makers, I am certain."

Klordia inclined her head toward Jorinda. "You have a garment maker at your disposal. A fine one."

Jorinda's cheeks became more heated at Klordia's compliment, and she mumbled an unhappy reply. "My thanks."

Wilash and Deineike laughed, and Deineike affected a mock stern tone. "Klordia, you must not praise her. It is an abomination to her."

Jorinda had never heard the word Deineike had used. "Another word I am unfamiliar with." For once, Wilash and Klordia agreed with Jorinda. They did not recognise the word either.

Deineike explained it to them. "It means you despise it."

Jorinda had wondered about Deineike's vocabulary before but had not raised it. "How do you know these words nobody else knows? Do you invent them?"

Deineike shook her head to accompany her denial of the accusation. "That I do not. I listen to others as they speak, and I am open to new things. Are you not open to new things?" She stared at Jorinda, her meaning unmistakable.

Jorinda's embarrassment brought peals of laughter to the parlour, and her cheeks reddened as she muttered to her tormentor. "You have lost control of yourself and should be locked in the privy." A strange realisation dawned on her. "You know these words, though few have ever heard them, yet you mangle common phrases. That is strange to me."

Deineike grinned back at her. "It is strange to me that you know so few words, but you can recall all the common phrases and know more than anybody I have ever met."

Jorinda laughed. "Ryl has many phrases. It is said that in Ryl, a phrase exists for every situation in life."

The humorous mood lifted Jorinda's spirits. None of them had asked about the incident on the stairs. Jorinda guessed it had embarrassed them, or they judged it might open further wounds in her to discuss it. They might have the right of it, but she had no explanation, after all else. She recalled the incident well enough, but it seemed as though she looked on from afar, not unlike a performance by actors at a festival. She attributed it to some further deterioration in her despondency, but it worried her to think back on it.

Jorinda's contentment had increased over the last few days. Things had become more relaxed between her and Deineike, although Jorinda still did not concede to herself they were reconciled. The death of the mariner in Torric intruded in her mind and her nightmares often, and she had not yet left the anger and guilt behind.

A knock at the front door interrupted her contemplation. Jorinda leapt to her feet in alarm—her dagger lay two flights of stairs above her. "You must answer it Klordia. You are the only one the Guild might not recognise."

Klordia spluttered, anxious. "M...Me? They would not know Deineike either."

Jorinda pointed to Deineike's leg. "She cannot answer the door. She is injured. Take your time, and delay whoever is outside as long as you can." Jorinda bounded up the stairs two at a time. She ran into the bedroom, snatched her dagger from her discarded boot, then peered around the doorframe and down the stairs.

Klordia had already opened the door, and Jorinda cursed to herself. She stood two flights of stairs away if the Guild had found them. Wilash loitered to one side of the door with his dagger in his hand, but she cursed again, for although he had concealed himself well enough, he had placed the door between himself and any would-be assailant. Jorinda sighed, frustrated. Must she alone always be the one with any capacity to care for them? It seemed so. She ran down to the next landing as Klordia opened the door wider.

The unmistakeable flash of a Portreeve's man's deep red tunic did not relax Jorinda. The Guild might dress in Portreeve's uniforms to make the fugitives feel comfortable enough to invite them into the house. She peered around the corner of the landing.

Klordia spoke to the person at the door. "Good morning. Can I help you?"

A man's voice replied. Jorinda did not recognise him or his voice, but that meant nothing. "Good day to you, madam. Raolos, Portreeve of Ort, asks you and your colleagues to attend his Offices as soon as possible. We have brought a cart, since we know one of you is injured and cannot move without difficulty."

Klordia looked around the door at Wilash. With one glance, she betrayed his position. Wilash shrugged and glanced up the stairs. Jorinda tried to signal that Klordia should close the door. Wilash seemed to understand and signalled something similar to Klordia, who stared at him for a heartbeat then gave an almost imperceptible nod of her head. What had become of the actor who had played the role of an old friend in the alleyway with such ease?

Klordia turned to the man outside the door again. "My thanks. Please wait a few moments while we ready ourselves." She tried to close the door, but he raised a hand to it, and Jorinda brought her dagger up, prepared to spring forward if necessary.

The tone of the man's voice did not change. "I am happy to wait, but please hurry. The Portreeve bids me tell you time is of the essence. Ominous news has come to him, and there is little more than an hour to devise a response." With that, he took his hand from the door and turned away. Klordia closed the door behind him.

Jorinda ran to the bedroom on the first floor whose window

looked down on the street below. She peered out and saw the cart, as the man had said; a purpose-built conveyance with velvet-covered benches along its length, steps at the rear, and shiny polished handles positioned either side of the steps. Two men in Portreeve's uniforms sat on the driver's bench at the front, and the third walked down the short path from the house and out into the street. None of them looked up at the house.

Jorinda ran down the stairs and into the parlour. Deineike sat where she had been when the knock had come at the door, while Klordia and Wilash stood nearby and stared out of the window, nervous. They turned to her as she entered.

Wilash fidgeted with anxiety. "What do you make of this?"

Jorinda summarised what she had seen. "There are three of them. They do not study the house, nor check whether we have counted their number. That means naught, however. Between you and I, we might take all three. There may be more of them hidden elsewhere nearby, of course."

Deineike did not rise, but she looked up at Jorinda as she voiced her opinion. "Or they may be three Portreeve's men, sent to bring us to Raolos."

Jorinda swept her brown hair from her forehead and held her fingers in it over her head as she turned the situation over in her head. "Mayhap."

Unlike Jorinda, Deineike seemed relaxed, unconcerned. "If the summons is genuine, it appears urgent, and time is wasted if we debate it."

Jorinda sighed, caught between doubt and uncertainty. "Very well, we will roll the dice again. We must roll ones at some point. It may as well be now as at some time in the future."

Klordia appeared mystified. "Ones?"

Wilash explained the phrase to her. "To roll two ones is a losing roll."

Klordia took a breath, then answered in a quiet voice. "I see."

For some reason, Jorinda doubted Klordia had understood, despite her answer.

Jorinda handed Deineike her staff, and they locked the door behind them as they left. As they walked down the short path, one of the men jumped down from the cart and joined the one already at the rear. Wilash and Jorinda motioned for Deineike and Klordia to ascend to the cart first, and the two Portreeve's men helped them both climb the steps. Jorinda stood apart from the others, ready to reach for her dagger in a heartbeat. She checked all around but saw nothing to alarm her.

Jorinda remained watchful as Deineike struggled with the steps, and the men attempted to give her such assistance as they could. They took great care to avoid any contact that might be deemed inappropriate. Deineike had one leg on the boards of the cart, but as she lifted her right leg from the step, she lost her balance, and the man who had come to the door reached for her, so she did not fall backward from the cart. His hand came to rest on her behind, and he shot a quick, nervous glance at Jorinda. His face reddened, and he moved his hand as far up Deineike's back as he could reach.

The interaction relaxed Jorinda. He had been concerned about more than the intimate touch without permission. He had looked to her in embarrassment, either from a knowledge she and Deineike were lovers, or because Jorinda represented unspeakable violence. Either reason suggested his instructions had come from the Portreeve. Guild members would have felt no shame about the touch, might have relished it. They may even have contrived it for simple gratification.

Wilash boarded the cart next before Jorinda climbed the steps last. The man who had come to the door stood on the lowest step and the other returned to the front bench. The driver snapped the reins over the backs of the two horses, one either side of the central shaft, and the cart lurched forward. No more men appeared and the two in front did not look back at them.

It did not take long to reach the Portreeve's Offices, and they descended from the cart. Jorinda offered to help Deineike, and the men appeared grateful, in particular the one who had touched her as she ascended. There had been nothing to fear, in truth, and Jorinda blew out a silent breath of relief, though it pained her that this might be their future, to fear and distrust any who came to their door.

Aides led them into Raolos's office without delay. He stood behind his desk as they entered. "My thanks that you came so soon. I am sorry if I disturbed your morning." They assured him it had been no imposition. "I trust the house is satisfactory."

Deineike smiled at him, warm and friendly. "It is magnificent. Our thanks."

Although Raolos smiled, he appeared anxious as he fidgeted with a scribing tool on his desk. "As a rule, we offer it to dignitaries and the like who visit Ort. That is not why I asked you to come here, however. Bad news has come south." Jorinda's heart sank. He must mean Zhanghar. Raolos confirmed it, and more. "Styrrach is here, in Ort."

Klordia slapped a hand to her mouth, and Wilash put an arm around her. Deineike slumped into one of the two chairs in front of Raolos's desk, while Jorinda clenched her teeth together and balled her fists. They were undone. How had Styrrach learned their movements so soon? She had been convinced it would be many days before he knew they had sailed to Ort.

Raolos continued. "He demands a meeting with me." Jorinda thought he sounded angry, and she had the right of it. "He is no more than a common murderer, but he has the arrogance to demand a meeting with me." Jorinda shot Wilash a glance full of exhortations to say nothing. "What is scribed, must be. My aides are skilled at the deflection of such demands from angry suitors— my every decision is not always well received." He smiled again.

"They told him I had been detained away from the Offices, but he insisted, and persuaded them to give him an appointment."

Jorinda slapped her thigh in anger and bitter disappointment. "When is this appointment?"

Raolos gave her an apologetic look. "In less than an hour."

His reply left Jorinda stunned. "An hour?" That left them no time to do anything other than flee at once.

Deineike looked close to tears. "What does he want?"

Raolos shrugged, the apologetic look still on his face. "That is a fine question, young lady. He did not say, but he told my aide that my interests would be best served if I accepted the meeting with him."

Klordia sounded almost hysterical. "You must arrest him. He is a killer."

The news had shocked them all, and Raolos nodded. "I would like to, but at this point, I have no proof he is anything other than an aggressive businessman."

Klordia spoke again. "He told you he would kill any business associate who created trouble."

Raolos cleared his throat. "That he did not, in fact. He hinted at it, I agree, but those precise words were not used. After all else, they did not come from him. He could claim the emissary misrepresented his intentions."

Klordia had not yet been defeated. "Jorinda can bear witness—he is a killer."

Raolos stared at Jorinda, many questions in his eyes, but he voiced only one. "Can you?"

Jorinda could not, in truth. She raised her hands to chest height, palms to the ceiling. "I have never seen him kill."

Klordia would not give up. "But you can say he ordered you to kill, can you not?" The woman had a stubborn streak wider than Jorinda's own.

Raolos waved a hand before himself, palm down. "Tread soft. In theory, if Jorinda confirmed she had killed on Styrrach's orders, I might convict him of the crime of collusion in murder. I would, however, be required to hang Jorinda as a confessed murderer."

After a stunned silence in the room, Deineike, half-hearted, came up with a new suggestion. "Can you not trick him into a confession?"

"I might, though there would be no witnesses. I am the Portreeve though, and my word is law here in Ort."

Jorinda's bitter sigh embodied all their frustration, she guessed. "I hope you left your bed early this morning, Raolos. If you did not, you would be hard-pressed to trip Styrrach. He is wily and careful. He will not fall into a trap like a fish, baited by trifles." Her mind had become a whirl of thoughts as she tried to piece together all the implications and options the news brought them.

Raolos's mouth turned down at the corners, a gesture of defeat. "I must try, nonetheless. My men will be close at hand, and I will trap him into some confession if I can. I tell you all this because I know it will affect your situation and your decision."

Wilash replied, despondent. "Our thanks." A pall seemed to have settled over them.

At that moment, a thought crossed Jorinda's mind. "Shroud." Raolos looked at her, incomprehension in his eyes. "If you can persuade him to talk about the shrouding, he might spill some information that could help you. You must prise such information from him with care. This business of the shroud is the last mystery, after all else, and I long to understand it since he ordered it for me."

Klordia squinted her confusion. "How would you come to understand it? We cannot be here. We must leave without delay. He may know of us and come for us after this meeting." She raised a hand to her mouth again. "He may be at the house as we speak." She glanced at Wilash, who rubbed a hand up and down her back.

Jorinda could not leave, not with Styrrach so near at hand. "You and Wilash must flee today; now. Take Deineike with you if she will go. I will stay and learn all I can." "*And kill Styrrach,*" she did not add.

Deineike replied without hesitation. "I will not leave without you." Jorinda had expected nothing less but wished she could have been wrong this once.

Wilash bowed his head, miserable. "If you must stay, then I will not abandon you."

Raolos looked from one to the other as though they had all lost their minds. "This is madness. You must all leave without delay. My cart will take you some distance from the city, or I will arrange a ship for you. You may decide which, but to stay here while he seeks you is a mistake. You must flee."

Jorinda's anger flared inside her, but she fought to control it, aware Raolos knew little of what lay between her and Styrrach. "You will not back down before him, but you would order us to do so?"

Raolos's reply sounded like a desperate plea for them to understand. "I do not order it. I will help you achieve it. Common sense orders it, in truth. You can all see that, can you not?"

Jorinda's conviction could not be shaken. She had to know about the shroud, even if it cost her life. "I will stay. I will hide somewhere where I can hear his explanation of the shroud. If it brings his downfall and arrest, so much the better. But I cannot live with this hole unfilled within me. I must know why he wished me dead. Arella lost her life thanks to it, and I must know. I do not ask any of you to stay. In truth, I implore you all to leave." She looked at Deineike. Tears dripped from the older woman's blue eyes.

An edge crept into Raolos's voice. "Hide? Where will you hide that he will not detect you?"

Jorinda stared about the room and walked around the desk in search of a place to hide. A deep recess beneath the desk accommodated Raolos's legs, and it sparked an idea. "I will hide in here. I am small and can hide deep in this recess. With you seated in your chair, there is little enough chance he will see me."

Raolos shook his head and muttered. "This is madness." Klordia, Wilash, and Deineike agreed with him, and some moments of heated debate ensued.

Jorinda stood on the edge of a precipice. The audacious plan to hide and learn why she had been marked for death might push her over the edge where she may die, cast down to the bottom by Styrrach's knife, but she could not run anymore without further enlightenment. The conflict tore at her, and she saw no solution that guaranteed satisfaction.

Jorinda turned to Deineike. "What word did you use? The one that implied contradiction?"

Puzzled, Deineike thought for a heartbeat before she replied. "Dichotomy?"

"That it is. This is a dichotomy. I can flee, but a part of me will be torn away, and I will never understand why Styrrach betrayed me and I ki..." She glanced at Raolos, aware of the mistake she had almost made. "I will never understand why that betrayal led to Arella's death. I can stay, learn why, and may still find no satisfaction. Or I can stay, and I might die. That is the dichotomy."

Despite the tangible tension in the room, Deineike smiled. "I do not think that is a dichotomy. My belief is only two contradictions are a dichotomy."

Raolos gasped aloud. "Does this matter? We bicker about a word while Styrrach's feet already doubtless cross the square."

Wilash must have reached a decision. "Deineike and Klordia will return to the house. I will stay and wait with your men if that suits." He glanced at Raolos, who gave a hopeless shrug of agreement. "Jorinda will hide. It may serve you well, in truth. If Styrrach makes some attempt on your life, as unlikely as that might seem, you have an ally in the room who can...who may be of some assistance." Jorinda could not repress a wry smile at Wilash's correction. They danced around her deadly art, and it both amused and frustrated her that the subject could not be spoken about with less pretence.

Raolos shook his head in apparent despondency. "The sand falls, and you remain bent on this ridiculous scheme. I should take you all into custody and lock you away somewhere to prevent you from any involvement in this. I will not do that, though I hope I do not come to regret it." He rang the bell, and an aide appeared. Raolos pointed to Deineike and Klordia. "These ladies will leave, and two men will escort them back to the house. The rest is as we discussed." Next, Raolos pointed to Wilash. "This man will wait with our men. Keep them out of sight but close by, as we arranged."

The aide nodded and held the door open. Deineike threw herself into Jorinda's arms. "I will not leave you."

"You cannot fit in there with me, and I cannot keep myself and Raolos safe if I am worried about you." Jorinda kissed Deineike's lips. "Go with Klordia. She will need you. We will all meet again soon, then we must leave Ort unless this has been resolved in our favour."

Deineike insisted she would not leave Jorinda to face danger alone, but at length, Klordia persuaded her they should return to the house together. Despite Deineike's obvious reluctance, they left, and Wilash followed the Portreeve's man out of the office. Only Jorinda and Raolos remained, and Jorinda turned to the Portreeve. "My thanks for this indulgence. I know you do not understand it."

"What will you do afterward? If I cannot trip him, he will walk from here a free man and doubtless spend all his energies to find you."

"That he will. If he cannot be brought to justice here, and if your offer of help still stands, we will make use of it and leave as soon as possible. Tonight, my guess, though we do not know where we will go."

Raolos looked thoughtful before he replied. "I will give you letters to take with you. Some towns exist where you should be safe enough for a time, and I will beseech the Portreeves of those towns to aid you as much as they can."

"You are a good man, Raolos. My thanks. Deineike and I regret we cannot settle here in Ort. You run a fine town."

"Ortfolk are fine people. The management of the town is simple enough. Any could do it." He smiled. "My thanks, nonetheless." A knock on the office door interrupted them. "Come."

An aide popped his head around the door. "He is here." Three small words that brought so much danger and tension into the Portreeve's Offices. The hour had come, and Jorinda heaved a long, slow breath as she calmed herself, ready for whatever might befall them.

NINETEEN

BLOOD IS SPILLED

Raolos nodded to his aide. "Very well. Give us a few moments, then show him in." The Portreeve glanced at Jorinda. "The moment is upon us. I trust I can pry some words from him that will bring you peace. More than that, I hope his neck will have a noose around it by nightfall, and all his accomplices will be named." He shook his head. "I hold little hope of that. It vexes me." He slapped the desk. "Now, you must scurry under here like a rat, and we will roll the dice."

Jorinda crouched and crawled into the recess. At the front, the desk extended all the way to the carpet, and Styrrach would never know she hid beneath it. Raolos sat in his chair and moved himself forward, his knees close to Jorinda's face. The space felt claustrophobic, and she could not emerge unless Raolos moved out of the way, but she needed to understand why her death had been ordered. Some part of her guilt for Arella's death must be assuaged.

Jorinda heard a knock at the door, and Raolos again said, "Come." The sounds were fainter than she had expected. The solid Ortwood of the desk deadened the noises. The door opened and closed. From beneath the desk, the thick carpet absorbed the sound of footfalls as Jorinda kept her breaths slow and soft—in through her nose, out through her mouth, to calm the rate of her heartbeat, and so Styrrach did not hear her. She guessed her foe stood mere spans from her, and she lowered a hand to her boot. Long ago, she had sewn a small flap in the inside of the boot where she tucked her fan when she carried it, and the dagger she had promised to name Wilke sat there now. She slipped it out into her hand. If things turned awry, she would be ready.

A disembodied voice spoke, muffled by the thickness of the wood, but familiar, nonetheless. She pursed her lips into a snarl as she recognised it. "I am Styrrach." Raolos did not answer, and Jorinda imagined Styrrach would notice the slight, which would add to his irritation. "This is my Senior Aide, Porl." A sorry turn, and one she should have anticipated. She could kill Styrrach alone if it came to it. Two trained killers, however, with Raolos to protect, and all while she crouched beneath the desk at the start of the combat—a serious disadvantage.

"You do not invite us to sit, but we will do so." Raolos had not yet spoken, and by good fortune, his shrewd move hurt Styrrach's ego. Jorinda guessed nothing more than Raolos's distaste for the man drove his incivility. How could she not hear them move, even as they sat on the chairs? She cursed the plush carpet and well-made furniture that yielded no clues as to what turned.

"What can I do for you?" Raolos broke his silence at last, and the contempt in his voice could have been devoured with a fork. Every word dripped with it.

Styrrach's voice gave no hint of any anger he might feel at

Raolos's treatment of him. "I have come to offer you one last opportunity to join our enterprise. Ort is an important river port, and we would like to avail ourselves of the convenience of its docks and the wealth of its merchants. Much coin awaits us all if you will drop this pretence of uprightness." Styrrach paused, but Raolos remained silent. "It is business, nothing more. It is good business, for us and for you. I imagine your position as Portreeve might become untenable if it emerged you had denied your citizens the wealth that could pour into the city."

Raolos paused a moment before he responded. "We are but a town."

Jorinda guessed what Styrrach would say next, and he did not disappoint. "That you are. That might change if you join us, however."

"The Duke himself is part of your…business, then?"

Styrrach's soft laugh made Jorinda 's skin crawl. She had heard that sardonic laugh before, and she did not care for it. "That he is not. He has wealth enough as it is. We have his ear, nothing more."

Raolos could not keep his distaste for Styrrach out of his voice, and Jorinda worried the Guildmeister, not known for his patience, might tire of the Portreeve's contempt. "Through the Bailiff?" Jorinda thought it risky to make such an overt accusation so early in the piece.

Styrrach's silence lasted for several heartbeats. "The Bailiff is a businessman. He recognises a good opportunity if he sees one. He would not be the Bailiff if he did not."

Raolos seemed bereft of any appropriate reply. "That is true enough, I imagine." Styrrach had not yet confessed to any crime. Much had been intimated, but Raolos had heard nothing that would allow him to call for his men and arrest Styrrach. The heat beneath the desk combined with the uncomfortable crouched position tested Jorinda's endurance, but she dared not risk any movement.

Porl had remained silent throughout, and that did not change as Styrrach pressed Raolos further. "What concerns you about our proposal? We are impressed by you and would like you to join us, but my patience grows thin."

Raolos seemed prepared to confront the intricacies of the scheme at long last. "I am not sure I have grasped it in full."

"There is little enough to understand. Goods will arrive, and your tally houses will buy them. They will then sell them at great profit."

"That is how things are already."

Styrrach paused for a heartbeat before he answered. "I feel certain that under my proposal, all who partake in it will see higher profit."

"Then?"

"The tally house owners will remit their levies to you, and you will keep what you need. The rest you will send to the Bailiff as proof Ort deserves its city charter."

Corelle tried to guess what looks the Guildmeister exchanged with Porl. That might give some clue as to what they intended if they could not persuade Raolos, as Jorinda knew they could not. To Jorinda's relief, Raolos appeared to feign interest. "These levies will be greater than they are today, I imagine."

A bead of sweat dripped from the end of Jorinda's nose onto the carpet. The heat beneath the desk had become oppressive, and the conversation seemed as though it would go on for the rest of the day. She dared not wipe her face in case the dagger made some noise against the wood as she moved.

Styrrach's tone did not change. It never had when she had worked for him. "That they will. The profits will be greater, and the extra profits will serve you well as you seek your city charter. You, of course, may keep as much of the levies as you feel you need to run the city, and pay yourself a wage for your efforts." Jorinda despaired, convinced she had heard nothing illegal in the proposal thus far. That appeared to have been the case all along, other than the Guild's mysterious involvement.

Raolos persisted in his search for some item he could use. "What is your part in this?"

Styrrach gave another of those irksome laughs. "I oversee the security of the arrangement, nothing more."

Jorinda detected a note of dejection in Raolos's voice. "What are these goods, that so much profit comes from them?"

"Exotic goods from the south. The citizens of Dur do love them and already pay enormous prices for them. Spices, cloths, jewellery, and the like. I guess your wife wears some fancy ornament in her ears, or a dress, all made from these goods. I see golden rings on your fingers. We will have imported the gold used to craft those rings. You already receive most of these goods, but there would be others that do not come to Ort yet. If you join us."

Why did Styrrach continue to press this? Jorinda knew little about Raolos, but she already knew he would never agree to this. It may not be illegal, but it bordered on immoral. He would not agree to become rich beyond the wildest dreams of avarice while his citizens paid the vast, inflated sums Styrrach hinted at. Styrrach showed he knew nothing of Raolos's nature.

Raolos changed course. Had he sensed defeat? "What will it cost to join this organisation?"

Styrrach maintained the same, disinterested tone. In truth, he made a terrible salesman, but he had the Guild to enforce his word, and with the Guild behind him, he could sell water to the sea. "There is no price to join. I take a fee from the profits for my part in it, as would you, and Ort will be what it should be, a city. The prestige..." Raolos said nothing, and Styrrach's next words intrigued Jorinda. "There is a favour you could do me, however."

"A favour?"

"A small thing. I seek an old friend. Corelle is her name. She arrived in Alcmouth about a pass ago, but I have lost touch. She may still be there, and I travel there tomorrow to seek her. She may arrive here, and if you do hear of her, I ask you to find some way to make her comfortable and send word to me. I shall come at once to be re-united with her."

Raolos kept his voice calm, although his heart must have raced. "I see." It seemed Styrrach might not know for certain they were in Ort after all else, although it might also be a bluff.

Styrrach had not finished. "One other thing will serve us both. She may be in the company of a man. Wilash, his name. They are implicated in the death of a Portreeve's man in Alcmouth. Corelle, I am sure, is innocent, and I wish to clear her name. Wilash killed the Portreeve's man, and you may hang him for his crimes. Witnesses aplenty will come forward."

"You killed a Portreeve's man?" Raolos sounded horrified, and he had slipped up. He had addressed his comment to her, Jorinda guessed. All may now be undone.

To Jorinda's relief, Styrrach appeared to draw the wrong conclusion. "I did not say I killed him. The man who travels with Corelle killed him. Not me, you may rest assured. Portreeves are my friends. I admire the work their men do, and it grieves me that one lost his life. Tragic." Jorinda yearned to heave a long sigh of relief but did not dare.

Raolos continued to search for something illegal and returned to the earlier track. "What if my friends wished to sell at unacceptable prices?"

Styrrach sighed and sounded even more impatient. "You will advise me, or my agent in the city, who will speak to them and ensure the arrangement is understood. They have, as they say, bitten the fingers that carve their meat." Jorinda felt happier now Raolos had manoeuvred the Guild into the conversation.

"I cannot shroud them?" Jorinda almost hit Raolos in the leg. Impatience must have got the better of him, and he had misspoken at the moment the conversation showed promise. Styrrach would leave now. Raolos ought to have teased the shroud out of him, not jumped in with such bluntness.

The silence that ensued reverberated around Jorinda until Styrrach spoke again. "Shroud? Where did you come by this term?"

Raolos did not reply straight away. "Your emissary let slip the word in this precise context." He played his highest hand, but with little chance of success. He would struggle to recover from the foolish mistake.

"My emissary used this word you say. How peculiar." Styrrach's voice seemed muffled or distant as though he cast about the room or some such. "I do not know what this word means. Regardless, other matters press on me, and time is short. I must have an answer from you if you will."

Raolos's legs moved as he shifted to his right, but he said nothing. Jorinda wished she could see his face and Styrrach and Porl's movements.

She struggled to catch Styrrach's next words. "Then we will depart and take up no more of your time, since I take your silence to mean you have no interest in my proposal." A metallic rattle followed before Styrrach spoke again. "The door is locked?"

Raolos sounded fearful now. "That it is. I keep it locked against unwanted interruptions when I take important meetings. I ring this bell to summon my aide and he will unlock it."

"Then do so now, if you will." Jorinda understood why Styrrach's voice sounded different. He had moved to the door.

Raolos seemed to abandon all caution. "You run the Guild, do you not? Tell me all now, and it may go easy for you. My men stand ready to arrest you." Jorinda cursed. He had lost and had played the low hand out of desperation. His life hung by a thread.

Styrrach shouted, "To me, men." Jorinda frowned in confusion, then realised Styrrach must have called for extra bodyguards who travelled with him and Porl. The plan had collapsed, and she must act.

The next few moments rushed by in a blur. Raolos moved backward and cried aloud as a shadow fell over him. Jorinda had already moved, and she pushed at his legs to propel him backward faster. Through the combination of his own movement and Jorinda's push, his chair toppled over, and he fell backward. As Jorinda emerged from beneath the desk, Porl swung a dagger at Raolos, and it proved fortunate that the Portreeve had fallen. The blade caught the arm he threw upward as he tried to retain his balance. It opened a deep cut, and he cried out in pain as blood gushed from the wound. He almost kicked Jorinda's face as he toppled backward.

Jorinda came up and slashed at Porl from a low position as soon as she had a chance to strike. Her dagger caught him across the chest and opened a deep welt from one side to the other. He seemed surprised at the sight of her, and he swung his blade at her in a defensive slash that whistled close but missed her. He grunted and raised his left arm toward his chest as though he might slow the blood that poured from him, but the arm never reached the wound. With a rapid circular motion of her dagger, Jorinda slashed downward and cut him from breastbone to stomach. The second blow cut even deeper as her weight moved forward and drove the blade deep into his flesh. He dropped his dagger and fell backward as blood flooded from the vermilion cross the two terrible strikes had opened on his body.

Raolos lay on the floor with a hand pressed to the bloody cut on his other arm. Jorinda turned at a crash from behind her as the door splintered inward. Styrrach turned away from the door to avoid fragments of wood that flew all around him, froze when he noticed Jorinda. He stared at her, disbelief on his face, his dagger in hand. Two men tumbled into the room, a Portreeve's man, and another whose face she recognised as one of the Zhanghar Guild members. They brawled on the floor and rolled out of her sight in front of the desk.

Jorinda sprang into action again. She tried to slide over the desk toward Styrrach but stumbled over Porl's leg and fell headlong onto the carpet next to the desk. Five paces from her, Styrrach ran through the shattered door into the outer office as she scrambled to her feet and yelled for somebody to stop him. The two men had struggled to their feet also, and the Portreeve's man, his back to her, stood between her and the Guild member.

The Guild member's dagger slashed, and a deep cut opened on the bicep of the Portreeve's man. He roared in pain and held his arms up, but the Guild member raised his hand to strike again, so Jorinda rose to a crouch and pushed past beneath one of the Portreeve's man's upraised arms to drive her dagger deep into the assassin beneath his ribcage on his right-hand side. He flicked his eyes toward her and snarled in recognition. She could not pull her dagger free from his body, and he swung his dagger downward toward her neck. In response, Jorinda stood upright, raised her left shoulder, and turned to the right. The dagger caught her high on the arm and opened a shallow cut half a span long. Her own dagger remained embedded in him, and her manoeuvres to avoid the blow had complicated its retrieval.

He raised his arm again, and Jorinda stared at her ruin. Instead, his eyes opened wide, glazed over, and the hilt of her dagger protruded from his right ear even as she tried to pull it free of his body. He crumpled to the floor as blood poured from his stomach and ear, and Wilash stood behind him. It had been his dagger, the twin of her own, that protruded from the man's head, after all else. With no time for conversation, Jorinda reached down, placed a foot on the man's body, and grunted as she pulled her dagger from his stomach.

Wilash stood rooted to the spot as she pushed past him through the door into the outer office. She could not see Styrrach. Two men in Portreeve's uniforms lay on the floor surrounded by blood, and one Guild member lay on his back on one of the desks. He groaned, and blood gushed from a terrible stomach wound. Another crouched, cornered by three Portreeve's men, two of whom held daggers toward him, while the other threatened him with a short sword. Jorinda saw no reason for the man to wield a sword in such close quarters combat.

Jorinda knew the Guild member, who could not survive if he fought on. She urged him not to squander his life. "Give yourself up."

He turned at the sound of her voice. "You." The Portreeve's man with the sword saw an opportunity in the man's distraction, and he drove his weapon to the hilt into the Guild member's stomach with both hands. The tip emerged from the Guild man's back with a spray of blood, and he slumped back against the wall. He still waved his dagger at his assailants, stared at Jorinda, and spat at her even as one of the other Portreeve's men drove his dagger into his throat. The Guild member slid to the floor, and a wide, bright red line on the wall followed him down to his ruin.

His spit landed short of Jorinda, and she steadied herself on one of the desks as she examined the carnage in the offices. The Guild member on the desk had fallen silent, and Jorinda imagined he had died. "*Wilash.*" She ran back into Raolos's office with a pained cry. Wilash sat on the floor with his head in his hands, and she knelt before him and placed her lips to his ear. Her words were whispered, and he alone heard them. "Flee. You cannot stay here. Flee. Take them both with you if they will go. Klordia at the least, if Deineike will not go."

He looked up at her. "I killed him." Tears pooled in his eyes.

"That you did, and you saved my life. My thanks. But you are in great danger. Styrrach told Raolos you killed the Portreeve's man in Alcmouth. You cannot stay here. You must flee, or Raolos will arrest you. Go, Wilash, I beg you." She took his head in her hands and stared into his eyes. "Go."

Jorinda stood and pulled at his arm to haul him to his feet. He rose, so slow that Jorinda wanted to scream. How could he not grasp the peril he found himself in? Once she had him on his feet, she moved behind him and pushed him toward the door. She manoeuvred him into the corridor, past the curious stares of the Portreeve's men.

Jorinda yelled at the men as she pushed Wilash down the corridor. "Your Portreeve lies in his office, injured. Call healers."

At last, Wilash seemed to understand, and he took off at a run. Jorinda, her hands still in the small of his back, almost fell on her face as he sprinted away from her, but she recovered her balance and watched until he turned a corner and vanished from sight. She ran into the office again, where Raolos lay on his back, soft moans of pain a welcome reassurance—he still lived. A quick glance at Porl confirmed the same. The wounded Portreeve's man also moaned in pain on the opposite side of the desk, out of sight, and Raolos paid Jorinda no attention.

Jorinda knelt over Porl, her knees in a pool of blood that spread across the plush carpet. Words rattled in his throat as his life flowed away from him. "Corelle. I am ended. Finish it."

With one last check nobody observed her, Jorinda snarled at him. "I am happy to send you wherever you travel to afterward, and good riddance." She drove the point of her dagger into the side of Porl's neck. His blood seeped from the fresh wound, and his eyes closed.

Jorinda turned her attention again to Raolos. He had fallen silent, and he stared up at the ceiling, but when she checked at his neck, she found a pulsing. She looked toward the office door and yelled, "Have you summoned healers?" Her body shook, and blood ran down her left arm. Raolos had suffered a long deep wound to his own arm, but it did not look fatal unless he bled to death. She turned back to Porl, cut a strip of cloth from the bottom of his tunic, and tied it around Raolos's upper arm to slow the loss of blood.

When she crawled around the desk, the Portreeve's man whimpered, and his hand clutched at his wound. She cut a strip of cloth from his tunic and tied it around his arm above the cut. He looked up at her and whispered. "Am I dead?"

"You complain too much for a dead man. You live, and help is on the way." He closed his eyes and groaned again. Furious, Jorinda shouted a third time. "Healers."

A man's voice cried out in response. "They come."

The man who replied stood in the doorway, and Jorinda turned to him. "Are any of the aides hurt?"

Fear turned his face ashen. "They left the outer office after they locked the door."

Frustrated by the inadequate answer, Jorinda snapped at the man. "Does that mean they are not hurt?"

He blinked, mayhap shocked by her aggressive tone. "That it does. They are unhurt."

With a sigh of relief, Jorinda stood and faced him. He still held his sword, and blood dripped from its blade onto the carpet. She softened her voice to comfort him. "You did well. A sword is not ideal in these close quarters, but you used it to good effect."

"My thanks. How does a woman do the things you have done here?"

"Do not ask."

He fetched up, and more people bustled into the office. One of them carried a bag and wore sombre black clothes, and he knelt beside Raolos and checked for a pulsing. Since Jorinda could do no more for the Portreeve or the other injured man, she walked into the outer office. The Portreeve's man who had come to the door of the house earlier stood there, and his eyes widened as he saw her.

Jorinda had not seen the Guildmeister since he ran through the shattered door. "Styrrach fled?"

The man's shoulders shrugged, non-committal. "We know not, in truth, but that is what we guess. Will Raolos live?"

Jorinda repeated her earlier gesture, palms up at chest height. "I am no chirurgeon. He suffered a deep wound, but he is in the care of healers now. Like as not he will."

"You remained in the office. You slew his assailant, the other that entered the office with Styrrach."

She nodded in agreement. "Porl, and that I did. I killed him." *"Curse me,"* she thought. *"I have killed again."*

"Our thanks. My thanks. All Ort thanks you. You saved him, it seems."

She shrugged. "I must go to my…to Deineike."

"You cannot."

Jorinda bridled. "That I will, and you will be wise not to attempt to prevent it."

"Forgive me, but you misunderstand. You cannot walk the streets like that. You are covered in blood. All who see you will be horrified. I will find you some clean clothes to wear."

She hung her head. "I apologise. This has been a difficult day."

"I understand. I will return as soon as I can." He strode off at a brisk pace, and Jorinda leaned back against a desk. Bodies still lay scattered around the office, although they had been covered with cloaks and cloths soaked by blood stains. Jorinda had never been in such a situation or seen so much brutality and carnage play out before her. Her entire body shook, and her hands trembled with such violence, she feared she would drop her dagger, so she bent to slide it into her boot as tears welled up and poured out of her eyes. Without shame, she fell forward, knelt with both hands on the floor, and wept.

The tears continued as the memory of the fight filled her mind. When she had killed Hiw and his companions, it had not been as visceral as all that had turned here. She had survived her first fight between multiple combatants. It had frightened her, but her training had carried her through. Without Wilash's intervention, though—

The man's voice interrupted her, and she struggled to her feet. "I found this dress." He held out a dress toward her. "One of the clerks had it. She intended to have it adjusted or some such, but now she donates it to you."

"My thanks. I will return it as soon as I may." Jorinda fumbled at the buttons of her tunic.

"Please." He turned away, embarrassed. "I will take you somewhere more private where you may change."

She managed a weak smile. "What is your name?"

He made a half-hearted attempt to return the smile. "Ibie."

"My thanks, Ibie. You are a good man. I am sorry some of your colleagues fell today."

His sad expression returned. "It has been a difficult day for us all." He led her to a small room, then left her alone. Jorinda sobbed as she cast the bloodied clothes from her and slipped the dress over her head. She cried alone in the room for long moments before she composed herself, pulled the door open, and set off down the corridor.

TWENTY
COMINGS AND GOINGS

Wilash froze as his former Guild colleague fell to the carpet with the dagger embedded in the side of his head. Corelle ran from the office, and Wilash's legs collapsed beneath him. He slumped to the floor and stared in horror as a pool of blood spread around the Guild member's head. He could not remember the man's name, a perpetual problem for him. Nearby, a man in a Portreeve's tunic moaned in pain as he clutched his arm, and blood seeped between his fingers.

Moments passed as shouts came from the other office, then silence descended, and Wilash hoped the horror had ended. He had killed a man, a man he once knew. Why had he ever joined the Guild? Styrrach hoodwinked him; there could be no other explanation. Wilash could never be a killer, and bile rose to his throat as he recalled the moment he drove his dagger into the man's head. He had acted out of instinct to help Corelle, or Jorinda rather—even in his shock, he knew he should relinquish her old name, which he clung to as a child clings to a favourite toy. The help he rendered her had made a killer of him. The thought sickened him, filled him with so much self-hatred, he could never face violence again in his life.

Jorinda ran in and whispered in his ear. He struggled to focus on her words, but he thought she urged him to flee.

Tears poured from his eyes. "I killed him."

Jorinda whispered more words he could not focus on, and she pulled his head around, then stared into his eyes. "Go." She stood and pulled at his arm.

He struggled to his feet. She pushed him, and he allowed her to guide him out of the office. More bodies and more blood lay strewn around the outer office, and Jorinda yelled something about healers and injured men, but her words did not register in Wilash's confused mind. She pushed him further until they reached the corridor.

In the Portreeve's office, she had told him to go. The word echoed in his mind, "*Go,*" and at last he understood. He took off and ran along the corridor until he saw another to the right. He turned and ran past startled people who milled about like lost children, ashen-faced and horrified. "*They are horrified at me. I have killed a man.*"

A door loomed ahead; he pushed it open and ran outside into the town square. Corelle's words came back to him, fragments of a conversation, like a dream half-remembered in the cold dawn. "*Flee. Take Klordia.*" He must reach the house and take Klordia to safety, away from all this blood and ruin. She might refuse to travel with him now he had become a killer. He must try to persuade her, no matter how difficult that proved. Klordia despised Corelle, whom she believed to be a heartless killer with nothing to redeem her. Would she now feel the same about him? She would loathe him, and he would lose her, the first woman he had ever cared for. Had ever…loved.

He stopped once he came within sight of the house. He must gather himself, or he would frighten Klordia. His breaths came in short gasps, and he struggled to suck air down his throat. He had never run so far in his life, though it had been little more than one street.

He calmed himself, nodded to Raolos's two guards, who seemed to recognise him, walked to the door of the house, and turned the handle. Locked. Of course; Klordia had locked it to keep herself safe. He searched his pockets but turned up no key, so he knocked on the door. Klordia pulled it open, and Wilash wrapped his arms around her. She buried her head in his chest as sobs shook her body.

Wilash kissed the top of her head. "I am unhurt."

"Thank the fates." Her voice sounded muffled against his chest.

He kissed the top of her head again and noticed Deineike in the entrance to the parlour, a hand over her mouth as tears poured from her eyes. She seemed unsteady on her feet. He had not given thought to her at all, wrapped up in his concern for Klordia and his own self-pity.

He reached a hand toward her. "Sweet girl. I am sorry. Forgive me." Deineike took a step backward and reached for the door frame as though to steady herself. Wilash had spoken ill-chosen words, and doubtless Deineike had misconstrued them. "Do not fret, sweet girl. I spoke without any thought. She lives. Corelle lives. I am sorry I have frightened you so." He cursed to himself. In his distress, he had called her Corelle again. Both women sobbed even louder, and Deineike slumped to the floor. Klordia ran to her, folded her into her arms, held her close.

Wilash did not know how to comfort them. His words should have been enough, he believed. He and Jorinda had survived the horrors of Raolos's office, but they must now leave this place as Jorinda had ordered. "We must flee."

Deineike looked up at him. "Where is Jorinda?" Her quiet, velvety voice sounded quieter than usual as she asked the question.

"She is still there, at the Offices."

Klordia, her arms still wrapped around Deineike, turned to Wilash. "What turned? Wilash, what turned? You have blood on your tunic. Are you hurt?"

Wilash shook his head as bewilderment turned his mind to mud. "I do not know what turned. It went awry. Core...Jorinda will know more, I feel certain. I am not hurt." He smiled at Klordia to reassure her. "We heard shouts and ran to Raolos's office. Three Guild members from Zhanghar attacked Raolos's door. I think they wanted to kill Raolos." He shook his head again. Shock, fear, and horror jumbled his words, and he could not explain with any clarity what had turned. His legs shook, and he needed to sit, lest he fall.

He walked into the parlour and collapsed into one of the armed chairs. A tear ran down his cheek, and Klordia slid across the floor to sit at his feet, reached up, and took his hands in her own. Deineike moved close to him and laid a hand on his shin. He must tell them more, but the next part would damn him in their eyes, and he feared to recount it.

He took a long breath. "Never have I seen such chaos; fights and screams and blood. Blood everywhere. Men fell to the ground left and right, and the door to the office opened somehow, so I ran in to look for Corelle." He shook his head, annoyed that he continued to call her by the wrong name. "Jorinda. She fought for her life against one of the men from Zhanghar." He stopped and looked down into Klordia's tear-filled eyes. "I killed him." Deineike squeezed his leg. "Klordia, I killed him."

Klordia leapt up onto his lap, wrapped her arms around his head, and pulled his face to her breasts. He could say no more for now. He surrendered to his grief, and the three of them wailed in misery.

He lost track of how long the three of them sat there, tearful and wrapped in one another's arms. The moment he had swung his dagger and thrust it into the head of the man replayed itself over and over in his mind. How could he be the same again? After the confrontation in Alcmouth, Klordia, Jorinda, and Deineike had persuaded him he had not killed the Portreeve's man, that he had done no more than injure the man, and Jorinda had killed him. They could not avoid the truth this time. He had killed and would be hanged for his crime.

Memories escaped from wherever his mind had buried them. Jorinda had said Styrrach or Raolos—he could not quite recall which—had demanded Wilash's arrest for the death of the man in Alcmouth, and he must escape. "We must flee. Jorinda said I will be arrested."

Klordia leaned back to look into his eyes. "You are to be arrested for the death of a man who threatened Jorinda and the Portreeve?"

Wilash blinked in surprise. Klordia had misunderstood, it seemed. "That I am not. For Alcmouth."

Klordia frowned in disbelief. "You did not kill that man, in truth. After all else, how have they learned of that here?"

Wilash clutched at fragments of memory that floated inside his head, tried to piece them together into some coherent picture of all that had turned in the Portreeve's Offices. "Styrrach, I believe. He played some part in it."

Deineike gasped. "Is Styrrach dead also?"

Wilash looked down into her upturned face. "I think not. He ran from the office, but I could not give chase. I wished to ensure Jorinda lived."

Klordia squeezed his hand. "You did the right thing. The man you killed would have harmed her had you not intervened." She paused, then, "Will he come here?"

"It is not possible. He is dead."

Deineike frowned, puzzlement in her voice. "You said he escaped."

"I said I killed him." He snapped his fingers as realisation dawned. "Hold. I see the confusion. I killed the man who fought with Jorinda. Styrrach escaped. You asked whether Styrrach will come here, not the man I killed." He shook his head, which scattered his thoughts even more. "This day confuses me."

Klordia shook, and her face had lost its colour. "Will Styrrach come here?"

Klordia appeared terrified, and Wilash pulled her close to him. "I think not. I do not know for certain."

Deineike laid her head against his leg. "You have your dagger if he comes. I think we will be safe."

"That I do not. I did not take it out of his…" He stopped, loath to describe the terrible vision that would not leave his mind.

Klordia shook her head as if to clear her mind. "We still have Raolos's guards outside. Raolos will not leave us unprotected."

Wilash had no idea how Raolos's fate had turned. "I do not know whether Raolos lives. I did not see him." Klordia pulled back and stared at him in horror.

Deineike raised a hand to her forehead, and her lips quivered. "Raolos might be dead?"

Despondency consumed him as he replied, ate at his heart and mind. "I know not. I did not see him."

After a momentary silence, Deineike spoke with a slight nod of her head. "Jorinda would not have allowed Styrrach to kill him."

Wilash's concern for their misery drove him to apologise. "Klordia, Deineike, I am sorry. I am a poor storyteller. Confusion and fear fog my recollection. I killed the man, and I can scarce recall anything afterward, except that Jorinda urged us all to flee."

Deineike shook her head and glared at him. "I will not leave without Jorinda. If she urged you to flee, then the two of you should, and must. She would not have said it unless she meant it. Go. Prepare to leave, I beg you."

Klordia shook her head. "Where will we go? How will we leave? We cannot rush out into the street and run heedless to who knows where."

"That we cannot." Wilash agreed with Klordia, but he also agreed with Deineike. "We can prepare, at the least. Let us gather our belongings then, in readiness." Klordia rose from his lap.

Deineike reached out and took Wilash's arm. "Did Jorinda say she would follow you here?"

He tried to recall all she had said. "I do not know. I am sorry. I think she said naught of her plans. I am dazed."

Deineike's eyes shone with compassion, though they were filled with tears. "She will come when she deems it right to do so. Prepare yourselves." She sat back on her haunches. "I will wait for her here." Wilash thought she said it to herself rather than him.

When Wilash entered the house alone, Deineike's heart skipped a beat. Jorinda had not returned with him, and his blood-spattered tunic implied something had gone awry. She saw it in his face, and Jorinda had not returned. Had she died? Deineike could not bear the thought, and she felt faint.

"Sweet girl. I am sorry. Forgive me." As he said it, his arms extended toward her. It could not be. Jorinda had been killed? Deineike staggered backward a step and reached for the door for support. Unbearable pain overcame her—her stomach tightened, her heart turned to stone in her breast, and tears poured from her eyes. For an hour or more, she had waited with Klordia in the house, unsure of what turned in the Portreeve's Offices, and now her life had unravelled.

It proved too much for her when Wilash told her Jorinda still lived. Her emotions overwhelmed her, and her legs gave way. She fell to the floor, and Klordia rushed over to hold her.

Confusion filled the next few moments. Wilash urged them all to flee as he recounted what he could recall of the incidents that had preceded his return to the house, but he seemed disoriented, and Deineike fought her frustration and her urgent need for information on Jorinda.

When Wilash suggested the Portreeve might have been killed, it horrified her, and anger boiled her blood when she learned Styrrach had fled. Deineike reminded herself Jorinda had been there and would have spent her own life to save Raolos. Jorinda still lived, so Raolos must also be alive. She knew it. She hoped it.

She could prise no further information from Wilash about Jorinda's intentions, He appeared so distraught, she chased the two of them away to their room where they could spend some time together and comfort one another, and where Deineike's needs would not intrude on their capacity to find some sense from all that had taken place on this extraordinary day.

Weary, she dragged herself up into the chair Wilash had vacated and reflected on the hand that had been dealt to her that night at Taro's farm. If she told her tale to anybody, they would ask why she loved Jorinda. *"The sum of all Jorinda has brought to you,"* they would say, *"is grief and pain."* It could not be denied, but they would not know Jorinda had helped Deineike to find herself. They could not know Deineike had blundered into Taro's farm a lost and broken thing after she had travelled through the rain and mud, aimless, desperate to find a purpose even as she had no idea what purpose she sought.

Jorinda brought her happiness, and Jorinda brought her sadness. Most of all, Deineike felt sadness for Jorinda herself, in truth. The younger woman needed somebody who would stand beside her through her worst moments, then guide her back toward the light that shone so bright within her in her best moments. Deineike would be that person. Jorinda had been at great pains aboard The Friendship to tell Deineike she needed Jorinda, but Deineike believed Jorinda had desperate need of her also. Jorinda brought her untold joy, and there could scarce be a warmer, more affectionate, and sensuous woman than Jorinda when not mired in her own self-induced hopelessness.

Two or three days ago, Jorinda had said one word from Deineike melted her. Deineike had not admitted it to Jorinda, but she felt the same whenever she looked at her. Jorinda had a kindness and compassion in her that few saw, to their loss. The younger woman had a complex nature, but Deineike imagined all great works of art to be the same. She knew little of art, but Jorinda seemed like a picture that needed more work to bring it to its full realisation. The incomplete version of Jorinda contented Deineike. How much more would she enjoy the final work when these trials that beset Jorinda ended, when Jorinda recovered herself and flowered into the magnificent bloom of the summer of her life?

The door opened, and Jorinda stood there, her hair dishevelled. She wore an unfamiliar dress many sizes too large for her and with blood on its left sleeve. Deineike covered her mouth with her hands, and tears flowed down her face like water tipped from a pail. Jorinda gazed at her for long moments, then held out her arms, and Deineike ran to her.

Jorinda walked from the square to the house and struggled to make sense of all that had turned. They had underestimated Styrrach, *she* had underestimated him, and it irritated her. They were unprepared for the possibility he might not come alone. He had brought at least four others, and she blamed herself for the oversight.

After all else, she had learned nothing she did not already know, and that irritated her the most. They already knew much of what Styrrach had said to Raolos. The Guildmeister revealed nothing of any illegality in his operation and little of the Guild's role in the enterprise. The Bailiff had not been compromised beyond doubt; nor had the Portreeves of Ryl, Zhanghar, Alcmouth, or Torric, unless they were guilty of greed. Even that had not been stated, in truth, and they were no further forward. Raolos had been injured, Wilash condemned, and men had died. It had been an absolute disaster.

Jorinda crouched, hidden beneath the desk, by chance, and that slender chance may have saved Raolos. Styrrach said he had been bound for Alcmouth, although his plans might change after all that had turned here. He had become a fugitive; the single ray of light in the whole sorry affair. The Guildmeister had played a part in the attempted murder of a Portreeve and must answer for that, at the least. Doubtless he could continue to run his operation in secret from elsewhere, but he would be sought for his part in the violence that had burst loose in Raolos's office.

Jorinda hoped Wilash heeded her words, had taken Klordia and Deineike away with him. Though it would devastate Jorinda not to see Deineike's blue eyes once she reached the house, Deineike's safety concerned her above all else. She stopped, surprised she had already come to the house. Now she had arrived, she did not wish to enter, did not want to search the enormous house in the vain hope Deineike had stubbornly refused to leave with Wilash and Klordia. It would break her heart if Deineike had left, even as she would be thankful her lover had heeded her wishes and fled to safety.

Heaviness squeezed her heart, as though a hand reached through her chest to taunt her as it crushed the life from her. Jorinda's anger over the death of the mariner in Torric had splintered her and Deineike apart, and now Jorinda cursed herself. If Deineike had indeed fled with Wilash, and Jorinda could not find her again, then Deineike would not hear the most important truth of all—the truth Jorinda only now grasped. She loved Deineike, wanted nothing more in this life than to feel her lover in her arms again, to be showered in the boundless love Deineike continually lavished upon her. How had she allowed a moment of fury to drive a wedge between her and this perfect woman without whose love she doubted she could last until nightfall?

With a heavy sigh, she dragged weary feet up the path past the two guards, who acknowledged her with grim faces, and opened the unlocked door. The instant she stepped inside, she saw Deineike seated in an armed chair, her legs tucked beneath her, alone in the parlour. Deineike's eyes were red-rimmed and full of tears, and she raised her hands to her mouth as she looked up at Jorinda, who gazed on her for some moments. Jorinda's heart threatened to burst from her chest with elation, and her breath became lodged in her throat as emotion constricted it. She raised her arms, and Deineike leapt from the chair to run to her.

They held each other for years without end as the passes of the moon paused. Deineike's sobs spasmed through her body while Jorinda stroked the dark hair that hung down Deineike's back. She pressed Deineike's head against her shoulder, felt her lover's tears soak into the dress.

At last, Deineike pulled her head back and gazed into Jorinda's eyes and whispered. "I feared you dead."

"I am not dead. I would not die unless I could hold you one more time."

Deineike smiled and wiped at her eyes. "I love you."

"As I love you. Without you, I am empty. You draw each breath from my body, and if you cease to do so, I will die." They kissed, and each held the back of the other's head as though to ensure there could be no escape, that the kiss would last for the rest of their lives and beyond, wherever they travelled to afterward.

Deineike pulled away from the kiss, took Jorinda's hand, led her to the couch in the parlour, and pulled her down next to her. She gazed deep into Jorinda's eyes for many moments, then examined Jorinda's body. "Did you change into this dress before you hid under the desk?"

"That I did not. I changed into it afterward. It is loaned and must be returned."

Deineike's brow furrowed. "You must have fought in it. There is blood on it."

Jorinda glanced down. Deineike's hand lay on the sleeve below the bloodstain. "I am injured."

Deineike cried aloud. "It is your blood? You are hurt?"

"It is nothing. A scratch, little more. It is nothing to worry about."

Deineike leapt up. "Remove the dress. I will attend to your wound."

Jorinda smiled up at her. "I see through you, wanton. You care nothing for the wound. You wish me to remove the dress so you may ravish me."

Deineike stared at her open-mouthed, then laughed. "You have unmasked my plan." She smiled, then an earnest look returned to her face. "Be serious, Jorinda. Let me see the injury. We must dress it."

Jorinda sighed, but she wished no disagreement, however small, between them at this moment. "You fuss over nothing." Deineike glared at her, and her resolve faltered. "Very well, fetch water." Jorinda stood and pulled the hem of the dress upward. The dress obscured her vision as it passed her eyes, and as it came over her head, Deineike stared past her, open-mouthed. Jorinda turned her head, and her own mouth fell open in horror. At the bottom of the stairs, Klordia stared at her in shock, and Wilash looked away in embarrassment. Jorinda froze, her arms still in the sleeves of the dress above her head.

Klordia shook herself from her stupor. "We must admire your figure for a second time." Jorinda pulled the dress downward to cover herself as best she could.

Deineike spluttered, no doubt as embarrassed as Jorinda. "We apologise. Jorinda is injured, and I am about to tend to her wound."

Klordia gasped. "You are hurt?"

Jorinda fussed with the dress as she tried to cover her nakedness. "It is nothing. A scratch.

Wilash took Klordia's arm and pulled her back toward the stairs. "We will give you some time."

Jorinda turned to Deineike and mouthed, "They are still here?"

Deineike nodded and turned from her. "I will fetch water and some cloths so we can clean you up. Jorinda sat on the couch and continued to hold the dress about herself for modesty. Deineike returned and knelt to wipe at Jorinda's arm with a cloth dipped into a pitcher of water. "The cut is not deep, thank the fates. I will fashion a bandage, and it should heal well enough, I think, though it will form an unpleasant scar."

"I would bear a thousand scars if I might never leave your side again."

Deineike paused her ministrations and stared into Jorinda's eyes. "You mean this? You have said otherwise in recent days."

Jorinda held her gaze. "Forgive me."

Deineike kissed her on the lips. "There is nothing to forgive. Rather, you must forgive me for all I brought about in Torric."

Jorinda smiled at her. "Come, finish your work on this scratch and let me put this dress on again. Wilash must leave, and there is no time to be wasted." Deineike frowned, but she cleaned the cut and reached down for Jorinda's dagger. She pulled it from Jorinda's boot, cut some strips from the cloths she had brought, then wrapped them around the upper arm as a bandage. Jorinda watched unperturbed, mindful she had never allowed anybody else to touch her fan but felt no such qualms with this weapon. Another conundrum piled on so many others. She dismissed the insignificant thought.

Deineike looked up from her work. "That should hold for now. I will attend to it in more detail when you allow me sufficient time."

Jorinda rose, slipped the dress back over her head, and called for Wilash and Klordia to come to the parlour. When they appeared, Wilash kept his head turned to one side until Klordia laughed and told him Jorinda had her clothes on.

Jorinda met his shy glance. "You saved my life." Jorinda could find no more appropriate words, and she walked over to embrace Wilash. He appeared surprised, but he wrapped his arms around her in turn. They held each other for a time until Jorinda stepped back.

From behind her, Deineike spoke. "There is much to be told, it seems."

Jorinda did not look away from Wilash's face. "That there is. There is no time for the tale, however, since Wilash and Klordia must leave at once. Every moment they spend here is perilous."

Wilash's eyes pleaded for some explanation. "You said as much earlier. I confess, I could not focus and cannot remember the full import of your words."

Jorinda gave as brief an explanation as she could. "Styrrach told Raolos you killed the Portreeve's man in Alcmouth." She held up a hand as Wilash drew a breath to protest. "I know, you did not kill him, but Styrrach claims to have witnesses who will testify you did. As false as the story is, Raolos is trapped. He must arrest you, and if Styrrach's witnesses convince him, as they will, mark my words, he must hang you for the murder of a Portreeve's man. You need to flee without delay."

Tears glistened in Klordia's eyes, and Deineike crossed the parlour to hold her.

Jorinda stared at Wilash. "Where will you go?" He shook his head, and Jorinda pondered the dilemma for a time, then came to a decision. "Dur City. You talked of it a while back, though that seems an eternity ago. There is no Guild there, if indeed the Guild exists any longer after today. You say it is a large place, so the Portreeve will find it hard to discover you there. After all else, Raolos might not pursue you with the same vigour with which he might pursue another who is not the dear friend of someone who saved his life."

A tear fell from Wilash's eye. "He lives? You saved him?"

"That I did. Now you must go. Are you prepared?"

Wilash nodded in confirmation. "That we are." He hesitated. "Come with us."

Jorinda took a breath to reply, then held it within herself, trapped along with the answer she had believed she could provide with ease. She owed him a response, so she relied on the truth, or a part of it, at the least. "You need to leave without delay, as I have explained. I still need answers, and I will not find them in Dur City. We will meet again, but for now, we must part." She did not add anything about her distaste for the prospect of Klordia's company for a heartbeat longer.

At the thought, however, Jorinda turned to Klordia, still wrapped in Deineike's arms. "Klordia, I beg you. We have little fondness for each other, but I beg you to care for this man, for I love him. He will tell you he killed today, but the truth is, he saved my life. I wish I had time to repay the debt I owe him, but I do not have that luxury. Farewell."

Klordia opened her mouth as if to speak, and questions formed in her eyes. Instead, she nodded and kissed Deineike's cheek. "It will be as you ask. Farewell, both of you."

Wilash placed a hand on Jorinda's arm. "What of Deineike? Are you content again, the two of you?"

Deineike answered the question. "That we are. Farewell. Take care of each other. You are special, both of you." Tears streamed from her eyes.

Wilash spat out a curse, and they all stared at him. "Curse it. I must ride that wretched rowboat to Eastort if we make for Dur City."

Deineike smiled, and they laughed even as tears ran down their faces. "That you do. I do not envy you."

Deineike and Jorinda followed them down the path and watched in misery as their friends walked off toward the docks, Deineike's pack slung over Wilash's shoulder. They had all but passed from sight when they both turned and waved, and Deineike and Jorinda waved back, unable to speak through the grief that overwhelmed them.

They stared after Wilash and Klordia for long moments, even though they could no longer see them. Jorinda took Deineike's hand, they turned, then trudged back into the house and sat again on the couch. Jorinda stopped to tell the guards they should leave and attend to the chaos in Raolos's Offices.

Deineike reached out and brushed Jorinda's hair back from her face with a hand. "Your hair is a mess."

Jorinda smiled as she answered. "Forgive me. I had no time to arrange it into a pleasant bun today. Other matters pressed me."

"I would learn of these matters, but first I will bring some water and some bread and cheese. I am hungry, and I am sure you must be also."

As the tension that had gripped her from the moment she pushed Raolos's chair backward faded, Jorinda's thoughts turned to other desires, and an itch between her thighs demanded satisfaction. "That I am, and for more than cheese."

Deineike slapped at her arm in jest. "Time enough for such hungers later."

Deineike rose and went to the scullery. She returned some moments later with a pitcher and two cups, set them on a table, then returned to the scullery and brought out a platter laden with bread and cheese. She sat on the couch and gave Jorinda a nod that indicated the tale should begin.

Jorinda reached for some bread and a piece of cheese. She took a breath, ready to start, then placed the cheese on the bread and swallowed it. Deineike smiled, and the tale began.

TWENTY-ONE

AN INVITATION IS RECEIVED

Delayed by the customary interruptions as Deineike sought to understand all that had turned, the hour grew late while Jorinda related all she could recall. Deineike quizzed her about small details until she seemed satisfied. More time passed as they discussed all the implications of what took place, and darkness closed around the house. At last, Deineike asked the most important question. "Are we safe?"

Jorinda considered her reply. The question seemed simple enough, but it had more than one potential answer. "I believe we are for now. Styrrach appeared surprised to see me, so it seems unlikely he knows we are in Ort. He has fled, I believe, for his life is in danger here now. Nothing of what turned this morning is known to anybody beyond Ort yet, and he will doubtless wish to be far away before such knowledge spreads throughout Dur."

Deineike pondered this. "Does this mean we can stay here, then?"

Jorinda had not considered that possibility. "It might, although much depends on how things turn with Raolos if he survives his injuries. Styrrach said nothing specific to compromise the Bailiff. We believe him involved, but to know and to prove are different things. Styrrach still seeks us and knows we are here." She sighed, and all her frustrations returned, as the morning follows the night. "We should have fled Dur after we left Torric. Instead, we became embroiled in things I now wish we had avoided."

Deineike sat in silence for a time. "That we did, but we cannot alter fates that are already written." She picked up the empty pitcher. "I will fetch more water. Are you still hungry?"

"That I am." Familiar desires stirred within Jorinda again, and she pulled the dress up to her waist. "Let us dine on each other. I need you more than I need food."

Deineike's face flushed as she gazed on Jorinda's exposed sex, and she reached out a hand. "Help me up the stairs then, and you may force yourself upon me."

They enjoyed each other as if for the first time, as though Jorinda discovered Deineike anew after all the tensions between them since the fateful incident aboard The Friendship. They roamed across each other's bodies for hours and tasted familiar and unfamiliar pleasures as they sought new ways to excite each other and took delight in all they found. They sated each other, then refused to stop, and they took each other beyond anything either of them had thought they could tolerate as they strove to bring even more pleasure to one another. To Jorinda, it seemed as though all they had borne since Taro's farm fell away behind them as they sailed together to new horizons through each other's bodies.

They lay spent at last, exhausted and unable to continue. The room filled with the smell of their passion, their sweat soaked the bed sheets, and strands of wet hair stuck to their faces, necks, backs, and each other. Deineike lay on her back with her head on Jorinda's stomach, and as the taller woman kissed the pale skin, small ripples of desire swept through Jorinda that she lacked the strength to act on.

Deineike's whisper disturbed the silence. "Are you asleep?"

Sleepy, Jorinda hoped she could persuade Deineike to abandon whatever she wished to discuss. "That I am."

"What brought you back to me?"

Jorinda did not need time to consider the question. "It is as I said to Wilash. He saved my life. I might have died but for him. The fight..." She strove to find words to explain, words that fluttered beyond her reach, an insect with bright coloured wings, easy to see, impossible to catch. "Brutal is the best word I can find to describe that fight. I am a killer, but I have never been involved in such a struggle, where so many slash at one another, and in the end, many lie dead or injured. The blood, its sight and smell, the cries of injured men, the fear; I have no words to describe the horror of it. It frightened me, Deineike—more than anything ever frightened me in my life." Deineike turned onto her stomach and moved so her chin lay on Jorinda's stomach, but she gazed into her lover's eyes. "Afterward, I stood there among the dead, and I cried. I had become even more frightened at that moment than I had been as the fight unfolded."

"How so?"

Jorinda waved at her in mock irritation at the interruption and Deineike held up a hand in apology. "The last words you hear from me should tell you how much I love you, but I had not said them when you left Raolos's office. I had urged Wilash to flee and take you with him—I might never see you again. Those realisations destroyed me. Everything I desired from life would leave with Wilash, and I might never see you again. Arguments and anger, the rights and wrongs of the things we do, these are nothing next to my love for you. I had to leave that place and hope against hope you waited for me."

Deineike sniffed, and one of her tears dripped onto Jorinda's stomach. "That I did. I would not have left without you, even if Wilash dragged me by the hair. I would sooner cut the hair from my head than leave."

"That pleases me. My life continues to be filled with interruptions." Jorinda laughed, embarrassed by the jest amidst such a solemn conversation. "I have no words for how happy I felt to see you when I opened that door. Happy is not the word, I know that. Ecstatic, elated, these are closer to how I felt. But I have betrayed you and killed again." Jorinda's throat constricted, and she fought back tears. "I am sorry, my love."

"You did not kill, you saved lives. You saved Raolos and the Portreeve's man. Two innocent lives saved, a few worthless lives the cost. A small price to pay, my guess. You told Wilash he had not killed, that he saved you, yet you will not allow yourself that same pardon. You must allow it Jorinda. I cannot stand to see you spend your life so angry at yourself."

Jorinda gritted her teeth as shame and guilt flooded her veins in place of her blood. "Death stalks me and seeks any opportunity it can find to use me as its instrument. That is why I am angry."

"We will hold it back from you together. We can do it if you will it. You must wish it though; I cannot force you to this."

They lay silent for a time while Deineike watched Jorinda and kissed her stomach from time to time as if some thought passed through her mind until Jorinda found words for a reply. "I wish it, Deineike. I wish to live a normal life."

Deineike grimaced. "I am not sure I know what 'normal' is."

Jorinda gave a small laugh. "Neither do I, but I wish it. I wish for the nightmares to end."

"Let that be our aim then. We must drive the nightmares from you."

They said nothing more, and Deineike's eyes closed as her breaths took on the rhythmic cadence of sleep. Weariness washed over Jorinda. There had been much frenetic activity and a great amount of fear, and it left her exhausted. She closed her eyes, and sleep claimed her within moments.

Despite Deineike's words, they failed to drive the nightmares away, for that night, at the least. The fight played itself out again, and in her dreams, Wilash stood before her after he had killed the Guild member. A huge sword swept his head from his shoulders. His decapitated body fell forward, and Deineike stood there, the sword in her hand. Deineike's voice drew her attention away from Wilash's body. "You killed my mother."

Jorinda hurried to defend herself. "Not I. Another killed her, one who resembles me." The sword swung and cleaved her hands from her arms before Deineike thrust it into her and drove it through her heart.

Arella appeared behind Deineike. "I killed your mother." Contempt and hatred dripped from her voice, and she slit Deineike's throat. Arella glanced between Deineike and Jorinda as both died, and she repeated the same three words. "I love you."

The morning brought relief as a small movement from Deineike woke Jorinda. "I am sorry, my love. I did not mean to wake you." The corners of Deineike's mouth turned down, a gesture of apology.

"I am relieved you did." Jorinda explained the nightmare and saw in Deineike's eyes the same pain she felt within herself.

"We will defeat them. Together, we will stop them and banish them from your sleep." Deineike kissed Jorinda. "Let us walk to the docks this morning."

Jorinda pursed her lips, doubtful. "That is a lengthy walk. I fear you will not cope well with it."

"A rest restores my stamina. We will break the journey into

smaller portions. Let our first stop be the pastry shop. I crave cake." Deineike smiled.

Jorinda gave her a gentle, playful shove. "Let us go then. This may take the entire day unless you walk faster today than I have seen for some time."

They rose and washed their faces. As Deineike rubbed the white paste around her mouth to sweeten her breath, she paused. "What do you imagine this paste to be made from?" She sprayed drops of the paste around with each word.

Jorinda reached for a cloth so she could wipe up the paste Deineike splashed onto the floor. "Sugar and little else, if its sweetness is any guide."

"There is more than mere sugar. Something binds it together." Deineike picked up the inexpensive cloth shop owners wrapped the paste in and turned it over in her hands. "I would be interested to know."

"I care not. It is cheap enough and I imagine it is little more than a device our vanity bids us use." The mundane subject bored Jorinda already.

Deineike had a twinkle in her eye. "You are right. You can be vain at times."

Jorinda sneered at her. "I see somebody who will arrive at the cake shop long after me to find I have bought and consumed all her favourites."

Deineike spat the last of the paste from her mouth into the bowl on the vanity stand. "You are cruel. Never again will I arouse you in a tavern."

Jorinda slid a hand inside her trousers. "I can arouse myself."

Deineike pushed her toward the bed, her eyes narrow, a pout on her lips. "Let us walk to the docks tomorrow."

An hour or more later, they rose and walked to the cake shop, bought some of their favourite pastries, and ate them seated on the same wall they had sat upon on previous occasions.

They visited the tavern on the journey home as they had done twice before. Syme seemed delighted to see them again and ushered them to a more private table at the rear of the tavernroom. "You will find this table more peaceful. I have received a cask of wine and wish you to sample it for me before I commit to it. Will you aid me?"

Jorinda smiled and nodded. "We would be delighted to." He scurried off.

Deineike leaned in close and whispered. "This table is more private. I might have been wrong earlier when I said I would not arouse you in a tavern."

The mere suggestion of a repeat of the excitement they had enjoyed the first time they visited the tavern stirred Jorinda's desire. "That you were, for you have already done so."

Deineike breathed into Jorinda's ear, and her hot breath flowed into Jorinda's stomach, where it swirled around and tied her innards in knots. "We seem to have more desire for one another than before."

Jorinda feared to trust her voice to speak. "That we do. It could be a temporary thing, some result of the difficulties aboard The Friendship." Deineike nodded, distracted, and placed a hand on Jorinda's thigh beneath the table.

Syme returned with two goblets of a blush red wine with a delightful, light aroma. It flowed over Jorinda's tongue, and she reasoned she could drink more of it than she ought with little diffi-culty. The innkeep sat opposite them and watched them drink. When they had each taken two mouthfuls, his impatience got the better of him. "Is it acceptable?"

Deineike licked her lips as she answered. "It is a better wine than the other you have served us, I think. I am no expert, but I like this more than the other."

He clapped his hands together. "Excellent. I shall sell this one in the future then. My favourite customers recommend it."

Jorinda felt the familiar warmth in her face. "You flatter us. We have only visited three times and will soon leave Ort."

Syme refused to be downhearted by the news. The smile did not leave his face. "Nonetheless, you brighten my tavernroom when you come in. My thanks for the joy you bring to my day. These louts are pleasant enough, but you are a delight." He left them, and they sipped at the wine.

Jorinda stared after Syme as he returned to the counter. "An unusual conversation."

"He is a nice man." Deineike slid her hand along Jorinda's thigh.

"'Nice' is a peculiar word. It is a compliment, yet it says little enough, I feel."

Deineike unbuttoned Jorinda's trousers beneath the table. "You think too much on such things."

Desire overwhelmed Jorinda, and she wanted to think of only one thing. "Then distract me, by all the fates."

Darkness had all but driven away the remnants of the daylight by the time they returned to the house, and they spent some time in the parlour. Jorinda lay on her back on the couch, her head in Deineike's lap, and Deineike ran her hands through Jorinda's hair as they talked of everything and nothing. They wondered how Wilash and Klordia had fared on the small rowboat and whether they were now on their way to Dur City. They discussed Raolos and hoped he would recover well from his injuries. Jorinda suggested they should visit the Portreeve's Offices in the morning and enquire after him. They climbed the stairs to the bedroom as the night wore on and made love again before they drifted off to sleep.

No nightmares assailed Jorinda that night, and she awoke more refreshed than normal. Deineike slept on, so Jorinda lay in the bed and contemplated the nightmares and how tired she often felt when she woke, which she decided must be related. Deineike woke, and they rose from the bed, dressed, and wandered down the stairs. Heartbeats after they reached the parlour, somebody knocked at the door. Jorinda peered from the window but could not see the person at the door, so she urged Deineike to stay out of sight.

When she opened the door, Ibie stood there, a glum expression on his face. Jorinda feared he carried bad news about Raolos, and she pulled the door open and invited him in. He would not enter but stood on the doorstep in apparent discomfort.

He coughed, and explained what brought him to the house. "I seek your companion, Wilash."

Jorinda kept her voice level. She had expected such a visit, in truth. "As do I, for I have not seen him since the trouble in Raolos's office."

"He has left then?"

"That he has, and his belongings with him." She opened the door a little further. "Would you like to check the house? I am his friend, and I would not be insulted if you thought I deceived you to protect him."

He shook his head and heaved a dramatic sigh, a twinkle in his eyes. "It is as Raolos feared. The fugitive has flown, and we have no clue as to where we might find him. I fear he may never be brought to justice."

Jorinda stifled a laugh as she replied. "A travesty." She paused. "Tell me, how is Raolos?"

Ibie stiffened, all business again. "On that matter, I have a further obligation. Raolos hopes you and Deineike will join him and his wife at his home for dinner tomorrow night. He has not returned to his office, which is in disarray as it is repaired and cleaned. Other than some pain, he is in good health, despite the serious wound he received."

An invitation to a Portreeve's own home must be a rare honour, one few would receive, even if they paid vast levies. It embarrassed and flattered Jorinda, and she stood with her head bowed, unsure how to respond to such a grand honour.

Deineike's reply startled Jorinda. "We would be delighted to attend."

Ibie battled to keep a smile at bay. "Excellent. We shall send a cart for you tomorrow as the sun reaches the three-quarter mark." He nodded, more a respectful acknowledgement than a confirmation.

Jorinda returned the nod. "We look forward to it."

Ibie half-turned, then seemed to have a further thought, turned to face them again, and continued, quieter. "One of my closest friends died in the fight at the Offices. Another suffered serious injuries but says you saved both him and Raolos. I have no words to say more than this. My thanks."

Jorinda glanced away for a heartbeat to hide her discomfort at his gratitude. "I am sorry for the loss of your friend. I wish I could have helped him also, and the other who fell. As for your thanks, they are unnecessary, but I appreciate them nonetheless."

He flashed a grateful smile and bade them good day. They closed the door and Jorinda turned to Deineike in frustration. "I told you to stay out of sight."

"That you did. You did not tell me to stay out of earshot, however."

Jorinda let out an exasperated sigh. "That I did not."

Deineike slid her arms around Jorinda's waist. "You see? You saved two lives. No guilt should attach to you over the death of this Porl. He brought his death on himself when he threw in his lot with the Guild and tried to kill Raolos."

Jorinda smiled at her, but the conflict between her guilt and Deineike's explanations discomforted her and required a change of subject. "Since we no longer need to visit the Portreeve's Offices, let us take that walk to the docks."

It took them the remainder of the morning to reach the docks, the journey broken by the now customary stop at the cake shop. The fresh air at the docks refreshed them as a breeze blew in from the river, and Jorinda sucked down deep breaths that served, for now, to clean the taint of death from her body. They found a stall that sold hot meats stacked on a piece of bread, and they each ate one as they wandered the length of the docks. Jorinda wondered if the meal owed anything to the way Taro ate cheese, or the other way around.

Ort might be smaller than Zhanghar or Alcmouth, but many of the ships that plied the river north or south seemed to stop there to re-provision or offload their goods. The docks were busier than Zhanghar's, almost as busy as Alcmouth. Most of the ships came from Dur, but two had travelled from other lands. They again wondered whether they bore goods onward to Zhanghar as part of Styrrach's enterprise.

Deineike pouted and wrinkled her forehead. "What happens to the goods those ships bring here?"

"They are sold to merchants, my guess."

"I realise that, but from what you said, they are sold onward here for less than in the cities Styrrach controls."

Jorinda could not see whatever connection Deineike had made. "That they are. They are sold cheaper than in those cities, which suggests—"

"A pair of trousers here would be less expensive than the same trousers in Zhanghar."

Deineike had finished the sentence for her, and Jorinda glowered at her for yet another interruption. The older woman had the right of it, nonetheless. "I imagine Styrrach wishes to redress that imbalance, which is why he attempted to persuade Raolos to join him. He wants to drive up prices here and scrape off his share of the coin."

Deineike looked thoughtful. "Everything that arrives in Dur is sold on from the tally houses at an inflated price and generates enormous profits. Those profits are sent onward as so-called levies to the Bailiff, and most of that coin is returned to Styrrach. He must be rich indeed."

Jorinda shook her head in frustration. "Meanwhile, the citizens of Dur pay more than they should for all they buy. It is disgraceful."

"That it is. Is it illegal though?" They looked at one another as if they sought an answer in the other's eyes.

Jorinda knew nothing of such financial matters, but she did know about murder, about death. She replied through clenched teeth. "That it is not. To kill someone who becomes an impediment is, however."

"That it is, and I am impressed."

Confused, Jorinda tilted her head to one side. "By?"

"Your use of 'impediment.' That is a big word for you."

Jorinda gave her hair a gentle tug. "I know many big words. I am not as stupid as you look."

Deineike laughed at the jest. "That you are not." She laid her head on Jorinda's shoulder.

Jorinda ducked away from her. "Not in public." The old anxiety returned in a heartbeat. Frustration flashed in Deineike's eyes, but she nodded, and they walked on.

They stopped at Syme's tavern for some wine on the way home. By the time they returned to the house, darkness had descended over Ort, and the exertions of the day had exhausted Deineike. She had done well, but for the first night since they arrived at the house, they did not make love. Sleep came to them both in moments.

TWENTY-TWO
A DINNER DATE

THE NEXT DAY PASSED WITHOUT EVENT. THEY FILLED THE TUB IN THE
privy with water heated on the fire in the room and bathed themselves. As the sun moved toward the three-quarter point of its
journey across the sky, they pulled on the dresses Jorinda had made
for them. Deineike thought hers might be a little flirtatious for such
a sombre occasion. Jorinda agreed but had no time to make another,
so she fashioned a shawl with some leftover materials. Deineike
draped it across her shoulders over the low neckline of the dress.
When Jorinda said she felt some embarrassment to wear the same
dresses they had worn when they first met Raolos, Deineike told
her not to dwell on the matter.

Jorinda's nerves at the importance of the event shook her body,
her arms, her hands, and by the time the same cart they had ridden
in three days earlier arrived, her mouth had become drier than

sand. The dresses made it difficult to climb into the cart with their modesty intact, but once seated the cart did not take long to reach Raolos's house. He lived in the rich quarter behind the square, no more than four streets away from their house.

Raolos lived in a house far larger and more grandiose than the one he had loaned to them. It stood some way back from the street, surrounded by an iron fence and reached by a wide path that led up to the front door, with a large circle in front of the house where carriages could turn. Small stones formed the path, and the colourful gardens had been tended with care. So many windows gazed out from the front of the three-storey house, Jorinda thought the house must have a room for every day of the year.

A servant welcomed them at the door and offered to take Deineike's shawl, but she chose to retain it. The servant showed them into a parlour filled with impeccable velvet chairs and couches positioned among Ortwood occasional tables and side-boards. Raolos possessed extraordinary wealth, it seemed. Silver candlesticks stood on every flat surface, and candles burned in them. The candles' flames sputtered in draughts as people passed or doors opened and closed, and they cast shadows that danced on the walls as though the furniture in the room had become intoxi-cated. The servant invited them to sit and said Raolos would be down to greet them before long. He asked if they would care for a drink while they waited, but they declined.

They did not have to wait long before Raolos entered the parlour. A cloth wrapped around his neck supported his right arm, but apart from that, he wore no visible sign of his injury other than a bulge beneath his tunic where his arm had been bandaged.

If he noticed they wore the same dresses, he did not mention it. He kissed Deineike on the cheek and pulled Jorinda into a one-handed embrace. She took great care not to touch his injured arm in the embrace, anxious not to cause any discomfort, and the sight of him in such good health pleased her. She smiled at him as he released her. "It is good to see you are well."

"That is because of you, in truth. My thanks." Jorinda blushed and looked down at her feet. "I thought it madness when you hid beneath my desk. I now thank the fates you did, or I might be dead."

Deineike pointed to his arm. "How is your wound?"

He grimaced. "Painful, I cannot deny it. I am not yet ready to return to work. I am required to drink some herb that befuddles me but relieves the pain. I wished to invite you here as soon as I could, however, as I owe Jorinda a great debt."

A tall, slender woman entered the room. She wore her shoulder-length light brown hair shaped around her face in a manner that accentuated her features: high cheek bones, full lips, and hazel eyes. She looked older than either Jorinda or Deineike and wore a simple red dress of good quality making and with little adornment. The quality of the making surprised Jorinda as the opulence of the house suggested the woman might have worn superior making.

Raolos smiled and gestured toward the older woman. "My wife, Pettra."

Pettra drew Jorinda into a warm embrace and kissed her cheek. "Welcome to our home. My thanks seem insufficient for all you have done, but you have them nonetheless." The attention embarrassed Jorinda, and she felt uncomfortable in the close embrace of a stranger. Pettra wore a powerful, pleasant scent that filled Jorinda's nostrils.

Deineike laughed. "Forgive Jorinda. She does not receive compliments well. They mortify her."

Pettra released Jorinda. "I am sorry. I did not realise. I am more grateful than I have words for, regardless. Were it not for your actions, I would be a widow now, and Raopul fatherless."

Jorinda gave Deineike a grateful smile. Her intervention had spared further embarrassment. Jorinda, anxious to deflect the conversation elsewhere, seized the opportunity to change the subject. "Raopul is your son?"

Raolos's face shone with pride as he answered. "That he is. He will join us at dinner. There is a matter I must discuss before we dine, though it pains me to bring it up. Wilash." Raolos did not elaborate.

Jorinda pondered what to say and how far to press the gratitude they had both shown to her so far. "He fled." She spoke the truth, no lie in her explanation that might catch her out.

Raolos glanced down, as though worried his eyes might betray him if his words disguised his true feelings. "Is it true? Did he slay a Portreeve's man in Alcmouth?"

Jorinda found herself caught between doubt and uncertainty, and the old Dur phrase had never seemed truer than at that moment. If she confirmed the tale, she condemned Wilash, who had saved her life. If she denied it, further investigation might implicate her. She glanced at Deineike in search of inspiration, but a grimace seemed to indicate Deineike had no more idea how to respond than Jorinda.

Jorinda looked down. The silence grew awkward, and Raolos did not seem ready to sweep the conversation in another direction to spare her. She came to a decision, took a deep breath, and looked up into Raolos's eyes. "He did not kill the Portreeve's man, though he did strike him. Another delivered the fatal blow. The incident in Alcmouth came as part of the same show you saw in your own office, acted out in another city." She hoped he would abandon the thread since she had saved his life in his office.

Pettra stared at her feet, fingers intertwined before her as though she wished herself anywhere but here. Deineike cast a worried glance at Jorinda. Raolos took some time to consider the answer, it seemed, then gave a curt nod of his head. "Wilash has flown. Styrrach's word is not to be trusted, and without Wilash to question, we are unable to pursue the matter further. Dinner is ready, and a goblet of wine might relax this mood somewhat." He smiled at a relieved Jorinda and extended his left arm toward her, somewhat bent.

Jorinda did not recognise the gesture and reasoned she should take his hand, but when she did so, Deineike tugged at her arm. Jorinda released Raolos's hand, and Deineike guided Jorinda's arm so her hand passed inside the crook of his elbow, then patted her hand down onto his arm before she apologised on Jorinda's behalf. "Forgive her. She is from Ryl." They all laughed as Deineike's jest brushed away the tension of Raolos's questions about Wilash.

Raolos shook her hand from his arm, then gripped it with his own, their fingers intertwined. "I think I prefer the Ryl custom." He smiled, and Deineike looked away and raised a hand to her eye, but the exchange left Jorinda baffled.

Raolos turned and led Jorinda to a door. When she looked back, Deineike and Pettra followed, Deineike's arm looped through Pettra's in the same way she had earlier guided Jorinda's own. Jorinda thought she now understood the gesture, but high society formalities were as strange as any she had encountered.

Raolos led them through into another large room occupied by a stained Ortwood table that could seat twelve people with ease. Jorinda had never seen such a big table, even in taverns. The legs had elaborate patterns carved into them, and different coloured woods in a floral pattern were inlaid into the outer edges of the table's surface. Five places were set, one at one end of the table and two on either side. So much cutlery had been set at each place, Jorinda imagined the neighbours must all have lent the Portreeve theirs for the evening.

A young boy already sat at the table in a high-backed chair, and he turned to watch them as Raolos guided Jorinda to the end of the table and held her chair while she sat. The boy stood as they approached, but he did not speak. Jorinda guessed he was around nine years. Pettra showed Deineike to the seat to Jorinda's right, then Raolos held out the chair next to Deineike for Pettra. He seated himself last, and a servant held out his chair until he had sat. The boy sat again once all the adults had taken their seats.

Raolos waved his arm toward the boy. "Jorinda, Deineike, may I introduce my son, Raopul?" As Raolos spoke, the boy bowed his head to each of them.

Jorinda did not know the polite way to respond. "I am pleased to meet you."

In a high, bright, polite voice, the boy replied. "And I you." He turned to his father. "Do you not sit at the head of the table tonight, Pada?" He had whispered the question so loud, they could have heard him in the parlour.

Raolos laughed. "That I do not, Raopul. Tonight, our honoured guest sits at the head of the table."

Raopul turned his gaze to Jorinda. "Ah. Jorinda, the hero of Ort." Heat burned in Jorinda's face as she blushed bright red, and she fought the impulse to look down in embarrassment. "You saved Pada."

The strange word confused Jorinda, and since Deineike did not rush to help her, she had no choice but to seek clarification. "Pada?"

Pettra laughed and Raolos patted his son's hand as he answered. "From his earliest years, he found it difficult to say 'Father'. 'Pada' became the best he could manage. The familiar name has stuck." Raolos's explanation brought forth a warm smile, and he ruffled the boy's hair, tender and affectionate.

Jorinda had never experienced the warm, tender familiarity that seemed to exist between the boy and his father. Her own parents had been business-like with her and almost never touched or held her, even if she hurt herself as a child. Her mother had not even explained the moon cycle to her.

Servants brought bowls of broth and placed them before each diner. The broth smelled delicious, spicy and muttony. Jorinda gazed in despair on the vast array of cutlery before her and wondered which to use.

Raopul came to her rescue. "Use them from the outside inward." Jorinda cursed her lack of knowledge on these etiquettes, and that it had been so transparent. She flashed Raopul a smile, grateful for his help, and picked up the spoon to the extreme right of the crowd of silverware that wandered away from the plate. A fork lay to the left and she wondered if she should use that also, but she had never eaten broth with a fork, so she rolled the dice. None of the others used a fork to consume the broth, and she congratulated herself on a successful roll.

The food, although delicious, proved richer than Jorinda's tastes could appreciate. All Raolos's food, other than the broth, arrived already cut into smaller pieces, and he wielded a fork or spoon with his left hand, clumsy and uncomfortable, as he ate his way through the various courses. The conversation remained light and cordial. Raolos and his family spoke to one other in a relaxed, easy manner in stark contrast to Jorinda's own home life, and she guessed it must have also been strange for Deineike, who had never known her father, and whose mother had been torn from her so early in her life.

Deineike resisted all attempts by the servants to take her shawl and kept it wrapped tight about her shoulders. She seemed embarrassed to reveal her cleavage in front of the young boy. Jorinda thought he might be too young to enjoy the delights of Deineike's small, sensitive breasts. She felt guilty as soon as the thought occurred to her, and a familiar tingle stirred within her.

Pettra gazed at Jorinda often, who guessed she fought the desire to gush her gratitude that Jorinda had saved Raolos's life. Jorinda had no desire to suffer further praise and its inevitable embarrassment, but after a time, Pettra complimented them on their dresses and asked if Jorinda had made them. Jorinda's consternation grew as Pettra heaped praise on her making skills, and Deineike gave a small, wicked grin that convinced Jorinda she could expect no rescue this time.

Pettra said she would love to wear a dress of Jorinda's making. Jorinda, desperate to end the uncomfortable conversation, offered to make a dress for her but cursed herself as soon as the words left her mouth. These people must have garment makers at their beck and call of such quality, her own work would be dowdy in comparison, and she had placed Raolos's wife in a difficult position with the offer. To her surprise, Pettra lowered her fork to her plate and looked at her, surprise on her face. "You would do that for me?"

For a moment, Jorinda wondered whether Pettra toyed with her. In truth, she thought it unlikely, given the warmth of their reception all night. "It would be an honour."

Pettra looked to Raolos, who gave a small nod. "The honour would be mine, to wear such making." Pettra turned toward Jorinda again. "My thanks. I will pay you for your work, of course"

Jorinda did not make an immediate reply. Why were these people so different from the only other Portreeve and his wife she had ever met? "That will not be necessary unless you wish some precious stone as embellishment that is beyond our coin, in which case some assistance with the cost would be appreciated."

Pettra shook her head. "I will pay you for your work. Your making will be more precious to me than any stone that might be attached to the dress."

Jorinda could stand no more, and she looked down into her lap.

Raolos chuckled. "Pettra, you have complimented our guest beyond her comfort, even though Deineike has warned you against this."

Pettra gushed a profuse apology, while Deineike stared into her food and would not meet Jorinda's eyes as she fought back laughter. Jorinda longed to pull her lover's long dark hair, although such behaviour would be viewed in a dim light at such a high table. She agreed a time for an appointment two days hence to measure Pettra and discuss her requirements.

The meal had almost drawn to close when Raopul frowned as he gave Deineike an earnest stare and asked, "Where are your husbands?"

Without hesitation, Pettra snapped at the boy. "Raopul. That is an impertinent question. Apologise this instant." His mother's stern tone brought a blush to the boy's cheeks, and he mumbled an apology.

Jorinda imagined the reprimand embarrassed Raopul, but her own discomfort must exceed his. The question landed in the centre of all the customs and traditions of Dur. In the circles in which his parents moved, it seemed unlikely any woman would ever go to dinner without her husband. A woman might not be invited to dinner in truth, other than as an attachment to her husband.

Raolos spoke in a softer tone than his wife. "Jorinda and Deineike are married to each other." His explanation caught Jorinda unawares. She could scarce believe a father in Dur would make such a bold statement.

The boy seemed to digest this information. "Is that allowed?"

Raolos sighed. "That it is not, in truth. Our society is not yet ready for this. They are, nonetheless. They love one another as your mother and I love each other." Pettra looked down at her lap as her husband spoke.

The boy nodded as though his child's simple mind found no fault with his father's explanation. "Then I imagine it is acceptable, as long as they are in love."

Deineike looked at Jorinda and not the boy as she joined the discussion. "Your parents must love each other a great deal, if they love as much as Jorinda and I love one another." Jorinda could not imagine any parents would permit their son to hear such words, but Raolos and Pettra appeared unconcerned. She did not know how her own parents had reacted to the letter she had sent to tell them she loved Arella, for the letter had never been answered.

Raopul turned to Jorinda. "I imagine when you are as great a hero as Jorinda, you may love whom you please." The boy showed no sign of mockery.

Though she felt herself blush again, Jorinda took Deineike's hand as she replied. "I do not love whom I please, Raopul. I love whom the fates have written for me to love. I did not find love; love found me. I had the good fortune to meet Deineike, and I found the love of my life." Deineike smiled back at her.

Raopul leaned forward, excited. "How did you meet her, Deineike? Did she save you also?"

"That she did." Deineike smiled into Jorinda's eyes. "She saved my life and has done so more than once since."

Raopul's face lit up. "That sounds really exciting. Tell me more, please."

A laugh in his voice, Raolos cut short his son's enthusiastic request for more stories. "I think it is time for some study, then bed for you, young man. I must talk with Jorinda and Deineike."

The excitement drained from the lad's eyes. "Pada business?"

"Pada business." Raolos laughed as Pettra stood and held out a hand to her son.

Raopul turned to Jorinda and Deineike. "Will you excuse me? I must bid you good night. It has been such a pleasure to meet you both."

"And we you." Jorinda cursed to herself that her tongue had betrayed her with such a clumsy response. The boy seemed not to notice, trotted round the table to take his mother's hand, and they left the room.

Deineike smiled across the table at Raolos. "Such a sweet boy. So polite."

"He is precocious, and of an age where all is a curiosity to him. My thanks for your kindness to him."

Deineike waved a hand toward Raolos. "Think nothing of it."

Raolos gestured toward the parlour. "Would you like to freshen up, then join us in the parlour for another goblet of wine?"

The wines had been extraordinary throughout the meal, and Jorinda had become quite light-headed already. "We would like to freshen up, though I do not think I want any more wine." She did not know for certain what "freshen up" meant, but it seemed to be expected of them.

Raolos beckoned to a servant who stood nearby and asked him to take the two women to the vanity room. The servant bowed to them and swept an arm before him in a clear indication they should precede him to a door to one side of the room. He showed them into a small room with a vanity bowl, soaps, cloths, and breath paste. A privy stood in another small room off the first.

As soon as the servant closed the door, Deineike whispered, "This house is enormous."

"That it is, but what is 'freshen up?'"

"I know not. I imagine we must freshen our breaths and wash our faces." Deineike giggled.

Jorinda also giggled. "Has the wine made you light-headed?"

"Has it made you amorous?" Deineike slid provocative arms around Jorinda's waist.

Jorinda tried to pull the arms from her waist. "Deineike, not here, please."

"You would deny me the chance to pleasure a hero?" Deineike kissed Jorinda's lips twice, her cheeks flushed.

Jorinda pushed her away. "You can pleasure me when we return home. You cannot do so here, or I shall die of shame."

"A hero and a killjoy." Deineike giggled again. "Quite the mystery, my Jorinda."

They splashed some water on their faces and sweetened their

breath. When they opened the door, the servant still stood there. Jorinda grimaced at Deineike, relieved they had not made love in the small room while the man stood there. They had not realised he waited for them.

The servant led them back to the parlour. Raolos and Pettra already sat on a couch, a goblet before each of them on a low table, and two empty goblets stood on another table before another couch perpendicular to theirs. As they sat, Jorinda declined more wine, though Deineike allowed her goblet to be filled.

Once the servant moved off, Raolos spoke. "My thanks that you came tonight. Your company has been delightful."

Jorinda gazed around the room, awestruck by its opulence. "It has been our pleasure. You have a beautiful home."

He inclined his head toward her. "My thanks. I will come straight to the point. I am indebted to you, a debt unlike any I have ever encountered, for mere coin will not settle it. I am also frustrated our encounter with Styrrach went so awry, and I hold myself accountable. We learned little enough, and there is still much work to be done to unravel this enterprise."

Jorinda tried to reassure him. "I know Styrrach, and you should not blame yourself for all that turned. He is a violent, repulsive man." She said nothing about Raolos's impatient mention of the "shrouding" as the cause of the violence.

Raolos gave a gracious nod. "The Bailiff seems to be implicated in the activities of this Guild, but I have no proof and no idea how I may obtain any. He schemes to replace me as Portreeve, and the deaths of my men, the injuries to many of us; all will be for naught if Styrrach's enterprise continues and expands into Ort. I am determined to stop it. This Guild must be destroyed. No more of Dur's citizens must die at their hands, and we must discover what lies behind their violence."

Jorinda had not expected the conversation to take this turn and had no answer prepared. "I am a fugitive from the Guild. Deineike also, for she travels with me. They are formidable, and I must protect Deineike from them."

He grunted as if in agreement with Jorinda's words. "I must be blunt. I need your help in their downfall. You know their ways, and unless I miss my guess, Deineike has a grasp of the financial aspects."

Jorinda looked down and wrung her hands in her lap. "I know their ways, but I remind you they are bent on my ruin."

Raolos seemed to ignore Jorinda's concerns. "You said you enjoy Ort. Stay a while."

Deineike and Pettra had said nothing, and they both looked from Jorinda to Raolos and back as each of them spoke. Jorinda sighed. "Deineike and I are not safe here. Styrrach knows we are in Ort—or I am here, at the least. He must guess Deineike still travels with me. The risks…" She fell silent.

Pettra leaned forward, anxiety in her eyes and a plea in her voice. "Jorinda, you saved my husband, and he has already admitted we cannot repay that debt. He is determined to pursue this, although I have urged him not to pick at it. I am worried, but I would worry less if you helped him."

Pettra fixed her gaze on Jorinda's eyes, and Jorinda could not decide why she felt so uncomfortable beneath the stare. She threw her hands up in despair. "How can I help him? I am a fugitive. I flee from more than the Guild, and I cannot tell you the full truth, or he would drag me from your house and hang me from the nearest tree."

Pettra seemed taken aback and sat back in the couch. Raolos placed a hand on his wife's lap as he replied. "Jorinda, we must speak of these things, and must do so in a way that does not compel me to do what you suggested. I realise it will be difficult for you. In truth, I did not follow what turned in my office after my injury, but I know you killed the monster who attacked me. Defence of a Portreeve whose life is threatened is no crime, but I doubt Pettra or Deineike could have taken him down. I conclude you have some…experience in these matters." He hesitated, and anxiety clouded his features. "I prefer not to understand it, in truth."

Jorinda laughed to herself at the irony. Raolos tip-toed around the issue with such care while he asked for her help. Other than to himself, he could not admit he might need her to kill on his behalf if necessary. The game seemed pointless, but she went along with it. "What words amount to a confession? If I say I have stolen your candle, that is a confession. If I say I have stolen but say naught of what, is that also a confession? Could I be prosecuted for this confession?"

He pondered the question, wrinkles on his brow, his mouth askew. "I would say not. It is not a crime to be a thief—it is only a crime if you steal. But beware; murder is a more serious crime, and I am unsure how I might react to any confession of that wrongdoing."

Jorinda stared at him and wished he would understand as she strove to find the correct words to use. She did not want to hang herself, but she respected Raolos and wanted to be as honest as she dared. "You know I am a killer, for you know I killed Porl after he attacked you. I am a killer, and I am not fit company for your wife, your son, or you. Death walks with me."

Deineike slipped an arm around her waist and laid her head on her shoulder. Pettra turned pale and stared into her wine. She could not have known everything Jorinda intimated.

Raolos's eyes burned into Jorinda's. "I hear your words. You chose them well. I have heard no confession of any crime."

The dance threatened to tie Jorinda in knots. One word out of place, and Raolos might hang her. She could not risk any further involvement if she intended to keep her past from Raolos's ears. "If I told my tale in full, you might do so. I cannot help you."

He drew in a sharp breath. "Styrrach stuck down and killed one of my men in the outer office as he fled, and he is now wanted for murder. If I can find him, I might extract information from him that will allow me to bring down those who worked with him; other Portreeves, the Guild, and the Bailiff, if I can plead a strong enough case to the Duke. I cannot do this alone. That is why I ask you for help."

"Styrrach struck down a part of my life that cannot be..." Jorinda paused as she felt her temper boil, and Raolos did not deserve her ire. "I am sorry for your men's deaths. Good men's lives have been wasted, and our hearts break for their loved ones, but I see no way to help you unless I place Deineike in grave danger. Besides, I know Styrrach. He would rather die than reveal all that lies behind his organisation. He would see any confession as weakness, and he tolerates that even less in himself than in others."

Raolos seemed to change the direction of his plea for help. "If I could obtain an audience with the Duke, would you be prepared to accompany me and tell him all you know of this enterprise?"

Jorinda sighed. She admired his persistence, but he had not heard her. "Raolos, do you ask me to stand before the highest authority in Dur and tell him I once belonged to an organisation that attempted to kill the Portreeve of Ort? My dinner tonight must have been the last meal of the condemned. To do such a thing would be madness."

He nodded. "I see this. What if I can arrange amnesty for any transgressions from your past in exchange for your assistance?"

Jorinda gave a sardonic laugh. "That might satisfy the Duke. I doubt it will impress the Guild. If Styrrach appeared before us now, my heart would be the first his dagger would seek. Your amnesty will count for little with them."

Pettra spoke again, the first time for some while. "How did you incur his hatred?"

Jorinda sneered. "I do not know, in truth. He betrayed me to the

Portreeve of Zhanghar, whose men came to hang me. Why Styrrach did this is unclear to me. It is some part of the 'shroud' I mentioned to your husband. The Guild betrays its own members to the Portreeve, but we do not yet know why."

Pettra shook her head, and Jorinda understood her confusion, for it made no sense even to her. They had reached an impasse, it seemed. The pleasantries of the early evening had been left behind, and this awkward disagreement lay between them.

Deineike's voice cut through the ominous silence. "Raolos, will you give us a day or two to think on this?" Jorinda could not understand why Deineike had decided to become involved and gave her a fierce stare. "We need time to consider whether there is a course of action that serves us all. The wine clouds our judgement tonight; we are unused to such fine food and drink. Jorinda wishes Styrrach brought to justice. She and I have a common interest in the reasons for her betrayal, for it cost us both dear."

He nodded. "That is reasonable. I cannot return to work for some days yet, I am sure, and I cannot act until I am further along the road to recovery. I long to bring him to justice, since my men gave their lives for his greed. I am sorry I pressed you so hard. You may stay in the house for as long as you need. Do you have coin?"

Deineike nodded confirmation. "We have some."

Raolos did not hesitate. "We will pay you some coin for your services in my office."

"We cannot accept it." Jorinda could never again take coin for her evil work, no matter how well-intentioned Raolos's suggestion had been. She did not dare to cross that line. "I served my own cause, not yours. I cannot accept coin for that."

Pettra had another thought. "For the dress, then. Can you accept coin for its creation?"

Jorinda sighed. She and Deineike had precious little coin, and if they needed to leave Ort for somewhere else, they would have little chance to earn any. There seemed no other way to come by any in the short term, but she would rather not take coin from them out of sympathy. Her pride railed against it. Her making, nonetheless, deserved a good price.

She decided to accept the offer, though it might trap her. "That would be acceptable."

Raolos exhaled as though her answer had pulled him back from the edge of some escarpment he had almost fallen over, and Pettra continued. "We will arrange for some to be brought to you in the morning. We keep little here."

Jorinda gave her a sad smile, full of all her doubt about the arrangement. "My thanks." Deineike finished the last of her wine, and Jorinda wished to leave. "It is late, and Deineike has not yet recovered from a fall. She tires by the end of the day."

Pettra gave her a warm smile. "Of course. The cart waits outside and will return you to the house. My thanks for your company tonight."

Jorinda returned the smile, grateful for the meal but anxious about the course the conversation had taken. "Our thanks for the delicious meal."

Raolos and Pettra showed them to the door, and one of the Portreeve's men came over to meet them. They said goodnight, and Jorinda suffered more embraces before the door closed behind them.

As they walked to the cart, Jorinda turned to the man. "We would like to walk, if that suits." He appeared taken aback. "It is such a pleasant evening, and it is difficult for Deineike to climb into the cart. Not long ago, she injured her leg in a bad fall."

He nodded. "I can send the cart away if you prefer, but will you allow me to escort you home? Ort is safe, but as recent events have shown, we never know what danger lurks in familiar places."

Jorinda had not the heart to deny him. "We would appreciate your company." He spoke to the cart driver, then fell into step beside them as they walked down the drive.

The walk did not take long even at Deineike's pace. Friendly and polite, they answered his enquiries about whether they had enjoyed their evening and the meal. At the house, he bade them goodnight as they closed the door.

Jorinda slumped into a chair in the parlour. Deineike perched on one of the chair's arms, placed her arms around Jorinda's neck, and kissed the top of her head. "You have a commission for your making. I am happy for you."

"It will take no more than a few days, then we can leave." Jorinda had little enthusiasm for the dress and regretted the offer, but the coin would be a help.

"You wish to leave Ort?"

"We are not safe here. We must leave."

Deineike twirled a piece of Jorinda's hair between her fingers. "Are you certain we are not safe? Styrrach has fled, a wanted murderer. He has no Guild here to do his vile work for him."

Weariness ached in every bone, and Jorinda had no strength to consider the matter further. "Deineike, I am tired. The food and wine were too rich for me, and my nerves gnawed at me the entire time. What if I used the wrong knife, or I slipped a careless word into the conversation that might see me arrested? They are fine people, but…" She ran out of objections.

Deineike kissed the top of her head again. "I understand, my love. Let us get you into bed and hope you wake happier. We have our lives ahead of us and do not need to rush into any decision."

Jorinda looked up at her and smiled. "I love you."

Deineike returned the smile. "Although you would not say those words to me for such a short time, it felt like a lifetime to me. I am happy to hear it again."

They made their slow way up the stairs. Although Deineike's leg flexed more each day, she had not regained full mobility. At the top, Jorinda stopped and looked down the stairs. "This house is too big for the two of us."

"That it is, but it is ours for now, and I will enjoy it. Once we leave here, we will not enjoy such grandeur again."

Jorinda smiled her agreement, though the urge to leave Ort ate at her like a meal that never satisfies a person's hunger. They pulled off their dresses, fell into the bed, and were asleep almost straight away.

TWENTY-THREE
A JOURNEY SOUTH

As everything turned to mayhem around him, Styrrach ran from the Portreeve's office and shoved aside anybody in his way. He should never have given the imbecile Portreeve a chance to join him, and it had brought him undone. When Corelle appeared from behind the desk, the Guildmeister cursed himself; he had not anticipated she would twist the Portreeve to her wiles. Porl fell, dead, he guessed, and as Styrrach ran from the office, he slashed one of the Portreeve's men across the stomach, then spotted the other traitor, Wilash. He might have killed Wilash, but with Corelle to contend with as well, he sacrificed his vengeance for the most important thing of all—his life.

He must leave Ort straight away. He had no time to waste, and he ran from the building into the square. He had never been to Ort before but recalled the journey he had taken from the docks with little effort. Doubtless the Portreeve's men would seek him now. With luck, Porl's dagger took the Portreeve before Corelle cut the Senior Aide down. Styrrach glanced backward, but with no sign of pursuit, he slowed to a walk. Unusual activity drew attention, and fewer people would notice him if he walked than if he ran.

He walked down the hill at a brisk pace, but it took longer than expected to reach the docks. Why had the town not built its square closer to the docks, as in the other towns and cities of Dur? He had much to contemplate and decide upon, but it must wait until whichever ship he boarded sailed out into the river. As he walked, he checked his surroundings and ensured none pursued him or attempted to detain him, but he did not bother with the usual evasive manoeuvres—the sand fell.

When he reached the dock, the vessel that had carried him from Zhanghar early that morning still stood at the docks. The three-masted ship came from a land to the south of Dur, had made excellent time on the voyage to Ort, and would now be bound for home. He guessed it took on fresh provisions before it set off on the long journey.

He strode up the ramp and pushed aside any mariners in his way as he sought out the master. The ship's crew spoke little Dur on the voyage south, but every master who sailed here to do business spoke the language of the land to some extent. Styrrach strode up to the master.

No need for the token; the man recognised him and stared at him, a question in his eyes. "Your companions remain in Ort?"

Styrrach shot out a command. "Cast off. We sail in moments."

The master seemed surprised. "This is not possible. We are not yet pro—"

"I care not what you believe possible." Styrrach scowled, and the man took half a pace backward. "Cast off or be thrown off in pieces. I give you the choice." He favoured the man with a sardonic smile.

The master tried to salvage his authority, and his tone became officious. "You do not own this ship."

Styrrach grabbed the front of the man's coat and pulled his face close to his own. "You know the token I carry, yet you claim I do not own this ship? I own everything this token portends, and that includes both you and your ship. I tell you again, cast off." Several members of the crew stood nearby, and Styrrach glared around at them. None held his gaze for long.

The master protested. "It is not possible. The tide."

Styrrach looked around, spotted another man nearby who wore an officer's coat, and asked him, "Are you an officer aboard this vessel?" The man nodded—he understood the Dur language also. "Do you wish to be the master of this ship?"

The man looked at the mariners around him in apparent confusion. "I am not master of ship. Gjorkan master." He pointed to the man whose coat Styrrach held balled in his fist. The officer did not grasp all the nuances of the language of Dur, it seemed.

Styrrach pulled his dagger from his belt and slid it beneath the master's ribs. The man's eyes widened, and he gave a howl of pain, but Styrrach would not release him. He stabbed the man four or five times, and the mariners cried in alarm in their native tongue. Styrrach let the man slide to the deck and pointed his dagger at the officer. "You are now master of this ship." He gestured at the body with the dagger. "Throw this over the side and cast off."

The officer looked on in horror, and Styrrach took a step toward him. "Cast off." He did not need to raise his voice to suggest great menace.

The man shouted some words in his native tongue, and mariners rushed about. They pushed the ramp down onto the dock and yelled at dockhands below them, who untied the ropes from the dockside. The ship moved out into the river. Styrrach scoured the dockside but saw none of the deep red tunics of the Portreeve. He had escaped, and now he must plot his next moves.

As the ship moved off and Ort fell away behind it, the new master stood transfixed where he had been as the former master had died. He yelled instructions and spoke quiet words to the handful of men who approached him. Styrrach did not care what they said. He would kill them all if he must, and with no remorse. If they possessed the spine to overpower him, they would already have done so. He understood the power of dominance. Show no weakness, no compunction as you dealt out rough justice, and all would fear you. Styrrach had built the Guild on that premise, but Ort's impudent Portreeve threatened to destroy all he had worked for, with Corelle's help. He cursed the day Arella proposed Corelle for Guild membership, and Wilash before her, who had introduced Arella and her deviancy. Porl had erred when he allowed Corelle to join, and Styrrach guessed Porl had now died under Corelle's blade. Styrrach saw some justice in that, but it brought him no satisfaction.

The ship had not left Ort behind yet. Did this new master play some game to slow Styrrach's escape? He walked up to the man. "Why do we travel so slow?"

The man swallowed hard before he answered. "Tide is against. Tide will turn in hours. Ship will make more…"

He seemed unable to find the word, and Styrrach helped him out. "Speed?"

The man blinked. "Speed, this is word. Ship will make more speed."

Styrrach knew nothing of the arts that moved a ship through the water. He did not know whether to believe the tale of the tide, but as the original master had said something similar, Styrrach would let the man live. "You will need a better grasp of our language now you are the master, if you wish to trade with us." He turned and faced south.

"Not travel Dur no more."

Styrrach did not care about the man's whispered words. Ships carried their goods to Dur at the order of others whom Styrrach had arrangements with, and it did not matter whether this master sailed one of them or not. For all Styrrach cared, this master could sail off into such sunsets as he wished.

Styrrach stayed near the wheel for some time so his menace remained visible, lest anybody considered a challenge. The longer they delayed, the more their resolve would weaken. Nobody moved the body of the former master, whose blood soaked into the wood of the deck.

The Guildmeister tried to unravel how things had turned so awry in the Portreeve's Offices. At the instant Raolos said the word "shroud," Styrrach guessed Wilash had already talked to the man. How else had he heard the word? He tried to leave, but someone had locked the door, and Styrrach realised something had turned awry. With a simple nod of the Guildmeister's head, Porl moved on the Portreeve while Styrrach called for aid from the three men who waited in the corridor. Then Corelle appeared, and things took a sorry turn.

How had Corelle and Wilash come to Ort so soon after the incident in Alcmouth? They must have taken ship, but they could not have used the token, for Styrrach had given express orders. Women who attempted to use the token were to be detained. How did they come by the coin to sail north? The cost would be exorbitant for Corelle and Wilash alone, and Corelle's deviant companion doubtless travelled with them; the woman who had been the mark of the failed gest also, he reasoned.

He would not dwell on fates he could not re-write. Porl had been a loyal Aide, but of late he had seemed less content with his lot and challenged Styrrach's orders at whiles. Senior Aides were ten a groat, and another would be simple enough to find. How Styrrach would run the Guild now he had killed the Portreeve's man in the outer office—and Porl might have killed the Portreeve— he could not yet know. He would lay low, and the coin would still accrue. Raolos had learned little enough, and he might be dead, unable to reveal what he had heard, in truth.

Corelle had heard, of course, and she knew more than Styrrach had told the Portreeve, but other Portreeves sought her for murders across the length and breadth of Dur. She could not bring about his demise, for she would hang from the gallows if she tried. In the four cities he controlled, he would order her killed on sight.

Styrrach had coin aplenty, after all else. He had been shrewd with the vast amounts of coin that rolled in from the Bailiff's Offices and had large quantities of it secreted around Dur. He always believed the jig might be up one day, and he would have to make his escape, so he decided long ago, no matter where he found himself when that day came, he would have access to great riches he could take south with him. He would live a life of luxury in some warmer land, away from this miserable, hard scrabble land with its innocent little denizens. They imagined their lives so peaceful, while he plundered coin before their eyes and killed any who stood in his way, and they never once guessed it.

The Guild network remained intact, and he could doubtless continue to run it if he wished. Of course, if he simply cut it all loose and took his coin, he would not care what became of all those who had clung to the tail of his tunic and grown richer through his endeavours. Let them all hang: the Portreeves, the Guildmeisters and above all that weasel of a Bailiff. What did it matter to Styrrach? Had he decided, after all else? He had vast amounts of coin stored around Alcmouth. He would gather it to himself and sail south.

Other considerations could not be ignored, of course. He still owed Corelle vengeance, first and last. He spat on the deck at the thought of her. She had been a stone in his boot since the day Arella had confessed she lay with Corelle, and he had ordered Corelle shrouded. He laughed to himself at the delicious irony. That had been the biggest mistake of his life. Who could have foreseen how much she could destroy as she blundered around Dur? To add insult to injury, she could not have guessed a whit of what she had undone, the vastness of the endeavour she pitted herself against. He despised her for her deviancy alone, but she had been fog in his fingers for more than a year now, and still he could not feed her to the flames.

Wilash. He spat again. Styrrach took pity on the young boy, nurtured and protected him, gave him a purpose, and in return, Wilash betrayed him. Styrrach owed him vengeance also, and it would be a dreadful fate.

Balgow too. That buffoon had her in his grasp and let her slip. Worse, he ordered an honour gest on her when Styrrach had issued explicit orders she should die under his blade and no other's. Styrrach resolved to visit the Alcmouth Guildmeister and ensure he understood full well he could not disregard his superior's orders with impunity.

Styrrach had built an enterprise the envy of anybody who could grasp his brilliance, but misfortune and the incompetence of others may have brought it down. Many had enriched themselves through his efforts, but not one of them had the ability to complete even the simplest task. Styrrach took all the risks, did all the work, while these others clung to the hem of his trousers. Some might have thought that unfair, but Styrrach always rolled loaded dice; he refused to accept unfairness, turned it instead to his own advantage. He had created the perfect way to make coin, and his generosity had been squandered by all those whom he invited to share in the bounty. It vexed him.

"Let them all hang," he thought again. They deserved it, for they had not been his equal, and they had created this turn. He decided to retire for the night and went in search of the new master, who had gone about his business at last. He tracked him down near the bow. "Show me to the cabin of your former master." The man took Styrrach to the master's cabin, where he explained the new situa-

tion the ship's new master. "This is my cabin until we reach Alcmouth. Once I leave the ship, it is yours. Do you understand?" The man gave him a glum nod, and Styrrach ushered him out, locked the door, and slid the master's heavy trunk up against it. Then he lay on the bunk and fell asleep.

When he woke the next morning, his precautions had been unnecessary, as he suspected. The crew must number no more than fifteen, mayhap one or two more or less. Most would not care who wore the master's coat as long as they received their pay, and if a few had been angry at the death of the master, they had been cowed by Styrrach's brutality, too frightened to act.

Styrrach went up onto the deck. The crew had removed the master's body, and a mariner on his hands and knees scrubbed at the deck to remove the bloody stain. Styrrach did not care what happened to the body, did not ask. Nobody looked at or spoke to him. When he went into the common area for food, nobody served him. They stood by, silent and sullen, until he had taken such food as he wanted.

As the ship sailed further south, he became more convinced he should continue his enterprise. Why walk away from all he had built for no reason other than the idiot in Ort who wished to arrest him? Styrrach had the Bailiff in his pocket, and Raolos could be replaced soon enough. Word of what had turned would spread slow, and not far, as all news did in Dur. It might come to the ears of other Portreeves, but he owned the most important of them, and they would take no action.

On balance, little enough damage had been done. Two Senior Aides had been lost, but it would be a simple job to find replacements for Porl and the idiot from Alcmouth with the foolish name. Any who suited the job needed more than an ability to kill—they must be loyal to Styrrach above all. They must possess discretion; a slip of the tongue in the wrong place could prove fatal. They must be prepared to shroud their members when it became necessary—

they must not become friendly with, nor care about, the ordinary members. Styrrach had made that mistake with Wilash, but he would never fall into that trap again.

Years before, Styrrach left Torric to establish the Guild in Alcmouth, and he now returned to resume that task. Nobody sought him in Alcmouth, and he had both the Portreeve and the Bailiff in his thrall. He would be safe enough, though he might keep a low profile for a time. He had always done so in truth, and it would be no hardship. More coin could be made, and after the loss of four men in Ort, he felt entitled to claim it.

Alcmouth had complications none of the other cities did, and he should never have left it in the hands of Balgow, who proved incapable. The capital city had always been the busiest of the four Guilds, and its docks saw the most business. Although Torric saw a great many ships, it did not match Alcmouth's size.

Violence and death had marked the start of his venture, but commerce drove it now. There were fewer deaths these days; outsiders whom his intelligence suggested showed more interest in his business than he felt comfortable with, or disillusioned tally house owners who wished for a larger share and could not be persuaded to be content with the agreed amounts. At times, some wished to leave the enterprise, and Styrrach permitted it in a way that ensured their knowledge of the organisation went with them wherever they travelled to afterward. Those whom Styrrach's Guild invited to become a part of the organisation either joined or died—no third option existed. The Portreeve in Ort should have been killed after he had rejected the first offer, but the death of such an important public figure might attract unwelcome attention, and it seemed less troublesome for the Bailiff to replace him. To Styrrach's frustration, Glailam had not yet done so.

Styrrach should never have left Alcmouth, and that decision now cost him this disturbance in his otherwise perfect scheme. He had grown weary of the capital and the Bailiff's tiresome interference, so he left for a simpler life in Zhanghar. He left Balgow in charge in the mistaken belief the man possessed the skills required to run the Guild in Alcmouth.

Styrrach must now take over and make things right again, and as soon as he disembarked in the capital city, he strode, purposeful and resolute, toward the Guild building, a nondescript house, as all Guild buildings were. It stood on Water Street in the poor quarter and had a front door but no rear entrance. Any who entered the building could do so from only one direction. A secret passageway led from the Guildmeister's office in case he needed to make a rapid exit, of course. Styrrach's safety always came first, and he had created the passageway. It opened into the building next door, which he also owned, though none knew it. Those who had created the passageway would not regale their grandchildren with tales of its construction. Styrrach had seen to that as soon as they finished the work.

The Guild never locked the front door of its buildings. Anyone who entered it uninvited could expect to be carried from it in the dark of night. When Styrrach walked into the parlour, the two members present drew their daggers and awaited him in a state of readiness. He did not recognise either of them.

"What business have you here, friend?" As one of them asked the question, the other sidled to one side of Styrrach. Their tactics were satisfactory so far, but the Guildmeister did not reply. The man continued. "You must be lost. Turn and head back whence you came."

Styrrach answered, calm, unafraid. "Where is your Guild-meister?"

"Guildmeister?" The man acted well enough; to all appearances, he did know what the word might mean.

Styrrach tired of the game. He had no need to raise his voice; his menace and his name would suffice. "Enough, I tire of this. You have performed well enough. I am Styrrach. If that name means nothing to you, then Balgow's list of failures grows longer."

The men froze and exchanged a swift glance. The name meant a great deal to them it seemed, but they did not put away their daggers, and Styrrach sighed his irritation. "Does he skulk in his office? Bring him to me."

Anyone who walked in might have heard Styrrach's name and profess to be him. Few would convey the threat Styrrach did, and he knew it. Any word he spoke, any movement he made; all carried menace and terror. He had worked over the years to cultivate a persona that intimidated all who met him. Guild members were trained killers with little fear, but most of them feared him—and that had come about by design, not by chance.

The man who had spoken slid his dagger into his belt. "He is not here, in truth. He left around an hour ago. He did not tell us where he went."

Styrrach became angrier. He felt insulted Balgow had not been here to greet him. It mattered little that his arrival had not been forewarned, Styrrach felt snubbed by Balgow's absence. "This Guild is in disarray. That will change. Does a courier still exist who carries messages to the Bailiff?"

"That he does." The first words the second man had spoken.

Styrrach sat in a battered armed chair against one wall of the parlour. "Fetch him."

The men exchanged glances again and Styrrach turned his head to one of them, opened his mouth to speak, but the man scurried from the building as soon as their eyes met.

The member who remained seemed nervous, anxious to please. "Do you wish anything? Food, or water?"

"If I needed those things, you would know it." Styrrach raised a hand and studied his nails. They had grown too long, he decided; not talons, but he liked to keep his nails short and neat and had neglected their care while on the ship. He took his dagger from his belt and trimmed his fingernails while the man stood, dejected, in the centre of the parlour. "Sit." Styrrach's focus never left his nails.

The door opened, and a man hovered in the corner of Styrrach's vision. He did not recognise the man, and he guessed another member had arrived. The man stopped short and glanced at the other, who now sat in a chair as far from Styrrach as any in the room. Styrrach thought the seated man shrugged, and the other moved a chair next to his colleague and sat on it. Styrrach did not speak to him.

Styrrach felt satisfied with his nails but dissatisfied with the fact that Balgow had not appeared. "Fetch such members as you can. Tell them to be here within the hour." He did not glance at the men.

They left without delay. Once outside, the latecomer would doubtless receive a full account of Styrrach's arrival, but the Guild-meister did not care. He cared that the members arrived an hour from now. He closed his eyes and continued to wait.

The door opened again, and footsteps entered the room. He did not open his eyes.

After a lengthy silence, the newcomer spoke. "You summoned me?"

When Styrrach stayed silent, others always felt compelled to break the silence. Fear, intimidation—Styrrach's key strengths. "I will meet with the Bailiff tonight. Does he still meet us in the rear of The Riverside Tavern?"

The man coughed, and Styrrach opened his eyes. He recognised the man's face; he had appointed this courier himself, many years ago. Styrrach had arranged for him to have access to the Bailiff at the time, and he should still have it today.

"The Bailiff has not met with Balgow for over a year. The Bailiff sends an emissary these days. He says direct contact with the Guild is unwise, and Balgow concurs. The meetings with emissaries do take place in that room, however." Styrrach stared at him but did not speak. The Guild must operate in a different manner from the days when he controlled it. Couriers should not know so much about Guild business as this man did, for instance. The man added, "Things have changed since you were the Guildmeister." Had he read Styrrach's thoughts?

"You are still here." Styrrach favoured the line. Over the years, those four words, delivered in the contemptuous tone he had perfected, had conveyed more menace than an army of assassins might. The dominance and humiliation the words heaped on one who had not leapt to carry out Styrrach's instructions at once could not be measured. No doubt, they railed and cursed him as they walked the streets after they had been dismissed and degraded by those words, but Styrrach did not care.

The man gulped down his humiliation and fear, then left. Styrrach had not mentioned an hour for the meeting—a deliberate move. The Bailiff would arrive at the sundown and Styrrach would arrive when it suited him to do so. The Bailiff would have no choice and would wait. Styrrach ran the organisation, and some people needed to be reminded of the fact.

He closed his eyes again and waited. At whiles, the door opened, and footsteps entered the parlour. Nobody spoke as they dragged chairs around. He guessed they all sat as far from him as they could, and he permitted himself a smile.

The door opened again. "Why are you all..." Balgow's irritated voice trailed off, and Styrrach guessed the idiot noticed him. When he opened his eyes. Balgow swallowed hard, then a resolute smile sprang to his face. "Styrrach. An honour. We did not receive notice you travelled to visit us."

"That you did not, for I sent none."

"Let us repair to my office. I will have food and drink brought to us."

Styrrach sought out the man who had offered him food and water earlier. He locked eyes with the man and nodded toward Balgow.

The man spluttered, nervous. "Styrrach has no need of refreshments. They have already been offered."

Styrrach smiled at the man, then gazed around the room. He counted eight members, plus Balgow. That might not be the entire complement of the Alcmouth Guild these days, but it would suffice. Balgow had provided no update on member numbers for some time.

Styrrach looked to the ceiling. "Have any fulfilled the honour gests Balgow assigned?" He waited for a reply, but none came, and he nodded once. He knew the answer before he asked the question. "Have none killed the woman, Corelle?" Still nobody replied. "It would surprise me to find an honour gest not completed, but to find four left incomplete baffles me. Are you not anxious for the prestige an honour gest confers? Are they everyday occurrences here that you accord little value?"

They all stared at their boots. Eight of them, nine with Balgow, all trained killers. They could overpower and kill Styrrach with ease, but the room remained as silent as the bedroom of someone who has gone wherever they travel to afterward. Such was Styrrach's menace, his threat. He turned his gaze to Balgow and could not keep his anger from his voice. "Have none completed the honour gest you placed on the woman whom I ordered must die under my knife, and my knife alone?"

Red-faced and uncomfortable, Balgow shifted from one foot to the other. "Styrrach—"

Styrrach had no patience for excuses. "She slipped through your fingers."

Balgow appeared to try to cast himself in a better light. "Wilash betrayed us, he whom you sent to us."

Several of the members gasped at Balgow's words, but Styrrach ignored Balgow's deflection. He turned his attention to another of Balgow's failures. "A gest went awry."

Balgow looked down in dejection. The members glanced

around among themselves. Nobody knew where the conversation might lead, as Styrrach had intended, the master manipulator in complete control of the room. He had not finished, however. "The death of your Senior Aide."

Balgow muttered but did not look up. "Sky."

"Sky? The sky fell on your Senior Aide?" Styrrach gave a short laugh, but nobody joined him.

Balgow coughed. Doubtless he longed for the floor to open and swallow him. "He called himself Sky. She killed him, and a Portreeve's man also."

"Did you not send letters to inform me of this?"

Balgow's tone brightened, no doubt in the belief Styrrach had praised him for his initiative. "That I did."

"Then why do you repeat it to me now? Do you think I have sufficient time to hear the same tale over and over?" Balgow's brief joy dissolved from his face. Styrrach yelled, and many in the room started as he raised his voice. "Do you?"

Balgow seemed near to tears. "That I do not. My apologies."

Styrrach closed his eyes again. "She killed a courier outside Torric, and two others with him."

"Word of this came to us. You dispatched Wilash to apprehend her, we heard. He failed you."

"That he did. She had threatened to kill the courier with a fork in a prior encounter." Styrrach opened his eyes and smiled at each man in the room in turn. Some responded with soft laughter, either amused by the tale or afraid they might offend him if they did not.

Styrrach returned his attention to Balgow, who did not laugh. Tired of the conversation, Styrrach launched himself from the chair, drove his dagger deep into Balgow's throat, and grasped one of his elbows so he did not fall to the floor. A collective gasp echoed around the room. Styrrach moved his face to within a finger of Balgow's and stared hatefully into the man's eyes as his life left him. "At the least, I did not use a fork." He released Balgow's elbow and allowed him to fall, the dagger still lodged in his throat. Blood gushed from the wound and spread around his head.

"He failed me." Styrrach looked about the room as he spoke to leave no doubt he meant Balgow, not Wilash. "Where is Nihl?" Nihl had been one of the first members Styrrach had recruited to the Alcmouth Guild as his idea grew and expanded but had not yet developed into the enterprise it had become today. He had never forgotten a name in his life, not over long years. Never a name, and never a grievance.

A voice answered. "The Portreeve hanged him, a year ago, or more." Styrrach did not notice which member had replied.

Balgow had shrouded Nihl? Styrrach tutted in annoyance. Nihl might have made an acceptable Senior Aide, but now he must take some time to find another. He pointed at the dagger that still protruded from Balgow's throat. "Clean that and bring it to me." He waved at Balgow's body. "Dispose of this mess." Styrrach turned and walked into the office, furnished by three wooden chairs and a small desk. He picked up two of the chairs and walked back to the open door. He threw them out into the parlour, and one of them shattered against the wall. Balgow had not known how to control men. One chair, no more; a chair nobody else would dare sit on.

Styrrach closed the door. Letters and parch lay strewn around the room, some torn up. A plate lay on the floor, some bread and cheese upon it. He gathered up the letters with a quick glance at each of them to determine their import. Most, he tore up. Those he wished to consider further, he stacked in a neat pile on the desk.

Someone knocked on the door, and the Guildmeister waited for the visitor to enter the office. At length, a man opened the door and peered in, tentative, Styrrach's dagger in his hand. Styrrach glowered at the man. "Your name?"

The man gave a hesitant answer. "Jakos." Styrrach had wanted to see which of them would grasp the initiative to attend to his dagger. He needed a Senior Aide, and he must seek one from the members in the parlour.

Styrrach gestured at the plate of food. "Remove this plate." Jakos bent and picked up the plate. "How long have you been a member?"

"Three years, I believe."

"I do not remember you from when I ran this Guild."

"That you would not. I have heard much of that time. None remain from then. All are dead."

Styrrach pondered this. Had Balgow shrouded all the members Styrrach left behind? He had not laid that failure on Balgow before he took his life. It seemed Balgow credited himself with more importance than he possessed, and Styrrach should have visited the three Guilds outside Zhanghar more often. Thanks to the unfortunate incident in Ort, he may not be as free to do so for a time. He would need a Senior Aide, and a dependable one. "How many gests have you fulfilled?"

Jakos shuffled his feet, embarrassed. "My apologies, I am uncertain."

"Can you read and scribe? Or comprehend numbers?"

"That I cannot."

Styrrach dismissed the man from his plans. His Senior Aide needed those skills, and Styrrach had neither the time or patience to train one who might have no aptitude for them. He sat at the desk and pointed to the parch he had torn up. "Take those scraps of parch and burn them. Then send me someone who can scribe."

Styrrach busied himself with the first letters from the pile he had created. The Bailiff had sent them soon after the disaster that saw Corelle kill Sky, the Senior Aide with the ridiculous name. The letters called for a meeting. Styrrach imagined an emissary had gone to the meeting, since the courier said the Bailiff no longer attended upon the Guild in person.

The sojourn the Alcmouth members had enjoyed under Balgow

would end today. The Guild existed to enforce discipline and instil fear in all those who served, or interfered, in Styrrach's organisation, and the members would learn soon enough, this must be their one focus.

Another knock at the door disturbed his study of the letters, and another member entered the office. Styrrach asked the newcomer the same question as Jakos. "Your name?"

"Gill."

Styrrach frowned as he noticed a close resemblance to the name of another of his members. "Gill? You know the Torric Senior Aide is named Gillar?"

Gill shrugged as though such coincidences held no interest for him. "That I do."

Styrrach grimaced for a heartbeat. The names sounded similar, but what of it? "You can scribe and read? You know numbers?"

"That I do."

"There are letters here. Balgow met with the Bailiff?"

Gill did not seem as afraid of Styrrach as Jakos had. "That he did not. He met with the Bailiff's emissary. It did not sit well with him that the Bailiff sent a junior, nor that the Bailiff made unreasonable demands of us."

Styrrach nodded. "Yet he did naught about it?" Gill did not reply but looked thoughtful. Styrrach encouraged him to elaborate. "Speak your mind."

"Balgow complained a lot more than he used to, and Sky had taken to ale. They did not behave as you have since you arrived but an hour ago."

Styrrach approved of the response. "How have I behaved?"

"Business. To you, this is a business, or it seems thus to me. You seem cold and indifferent toward the members."

Styrrach held up a hand. "You seek to insult me?"

Gill's face flushed and a hint of fear crept into his eyes. "That I do not."

Styrrach laughed once. "You did not insult me. I care about one person in this life, and it is me. I have built far more than this Guild, and you know precious little of it." He did not waste time. Decisions must be made. "I will now manage this Guild, and I need a Senior Aide. As you have already guessed, things will not be as they were under Balgow. I offer you the chance to fill the role. I will judge your performance, and if you satisfy me, you may become the Senior Aide on a permanent basis. If you do not, you will be replaced by another until I find one who meets my expectations." Styrrach would try this Gill on for size, reveal little, but test him by degrees. "I demand loyalty. Absolute loyalty. There will be hard choices. Falter and fail, Gill. Falter and fail. Those three words will be the last time you will hear me repeat a command, for those words are vital. I say things once. If you do not grasp my words, another will be found who does."

Gill stood silent for a moment. "What would you have me do next?"

"Are there gests to be assigned?"

"The honour gests only."

"Balgow's are rescinded, as is my order about the deviant. I now call honour gests of my own on them all. In addition, any who bring me the severed head of Corelle will be paid fifty regals. They were last seen in Ort, and I wish to know how they arrived there. Couriers may find some information in the town, although they will be unlikely to find the fugitives there. You may tell the others this news and they may leave. Leave the door open." Fifty regals; a vast sum, but worth it to rid himself of the deviant.

Gill returned to the parlour and gave the news to the members. None questioned his authority as he spoke. Styrrach had ordered the door left open for one simple purpose. It would be obvious he heard Gill's words, and if Gill lied, Styrrach would act. This simple act imbued Gill's words with Styrrach's own authority, and he need do nothing. The members shuffled out, and Gill returned to the office.

Styrrach looked up at him. "I will meet with the Bailiff tonight. I will go alone, for I must discuss things with him I will not yet entrust you to know. You will remain here. If gests arise, you will assign them. Know this, Gill. I will never ask you do anything. I will tell you what must be done, and you will do it. Do not question me."

Gill nodded and Styrrach returned his attention to the letters. Gill returned to the parlour, sat in a chair in sight of the door, and his eyes closed as though he might take a short sleep. Styrrach thought, *"So far so good."* He wondered how Balgow had not seen this man's potential when his own Senior Aide took to drink. It puzzled him, but Balgow had been disposed of, and his deficiencies no longer concerned Styrrach.

Darkness fell. None of the members returned to the building, which satisfied Styrrach. He had created the impression he intended. Among the letters, there had been some items that would demand his attention over the next days, items Balgow ought to have resolved already.

The Bailiff had waited long enough. Styrrach walked out of the building and headed for The Riverside Tavern.

TWENTY-FOUR
A POUCH IS DELIVERED

Deineike woke early, Jorinda still asleep beside her. The previous night had drained the younger woman. Raolos pressed her hard to help him, but she seemed resolved to leave Ort and abandon any further attempt to unmask Styrrach and those who colluded with him. Deineike thought she understood—Jorinda had become a killer, and it ate at her, gnawed at her sense of self.

Deineike did not much care whether Styrrach and his accomplices became rich or poor as long as Jorinda found peace. Whether it would give Jorinda more satisfaction to bring down Styrrach and learn why he had shrouded her that night in Zhanghar, or to find relaxation and solitude in a far-flung town where she could settle to a life with no violence, no constant glances over the shoulder, and no need to flee at a heartbeat's notice if they were discovered, Deineike could not say. The two might go hand in glove.

Deineike worried about Raolos and his family. The Portreeve seemed a fine man who wanted nothing more than to sweep the shadow of deception, greed, and death from the land. Though it would hurt him to abandon that objective, he might feel compelled to do so unless Jorinda helped him, but Jorinda seemed determined not to provide the help he sought.

Jorinda stirred, and her eyes opened. Deineike turned and drew her into an embrace. "Good morning my love. How did you sleep?"

Jorinda looked tired, drawn. "Nightmares."

Deineike kissed her forehead. "We will drive them from you in time, do not fear."

"How will we do this?"

Jorinda sounded irritable, and Deineike strove to keep her voice gentle, hopeful. "When you find peace, I feel certain the nightmares will leave you. We must find a way to drive out the pain from within you. The nightmares will depart then, I am certain."

"Is that all? We need do nothing more than cure the pain that burns my insides? We should complete this task in time for a pleasant lunch." Jorinda rolled away.

The sarcastic rebuff hurt Deineike, but she did not wish to add to Jorinda's pain with ill-chosen words. "My love, I am sorry. I do not mean it will be a simple task. We must do it, however, and for more than the nightmares. We must do it for you. You will be destroyed otherwise."

Jorinda stayed silent for a time, and Deineike lay close, her arms once more around her. Jorinda's next words surprised Deineike. "What is 'the head of the table?'"

Deineike lay stunned and silent for a moment, then laughed. "I do not know. The table had no head—although it did have legs." The anatomical conundrum made no sense. "Tables are a mystery."

"It could mean the most important person at the table. The head may refer to the leader."

"It cannot be that. You are not important, but Raolos named you the head of the table." Jorinda's elbow struck Deineike in the stomach, and a whoosh of air burst from her mouth. Jorinda laughed as Deineike sucked air into her lungs, nauseous.

Soft, mayhap remorseful, Jorinda asked, "Are you hurt?"

"That I am not, and my jest earned it if I were."

Although she did not turn to face Deineike, Jorinda continued with her questions about the previous evening. "How did you know about this strange business with the linked arms? I knew nothing of how to respond, yet you took to it like the daughter of the Duke himself."

"I may be his daughter. Who can know?" Deineike laughed at her own jest, and Jorinda laughed with her. Deineike revelled in the shared moment of levity before she explained. "I have seen others do it. Have you not noticed it? At Springfest in Vjort, for example, many couples roamed the marketplace in this fashion. The well-dressed ones at the least; rich also, I imagine. Of course, you did not notice it there. You had eyes only for me." She moved backward lest another elbow be aimed at her stomach.

"You are correct. I had eyes for none but you. I never do." Jorinda turned to face her at last. "You are beautiful, and I cannot keep my eyes from you."

"Or your hands, it seems." Deineike gasped as Jorinda's finger caressed her. She parted her legs.

"You wish me to stop?"

"That I do. In an hour or so." She pushed Jorinda back, lay on top of her, and Jorinda massaged her nub as Deineike ground her hips in time with the delicious torment. Her breaths became faster and heavier as Jorinda stimulated her, and her passion burst within her. She moaned as she craved further pleasure. "More." Jorinda's finger slid inside her, and Deineike teased at Jorinda's full breasts as she rode another surge of satisfaction to its peak.

When she had taken sufficient satisfaction, she turned her attentions to her lover and returned the pleasure to Jorinda time after time until they lay contented in each other's arms.

Deineike had little breath left with which to speak. "We cannot leave Ort."

"Why is that?"

"We cannot leave one another alone for longer than a few hours. A long journey filled with passionate interludes and nights under the lights of the night sky might require the rest of our lives before we even reached Delcan."

Jorinda frowned. "Why Delcan?"

"It is a place I have visited. I did not mean we should go there. I mentioned it to illustrate the point."

Jorinda appeared to reflect on her words. "It would be a journey I would be happy to take, though it took all our days."

"As would I." Deineike kissed Jorinda's nose. "But a person travels on her stomach, I have heard. The cake shop calls me."

"We cannot leave yet. Pettra will send coin this morning. She said as much last night. We cannot be away from the house when they arrive with it."

Deineike sat upright, alarmed. "Do you think she will bring it here? We cannot be naked and dishevelled when she comes." She sprang from the bed.

Jorinda laughed. "I doubt she will bring it. One of Raolos's men will do so, my guess. Tell me though; will you answer the door to Ibie naked and dishevelled, where you will not for Pettra?"

Deineike picked up her dress and draped it over Jorinda's head. "Still your tongue, bully." She laughed and headed for the privy.

Downstairs, they ate some bread and cold meats, along with some fruit left over from the previous day. Deineike wanted to return to the topic of their intentions. They must decide one way or the other. "Will you refuse to help Raolos?"

"That I will."

The answer saddened Deineike for some reason. Her heart told her Jorinda could not find peace if they ran for the rest of their days from the concerns that tore at her. They had been on the run together since Taro's farm, and Jorinda's state lurched from bad to worse at every turn. "You know I love you and will stand with you whatever you do."

"But?" Jorinda suspected more followed, it seemed.

Deineike sought for words that captured her thoughts but did not stir Jorinda's disposition toward anger. "We have spent nights on the ground and in inns. We have worked and loved. I have fetched up into the water countless times aboard ships between Torric and Ort. What an adventure it all sounds, to any who heard that part alone." Silent and earnest, Jorinda gazed into Deineike's eyes as she continued. "We have found no real peace. We have been unable to settle anywhere, dogged by the Guild at every turn. We have evaded them, but we must run out of luck at some point. There can be no other conclusion."

"You are correct, but any help I give Raolos will bring us into direct conflict with Styrrach and all his resources. The Guild is not torn down. He has many trained killers at his call, while only one of us has ever killed, and she longs never to do so again."

"You could travel to Alcmouth and visit the Duke with Raolos."

Jorinda sighed. "That I could if he obtains the audience he believes he can. Even now Styrrach will pour poison into the ears of the Bailiff, second only to the Duke in the entire land. To go to Alcmouth increases the danger beyond measure."

Deineike could not fault Jorinda's logic, but unless they stood up for themselves, they would run for ever with no end in sight. "Do you fear him—Styrrach?"

Her lips set in an angry line, Jorinda answered. "That I do not, for myself. I believe I could bring his ruin, though if I failed, I would die. That would put an end to my pain." Deineike shook her head in violent denial of Jorinda's words. She loathed to hear Jorinda talk of her own death. Jorinda's face softened as she went on. "I fear him for you. I might fail to kill him, for he is not unguarded as I am, and if I fail, he might come for you."

Deineike doubted Styrrach would search for her. "He does not know me, and Wilash said he does not care about me."

"He would if you sought vengeance, or would you shrug your shoulders, accept the fates, and forgive him for my death?"

"I cannot answer that question. I have never killed anyone. The hair I tore from that man in desperation in Alcmouth may be the first time I have injured another person on purpose. If Styrrach snatched you from me, I cannot say how I would react." Deineike fell silent. Violence had never been a part of her life, and now she considered it, she doubted she could kill, even under such extreme circumstances as the murder of Jorinda. In Torric, when Deineike had seen the mariner and believed him the man who killed her mother, she had accepted that violence did not dwell in her, despite the young Deineike's pledge to exact revenge on him. *"His eyes stare into yours even as the life leaves them. You could not do it,"* Jorinda had said, and in her heart, Deineike had accepted her lover had the right of it. To her surprise, she felt both shame and pride that she could not kill, not even to avenge Jorinda.

Jorinda gave her a sad smile. "You could not kill him, and to try would bring your ruin. I would not wish that. I cannot help Raolos, though it grieves me that if he is replaced as Portreeve, then he and his family will be in danger. We rolled the dice that we could bring Styrrach down, but we rolled ones. He escaped unscathed, the loss of Porl and three of his men the sole injury to him. He will find no shortage of men enthusiastic to kill, though few in Dur would acknowledge that. Porl's shoes will be more difficult to fill, but he will fill them. The Bailiff remains unexposed, and the coin continues to pour into their coffers."

The mood seemed to turn more sombre than the night before, and Deineike offered a miserable reply, "Raolos will not take this news well."

Jorinda agreed. "That he will not. He trusted us and it brought him naught."

Deineike shook her head in defiance. "That is not true. Styrrach might have tried to kill him anyway, and you would not have been there to defend him, had things been different."

Jorinda looked down in despondency. "That is incorrect. He brought himself undone when he mentioned the shroud and the Guild. Since he learned of those things from me, he would have declined their offer had we never arrived here, and they would have gone on their way. The Bailiff would have removed him; he still will, I imagine. I brought about the attack. It is fortunate he did not die, for had he done so, his death would have been laid at my feet as if I robbed him of all his tomorrows with my own blade."

Deineike recognised defeat. She had seen it too many times in her life not to know it. "Where will we go?"

"Dur City? We have an ally there in Wilash if need arises."

A knock came at the door. Jorinda held a finger to her lips and ran to the window. "It is Ibie." Deineike heard the relief in her voice.

When they went to the door together, Ibie stood part way down the path. "Good day to you both."

He sounded jovial, and Deineike tried to emulate his cheeriness. "And to you."

He held out a pouch. "Raolos sends this for you."

Jorinda took it from him. "My thanks. Will you come in for some refreshment?"

"That I will not, for I am on duty and must continue my patrol. My thanks for the offer, nonetheless." He walked down the path, turned onto the street, and disappeared from their sight.

They went back inside, and Jorinda looked into the pouch. Eyes wide, she glanced up, pursed her lips, and blew out a soft, almost sad breath. "This is a ridiculous amount of coin for one dress if her tastes run to nothing more elaborate than the dress she wore last night."

"She may wish some complex dress for a ball or some such."

The surprise did not leave Jorinda's face. "It is still a lot of coin."

Deineike laid a hand on Jorinda's cheek. "Raolos pays you extra in his gratitude, no doubt. It would be an insult to refuse."

"He pays me for the death of Porl." Jorinda looked up, her surprise replaced by horror. "I cannot accept it, Deineike. That would make me no better than when I took coin from Styrrach for gests."

Deineike fought back tears. She had not considered the implications of the coin. At all turns, Jorinda's own mind cursed her, but she had the right of it this time, at the least. They must leave Ort, and soon. As she thought of Pettra and Raopul, Deineike could not contain her tears any longer at what might happen to them if the Bailiff removed Raolos from his position. Jorinda must be her concern, after all else. She could cry for the Portreeve and his family, but she must act for Jorinda.

Deineike looked at Jorinda, who cried also. "Let us go to the cake shop. I have need of some fresh air."

Jorinda responded with a glum nod, Deineike picked up the key, and they locked the door behind them. They left the pouch of coin on a small table in the entrance lobby of the house.

TWENTY-FIVE

IN THE ARMS OF DISCOMFORT

JORINDA AND DEINEIKE BOUGHT CAKES AND ATE THEM SEATED ON THE usual wall, then wandered back to the house and spent the rest of the day in bed. They made frantic love, the passion not reduced, but something else intruded. It seemed they sought to arouse one another to drive away their pain, and they gave each other furious pleasure until they were spent.

Jorinda ran down the stairs and brought some food back to the bedroom. They ate in bed, then as darkness closed in, they chatted about small matters until they fell asleep.

The next day, Jorinda readied herself to leave for Raolos's house to measure Pettra. Deineike wanted to go with her, but Jorinda would have no part of it. "That would be inappropriate. She will need to remove her clothes for me to take accurate measurements."

"I imagine you will go into some private room for this while I sit in the parlour with Raolos."

"Raolos might not be there. It is better you do not come with me. I will not be gone long. After lunch, you and I can visit a shop and buy the materials." Deineike pouted, but Jorinda would not be swayed.

Jorinda's making set did not compare to the days in her father's shop—a tape for measurements, parch to scribe designs and measurements onto, and some lengths of simple cloth she used to create small approximations of the design as she realised it in her mind, all in a small, crude sack alongside some making pins, needles, thread, and scissors. Since she left Ryl with Arella a lifetime ago, the simple set had sufficed for the clothes she created as she travelled across Dur. She took the sack, kissed Deineike, and walked to Raolos's house.

Pettra ushered Jorinda into the house and embraced her. Pettra wore the same scent she had worn on the night of the dinner. Jorinda hoped not to see Raolos, so she suggested they work in a private room. Pettra led her up one flight of stairs and into a small room.

Deineike had the right of it; Pettra wanted a dress for an upcoming ball, and she wanted to be the best-dressed woman there. Jorinda pointed out several times that there must be better garment makers in the town if Pettra preferred to use them, but Pettra remained set on the commission of Jorinda's making. She desired a fitted, strapless bustier dress. Jorinda thought this too bold for a society ball and said so. Despite Pettra's initial insistence, Jorinda convinced her to accept a more restrained gown with a lower neckline, similar to the dress she had made for Deineike. Pettra would not compromise on the fitted bodice of the dress, so Jorinda asked her to remove her dress so she could take accurate measurements.

Measurements for clothes used a definition of the span, in the same way they did for buildings or anything that required precision. Jorinda had spans marked on her tape, and within each span Jorinda used her left index finger as a measure of smaller distances. Her definition of a span might not match that of another person, but that mattered little provided she always used her own tape in the making.

Pettra seemed unconcerned by Jorinda's sexual preferences, and she removed her clothes with no evidence of embarrassment. Her faultless figure could steal the breath from any who saw it, with full firm breasts, a slender waist, and perfect, rounded hips. Jorinda kept her focus on her work and off Pettra's figure as she measured with precision. Pettra insisted the dress be as fitted as possible. With no hint of boastfulness, she told Jorinda, "I wish to ensure all at the ball know I am still a desirable woman. The midyears should not diminish a person's looks, nor their importance in life, I think."

Jorinda muttered a distracted agreement, her scribing tool gripped between her lips, but Pettra reached up and took the tool. "Am I an attractive woman?"

Jorinda froze, her tape beneath Pettra's breasts as she took the measurements for the bodice. How should she respond to the question? Did Pettra thirst for reassurance? Pettra had a fine husband and a wonderful son, and Jorinda hoped Pettra had only asked the question in search of some compliment. "That you are."

Pettra slid her arms around Jorinda's waist. Her naked breasts now pressed against Jorinda's own, and Jorinda's heart pounded in her chest, her disquiet increased. "Do you find me attractive?" The older woman breathed the seductive question into her ear.

"Pettra..." Jorinda felt a familiar heat in her cheeks.

Heartbeats passed before Pettra moved back, her hands still on Jorinda's hips. "Forgive me. My behaviour is inappropriate. You love Deineike, and I am married. The fates know you are a remarkable woman, and I forgot myself for a heartbeat." Pettra's hazel eyes blazed with desire, her lips pouted, and Jorinda suspected the apology might be shallow, that if its surface were scratched away, nothing but Pettra's disappointment at Jorinda's rejection of her advances might remain.

Jorinda shuffled her feet and wracked her brain for some appropriate response, but she found none. She looked down, could no longer meet Pettra's gaze.

Pettra's whisper returned, breathy, husky. "Is it wonderful to lie with another woman?"

Jorinda looked up into her eyes at the question as she searched for a way to end the awkward situation. "It is wonderful to lie with the person I love."

Pettra's breathy arousal did not diminish. "There can be little more beautiful than love that exists in this way, between two women."

"That there is not, but there is nothing beautiful about a woman who must hide the truth of her love for fear of society's revulsion. The land is slow to understand behaviours it finds unacceptable." Anger welled up inside Jorinda at the injustice, a rage matched by her confusion and anxiety at Pettra's behaviour. She hoped Pettra would remove her hands from her hips before Jorinda had to push them away.

Pettra paused before she spoke again. Doubt clouded her face, as though Jorinda's answer prompted more questions; questions the Portreeve's wife could not trust herself to ask. "Forgive me. Please do not allow my moment of stupidity to deter you from your work on the dress, I beg you. Continue, please." Her hands lingered on Jorinda's hips a touch longer, then Pettra slid them down Jorinda's thighs, intertwined her fingers in the space between her and Jorinda, looked away, and worried at her lower lip with her teeth.

Jorinda resumed her measurements, desperate to dispel the tension that had settled on the room. Pettra seemed embarrassed, anxious to put the matter behind them mayhap, and she hummed in distraction as Jorinda measured her. The melody captivated Jorinda, and she wondered whether some discussion of the song would lighten the atmosphere. "What is that song?"

"I heard it at a social event hosted by a friend several days ago. She spent a great deal of coin to hire a popular minstrel who sang to us as we ate cake and drank fine wines. The singer is Khittie, a minstrel from Ort."

Jorinda stared at Pettra in astonishment. "I heard this woman sing at Springfest in Vjort some passes ago."

Pettra continued the tale, a distant look in her eyes and a smile on her lips. "She has such a beautiful voice. She sang a sad song, I thought. How did it go?"

"I am sometimes good and more times trouble, my life is never what it
seems.
My heart is somewhere in the rubble of thwarted plans and faded dreams."

The song petered out, and Pettra smiled, though her face bore the misery of the song's mood. "It began with those words if memory serves."

Pettra sang the melody well, but Jorinda imagined Khittie would have done it more justice. One word confused her, however. "What is 'rubble?'"

Pettra smiled. "It is a large pile of broken things." She cocked her head to one side. "That is the best way I can explain it to you." Her mouth skewed, and her eyes again stared into some imagined distance.

Jorinda ignored the note of condescension she fancied she heard in Pettra's voice as she explained the word. Enough trouble had already passed between them. The song might have been composed for Jorinda and her thoughts about herself, but she did not wish the mood to turn solemn again, so she changed the subject. "You must not eat your friend's cake between today and the day of the ball. The dress might not fit on the day otherwise." They laughed together over the jest.

Pettra smiled, and the awkwardness appeared to have dissolved. "You will be here for last-gasp adjustments, I imagine."

The ball would not be for two weeks, but Jorinda had not the heart to tell her they would be gone before then. "Eat no cake, nonetheless."

They discussed the skirt of the dress. Pettra wanted no hoop, and though Jorinda once more felt a straighter design would be inappropriate for the ball, Pettra would not relent. She insisted that as she had compromised on the bodice, she would have her way on the skirt. Jorinda sighed and abandoned her quest to persuade Pettra to wear something more restrained.

Pettra wanted the dress made from taffeta, although few makers used the material, the price of which would be exorbitant. Jorinda knew a little of the small worms from which those who manufactured taffeta harvested the silk used in its creation, and she imagined it a long and complex process. She wished Pettra had not chosen taffeta; it came from lands to the south, and to create the dress would doubtless enrich Styrrach, but the customer must have what the customer desires, as her father had always told her. The pouch of coin no longer seemed quite so generous; the taffeta would cost a considerable sum. Pettra also wanted a shawl of the same material for warmth on evenings that grew ever colder as summer faded from the land.

Her work finished, Jorinda wandered back to the house, happy she had not met Raolos in the house but miserable about the encounter with Pettra. She resolved to say nothing to Deineike. How could she explain her shock or her sense of betrayal? Worse, she had felt a surge of arousal as Pettra pressed her naked breasts against her own and breathed into her ear. Deineike sat in the parlour, and Jorinda showed her the sketches she had created as she took the measurements. The suggestive nature of the dress also surprised Deineike, more so when Jorinda recounted Pettra's original desire for a bustier top.

They set out in search of sufficient taffeta for the making, a task that proved difficult. They found none that day, although one shopkeeper gave them an address of a shop he thought might stock it in large quantities. Few shops would hold such an expensive item against a prospective sale, and the material might have to be sourced elsewhere. The imminent ball might see the wealthy rush to have dresses made, however, so shop owners might roll the dice and carry such expensive cloth against a possible commission.

The next day, they had the good fortune to find a shop with enough taffeta and arranged for the owner to dye it the golden brown Pettra desired. It would match her eyes, of course, but would be a difficult colour to create in a dye for a cloth, and the total cost proved exorbitant by the time Jorinda had completed the purchase.

Back at the house, Jorinda sat on the floor to lay out a making schedule. To dye the cloth would take two days, so she could begin the making in three days. The dress might take a further two or three days to complete, since she must take great care with such expensive material. Mistakes would be costly, and she would need to be more meticulous than when she had crafted the clothes for the meeting with Raolos.

Jorinda gazed into the pouch with a sad sigh. "Little coin remains after so much outlay. My reward for the work is not so outrageous after all else."

Deineike smiled. "I am glad, though I find it disgraceful she would spend such a vast sum on one dress while others struggle for a piece of bread to keep them from wherever they travel to afterward."

"That is not our judgement to pass. I am used to the excesses of the wealthy and their dresses."

"Will you make me an elaborate dress one day so I may parade myself before all the jealous women of high society?"

Jorinda laughed. "You are unhappy with the one I made for you?"

"That I am not, but I would like another. I wish to turn heads as I walk past." Deineike's eyes sparkled, and the idea seemed to captivate her imagination.

"Deineike, you could dress in a cast-off cloth from the docks, and every head would turn. You are remarkable."

Deineike pushed her back onto the floor. "Very well. You have flattered me and have once again earned your reward." She nibbled at Jorinda's earlobe and worked on the buttons of her tunic.

TWENTY-SIX
DRESSES AND DEPARTURES

THE DAY AFTER THEY HAD FOUND THE TAFFETA, IBIE AGAIN CAME TO the house. Raolos wished to meet with Jorinda if she had time, so she asked him to wait while she discussed their schedule with Deineike. Despondent, Jorinda told Deineike she had hoped to slip away unnoticed.

Deineike shook her head. "That would have been ill-mannered. Tomorrow, I would like to walk once more to the docks with you, then you will be occupied for three days with the dress. Once it is delivered, we will leave. This is your last chance to tell him. You must go."

"Come with me, please." Jorinda needed some moral support, and Deineike nodded. Jorinda told Ibie they could meet Raolos later that day. Raolos had now returned to the Portreeve's Offices to conduct his meetings, although he used a different office.

As the day wore on, a sadness settled on them both, and they could not shake it with either jests or optimistic conversations about a prospective reunion with Wilash if they travelled to Dur City. They wandered, morose, toward the square. Deineike's leg had healed well, her pace improved, and Jorinda smiled at the bitter irony that the leg did not slow them today as it once had, although she had would have welcomed it this one time.

Raolos's temporary office had neither the splendour nor size of his original one. Much of the furniture from his original office had been crammed into it, nonetheless. The carpet did not seem as plush as in his normal office, and as the Portreeve bade them take a seat in the armed chairs, Jorinda wondered who had made each of the carpets and how much they had cost.

Raolos wasted no time on formalities beyond his joy to see them again. "Have you arrived at any decision?"

Jorinda replied. "That we have."

His head dropped even as Jorinda spoke. "You will not stay. You will not aid me."

Jorinda wiped at her eyes, saddened beyond measure by his dejection at her answer. "It is more that we cannot help you. We are sorry, Raolos. You are a decent man, everything Styrrach is not, but I cannot place Deineike at risk, which I will do if I help you."

He sat silent, his head bowed, for so long, Jorinda wondered if he had fallen asleep. At last, he looked up with a brave smile. "I understand. You must protect her, for she is precious. You must also take care to keep yourself safe, and I know there are things in your past that might cause problems if brought into the open."

Deineike sniffed and wiped at her eyes also. "What will you do?"

"I will serve the good people of Ort for as long as I can. Styrrach will not find Ort an easy outlet for his greed while I remain Portreeve. He may have abandoned his plot and fled Dur. There is still a chance we have brought him undone."

Jorinda doubted it but could not bring herself to snatch all his hope from him in one blow. "That there is." It sounded weak, but she had no more encouragement to offer him.

He brightened, and Jorinda admired his resolve, a skill she imagined must be necessary for a leader. "How goes the dress?"

Jorinda copied his brighter mood. "The cloth should be dyed soon. Your wife has rare tastes." He smiled at this. "I will start the making the day after tomorrow, and she will have the dress in good time. You must stay by her side throughout the ball, for the dress will draw all eyes to her, and somebody may try to whisk her away from you."

He laughed without reserve. "Oh Jorinda, how I wish you would stay. Pettra would have me install you as her personal dressmaker and grant you an extravagant salary. I will miss you both." Jorinda's guilt at the embrace between her and Pettra grew stronger, but she could not mention it.

They swore to send him their address once they settled in Dur City. Once more, he offered them letters to aid them with their safety, then bade them good day. Jorinda looked back as she reached the door, but he stared out of the window, and she thought he wept. She cursed herself and followed Deineike back to the house. They spent a tearful evening in the parlour, unable to summon any enthusiasm for anything but to lie on a couch in each other's arms.

The next day, they walked to the docks and stopped along the way for the customary cake. They sat on a bench when they reached the docks on a grey, overcast day that spoke of the imminent arrival of the wet season. A cold wind drove in from the river, and they pulled their cloaks about them. The wind carried the smell of the river and the dank, damp odour of the rain that hovered in the clouds, ready to soak everything below it.

A small rowboat struggled toward the dock. Four men rowed it while five others huddled on plain wooden benches. The wind whipped the waters into a powerful swell that threatened to swamp the boat with every new wave.

Jorinda broke the silence. "That must be the boat from Eastort."

"It is not as small as I imagined, but it is small."

The waves tossed the boat about, and the rowers bent their backs to their oars as they struggled to bring it to the docks. Jorinda and Deineike held their breaths each time the little boat crested the swell, exhaled in relief when all within were not cast from it. When it reached the docks at last, the five passengers disembarked. The rowers came up onto the dock and took some water and food from a woman who stood there. Some people huddled nearby, passengers for the return journey, Jorinda guessed.

As they departed the docks, two of the passengers from the boat walked past Jorinda and Deineike. They had a bilious colour in their faces, and Deineike turned to Jorinda in alarm. "I cannot face that trip."

Jorinda understood but saw no alternative. "I know of no other way to cross the river."

"Some other way must exist."

"Ships might sail from Zhanghar or Alcmouth to eastern ports I have not heard of, but it is too dangerous for us to travel to either city."

Deineike shook her head, terror in her face. "Jorinda, I swear it. I am afraid to enter that boat. I cannot do it. I am sorry."

Jorinda leaned forward and held her head in her hands as she pondered what lay before them. Deineike feared to journey in the little rowboat, and after all she had been through since they had met, Jorinda could not force her to undertake a journey that terrified her. Deineike's stomach had proved a hopeless passenger on any vessel, and the rowboat would be too much. Resignation in her voice, she accepted the inevitable. "We will buy horses. We have ridden across Dur before and will do so again, though they will take a large portion of our coin."

Anxiety creased Deineike's forehead. "Where will we go?"

Jorinda had no ready answer. "Vjort would be as unfriendly now as when we left, though we are fond of it. What is Delcan like? I recall you have been there."

"It is small, compared to Ort. I did not care for it, but I did not have you to share it with me." Deineike smiled. Her optimism could not be crushed.

"What lies beyond Delcan?" Jorinda knew nothing of the west of Dur.

Deineike sounded almost bitter. "Towns so enormous, we have never heard of them."

"Is there a land to the west where we might find safety?" In truth, Jorinda had the question as much of herself as Deineike, but she reached a decision. "Time is short. The boat is unacceptable. We will ride to Delcan. If we dislike it, we will strike out west and see what fates await us."

Deineike smiled at her. "That we will."

Jorinda worked on the dress over the next three days; she took frequent breaks to keep her mind focused on the work and avoid expensive mistakes. Deineike often walked around the town alone, but she heaped praise on Jorinda's making as the dress took shape. At last, Jorinda finished the dress and its shawl, and they walked together to Raolos's house to deliver both.

Deineike continued to praise the dress as they drew close to Raolos's house. "It is a remarkable dress. I would like to be at the ball and observe the reactions it draws. It is so audacious. I admire her, that she would take such a bold approach to her gown."

Jorinda fought to keep her emotions under control. Despite her previous reluctance for Deineike to attend the fitting session, she insisted Deineike must be present when Pettra tried the dress on. She claimed Deineike's help would make the dress easier to carry. There would be no repeat of the earlier, awkward moment. "As do

I, although I fear it will scandalise her friends. That is hers to bear though, not ours."

At the house, Pettra ushered them in. She demanded to see the dress in the parlour before she tried it on, then led them into the small room at the top of the first set of stairs and slipped her own dress off. Deineike looked away for modesty as Jorinda helped Pettra into the dress.

Pettra admired herself in a reflecting glass. "It is exquisite."

Deineike sighed her praise. "It is more than exquisite. With you in it, it is sensational." Jorinda fussed at parts of the dress that needed small adjustments and tried not to be distracted by how much the dress accentuated Pettra's figure.

Pettra removed the dress and pulled her own on. "I will be the centre of attention at the ball. My thanks, Jorinda. You are skilled beyond comprehension. Will you please stay in Ort and be my personal dressmaker?"

Jorinda felt another wave of sorrow and guilt wash over her. "We cannot. We leave the day after tomorrow. Our plans have changed, and we will ride west. Deineike's stomach is incompatible with the rowboat."

Pettra cried despite Jorinda's attempted jest, a crumpled shadow of the woman she had been as she paraded the dress before the reflecting glass. "What will become of us all?"

Jorinda had no words of comfort to share. Her heart broke for Pettra and her family, but Styrrach had beaten them, and it tore at her insides. "I know not." She had nothing more to offer.

As they left, Pettra handed Jorinda sealed letters Raolos had left for her, and they headed back to the house. Their misery crushed them, and the next day brought no improvement to their mood. Styrrach must have reached Alcmouth by now, and if he planned to remain in Dur and seek her, he must already employ all his resources to search for her. Neither news nor assassins could reach

Ort for some days yet, so they would be gone before danger sailed up to the docks.

To their surprise, Raolos's cart arrived at the house early the next morning, and Ibie drove them to a stable. Raolos had arranged for them to be provided with two sturdy horses, complete with tack. The generous gift took them by surprise, and to their further astonishment, Raolos, Pettra, and Raopul arrived to say farewell. They exchanged many embraces and cried even more tears before Jorinda and Deineike kicked the two horses forward, and they rode toward the town's western gate. Ever fewer houses surrounded them as they rode westward in silence. Jorinda had forgotten that the town ended not far beyond the gate. They rode on, and by the midday, they were into the Ortlands.

Even close to the town, the Ortlands felt similar to those they had ridden through after they departed Taro's farm little more than a year ago. The sun dropped low in the sky, and Jorinda, who had ridden in silence since they left the town, reined her horse to a stop.

Deineike pulled her own horse to a halt. "Do we break our journey already?"

Jorinda studied Deineike, all she loved in the land. She recalled Raolos, Pettra, and Raopul as they waved them goodbye, imagined Wilash and Klordia as the river tossed them around in the little rowboat, and pictured Wilash as he fetched up with every wave that struck the tiny vessel.

"Soon. I recall a village with an inn. It lies not far ahead. We shall spend the night there."

Deineike nodded. "You remember this road from your journey with Taro?"

"That I do." Sadness washed over Jorinda at the memory of that day when Taro had sat on the dun with her until it tired, then dismounted and walked alongside her. She had little idea of her plans that day, and she had little idea today.

Deineike reached out a hand. "Let us ride to this inn. There you can ravish me all night."

Jorinda laughed and gazed on the dark-haired woman. "That I will not."

Deineike looked surprised. "You turn me down?"

Jorinda gave a wicked laugh. "You shall ravish me all night instead." She touched Deineike's cheek, and they spurred their horses on toward whatever unknown fates lay ahead of them.

The following morning, Jorinda sat on her horse with the reins of Deineike's mount in her hands as she waited for the older woman to appear. The sun hid behind grey clouds, and the morning slipped by. The inn's faded sign swung back and forth in the stiff breeze and gave off a loud squeak they had heard all night from their room. Their sleep had been fitful as a result, and she hoped they would never spend another night at the inn.

Summer had ended. The wet season would arrive soon, and the air smelled musty, the threat of rain later in the day. A chill wind from the north threatened to freeze Jorinda's blood in her veins, and she pulled her cloak tighter about her. Cramps delayed Deineike as her moon cycle woke her early, and she had returned to the inn to make herself as comfortable as she could before they set out on the road. Jorinda thought back several days. She could not shake the incident with Pettra from her mind, and her guilt increased with each recollection. Jorinda did not believe she had done anything wrong but felt ashamed, concerned her guilt might drive her to confess to Deineike. How Deineike would respond she had no idea, and no desire to find out.

Deineike clutched her cloak tight about herself as she emerged and approached her horse. She smiled up at Jorinda, took her horse's reins, and swung herself up into the saddle. Jorinda did not help her. Deineike's leg had healed, and her mobility had all but been restored.

Jorinda ensured Deineike felt ready to ride on. "Are you comfortable?"

Deineike smiled again and nodded. "That I am, although I curse this cycle."

"As do I. Shall we ride on? I do not know where we might strike another inn along the road, and although I do not doubt one will exist, the hour is late, and we may not reach it before dark."

"I am sorry. I have delayed us."

Jorinda shook her head. "Such things cannot be helped. We are cursed to endure them." She pressed her heels to the flank of her horse, and they rode off.

Deineike shivered in the unfriendly chill of the air. "It is cold today. How long will it take us to reach Delcan?"

Jorinda had never been to Delcan and did not know with any certainty. "I know not. I hoped you would have more of an idea, in truth. You have been there, and you rode this road when you left."

Deineike laughed, a soft tinkle that rang in Jorinda's ears like rain on a window glass. "That I did, but the rain fell without end, and I did not mark the days."

Jorinda returned the laugh. "That you did not. You have never done so."

Deineike rode in silence for a time as though she cast her mind back. "Six, seven, or eight days, I think, before I reached the farm. How far that farm is from Ort, you can reckon better than I, for you took that journey with Taro."

"That I did, although Taro walked much of the way, and it took us two long days. We will pass the farm later, I imagine."

Deineike reached out and touched Jorinda's arm. "We have not yet passed the road to Vjort, and it lay half of a day from the farm. We saw no villages between the farm and the road. I hope we will not have to spend a night on the ground. Your back…"

Jorinda laughed in reply. Their journey south to Torric less than a year ago had involved many nights in barns or on the hard ground, and she had no wish to revisit either experience. "Let us see if we can persuade these creatures to greater speed." She kicked at the horse, which pricked up its ears and trotted faster. It would be risky to ride at too great a speed as Jorinda had poor skills on horseback and had not ridden in some time. She had no wish to sleep on the ground, but it appealed to her more than the risk of a fall from the horse.

The morning wore on, and as they passed the road to Vjort, Jorinda could not remain silent. "Road to Vjort." Her uncontrollable laughter compelled her to recount the tale of Taro's concise comment as they had passed the road a year or more ago. Deineike seemed to enjoy the jest, and they laughed as they rode on, cheerier today than they had been almost a year ago when they turned their horses south onto that road.

Darkness drew near, and a misty rain arrived that soon soaked their cloaks. Jorinda's earlier concern they might not find an inn in which to spend the night gnawed at her. The unfortunate delay due to Deineike's moon cycle might require them to spend a night on the ground, and her back already ached at the prospect. At that moment, she spotted a lane that led from the road and reined her horse to an immediate halt. Deineike rode on a pace or two, then seemed to realise Jorinda had stopped, reined her horse to a stand-still, and turned in the saddle. "What is…" She paused and flicked a glance to the lane.

Jorinda's heart grew heavy. She recognised the lane, and painful memories of the dreadful morning she and Deineike had ridden out of it onto the road washed over her, brought guilt and remorse with them.

"Let us ride on, my love." Despite Deineike's soft words, Jorinda's legs betrayed her, and she could not compel them to kick the horse forward along the road. "Jorinda?"

"It rained that night as it rains now." Jorinda recalled every detail of the night: her fear that the Guild had tracked her down, her desire for the tall woman, and her frustration that Taro stood between her and the fulfilment of that desire. He had not stood in the way of her need for long, and it cost him his life. Yet another whose breath Jorinda had stilled. A tear spilled from her eye and trickled down her cheek. "I must."

Deineike sighed. "Nothing here can bring you joy, Jorinda. Do not ride down the lane, I beg you."

"I must." Jorinda pulled the reins and turned the horse toward the lane. She kicked at its flank, and it walked down toward the farmhouse, no more than a shadow in the gloom. Jorinda did not look back but sensed Deineike had followed her.

Her hair hung damp and lank past her shoulders, and the rain ran from it down her cloak. Her trousers were soaked, but her black mood owed nothing to the weather. She could not understand what drove her to push her horse down toward the house, but she must go. An innocent man died at her hand here, and she could not ride past the lane as though nothing had turned. Doubtless others lived here now—the mysterious cousin, or some other. What would she say to those residents? She did not know, but she must look on the house again and hope to find some forgiveness for her crime. One of many such crimes, she reminded herself, and she cursed herself again as she did almost every waking moment. Others cursed her while she slept, came to her in nightmares that laid before her all the evil she had become.

Deineike spoke again as Jorinda's horse turned the corner of the farmhouse. "Jorinda, stop, I beg you. Let us ride back to the road."

Jorinda looked back at Deineike, who cried, desolation in her eyes. "*She is concerned for me,*" Jorinda thought, "*but she must bear that concern for a while.*" She shook her head, and as raindrops scattered from her hair, she hoped each one carried away some part of her evil past. "I must." The third time she had said it. The farmyard lay in ruin, and abundant weeds and grass grew everywhere. The house remained intact, but the door lay askew, torn from one hinge;

Jorinda could not guess how. The barn doors hung open as they had left them when they rode away that fateful morning. Bones lay in the pens beside the barn, bleached by the sun, although the rails of those pens lay broken and strewn about nearby. The bones must be the remains of the animals Jorinda abandoned that day.

Deineike reined to a halt beside her and gazed around at the devastation that now cloaked the long-abandoned farm. Jorinda handed Deineike her reins and dismounted. She moved toward the door of the house and noticed more bones near the door; a small animal, she thought. Taro's dog, she imagined. Another abandoned creature, now dead because of her.

"Jorinda, please. Do not enter. He may still..." It seemed Deineike had not the heart, or the will, to accept that Taro might lie dead and undiscovered in the bed he had shared with his ruin—Jorinda, the woman who had brought his death to him. It had not been her intention, but he had died in his sleep, nonetheless, sedated by her. He slept while she lay with Deineike in the barn, and his fate was written never to awaken.

Jorinda glanced back at Deineike. They both wept, and their tears mingled with the rain on their faces. The rain treated them both with equal disregard, but they shed their tears for reasons that were as different as day is from night. Jorinda gave Deineike an apologetic smile and took a step into the gloom of the parlour.

The table and chairs still stood as she had left them. The fireplace where she had cooked meals for her and Taro lay undisturbed, and the pot in which she had created the broth, laced with valerian, stood next to it. The valerian put him to sleep, and he went wherever he travelled to afterward.

A thick layer of dust covered the meagre furniture and the stairs. To her surprise, the window glass had survived better than she would have guessed, other than a few broken squares. Did she dare to ascend those stairs? If Taro had never been discovered, his remains might lie in the bed at the top of the stairs.

"Jorinda?" Deineike's voice broke into her thoughts, and she turned at the sound of it. The taller woman stood in the parlour behind her, anxiety on her face as she rubbed her hands together before her.

"Where are the horses?"

Deineike inclined her head toward the shattered door. "Tied to the rail."

"There is a rail?" Jorinda could not recall a rail when she cast her mind back. She had lived here for five or six passes but had no memory of the rail.

A wretched misery wreathed Deineike's face, sighed in her every word. "That there is. My love, let us ride on now. Nothing but pain dwells here for you."

Jorinda faced the stairs again. "He must have been discovered. We fled with such urgency because I feared somebody might discover him. He cannot still lie up there, can he?"

"That he cannot. Let us not investigate further."

Jorinda cried aloud. "Taro, are you there?" Deineike sighed, and Jorinda turned to her. "He does not answer. He cannot be here, after all else." Her mind whirled, twisted thoughts of Taro, Deineike, and the urge to escape on that fateful morning.

Deineike moved forward and wrapped Jorinda in her powerful arms. "That he is not." She nuzzled into Jorinda's neck. "Let us leave."

"We could spend the night here. There is a bed here, and it is more comfortable than the ground." Memories of the bed returned to her, and she muttered. "Although not much."

Deineike held her so tight it had become difficult to breathe. "There is no blanket. You took it with you."

Jorinda kissed Deineike's cheek. "I need no blanket. I have you to keep me warm."

Deineike took her hand and pulled her toward the door. "There is hay in the barn, and we first enjoyed each other there. Let us recapture that night." She gave a suggestive smile, and Jorinda allowed the tall woman to lead her to the barn. They tugged the horses behind them.

The black of the night absorbed the last light of a grey day as they entered the darkened barn. They needed no lantern for that which they intended, and they had not forgotten the whereabouts of the pile of hay that had been their first bed. They pushed the horses into the stall at the rear of the barn, and Deineike drove thoughts of Taro from Jorinda with fingers and a tongue that carried her to exhaustion and a troubled sleep.

Jorinda awoke from a nightmare in which Taro watched her make love to Deineike while he pleasured himself in the horse stall. Blood seeped from a vermilion ribbon across his gashed throat, but still he caressed himself as Deineike brought forth waves of pleasure that crashed over Jorinda time and again.

Deineike had already woken. "Did I wake you?"

"I know not, in truth. Is it late?"

"I cannot tell. It is wet and grey outside, and I fear we have a rainy day ahead of us. We should stop at the first inn we come to and take a warm bath and a hearty meal. We can put the memory of this place behind us."

"I must know, Deineike. I cannot leave unless I know."

Deineike sighed and lay motionless other than a hand that caressed Jorinda's hair. After some time, she seemed to come to a decision. "Very well. I will look. You will not come. Wait here for me." Jorinda tried to object but Deineike held up a hand to her lips to silence her. "I will look alone, or I will ride on alone. Which is it to be?"

Jorinda smiled and buried her head in Deineike's breast. "You are a bully."

"That I am." Deineike extricated herself from the hay and Jorinda's arms.

Jorinda lay in the hay after Deineike left the barn. She did not count the many heartbeats that passed, and Deineike did not return. What if she had fallen? Although her leg had improved, it might have given out on the stairs. At last, footsteps trudged through the mud outside the barn, and Jorinda propped herself up on her elbows as Deineike returned. She had a pale complexion, her face set in equal parts revulsion and pity.

Jorinda inhaled a sharp, disappointed breath. "He lies there still?"

Deineike nodded. "That he does."

Aghast, Jorinda gasped, "None came to check on him?" Devastation washed over her like a mighty wave of water that cannot be resisted as it carries away all trace of those it gathers up before it. "Nobody cared whether he lived or died, gave him a Pyre, or spoke a Sending. It is inconceivable, is it not?" Deineike shrugged, and Jorinda remembered the conversation with Taro in the tavern in Ort. "The cousin might not exist after all else."

"Mayhap they were estranged."

Jorinda nodded at Deineike's suggestion, since Taro had talked of a fight between them at one time. She felt the sting of tears again. Taro died alone while she lay with Deineike in the barn, a dalliance in the hay mere footsteps from where his life fled from him. It seemed unjust, but so did much she had wrought since the ill-conceived notion to join the Guild entered her head one day in The Ship's Yard in Zhanghar. She came to the farm to flee the Guild, then fled the farm for fear the Guild would track her here, and now she returned as she fled them yet again.

The Guild also threatened Raolos, Pettra, and Raopul's lives. Jorinda and Deineike might never escape their incessant pursuers, for Styrrach seemed determined to bring her under his knife, and darkness take any with her or who crossed her path. How many more innocent deaths must there be? Taro had died, she had abandoned his body, and now, all but a year a later, he still lay where she had killed him. Would that same fate be written for Raolos and his family? She could not bear the thought of it. "We should not have abandoned Raolos."

Deineike gazed down on her, pain etched in every line on her face. "You thought it too dangerous to stay."

"You did not. I should have listened to you. I abandoned them and heeded no advice but my own. Again."

"That is not true." Deineike knelt and took Jorinda's face in her hand. "You left because of concern for me."

"You did not share that concern." Jorinda sat up in the hay. "You thought of them, not yourself. It is your way."

Deineike sighed. "What do you wish to do, my love?"

Jorinda bit at her lower lip before she whispered her answer. "We return to Ort."

THE END

ACKNOWLEDGMENTS

"Sometimes/More Times"
Performed by Adventures With Alice feat. Catherine Porter
Written by Debbie Rollason
© Hand Elephant Records 2020
Lyrics reprinted by permission

Cover by Jamie Flack - https://www.catandcrown.com

Cover models:
Corelle/Jorinda - Erin https://www.instagram.com/afaerytalecos/
Deineike - Katya https://www.instagram.com/katyafern/

Map and scene divider created by André Barbeto
Edited by Malory Wood of The Missing Ink

SPECIAL THANKS

Ailsa, whose unfailing dedication to my creative ideas never ceases to amaze me.

Malory Wood, for her insightful edits.

Jo & Rob, whose support over the years means more than I can say.

The Beta Bunnies: Ailsa and Danae, for the test readings, and the feedback.

Andre, for the map and scene divider.

Jamie, Erin and Katya, for another staggering cover.

My street team, for their support and enthusiasm.

Bec, for her tireless advocacy on behalf of my books.

Everybody who has read my work since I set out on this journey. I am humbled by every positive word I hear.

Christopher Cross, for his music, which I listened to every day as I wrote. Again.

Alan Rickman, RIP. (Did you spot it?)

Rosie, who added quite a few paw words to this manuscript.

LINKS

Thank you for reading The Vermilion Cross. It humbles me that you took a chance on my work. I hope you enjoyed it.

You might consider subscribing to my newsletter, which will keep you informed of all my writing news, as well as giving you access to giveaways and insider views of my journey through The Vermilion Saga and beyond. The newsletter sign-up form is on my website (link below).

My website: https://hayleyprice.net

Download Sometimes/More Times free: https://go.wetransfer.com/t-0zGDALnPAX

Pre-order The Vermilion Triangle: https://geni.us/TheVermilionTriangle

Please leave a review for this book at: https://geni.us/The_Vermilion_Cross